W9-DHU-286

CRADLE

CRADLE

Arthur C. Clarke
& Gentry Lee

WARNER BOOKS

A Warner Communications Company

Grateful acknowledgement is given to quote from the following: "Light My Fire," copyright ©
1967 by Doors Music Inc.

"Time after Time," copyright © 1983 by Cyndi Lauper and Bob Hyman, Dub Notes and Rellla
Music Co. All rights on behalf of Dub Notes Music. Administered by Warner Bros. Music
Corp. All rights reserved. Used by permission.

"Memory," lyrics copyright © 1981 by Trevor Nunn. Administered by Screen Gems/EMI.

Warner Books, Inc., 666 Fifth Avenue, New York, NY 10103

 A Warner Communications Company

Printed in the United States of America
First printing August 1988
10 9 8 7 6 5 4 3 2 1

Book design: H. Roberts

Library of Congress Cataloging-in-Publication Data

Clarke, Arthur Charles, 1917–
    Cradle.

    I. Lee, Gentry. II. Title.
PR6005.L36C7 1988   823'.914   87-37283
ISBN 0-446-51379-2

This book is dedicated to the four youngest
children in our families,
Cherene, Tamara, Robert, and Patrick.
May their lives be filled
with joy and wonder.

CREDITS

Executive Producer .... Peter Guber

Production Executives........................... Roger Birnbaum
Lucy Fisher

Production Designer............................. Arthur C. Clarke

Location Manager....................................... Gentry Lee

Logistics and Catering.......................... Hector Ekanayake
Valerie Ekanayake

Research Assistants.................................. Gerry Snyder
Alan Ladwig

Story Consultants .... Cooper Lee
Austin Lee

Casting Director.............................. Stacey Kiddoo Lee

Assistant Director .... Russell Galen

Producer .... Gentry Lee

Director .... Arthur C. Clarke

CRADLE

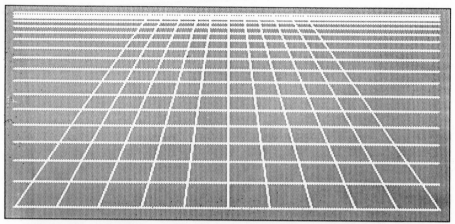

ENDANGERED SPECIES

THE emerald water smashes against the dark volcanic cliffs. Fine white spray hovers over the harsh rock, creating a misty veil that glimmers in the fading light. In the distance, two yellow suns set simultaneously, separated by about forty degrees as they disappear together below the horizon. Across the blue-black sky, on the opposite side of the isthmus that slopes gently downward from the volcanic cliffs to another ocean, a pair of full moons rise as the two suns vanish. Their twin moonlight, although much weaker than the shine of the disappearing suns, is still strong enough to create dancing moonshadows on the ocean beneath the rocky overhang.

As the dual moons rise on the eastern side of the isthmus, light begins to glow on the horizon beside them, about twenty degrees to the south. At first the glow looks like the light of a distant city, but with each passing moment it brightens until it spreads across the sky. At length an awesome third moon, its first chord coming over the horizon when the twin moons are maybe ten degrees into their arc, begins to rise. Calm descends on both oceans for a few seconds, as if the world beneath the giant orb has paused to give homage to the spectacular sight. This great yellow moon, its face clearly scarred by craters, appears to be surveying its dominion as it slowly rises in the sky and bathes the emerald oceans in a mysterious reflected light. It is a hundred times the size of the smaller twin moons and its wide swath through the sky is greater in size than that cut minutes before by the pair of setting suns.

Below the cliffs, in the shadow of the newest moon, a long sinuous object arcs its way out of the water, rising nearly twenty feet above the surface. The slender apparition twists itself toward the cliffs and thrusts itself forward as the piercing sound of a trumpet, a solo blast, reverberates against the rocks and carries across the isthmus. A moment later another sound is heard, a muted echo or possibly a reply from the other sea. The creature swims gracefully into the moonlight, its long, lithe neck a cobalt blue above a gray body mostly submerged in the ocean. Now the bluenecked serpent extends itself upward again and leans toward the land, its face revealed in the expanding moonlight. The facial features are convoluted and complex, with rows of orifices of unknown purpose. At the peak of its extension, the creature contorts its face and a medley of sounds is heard; the trumpet blast is now accompanied by an oboe and an organ. After a short pause a muted response, quieter but with the same rich complexity of sound, comes back across the isthmus.

The serpent swims north along the shore. Behind it in the moonlight half a dozen other swirling necks rise from the ocean. These creatures are a little smaller, the hues of their cobalt necks not quite so vivid. This ensemble turns as one, on cue, and blasts six trumpet calls to the east. Again a pause precedes the expected response, the sound of several smaller trumpets from across the land. Immediately the six new creatures and their distant friends begin a complex, interleaved musical pattern, slowly building in intensity until the overture reaches an inevitable crescendo and then abruptly abates.

After a few moments more the oceans on both sides of the isthmus become alive with teeming serpents of all sizes. Hundreds, even thousands, of serpents, covering the water for as far as the eye can see, begin languorously extending their necks, twisting as if looking around, and joining in the singing. The serpents of the eastern sea are slightly smaller than their western cousins. The necks of the eastern serpents are pale blue instead of cobalt. These pale blue serpents are also joined by a nursery of tiny creatures, the palest of blue markings on their necks, whose singing is high-pitched and a trifle erratic and sounds like piccolos interspersed with crystal bells.

The waters of the emerald oceans begin to surge forward in tidal frenzy, now rapidly moving up the rocky cliffs on the western side and quickly submerging great chunks of land on the sloping side that runs to the eastern ocean. The concerted pull of all the moons produces a tide that will eventually cover the isthmus completely, uniting the two oceans. As the waters draw ever closer together, the music from the thousand singing serpents swells to magnificence, flooding the entire area with a sound of mesmerizing beauty. It is also a plaintive sound of longing and anticipation, the universal cry of long-suppressed desire on the verge of being satisfied.

The great longnecked serpents of Canthor conclude their annual mating symphony as the two oceans become one and the inhabitants of each ocean seek out their lifelong mates in the united waters. There are five nights out of each Canthorean year when the tidal forces act together to submerge the isthmus and permit the sexual mixing of the serpents. Five nights of love play and frolicking, of renewal and promise, before the requisite return to the separate oceans and a year of waiting for the great tide to come again.

For the little ones, the new serpents placed into gestation by the last annual gathering and hatched by their mothers in the eastern ocean, the great tide is a time of excitement and sadness. They must now separate from their playmates, leave their infancy behind. Half must depart from their mothers as well and go to swim among the cobalt blue adults that they have never met.

This half, having lived their lives among their mothers' friends exclusively, will swim above and across the isthmus on the fifth night alongside their fathers. Once into the western ocean, their pale blue necks will begin to deepen in color as they begin the transition through puberty into adulthood. And next year, their tiny voices will have matured just enough that each of them may detect some arousing and positive response to his call during the mating symphony.

Thousands of years pass on the planet Canthor. The forces of change conspire against the beautiful bluenecked serpents. First a major ice age comes to the world, locking up more of the planet's water in perennial polar caps and lowering the seas. The number of days that the great tide submerges the isthmus is reduced to four, then three, and finally only two. The elaborate mating ritual of the serpents, worked out over hundreds of generations, works best for a five-night courtship. For the several hundred years that only two nights are available for mating, the number of serpent offspring produced each year drops precipitously. The total number of Canthorean serpents becomes dangerously small.

At length the radiative output of the dual suns increases slightly again and Canthor emerges from its ice age. The sea level rises and the number of days for mating returns eventually to five. The serpent symphony, which had added a saddened counterpoint during the trying years of reduced mating nights, again becomes charged with joy. For several generations the number of serpents increases. But then the lovely creatures encounter another foe.

Evolving elsewhere on Canthor for almost a million years has been another intelligent species, a fierce, squat creature with an insatiable appetite for control. The ice age stimulated the rapid evolution of these trolls by enforcing a strict survival of the fittest that naturally selected those individuals with the most resources (intelligence and power primarily) and, in a sense, purified the troll gene pool.

The troll species that emerges from the thousands of years of ice domination on Canthor is sharper and more capable of dealing with the rest of its environment. It has become a tool maker and has learned how to use the riches of the planet for its benefit. No other living creatures on Canthor can match the cleverness of the trolls or threaten their existence. So the trolls proliferate around the planet, dominating it completely with their rapaciousness.

The bluenecked serpents have had no natural enemies on Canthor for hundreds of millennia. Therefore they have not retained the aggression and territoriality necessary to survive when threatened. Their diet has always consisted primarily of plants and animals that fill the Canthorean oceans. The seas provide a virtual cornucopia of food, so it does not make much of an impression upon the serpents when the trolls begin to farm the oceans for their own food. To the trolls, however, whose greed for territory knows no bounds, the serpents represent at least a rival for the plenty of the oceans and possibly, because of their size and intelligence, even a survival threat.

It is again the time of the great tide and the male longnecked serpents have completed their ocean migration on time, swarming as usual just opposite the great volcanic cliffs. There are only a few hundred male serpents now, down markedly from the halcyon years when they were so numerous they stretched as far as the eye could see. The giant full moon rises as it has for thousands of years, following the twin smaller moons into the sky, and the overture announces the coming mating symphony. But as the tide rolls in to submerge the isthmus, the serpents sense that something is wrong. A growing cacophony creeps into the mystical mating song. Anxiety spreads by sound across both sides of the land separating the serpents. When the tide finally surges over the top of the volcanic rocks, the point in the original mating symphony for the magnificent final crescendo, the sound of the serpents' pleading wail fills the Canthorean night.

The trolls have erected a huge barrier down the spine of the isthmus. Carefully calculated to be just tall enough to preclude passage to the largest of the serpents, this oppressive barrier allows the lovely bluenecked creatures, if they strain, to sense one another at close range but not to touch. The nights of the great tide are extremely painful to watch. From both sides the serpents hurl themselves repeatedly and ineffectually at the wall, trying desperately to make contact with their mates. But it is all in vain. The barrier holds. The serpents are unable to mate. Both sexes return eventually to their respective oceans, deeply saddened and profoundly aware of the implications of the barrier for their future.

Some of the serpents batter themselves nearly senseless as they try to break down the wall. These wounded ones on both sides of the isthmus remain behind to recover while the rest of the species, resuming the annual migration as if the normal mating had indeed taken place, slowly and sadly swim away, each sex heading for a separate reach of Canthor.

It is two nights after the great tide has stopped submerging the land between the oceans. Two older male serpents, their necks still bruised from the repeated bootless hammerings against the hated barrier, are swimming slowly together in the moonlight. A strange light in the sky comes swiftly upon them from above. It hovers over the serpents, seeming to spotlight them as they crane their necks to see what is happening.

In a moment the graceful necks keel forward and slap down upon the moonlit ocean. From out of the light above them comes an object, a basket of some kind, that descends to the water. The two serpents are scooped up, lifted silently out of the sea into the air, reeled in by some unknown fisherman in the sky above them. The same scene repeats a dozen times, first in the western ocean with the wounded serpents whose necks are cobalt blue, then in the eastern ocean with their pale blue counterparts. It is as if a great roundup is taking place, removing all the exhausted serpents who had been unable to take their place with the rest of the species in the annual migration.

Far above Canthor a gigantic cylindrical spaceship awaits the return of its robot minions. Twenty miles on a side, this traveling planet opens itself to a fleet of returning vehicles the size of large airplanes that bring back the quarry from Canthor. The cylinder rotates slowly as Canthor and its giant moon shine in the background. A solo laggard vehicle returns, a door opens to receive it in the back of the larger craft, and for a while there is no more activity. At length the cylinder tips over on its side and fires several small rockets. It is out of sight in seconds, departing Canthor for other worlds.

The snow falls steadily on the huge man trudging silently through the forest. Clad in skins, carrying a heavy load on his back and a large spear in one hand, he turns his hairy, unkempt face toward the others behind him, his family, and grunts at them to hurry. There are five altogether, an infant carried by the woman and two teenage children. The teenagers are wearing skins like their parents and have large bundles slung across their backs. The teenage boy is also carrying a spear. At close distance all of them look very weary, almost exhausted.

They break free from the forest for a moment and enter a meadow that surrounds a frozen pond. The snow continues to fall, adding to the three inches that already cover the ground. The father motions to his family to stop and approaches the pond gingerly. As the others huddle together against the cold, the man takes a crude tool from his bundle and, after brushing the snow off the surface of the pond in a small area, begins to cut the ice. Almost an hour passes. Finally he succeeds, utters a grunt of happiness, and bends down to drink the water. He pulls out a skin, fills it, and brings the water to his wife and children.

The teenage daughter smiles at her father, a smile of love and admiration, as he offers her the water. Her face is tired, etched with the lines of sun and wind and cold. She reaches up to take the skin. Suddenly her face contorts with fear, she screams, and her father turns just in time to protect himself from a snarling wolf, midair in an attack. He strikes the wolf full force with his powerful arm, knocking it away from its target, and then stumbles toward his spear on the ground beside the pond. He grabs the spear and turns around quickly, prepared to defend his family.

Three wolves have attacked them. His son has deftly impaled one of the wolves through the midriff with his spear, but now a second wolf has pinioned the boy, defenseless in the snow, before he has been able to withdraw his weapon and strike again. In a frenzy, the father jumps forward and thrusts his spear into the wolf attacking his son. But it is too late. The hungry wolf had already found the boy's throat, severing the jugular vein with one quick snap of his powerful jaws.

Whirling around, the caveman moves against the last of the wolves. His wife lies bleeding in the snow and his infant child is unprotected, screaming in its wrappings some twenty feet from the mother. The last wolf, wary of the huge man, feints an attack against the father and then leaps for the baby. Before the man can respond, the wolf has grabbed the baby by its clothes and headed off for the forest.

The young girl was spared physical injury in the attack but was devastated by the near instant death of her brother and the disappearance of her tiny sister. She holds her dead brother's hand and sobs uncontrollably. The father stuffs virgin snow in the wife's wounds and then lifts her upon his back along with the heavy bundles. He grunts a couple of times to his daughter and she finally, reluctantly, picks herself up and starts gathering what remains of the family's things into another bundle.

As night falls the three surviving members of the family are approaching some caves at the edge of the forest. The father is near exhaustion from the weight of his wife and the family's meager belongings. He sits down to rest for a moment. His daughter stumbles down beside him, placing her head in his lap. She cries silently and her father tenderly wipes away her tears. A bright light suddenly shines down on them from above and an instant later all three are unconscious.

A tethered metallic basket about fifteen feet long and five feet wide descends in the eerie snowy light and comes to rest softly on the ground beside the three humans. The sides of the basket drop and metal belts extend themselves outward, wrapping around each of the people. They are pulled into the basket, the sides of the basket are closed, and the strange object then ascends into the snowy night. Seconds later the spotlight disappears and life returns to normal in the prehistoric forest.

Above the Earth the giant cylinder sits quietly, waiting for its messengers to return. The planet below is nearly cloudless and the great blue stretches of ocean tremble like jewels in the reflected sunlight. Near the evening terminator, the low sun angles show a vast expanse of ice extending down from the North Pole, covering almost all of a large continent. To the west, across a great ocean and an all white northern island, the midday sun shines on another large continent. It is also mostly covered by ice. Here the ice extends southward across two thirds of the land mass and only disappears completely as the continent begins to taper and the southern sea is reached.

The hunting shuttles sent out from the great cylinder return to their base and unload their prey. The father, injured mother, and teenage daughter are inside the small shuttle craft along with fifty to sixty other humans, obviously selected from disparate points around the world. None of the humans is moving. After the shuttle safely docks with the mother ship, all the prehistoric humans are moved in a large van to a receiving station. Here they are admitted and catalogued, and then taken inside a vast module that re-creates the environment of Earth.

Far above the Earth, the last of the drone scouts returns to the giant cylinder. There is a momentary pause, as if some unknown checklist were being verified, and then the cylindrical space vehicle disappears.

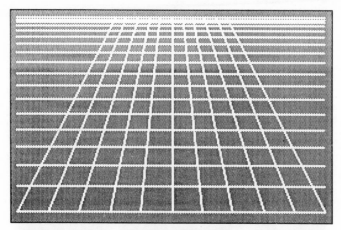

THURSDAY

THEY were there on the beach at sunrise. Sometime during the night seven whales had run aground at Deer Key, five miles east of Key West. The powerful leviathans of the deep, ten to fifteen feet long, looked helpless as they lay floundering on the sand. Another half dozen members of this misguided pod of false killer whales were swimming in circles in the shallow lagoon just off the beach, obviously lost and confused.

By seven o'clock on the clear March morning, whale experts from Key West had arrived and were already beginning to coordinate what would later become a concerted effort by local fishermen and boating enthusiasts to push the beached animals back into the lagoon. Once the whales were off the beach, the next task would be to coax the entire pod into the Gulf of Mexico. There was little or no chance that the animals would survive unless they could be returned to open water.

Carol Dawson was the first reporter to arrive. She parked her sporty new Korean station wagon on the shoulder of the road, just off the beach, and jumped out to analyze the situation. The beach and lagoon at Deer Key formed a cove that was shaped like a half moon. An imaginary chord connecting the two points of land at the ends of the cove would extend almost half a mile across the water. Outside the chord was the Gulf of Mexico. The seven whales had penetrated the cove in the center and were beached at the point farthest from the open sea. They were about thirty feet apart and maybe twenty-five feet up on the sand. The rest of the whales were trapped in the shallows no more than a hundred feet offshore.

Carol walked around to the back of her station wagon. Before pulling out a large photographic case, she stopped to adjust the strings on her pants. (She had dressed quickly this morning when awakened in her Key West hotel room by the call from Miami. Her exercise sweat suit was hardly her usual working attire. The sweats hid the assets of a shapely, finely tuned body that looked more like twenty than thirty.) Inside the case was a collection of cameras, both still and video. She selected three of the cameras, popped a couple of M & Ms from an old package in her mouth, and approached the beach. As she walked across the sand toward the people and the beached whales, Carol stopped occasionally to photograph the scene.

Carol first approached a man wearing a uniform from the South Florida Marine Research Center. He was facing the ocean and talking to two Naval officers from the Marine Patrol section of the U.S. Naval Air Station in Key West. A dozen or so local volunteers were in close orbit around the speakers, keeping their distance but listening intently to the discussion. Carol walked up to the man from the research center and took him by the arm.

"Good morning, Jeff," she said.

He turned to look at her. After a moment a vague smile of recognition crossed his face.

"Carol Dawson, *Miami Herald*," she said quickly. "We met one night at MOI. I was with Dale Michaels."

"Sure, I remember you," he said. "How could I forget a gorgeous face like yours?" After a moment he continued, "But what are you doing here? As far as I know, nobody in the world knew these whales were here until an hour ago. And Miami is over a hundred miles away."

Carol laughed, her eyes politely acknowledging and thanking Jeff for the compliment. She still didn't like it but had grudgingly grown to accept the fact that people, men especially, remembered her for her looks.

"I was already in Key West on another story. Dale called me this morning as soon as he heard about the whales. Can I interrupt you for just a minute and get some expert comments? For the record, of course."

As she was speaking, Carol reached down and picked up a video camera, one of the newest models, a 1993 SONY about the size of a small notebook, and began interviewing Dr. Jeff Marsden, "the leading authority on whales in the Florida Keys." The interview was standard stuff, of course, and Carol could have herself supplied all the answers. But Ms. Dawson was a good reporter and knew the value of an expert in situations like this.

Dr. Marsden explained that marine biologists still did not understand the reasons for whale beachings, although their increased frequency in the late eighties and early nineties had provided ample opportunities for research. According to him, most experts blamed the beachings on infestations of parasites in the individual whales leading each of the unfortunate pods. The prevailing theory suggests that these parasites confuse the intricate navigation systems telling the whales where to go. In other words, the lead whale somehow thinks his migration path is onto the beach and across the land; the others follow because of the rigorous hierarchy in the pod.

"I've heard some people say, Dr. Marsden, that the increase in whale beachings is due to us and our pollution. Would you care to comment on the accusation that our wastes as well as our acoustic and electronic pollution have undermined the sensitive biosystems that the whales use to navigate?"

Carol used the zoom on her tiny video camera to record the furrowing of Jeff Marsden's brow. He was clearly not expecting such a leading question from her this early in the morning.

After thinking for a moment, he answered. "There have been several attempts to explain why there are so many more beachings now than were recorded in the past. Most researchers come to the inescapable conclusion that something in the whales' environment has changed in the last half-century. It is not too farfetched to imagine that we may well have been responsible for the changes."

Carol knew she had the right quotes for a perfect short piece for television. She then quickly and professionally wrapped up the interview, thanked Dr. Marsden, and walked over to the onlookers. In a minute she had plenty of volunteers to take her out into the lagoon so that she could take some close-up photographs of the confused whales. Within five minutes not only had Carol finished several discs of still photographs, but she also had rigged up her video camera with a stabilizing tripod on one of the little boats and done a video clip of herself explaining the beachings.

Before leaving the beach at Deer Key, Carol Dawson opened up the back of her station wagon. It served her well as a portable photo laboratory. She first rewound and checked the video tape that she had taken, listening particularly to hear if the splashing of the whales could be heard behind her while she was in the boat. Then she popped the discs from the still cameras into readers to see if she liked all the photographs. They were good. She smiled to herself, closed the back of the station wagon, and drove back to Key West.

AROL finished the redundant transfer of the videotape through the modem to Joey Hernandez in Miami and then called another number. She was sitting in one of the private cubicles inside the large new communications room at the Key West Marriott. The screen in front of Carol indicated that the connection for her new number had been made, but there was not yet any picture. She heard a woman's voice say, "Good morning, Dr. Michaels' office."

"Good morning, Bernice, it's Carol. I'm on video."

The monitor cleared up in a second and a pleasant, middle-aged woman appeared. "Oh, hi, Carol. I'll tell Dale you're on the line."

Carol smiled as she watched Bernice swivel her chair and roll over to a panel of buttons on her left. Bernice was almost surrounded by her desk. In front of her were a couple of keyboards connected to two large screens, a variety of disc drives, and what looked like a phone embedded in another monitor. Apparently there had been no room for the communications panel right next to the phone, so Bernice had to roll three to four feet in her chair to signal to Dr. Dale Michaels that he had a call, that it was on video, that it was Carol, and that it was coming from Key West. Dr. Dale, as he was known by everyone except Carol, liked to have plenty of information before he answered the phone.

Both to Bernice's left and right were perpendicular extensions to the desk, upon which were arrayed stacks of floppy discs of different sizes (the stacks were labeled "read" or "file" or "outgoing correspondence"), interleaved with groups of magazines and manila folders containing hard copy printout from the computers. Bernice pushed a button on the panel but nothing happened. She looked apologetically at Carol on the screen above the phone.

"I'm sorry, Carol." Bernice was a little flustered. "Maybe I didn't do it right. Dr. Dale had a new system installed this week again and I'm not certain . . ."

One of the two large monitors flashed a message. "Oh good," Bernice continued, now smiling, "I did it right. He'll be with you in a minute. He has someone in there with him and will finish quickly so he can see you and speak with you. I hope you don't mind if I put you on hold."

Carol nodded and Bernice's image faded away from the screen. On the monitor Carol now watched the beginning of a short tutorial documentary on oyster farming. The piece was beautifully filmed underwater using the most advanced photographic equipment. The narration featured the mellifluous voice of Dr. Dale and the video pointed out the connection between the inventions at MOI (the Miami Oceanographic Institute, of which Dr. Dale Michaels was the founder and chief executive officer) and the rapid rise of sea farming of all kinds. But Carol had to laugh. Playing quietly behind the narration, and increasing in volume during periods of narrative silence, was Pachelbel's "Canon." It was Dale's favorite piece of mood music (he was so predictable—Carol always knew what was coming next when Dale put Pachelbel on the CD player in his apartment), but it seemed strange to her to listen to the lilting strings as the cameras moved in for close-ups of growing oysters.

The oyster story was abruptly discontinued in medias res and the screen dissolved to the interior of a large executive office. Dale Michaels was sitting on a couch, across the room from his modern desk, looking at one of three video monitors that could be seen in the room. "Good morning again, Carol," he said enthusiastically. "So how did it go? And where are you? I didn't know that they had videos in the Marriott rooms yet."

Dr. Michaels was tall and slim. Blond, his hair was slightly curly and receding just a trace at the temples. He flashed a ready smile that was too quick, almost practiced, but his green eyes were warm and open.

"I'm down in the comm room here at the hotel," Carol answered. "I just sent the whale beaching story off to the *Herald* on disc. Jesus, Dale, I felt so sorry for those poor animals. How can they be so smart and still get their directions so fouled up?"

"We don't know, Carol," Dale replied. "But remember that our definition of intelligence and the whales' definition are almost certainly completely different. Besides, it's not that surprising that they trust their internal navigation system even when it leads them to disaster. Can you imagine a situation in which you would essentially disregard information that your *eyes* were giving you? It's the same thing. We're talking here about a malfunction in their primary sensor."

Carol was quiet for a moment. "I guess I can see what you're saying," she said finally, "but it hurt to see them so helpless. Oh, well, anyway, I got the story on video too. Incidentally, the new integrated video technology is superb. The Marriott here just installed a new higher data rate modem for video and I was able to transfer the entire eight-minute piece to Joey Hernandez at Channel 44 in only two minutes. He loved it. He does the noon news, you know. Catch it if you can and tell me what you think."

Carol paused just a beat. "And by the way, Dale, thanks again for the tip."

"Just glad to help." Dale was beaming. He loved it when he could help Carol with her career. He had been pursuing her single-mindedly, in his left brain scientific way, for almost a year and a half. But he had been unable to convince her that a permanent relationship would be mutually beneficial. Or at least he thought that was the problem.

"I think this whale thing could be a great cover," Carol was saying. "You know I was worried about attracting too much attention with your telescope. And the treasure hunter bit just doesn't fit if someone down here recognizes me. But I think I can use a whale follow-up story as the pretense. What do you think?"

"Sounds reasonable to me," Dale answered. "Incidentally, there have been a couple of other whale irregularities reported as well this morning—a partial pod beaching up at Sanibel and a supposed attack on a fishing boat north of Marathon. The owner was Vietnamese and highly excitable. Of course it's almost unheard of that false killers attack anything related to humans. But maybe you can use the whole thing somehow."

Carol saw that he was already up from the couch and walking around his office. Dr. Dale Michaels had so much energy it was almost impossible for him to sit still or relax. He was just a few months away from his fortieth birthday but he still had the zest and enthusiasm of a teenager.

"Just try not to let anyone from the Navy know that you have the telescope," he continued. "They called again this morning and asked for a third set of equipment. I told them the third telescope was loaned out and being used for research. Whatever it is that they're looking for must be very important." He turned and looked at the camera. "And very secret. This guy Lieutenant Todd reminded me again this morning, as soon as I made a normal scientific inquiry, that it was Navy business and he couldn't tell me anything about it."

Carol made some notes on a small spiral pad. "You know, Dale," she began again, "I thought this story had tremendous potential as soon as you mentioned it to me yesterday. Everything indicates that something unusual and secret is going on with the Navy. I myself was amused by the amateur way that Todd stonewalled me on the phone yesterday and then demanded to know who had given me his name. I told him that a source in the Pentagon had suggested that there was some high-priority activity at the Naval Air Station in Key West and that he, Todd, was associated with it. He seemed to buy it. And I'm convinced that the bozo Navy public affairs guy here knows nothing at all about anything that might be happening."

Carol yawned and quickly put her hand over her mouth. "Well, it's too late to go back to bed. I guess I'll exercise and then go find that boat we talked about. I feel as if I'm looking for a needle in a haystack, but your guess could be right. Anyway, I'll start with the map you gave me. And if they really have lost a cruise missile somewhere down here *and* are trying to cover it up, it would certainly be a great scoop for me. Talk to you later."

Dale waved goodbye and hung up. Carol left the communications area and walked out to the end of the hotel. She had an oceanfront room on the first floor. The *Herald* wouldn't pay for that kind of luxury, but she had decided to splurge anyway this time and pamper herself. As she was changing into her skintight workout swimsuit, she mused to herself about her conversation with Dale. *Nobody would ever know,* she thought, *that Dale and I are lovers. Or at least sex partners. It's all so businesslike. As if we're teammates or something. No darlings or dears.* She paused for a moment and then completed her thought. *Did I make it that way?* she wondered.

It was almost nine o'clock and the resort was in the process of waking up when Carol walked out of her room and onto the hotel grounds. On the beach, the staff had just arrived and were setting out the chaises and umbrellas on the sand for the early risers. Carol walked over to the young man in charge (a typical Charlie Terrific, Carol thought sarcastically as she watched him strut along in front of his concession shack) and informed him that she was going for a long exercise swim. Twice at hotels previously she had forgotten to tell the guardians of the beach that she was going to swim a half mile away from the shore. Both times she had been "rescued," much to her dismay, and had created an untoward scene.

As Carol worked into the rhythm of her freestyle stroke, she began to feel the release of tension, the loosening of the knots that bound her most of the time. Although she told most other people that she exercised regularly to stay fit, the real reason Carol spent at least forty-five minutes each morning running, swimming, or walking briskly was that she needed the exercise to deal with her fast-paced life. Only after hard exercise could she really feel calm and at peace with her world.

It was normal for Carol to let her mind drift idly from subject to subject while she was swimming long distances. This morning she remembered swimming long ago in the cold waters of the Pacific Ocean near Laguna Beach in California. Carol had been eight years old at the time and had gone to a birthday party given by a friend, Jessica was her name, whom Carol had met at soccer camp during the summer. Jessica was rich. Her house had cost more than a million dollars and Jessica had more toys and dolls than Carol could possibly imagine.

Hmm, Carol was thinking as she recalled Jessica's party and the clowns and the ponies. *That was when I still believed in fairy tales. That was before the separation and divorce . . .*

Her watch alarm sounded, breaking her reverie, and Carol turned around in the water and headed back to shore. As she did so, she saw something strange out of the corner of her eye. No more than twenty yards from her a great whale broke the water, sending chills down her spine and adrenaline rushing into her system. The whale disappeared underwater and, despite the fact that Carol treaded water for a couple of minutes and scanned the horizon, she never saw him again.

At length Carol began swimming back toward shore. Her heart rate had started to return to normal after the bizarre encounter and now she was thinking about her lifelong fascination with whales. She remembered having a toy whale from Sea World, in San Diego, when she was seven. What was his name? Shammy. Shamu. Something like that. Then Carol remembered an earlier experience, one she had not thought about for twenty-five years.

Carol was five or six and sitting in her room, ready for bed as requested, and her father came into the room carrying a picture book. They sat together on the bed and leaned against the wallpaper with yellow flowers while he read to her. She loved it when he put his arm around her and turned the pages in her lap. She felt protected and comfortable. He read to her a story about a whale that seemed human and a man named Captain Ahab. The pictures were frightening, one in particular showed a boat being tossed about by a giant whale with a harpoon stuck in his back.

When her father tucked her in that night he seemed to linger in the room, showering her with tender hugs and kisses. She saw tears in his eyes and asked him if anything was wrong. Her father just shook his head and told her that he loved her so much, sometimes it made him cry.

Carol was so deep in this vivid memory that she wasn't paying attention to where she was swimming. She had drifted west with the current and could now barely see the hotel. It took her a few minutes to orient herself and head back in the right direction.

LIEUTENANT Richard Todd waited impatiently while the data processing assistant made the last corrections on the master sheets. "Come on, come on. The meeting is supposed to start in five minutes. And we have a couple more changes to make."

The poor girl was clearly hassled by the Navy officer hanging over her shoulder while she worked at the design monitor. She corrected a couple of spelling errors on one sheet and pushed the return key. On the screen in front of her appeared a computer line-drawn map of South Florida and the Keys. With a light pen she tried to follow Lieutenant Todd's instructions and highlight the specific areas described by him.

"There," he said finally, "that's good. That finishes the group. Now hit the hard copy repro button. What's the initial key? 17BROK01? Good. On the Top Secret data base? All right. Today's password?"

"Matisse, Lieutenant," she answered, standing up to walk around the machine and pick up a single collated hard copy of his presentation. Todd had a blank look on his face. "He was a French painter," the girl said sarcastically, "M-A-T-I-S-S-E, in case you're wondering."

Todd signed out for his copy of the material and then scribbled the spelling of Matisse on a sheet of scratch paper. He awkwardly thanked the girl in a minimal way and left the room, heading out of the building and across the street.

The conference center for the U.S. Naval Air Station in Key West was next door. It was a brand-new building of modern design, one of the few edifices on the base to break the architectural monotone that could best be described as "white stucco, World War II." Lieutenant Todd worked in one of the nondescript white buildings as head of Special Projects for the site. Todd and his group were essentially troubleshooters for the command, crackerjack systems engineers who were moved from project to project depending upon where they were needed. Todd himself was twenty-eight, an Annapolis graduate in aerospace engineering, a gung-ho Navy bachelor who had grown up in Littleton, a suburb of Denver in Colorado. Todd was ambitious and in a hurry.

He felt as if he were out of the mainstream down here in Key West and longed for a chance to move to somewhere he could really prove his mettle, a weapons design center, for example, or even the Pentagon.

The sign on the door in the conference center read TOP SECRET—BROKEN ARROW. Lieutenant Todd checked his watch. One minute remained before 0930, the time for the meeting. He entered an alphanumeric code into the door lock and walked into the back of a midsized conference room with three large screens in the front. His group of five younger officers and a couple of members of the senior staff had already arrived. They were standing around the coffee and donuts that were on a table at the left. Commander Vernon Winters was sitting alone at the center of a long table that ran across the room and virtually bisected it. He was facing the screens with his back to the entrance.

"All right, all right," Winters said, first looking around the room and then at the digital time printout in the upper left corner of the front wall, "let's get started. Are you ready, Lieutenant Todd?" The other officers sat down at the table. At the last minute another senior staff officer entered the room and took a seat in one of the chairs at the back.

Todd walked around the table to the front of the room, to a podium with a built-in keyboard underneath a small monitor, and eyed Commander Winters. "Yes, sir," he answered. He activated the computer system in the podium. Todd indicated that he wanted access to the Top Secret Data Base. He then entered a complicated keyed input that was the first part of a password system. The interactive monitor in the podium next requested the password of the day. Todd's first attempt was unsuccessful, for he hadn't remembered the correct spelling. He began to search his pockets for the piece of scrap paper.

The only other keyboard in the room was in the center of the long table where Winters was sitting. While Lieutenant Todd fumbled around at the podium, the commander smiled, entered the password, and then added some code of his own. The center screen came alive in vivid color and showed a stylized woman in a yellow dress, sitting at a piano, while two young boys played checkers behind her. A sense of red flooded forth from the picture. It was a reproduction of one of Matisse's paintings from his late years in Nice and was magnificently projected at the front of the room. Lieutenant Todd looked startled. A couple of the senior officers laughed.

Winters smiled engagingly. "There are some fairly amazing things that can be done with the resolution power of a 4K-by-4K image and a nearly infinite data base." There was an awkward silence and then Winters continued. "I guess it's hopeless to keep trying to expand the education of you young officers on this base. Go on. Continue. I've put you already into the Top Secret Data Base and any new input will override the picture."

Todd composed himself. *This man Winters is certainly a queer duck,* he thought. The admiral who was the commanding officer of the Key West base had assigned the commander last night to lead this important Panther missile investigation. Winters had an impressive background in missiles and in systems engineering, but whoever heard of starting such a critical meeing by calling a painting up on the screen? Todd now entered 17BROK01 and, after counting the people, the number nine. In a few seconds a machine in the back corner of the room had copies of the presentation collated and stapled for the use of the participants. Todd called his first image (entitled "Introduction and Background") to the center screen with another touch of the keyboard.

"Yesterday morning," he began, "a demonstration test for the new Panther missile was conducted over the North Atlantic. The missile was fired at 0700 from an airplane at eighty thousand feet off the coast of Labrador. It was aimed at a target near the Bahamas, one of our old aircraft carriers. After flying a normal ballistic trajectory into the region where the ship was located, the Panther was supposed to activate its terminal guidance that uses the Advanced Pattern Recognition System or APRS. The missile should then have found the aircraft carrier and, using the reaction control jets as its primary control authority, made whatever vernier corrections were necessary to impact the old carrier on the main deck."

Todd pushed a key on the podium and a line drawing map of the American east coast, including the area from Labrador through Cuba, appeared on the left screen. "The missile was a final test version," he continued, "in the exact configuration of the production flight vehicle, except for the command test set and the warhead. This was to be the longest test flight yet conducted and was designed to demonstrate thoroughly the new 4.2 version of the software that was recently installed in the APRS. So of course the missile was not armed."

The lieutenant picked up a light pen from the podium and marked on the small monitor in front of him. His markings were immediately translated to the larger screen behind him so that everyone could easily follow his discussion. "On the screen you all can see the predicted versus actual overflight path of the bird yesterday. Here, roughly ten miles east of Cape Canaveral on what appeared to be a nominal flight, the sequencer turned on the cameras. After a couple of hundred calibration images, sort of a self-test of the APRS, the terminal guidance algorithms were activated as scheduled. As far as we can tell from the realtime telemetry, nothing strange had occurred until this time."

The right screen now showed a detailed map of south Florida and the Keys that included the target in the Bahamas. The maps on the two flanking screens remained in view during the rest of his presentation but Lieutenant Todd constantly changed the word charts in the middle to keep up with the discussion. "The a priori location of the target, which was where the cameras should first have looked for the aircraft carrier, was here at Eleuthera, in the Bahamas. The search algorithm should have fanned out in a circle from there and, if it had operated properly, found the target in about fifteen seconds. This (Todd pointed toward a dotted line on the more detailed map) *should* have been the impact trajectory.

"However," Todd continued dramatically, "based on the telemetry data that we have analyzed to date, it appears that the missile veered sharply westward, toward the coast of Florida, soon after the terminal guidance system was activated. We have only been able to reconstruct its path up to this point, where it was about three miles west of Miami Beach at an altitude of ten thousand feet. After that the telemetry becomes intermittent and erratic. But we do know that all the terminal guidance engines were on at the time we lost complete data. Projecting the total control authority for the missile, the area highlighted here, covering the Everglades, the Keys, and even as far south as Cuba, represents where the bird might have landed."

Lieutenant Todd paused for a second and Commander Winters, who had been writing down major points in a small notebook during the presentation, immediately jumped in and started taking charge of the meeting. "A couple of questions, Lieutenant, before we proceed," Winters began in a businesslike manner with an obvious overtone of authority. "First, why was the missile not destroyed soon after it veered off course?"

"We're not exactly certain, Commander. The command test set and the small ordnance had been installed, of course, specifically for that purpose. The change in the motion of the vehicle was so sudden and so unexpected that we reacted a little slowly at the beginning. By the time we sent the command, it's possible that we were out of range. All we know is that we never saw an explosion of any kind. We can only assume—"

"We'll come back to this operational error later," Winters interrupted him again. Todd blanched at the word "error" and fidgeted behind the podium. "Where would the impact point have been according to the guidance constants active at the time of the last complete telemetry packet? And how long is it going to take us to extract additional information from the intermittent data?"

Lieutenant Todd noted to himself that the commander was sharp. Winters had obviously been associated with anomaly investigations before. Todd then explained that if the active guidance constants had not changed again, the continued firing of the terminal engines would have brought the missile to an impact point about twenty miles south of Key West. "However," Todd added, "the constants were allowed, by the software, to change every five seconds. And they had changed in two of the last five internal data updates. So it's unlikely they stayed the same as they were when our complete telemetry terminated. Unfortunately, although all the constants—even the future predicted ones that are being calculated by the APRS—are stored in the onboard computer, because of bandwidth limitations we only transmit the active constants with the realtime telemetry. We are now going through the dropout data manually to see if we can find out anything more about the constants."

One of the other staff officers asked a question about the probability of the missile actually having reached Cuba. Lieutenant Todd answered "very low" and then activated an electronic overlay that placed a dotted and blinking trajectory on the right screen inset map. The blinking dots followed a path that started just off Coral Gables, south of the city of Miami, and then continued across a portion of south Florida, into the Gulf of Mexico, across the Keys, and finally into the ocean again. "It is along this line that we intend to concentrate our search. Unless the bird suddenly changed its mind, its general heading would have been consistent with a perceived target located anywhere along this path. And since we have no reports of any land impact near a populated area, we assume that the missile landed in the Everglades or the ocean."

Lieutenant Todd had consulted briefly with Winters the previous evening on the agenda for the meeting. It had been scheduled to last only an hour, but the number of questions caused it to stretch to an hour and a half. Todd was thorough and precise in his presentation but was obviously dismayed by Winters' continued probing into the possibility of human error. The lieutenant freely admitted that they had blown the procedure to destroy the missile when it went awry, but defended his men by citing the unusual circumstances and the nearly perfect previous record enjoyed by the Panther missile. He also explained that they were going to equip their search vessels with the best possible instrumentation ("including the new ocean telescope developed by the Miami Oceanographic Institute") and begin searching the outlined areas in earnest the next day.

Winters asked many questions about the possible cause of the missile's strange behavior. Todd told him that he and his staff were convinced that it was a software problem, that some new or updated algorithm in the 4.2 version of the software had somehow scrambled both the initialization sequence and the optically stored target parameters. Winters accepted their opinion eventually, but not until he ordered them to prepare a "top down" failure modes analysis that would list every possible hardware, software, or operational error (Todd winced when Winters mentioned operations again) that could lead to the kind of problem observed.

Toward the end of the meeting Winters reiterated the secrecy of the activity and pointed out that the Broken Arrow project was to remain completely unknown to the press. "Commander," Todd broke in while Winters was explaining the press policy. The lieutenant had begun the meeting with confidence but was feeling increasingly unsettled. "Sir, I had a call late yesterday afternoon from a reporter, a Carolyn or Kathy Dawson I think, from the *Miami Herald*. She told me that she had heard of some special activity down here and that I was supposedly connected with it. She claimed her source was someone in the Pentagon."

Winters shook his head. "Shit, Lieutenant, why didn't you say something before this? Can't you imagine what will happen if the word gets out that one of our missiles wandered over Miami?" He paused. "What did you tell her?"

"I didn't tell her anything. But I think she is still suspicious. She called the public affairs office after she talked to me."

Winters gave an order that the existence of the Broken Arrow investigation was to be kept classified and that any and all inquiries about it were to be referred to him. He then called for the next status meeting at 1500 on the following day, Friday, by which time (he told Lieutenant Todd) the commander expected to see the results of the analysis of the intermittent telemetry, a more complete logic breakdown of the failure modes, and a list of recent open items with the 4.2 software.

Lieutenant Richard Todd left the meeting aware that this assignment was going to have a significant impact on his career. It was clear to the lieutenant that his personal competence was already being questioned by this Commander Winters. Todd intended to respond to the challenge in a positive way. First he called a small postmortem meeting of the junior officers in his group. He told them (they were all young ensigns, just out of the university after completing a Navy ROTC program) that their collective ass was on the line. Then he defined a series of action items that would keep all of them up working for most of the night. It was imperative to Todd that he be properly prepared for the next meeting.

K
EY West was proud of its new marina. Completed in 1992 just after the explosion in cruises had brought an influx of new visitors to the old city, the marina was thoroughly modern. Scattered around the jetties on high towers were automatic cameras that constantly surveyed the marina. These cameras and the rest of the electronic surveillance systems were just one facet of an elaborate security setup that protected the slips when the boat owners were absent. Another of the new features of the Hemingway Marina (it was naturally named after the most famous resident of Key West) was a centralized navigation control center. Here, using a virtually automatic traffic control system, a single controller was able to pass instructions to all the vessels in the harbor and provide for efficient handling of the burgeoning water traffic.

The marina was built on Key West Bight, on what had been a decaying part of the waterfront. It had slips for almost four hundred boats and its completion changed the nature of the city's commerce. Young professionals wanting to be near their boats at the marina quickly purchased and upgraded all the wonderful nineteenth-century houses that lined Caroline and Eaton streets on what was known as the Pelican Path. Smart shops, tony restaurants, even little theaters crowded into the area around the marina to create an atmosphere of bustle and excitement. There was even a new Japanese hotel, the Miyako Gardens, which was famous for its magnificent collection of tropical birds that played in the waterfalls and ferns of its atrium.

Just before noon Carol Dawson walked into the marina headquarters and approached the circular information desk in the middle of the large room. She was wearing a sharp silk blouse, light purple in color, and a pair of long white cotton slacks that covered the tops of her white tennis shoes. Two petite ruby and gold bracelets were wrapped around her right wrist, and a huge amethyst set in a gold basket at the end of a neck chain dangled perfectly at the vertex of the "V" in her open blouse. She looked stunning, like a well-heeled tourist about to rent a boat for the afternoon.

The young girl behind the information desk was in her early twenties. She was blonde, fairly attractive in the clean-cut American style originally typified by Cheryl Tiegs. She watched Carol with just a tinge of competitive jealously as the journalist moved purposefully across the room. "Can I help you?" she said with feigned cheer as Carol reached the desk.

"I would like to charter a boat for the rest of the day," Carol began. "I want to go out to do a little diving and a little swimming and maybe see some of the interesting shipwrecks around here." She planned to say nothing about the whales until she had picked the boat.

"Well, you've come to the right place," the girl responded. She turned to the computer on her left and prepared to use the keyboard. "My name is Julianne and one of my jobs here is to help tourists find the boats that are just right for their recreational needs." Carol noted that Julianne sounded as if she had memorized the little speech. "Did you have any particular price in mind? Although most of the boats here at Hemingway are private vessels, we still do have all sorts of boats for charter and most of them meet your requirements. Assuming of course that they're still available."

Carol shook her head and in a few minutes she was handed a computer listing that included nine boats. "Here are the boats that are possible," the girl said. "As I told you, there's quite a range in price."

Carol's eyes scanned down the list. The biggest and most expensive boat was the *Ambrosia*, a fifty-four-footer that chartered for eight hundred dollars a day, or five hundred for a half day. The list included a couple of intermediate entries as well as two small boats, twenty-six-footers, that rented for half the price of the *Ambrosia*. "I'd like to talk to the captain of the *Ambrosia* first," Carol said, after a moment's hesitation. "Where do I go?"

"Do you *know* Captain Homer?" Julianne replied, a strange smile starting to form at the corner of her mouth. "Homer Ashford," she said again slowly, as if the name should be recognized. Carol's mind began going through a memory search routine. The name was familiar. Where had she heard it? A long time ago, in a news program . . .

Carol had not quite retrieved the memory when the girl continued. "I'll let them know that you're coming." Below the desk counter on the right was a huge bank of relay switches, several hundred in all, apparently connected to a speaker system. Julianne flipped one of the switches and turned to Carol. "It should only be a minute," she said.

"Vat is it, Julianne?" a booming feminine voice inquired within about twenty seconds. The voice was foreign, German judging from the way the first word was pronounced. And the voice was also impatient.

"There's a woman here, Greta, a Miss Carol Dawson from Miami, and she wants to come down to talk to Captain Homer about chartering the yacht for the afternoon."

After a moment's silence, Greta was heard again, "Ya, okay, send her down." Julianne motioned for Carol to walk halfway around the circular desk to where a familiar keyboard was sitting in a small well on the counter. Carol had been through this process many times since the UIS (Universal Identification System) was first introduced in 1991. Using the keyboard, she entered her name and her social security number. Carol wondered which verification question it would be this time. Her birthplace? Her mother's maiden name? Her father's birth date? It was always random, selected from the twenty personal facts that were immutable and belonged to each individual. To impersonate someone now really took an effort.

"Miss Carol Dawson, 1418 Oakwood Gardens, Apt. 17, Miami Beach." Carol nodded her head. Blonde Julianne obviously enjoyed her role of checking out the prospective clients. "What was your birth date?" Carol was asked.

"December 27, 1963," Carol responded. Julianne's face registered that Carol had given the correct answer. But Carol could see something else in her face, something competitive and even supercilious, almost a "Ha-ha-de-ha-ha, I'm lots younger than you are and now I know it." Usually Carol didn't pay attention to such trivia. But for some reason, this morning she was uncomfortable about the fact that she was now thirty. She started to indicate her annoyance to smug little Julianne but thought better of it and held her tongue.

Julianne gave her instructions. "Walk out that door over there, at the far right, and walk straight until you come to Jetty Number 4. Then turn left and insert this card in the gate lock. Slip "P" as in Peter is where the *Ambrosia* is berthed. It's a long walk, way down at the end of the jetty. But you can't miss the yacht, it's one of the largest and most beautiful boats at Hemingway."

Julianne was right. It was quite a hike to the end of the Jetty Number 4. Carol Dawson probably passed a total of thirty boats of all sizes, on both sides of the jetty, before she reached the *Ambrosia*. By the time Carol could discern the bold blue identifying letters on the front of the cabin, she had started to sweat from the heat and humidity of late morning.

Captain Homer Ashford walked up the gangplank to meet her when she finally reached the *Ambrosia*. He was in his mid to late fifties, an enormous man, well over six feet tall and weighing close to two hundred and fifty pounds.

His hair was still thick, but the original black color had now almost completely surrendered to the gray.

Captain Homer's wild eyes had followed Carol's approach with undisguised lubricious delight. Carol recognized the look and her reaction was one of immediate disgust. She started to turn around and go back to the marina headquarters. But she stopped herself, realizing that it was a long walk back and that she was already hot and tired. Captain Homer, apparently sensing her disapproval by the change in her gait, changed his leer to an avuncular smile.

"Miss Dawson, I presume," the captain said, bowing slightly with fake gallantry. "Welcome to the *Ambrosia*. Captain Homer Ashford and his crew at your service." Carol reluctantly smiled. This buffoon in the outrageous blue Hawaiian shirt at least did not appear to take himself too seriously. Still slightly wary, she took the proffered Coke from his outstretched hand and followed him along the smaller side jetty beside the boat. The two of them then descended onto the yacht. It was huge.

"We understand from Julianne that you are interested in a charter for this afternoon. We would love to take you out to one of our favorite spots, Dolphin Key." They were standing in front of the wheelhouse and the covered cabin area as they talked. Captain Homer was clearly already into his sales pitch. From somewhere nearby Carol could hear the clang of metal. It sounded like barbells.

"Dolphin Key is a marvelous isolated island," Captain Homer continued, "perfect for swimming and even nude sunbathing, if you like that sort of thing. There's also a sunken wreck from the eighteenth century not more than a couple of miles away if you're interested in doing some diving." Carol took another drink from her Coke and looked at Homer for an instant. She quickly averted her eyes. He was leering again. His peculiar emphasis on the word "nude" had somehow changed Carol's mental picture of Dolphin Key from a quiet tropical paradise to a gathering place for debauchery and peeping Toms. Carol recoiled from Captain Homer's light touch as he guided her around the side of the yacht. *This man is a creep*, she thought. *I should have followed my first instincts and turned around.*

The clang of metal grew louder as they walked past the entrance to the cabin and approached the front of the luxurious boat. Carol's journalistic curiosity was piqued; the sound seemed so out of place. She hardly paid attention as Captain Homer pointed out all the outstanding features of the yacht. When they finally had a clear view of the front deck of the *Ambrosia*, Carol saw that the sound had indeed been barbells. A blonde woman with her back toward them was working out with weights on the front deck.

The woman's body was magnificent, even breathtaking. As she strained to finish her repetitive presses, she lifted the barbells high over her head. Rivulets of sweat cascaded down the muscles that seemed to descend in ripples from her shoulders. She was wearing a low-cut black leotard, almost backless, whose thin straps did not seem capable of holding up the rest of the outfit. Captain Homer had stopped talking about the boat. Carol noticed that he was standing in rapt admiration, apparently transfixed by the sensual beauty of the sweaty woman in the leotard. *This place is weird,* Carol thought. *Maybe that's why the girl asked me if I knew these people.*

The woman put the weights back on the small rack and picked up a towel. When she turned around Carol could see that she was in her mid to late thirties, pretty in an athletic sort of way. Her breasts were large and taut and clearly visible in the scant leotard. But it was her eyes that were truly remarkable. They were gray-blue in color and they seemed to look right through you. Carol thought that the woman's first piercing glance was hostile, almost threatening.

"Greta," said Captain Homer, when she looked at him after her first glance at Carol, "this is Miss Carol Dawson. She may be our charter for this afternoon."

Greta did not smile or say anything. She wiped the sweat off her brow, took a couple of deep breaths, and put the towel behind her neck and over her shoulders. She squared herself off to face Carol and Captain Homer. Then with her shoulders back and her hands on her hips, she flexed her chest muscles. With each flexure her abundant breasts seemed to stretch up toward her neck. Throughout this routine her incredibly clear eyes evaluated Carol, checking out her body and clothing in minute detail. Carol squirmed involuntarily.

"Well, hello, Greta," she said, her usual aplomb strangely absent in this awkward moment, "nice to meet you." *Jesus,* Carol thought, as Greta just looked at Carol's outstretched hand for several seconds, *let me out of here. I must be on a strange planet or having a nightmare.*

"Greta sometimes likes to have fun with our customers," Captain Homer said to Carol, "but don't let it put you off." Was he irritated with Greta? Carol thought she detected some unspoken communication between Greta and Captain Homer, for at length Greta smiled. But it was an artificial smile.

"Velcome to the *Ambrosia,*" Greta said, mimicking Captain Homer's first remarks to Carol. "Our pleasure avaits you." Greta lifted her arms over her head, watching Carol again, and began to stretch. "Come vit us to paradise," Greta said.

Carol felt Captain Homer's burly hand on her elbow, turning her around. She also thought she saw an angry glance from Homer to Greta. "The *Ambrosia* is the finest charter vessel in Key West," he said, guiding her back toward the stern and resuming his sales pitch. "It has every possible convenience and luxury. Giant screen cable television, compact disc player with quad speakers, automatic chef programmed with over a hundred gourmet dishes, robot massage. And nobody knows the Keys like Captain Homer. I've been diving and fishing these waters for fifty years."

They had stopped at the entrance to the cabin area in the middle of the yacht. Through the glass door Carol could see stairs descending to another level. "Would you like to come down and see the galley and the bedroom?" Captain Homer said, without a trace of the earlier suggestiveness. He was a clever chameleon, there was no doubt about that. Carol revised her earlier judgment of him as a buffoon. *But what was this business with musclebound Greta, whoever she is,* Carol wondered. *And just what is going on here? Why are they so strange?*

"No, thank you, Captain Ashford," Carol saw her opportunity to exit gracefully. She handed him what was left of the unfinished Coke. "I've seen enough. It's a magnificent yacht but I can tell it's much too expensive for a single woman wanting to spend a relaxing afternoon. But thanks a lot for your time and the brief tour."

She started to walk toward the gangplank to the jetty. Captain Homer's eyes narrowed, "But we haven't even discussed price, Miss Dawson. I'm certain that for someone like you we could make a special deal . . ."

Carol could tell that he was not going to let her go without some additional discussion. As she started to leave the yacht, Greta came up beside Captain Homer. "It vould give you sometink to write about for your paper," Greta said with a bizarre smile. "Sometink unusual."

Carol turned, startled. "So you recognized me?" she said, stating the obvious. The strange pair grinned back at her. "Why didn't you say something?"

Captain Homer simply shrugged his huge shoulders. "We thought maybe you were traveling incognito, or were looking for some special fun, or maybe even were working on a story . . ." His voice trailed off. Carol smiled and shook her head. Then she waved goodbye, mounted the gangplank, and turned on the jetty toward the distant marina headquarters. *Who are those people?* she asked herself again. *Now I'm certain that I have seen them before. But where?*

Twice Carol looked over her shoulder to see if Captain Homer and Greta were still watching her. The second time, when she was almost a hundred yards away, they were no longer in sight. She sighed with relief. The experience had definitely unnerved her.

Carol walked on slowly. She pulled the computer listing that Julianne had given her from a small purple beach bag. Before she could look at it, she heard a telephone ring on her left and her eyes lifted naturally to follow the sound. The telephone was ringing on a boat just in front of her. A husky man in his early thirties was sitting in a folding chair on the same boat. Wearing only a red baseball cap, a pair of swim trunks, dark sunglasses and some thongs, the man was intently watching a small television propped up on a flimsy tray of some kind. He held a sandwich in one hand (Carol could see the white mayonnaise oozing out between the slices of bread even from her distance of ten yards or so) and a can of beer in the other. There was no sign that the man in the red cap even heard the telephone.

Carol moved closer, a little curious. A basketball game was in progress on the television. On about the sixth ring of the phone, the man gave a small cheer (with his mouth full of sandwich) in the direction of the six-inch picture tube, took a swig from his beer, and abruptly jumped up to answer the call. The telephone was underneath a canopy in the center of the boat, on a wooden paneled wall behind the steering wheel and next to some built-in counters that appeared to contain the navigation and radio equipment for the boat. The man fiddled with the steering wheel unconsciously during the brief conversation and never took his eyes off the television. He hung up, issued another short cheer, and returned to his folding chair.

Carol was now standing on the jetty, just inches away from the front of the boat and no more than ten feet away from where the man was sitting. But he was oblivious to her, totally absorbed in his basketball game. "*All right*," he shouted all at once, reacting to something pleasing in the game. He jumped up. The sudden movement caused the boat to rock and the jerrybuilt tray underneath the television gave way. The man reached out quickly and grabbed the TV before it hit the ground, but in so doing he lost his balance and fell forward on his elbows.

"Shit," he said to himself, wincing from the pain. He was lying on the deck, his sunglasses cocked sideways on his head, the game still continuing on the little set in his hands. Carol could not suppress her laughter. Now aware that he was not alone for the first time, Nick Williams, the owner and operator of the *Florida Queen*, turned in the direction of the feminine laugh.

"Excuse me," Carol began in a friendly way, "I just happened to be walking by and I saw you fall . . ." She stopped. Nick was not amused.

"What do you want?" Nick fixed her with a truculent glare. He stood up, still holding (and watching) the television and now trying as well to put the tray back together. He didn't have enough hands to do everything at once.

"You know," Carol said, still smiling, "I could help you with that, if it wouldn't injure your masculine pride." *Uh oh*, Nick thought in a flash, *Another pushy, assertive broad.*

Nick put the television down on the deck of the boat and began to reassemble the tray. "No thank you," he said. "I can manage." Obviously ignoring Carol, he set the TV back on the tray, returned to his folding chair, and picked up his sandwich and beer.

Carol was amused by what Nick had clearly intended as a putdown. She looked around the boat. Neatness was not one of the strengths of the proprietor. Little odds and ends, including masks, snorkels, regulators, towels, and even old lunches from fast-food restaurants were scattered all over the front of the boat. In one of the corners someone had obviously taken apart a piece of electronic equipment, perhaps for repair, and left the entire works a jumbled mess. Mounted on the top of the blue canopy were two signs, each with a different type of print, one giving the name of the boat and the other saying THANK YOU FOR NOT SMOKING.

The boat looked out of character for the sleek modern marina and Carol imagined the other boat owners reacting with disgust each day as they passed the *Florida Queen*. On an impulse Carol looked at the computer listing in her hand. She almost laughed out loud when she saw the boat listing as one of the nine available for hire.

"Excuse me," she began, intending to start the discussion about chartering the boat for the afternoon.

Nick heaved an exaggerated sigh and turned away from his televised basketball game. The miffed look on his face was unmistakable. It said, What? Are you still here? I thought we'd finished our conversation. Now go away and let me enjoy the afternoon on my boat.

Mischievous Carol couldn't resist the opportunity to harass the arrogant Mr. Williams (she assumed that the name on the computer listing and the man in front of her were the same, for she couldn't imagine a crew member acting with such apparent confidence and authority on someone else's boat). "Who's playing?" she said cheerfully, as if she had no idea that Nick was trying to get rid of her.

"Harvard and Tennessee," he answered gruffly, amazed that Carol hadn't got the message.

"What's the score?" she said quickly, now enjoying the game she had just created.

Nick turned around again, his quizzical look acknowledging his exasperation. "It's 31–29 Harvard," he said sharply, "just before the end of the first half." Carol didn't move. She simply smiled and returned his fierce stare without blinking. "And it's the first round of the NCAA tournament and they're playing in the Southeast Regional. Any more questions?"

"Just one," she said. "I would like to charter this boat for the afternoon. Are you Nick Williams?"

He was taken by surprise. "Whaat?" Nick said. At that minute Tennessee tied the basketball game again, distracting Nick even further. He watched the game for a couple of seconds and then tried to collect himself. "But I have had no calls from Julianne. Anyone who wants to charter a boat here at Hemingway has to sign in at the desk and . . ."

"I came down to look at another boat first. I didn't like it. So I stopped by here on the way back." Nick was watching the television again and Carol was losing her patience with him. At first he had been amusing. *At least I don't have to worry about his pawing me*, she thought. *The guy can't even concentrate on me enough to get his boat chartered.* "Look," she added, "do you want a charter for this afternoon or not?

The first half of the basketball game ended. "All right . . . I guess so," Nick said slowly, thinking to himself, *only because I need the money*. He gestured to Carol to descend onto the deck of the boat. "Let me just call Julianne and make sure you're legit. You never know these days."

While Nick confirmed Carol's identification with the marina headquarters, a jaunty young black man in his early twenties came down the jetty and stopped just opposite the *Florida Queen*. "Hey, Professor," he said, the moment Nick was off the phone, "am I in the wrong place?" He motioned to Carol. "You didn't tell me you were entertaining beauty, style, and class today. Wooee! Look at that jewelry. And that silk blouse. Should I go now and come back to hear your stories later?" He winked at Carol. "He's no good, angel. All his girlfriends eventually end up with me."

"Cut the crap, Jefferson," Nick reacted, "this woman is a potential customer. And you're late, as usual. How do you expect me to run a charter dive boat when I don't have any idea when or if my crew is going to show up?"

"Professor," the newcomer jumped down on the boat and walked up to Carol, "if I had known that you had something that looked like *this* down here, I would have been here before dawn. Hello, there, young lady, my name is Troy Jefferson. I am the rest of the crew on this lunatic asylum of a boat."

Carol had been slightly discombobulated by the arrival of Troy and the quick repartee that followed. But she adapted swiftly and regained her composure. She took Troy's outstretched hand and smiled. He immediately leaned up and almost brushed his cheek against hers. "Oooeee," Troy pulled back grinning. "I just caught a whiff of Oscar de la Renta. Professor, didn't I tell you this woman had class? Well, angel," he looked at Carol in mock admiration, "I just can't tell you how much it means to me to finally meet up with someone like you on this tub. Usually we get old ladies, I mean *old* ladies, who want to—"

"Enough, Jefferson," Nick interrupted him. "We have work to do. It's almost noon already and we're still at least half an hour away from being ready to leave. We don't even know what Miss Dawson wants to do."

"Carol is fine," she said. She paused for a moment, assessing the two men in front of her. *Might as well*, Carol thought, *nobody is going to suspect anything if I'm with these two*. "Well, I told the desk that I wanted to go out to do some swimming and diving. But that's only partially true. What I really want to do is go out here (she pulled a folded map out of her beach bag and showed them an area of about ten square miles in the Gulf of Mexico to the north of Key West) and look for whales."

Nick's brow furrowed. Troy peered over Carol's shoulder at the map. "There have been numerous irregularities in the behavior of whales in this area lately, including a major beaching at Deer Key this morning," Carol continued. "I want to see if I can find any pattern in their actions. I may need to do some diving so one of you will have to accompany me. I assume that at least one of you is a licensed diver and that your dive gear is onboard?"

The two men regarded her with disbelieving stares. Carol felt on the defensive. "Really . . . I'm a reporter," she said as an explanation. "I work for the *Miami Herald*. I just did a story this morning on the Deer Key beaching."

Troy turned to Nick. "Okay, Professor, I guess we have a live charter here. One who says she wants to look for whales in the Gulf of Mexico. What do you say? Should we accept her money?"

Nick shrugged his shoulders indifferently and Troy took it as assent. "All right, angel," Troy said to Carol, "we'll be ready in half an hour. We're both licensed divers if we're really needed. Our gear is onboard and we can get more for you. Why don't you pay Julianne at the desk and get your things together."

Troy turned and walked over to the jumbled mess of electronics at the front of the boat. He picked up one of the boxes with its housing partially removed and began toying with it. Nick pulled another beer out of the refrigerator and opened the built-in counters, exposing racks of equipment. Carol did not move. After about twenty seconds Nick noticed that she was still there. "Well," he said in a tone of dismissal, "didn't you hear Troy? We won't be ready for half an hour." He turned around and walked toward the back of the boat.

Troy looked up from his repair work. He was amused by the friction already developing between Nick and Carol. "Is he always so pleasant?" Carol said to Troy, nodding in Nick's direction. She was still smiling but her tone conveyed some irritation. "I have a few pieces of equipment that I want to bring onboard. Can you give me a hand with it?"

Thirty minutes later Troy and Carol returned to the *Florida Queen*. Troy was grinning and whistling "Zippity-Do-Dah" as he pulled a cart down the jetty and came to a stop in front of the boat. A partially filled footlocker was resting on the cart. Troy could hardly wait to see Nick's face when he saw Carol's "few pieces of equipment." Troy was excited by the turn of events. He knew that this was no casual afternoon charter. Reporters, even successful ones (and Troy's street intelligence had quickly informed him that Carol was not just an ordinary reporter), did not have everyday access to the kind of equipment that she was carrying. Already Troy was certain that the whale story was just a cover. But he wasn't going to say anything just yet; he wanted to wait and see how things developed.

Troy liked this confident young woman. There was not a trace of superiority or prejudice in her manner. And she had a good sense of humor. After they had opened the back of her station wagon and she had showed him the footlocker full of equipment, Troy had demonstrated to Carol that he was fairly sophisticated about electronics. He had recognized immediately the MOI insignia on Dale's ocean telescope and Troy had even guessed the meaning of the MOI-IPL acronym on the back of the large monitor and data storage system. When he had looked at her for an explanation, Carol had just laughed and said, "So I need some help finding the whales. What can I say?"

Carol and Troy had loaded the gear on the cart and wheeled it through the parking lot. She had been a little dismayed at first by Troy's recognition of the origin of the equipment and his friendly, probing questions (which she handled adroitly with vague answers—she was helped by the fact that Troy wanted mostly to know how the electronics worked and she, in truth, didn't have the foggiest idea). But as they talked, Carol developed a comfortable feeling about Troy. Her intuitive sense told her that Troy was an ally and could be counted on to be discreet with any important information.

Carol had not, however, planned for a security check inside the Hemingway Marina headquarters. One of the primary selling points of the slips at the new marina had been the almost unparalleled security system offered the boat owners. Every person who went in or out of the marina had to pass through computerized gates adjacent to the headquarters building. A full listing of each individual entrance and exit, including the time of passage through the gate, was printed out each night and retained in the security office files as a precaution in case any suspicious or untoward events were reported.

Materiél entering and leaving the marina was also routinely scrutinized (and logged) by the security chief to prevent the theft of expensive navigation equipment and other electronics. Carol was only mildly irked when, after she paid for the charter, Julianne asked her to fill out a sheet describing the contents of the closed footlocker. But Carol really objected when the summoned security chief, a typical Boston Irish policeman who had retired in the Key West area, forced her to open the locker to verify the contents. Carol's objections and Troy's attempts to help her were to no avail. Rules were rules.

Because the cart would not fit through the door into the adjacent security office, the footlocker was opened in the main clearing room of the marina headquarters. A couple of curious passersby, including one giant, friendly woman about forty named Ellen (Troy knew her from somewhere, probably she was one of the boat owners, Carol thought), came over and watched while Officer O'Rourke carefully compared the contents of the locker with the list that Carol had prepared.

Carol was a little rattled as she and Troy pulled the cart down the jetty toward the *Florida Queen*. She had hoped to attract as little attention as possible and she was now angry with herself for not anticipating the security check. Nick, meanwhile, after performing a few routine preparations on the boat and opening another beer, had become engrossed again in the basketball game. His beloved Harvard was now losing to Tennessee. He did not even hear Troy's whistling until his crewman and Carol were just a few yards away.

"Jesus," Nick turned around, "I thought you had gotten lost . . ." His voice trailed off as he saw the cart and the footlocker. "What the fuck is that?"

"It's Miss Dawson's equipment, Professor," Troy answered with a big grin. He reached into the locker, first picking up a cylinder with a clear glass face, a large flashlight-looking object on a mounting bracket. It was about two feet long and weighed about twelve pounds. "Here, for example, is what she tells me is an ocean telescope. We attach it to the bottom of the boat by this bracket and it takes pictures that are displayed on this here television monitor and also stored on this other device, a recorder of some—"

"Hold it," Nick interrupted Troy imperiously. Nick walked up the gangplank and stared incredulously into the locker. He shook his head and looked from Troy to Carol. "Do I have this right? We are supposed to set up all this shit just to go out into the Gulf for one afternoon to look for whales." He scowled at Troy. "Where is your head, Jefferson? This stuff is heavy, it will take time to set it up, and it's already after noon.

"And as for you, sister," Nick continued, turning to Carol, "take your toys and your treasure map elsewhere. We know what you're up to and we have more important things to do."

"Are you through?" Carol shouted at Nick as he walked back down the gangplank onto the *Florida Queen*. He stopped and turned partially around. "Look, you asshole," Carol raged, giving vent to the frustration and anger that had been building inside of her, "it is certainly your right to deny me the use of your boat. But it is not your right to act like God almighty and treat me or anyone else like shit just because I'm a woman and you feel like pushing somebody around." She stepped toward him. Nick backed up a step in the face of her continued offensive.

"I told you that I want to look for whales and that's what I intend to do. What you might think I'm doing is really of no significance to me. As for the important things that *you* have to do, you haven't moved from that goddamn basketball game in the last hour, except to get more beer. If you'll just stay out of the way, Troy and I can set all this gear in place in half an hour. And besides," Carol slowed down just a bit, starting to feel a little embarrassed about her outburst, "I have already paid for the charter and you know how hard it is to straighten out these computer credit card accounts."

"Oooeee, Professor," Troy grinned wickedly and winked at Carol. "Isn't she something else?" He stopped and became serious. "Look, Nick, we need the money, both of us. And I would be happy to help her. We can take off some of the excess diving gear if it's necessary to balance the weight."

Nick walked back to the folding chair and the television. He took another drink from his beer and did not turn around to look at Carol and Troy. "All right," he said, somewhat reluctantly. "Get started. But if we're not ready to sail by one o'clock it's no deal." The basketball players swam in front of his eyes. Harvard had tied the game again. But this time he wasn't watching. He was thinking about Carol's outburst. *I wonder if she's right. I wonder if I do think that women are inferior. Or worse.*

COMMANDER Vernon Winters was trembling when he hung up the phone. He felt as if he had just seen a ghost. He threw his apple core in the wastebasket and reached in his pocket for one of his Pall Malls. Without thinking, he stood up and walked across the room to the large bay window that opened onto the grassy courtyard of the main administration building. Lunch hour had just finished at the U.S. Naval Air Station. The crowds of young men and women heading either toward or away from the cafeteria had died out. A solitary young ensign was sitting on the grass reading a book, his back against a large tree.

Commander Winters lit his nonfilter cigarette and inhaled deeply. He expelled the smoke with a rush and quickly took another breath. "Hey, Indiana," the voice had said two minutes before, "this is Randy. Remember me." As if he could ever forget that nasal baritone. And then, without waiting for an answer, the voice had materialized into an earnest face on the video monitor. Admiral Randolph Hilliard was sitting behind his desk in a large Pentagon office. "Good," he continued, "now we can see each other."

Hilliard had paused for a moment and then leaned forward toward the camera. "I was glad to hear that Duckett put you in charge of this Panther business. It could be nasty. We must find out what happened, quickly and with no publicity. Both the secretary and I are counting on you."

What had he said in response to the admiral? Commander Winters couldn't remember, but he assumed that it must have been all right. And he did remember the last few words, when Admiral Hilliard had said that he would call back for an update after the meeting on Friday afternoon. Winters had not heard that voice for almost eight years but the recognition was instantaneous. And the memories that flooded forth were just a few milliseconds behind.

The commander took another drag from his cigarette and turned away from the window. He walked slowly across the room. His eyes slid across but did not see the lovely, soft print of the Renoir painting, "Deux Jeunes Filles au Piano," that was the most prominent object on his office wall. It was his favorite painting. His wife and son had given him the special large reproduction for his fortieth birthday; usually several times a week he would stand in front of it and admire the beautiful composition. But two graceful young girls working on their afternoon piano lessons were not the order for the day.

Vernon Winters sat back down at his desk and buried his face in his hands. *Here it comes again*, he thought, *I can't hold it back now, not after seeing Randy and hearing that voice*. He looked around and then stubbed out the cigarette in the large ashtray on his desk. For a few moments he played aimlessly with the two small framed photographs on his desk (one was a portrait of a pale twelve-year-old boy together with a plain woman in her early forties; the other was a cast photo from the Key West Players' production of *Cat on a Hot Tin Roof*, dated March 1993, in which Winters was dressed in a summer business suit). At length the commander put the photographs aside, leaned back in his chair, closed his eyes, and succumbed to the powerful pull of his memory. A curtain in his mind parted and he was transported to a clear, warm night almost eight years before, in early April of 1986. The first sound that he heard was the excited nasal voice of Lieutenant Randolph Hilliard.

"Psst, Indiana, wake up. How can you be asleep? It's Randy. We've got to talk. I'm so excited I could shit." Vernon Winters had only fallen asleep himself about an hour before. He unconsciously looked at his watch. Almost two o'clock. His friend stood next to his bunk, grinning from ear to ear. "Only three more hours and we attack. Finally we're going to blast that A-rab lunatic and terrorist supporter into heaven with Allah. Shit, big buddy, this is our moment. This is what we worked our whole life for."

Winters shook his head and began to come out of a deep sleep. It took him a moment to remember that he was onboard the USS *Nimitz* off the coast of Libya. The first action of his military career was about to occur. "Look, Randy," Winters had said eventually (on that night almost eight years ago), "shouldn't we be sleeping? What if the Libyans attack us tomorrow. We'll have to be alert."

"Shit no," said his friend and fellow officer, helping him to sit up and handing him a cigarette, "those geeks will never attack someone who can fight. They're terrorists. They only know how to fight unarmed people. The only one of them that has any guts is that Colonel Gaddafi and he's nutty as a fruitcake. After we blow him to kingdom come, the battle will be over. Besides, I have enough adrenaline flowing that I could stay awake for thirty-six hours with no sweat."

Winters felt the nicotine coursing through his body. It reawakened the eager anticipation that he had finally conquered when he had fallen asleep an hour earlier. Randy was talking a blue streak. "I can't believe how goddamn lucky we are. For six years I have been wondering how an officer can stand out, distinguish himself, you know, in peacetime. Now here we are. Some loonie plants a bomb in a club in Berlin and we just happen to be on duty in the Med. Talk about being in the right place at the right time. Shit. Think how many other midshipmen from our class would give their right nut to be here instead of us. Tomorrow we kill that crazy man and we're on our way to captain, maybe even admiral, in five to eight years."

Winters reacted negatively to his friend's suggestion that one of the benefits of the strike against Gaddafi would be an acceleration in their personal advancement. But he said nothing. He was already deep in his own private thoughts. He too was excited and he didn't fully understand why. The excitement was similar to the way he had felt before the state quarterfinals in basketball in high school. But Lieutenant Winters couldn't help wondering how much the excitement would be leavened by fear if they were preparing to engage in a real battle.

For almost a week they had been getting ready for the strike. It was normal Navy business to go through the preparations for combat and then have them called off, usually about a day ahead of the planned encounter. But this time it had been different from the beginning. Hilliard and Winters had quickly recognized that there was a seriousness in the senior officers that had never been there before. None of the usual horsing around and nonsense had been tolerated in the tedious and boring checks of the planes, the missiles, and the guns. The *Nimitz* was preparing for war. And then yesterday, the normal time for such a drill to be called off, the captain had gathered all the officers together and told them that he had received the order to attack at dawn. Winters' heart had skipped a beat as the commanding officer had briefed them on the full scope of the American action against Libya.

Winters' last assignment, just after evening mess, had been to go over the bombing targets with the pilots one more time. Two separate planes were being sent to bomb the residence where Gaddafi was supposedly sleeping. One of the two chosen pilots was outwardly ecstatic; he realized that he had been given the prime target of the raid. The other pilot, Lieutenant Gibson from Oregon, was quiet but thorough in his preparations. He kept looking at the map with Winters and going over the Libyan gun emplacements. Gibson also complained that his mouth was dry and drank several glasses of water.

"Shit, Indiana, you know what's bothering me? Those flyboys will be in the battle and we'll be stuck here with no role unless the crazy A-rabs decide to attack. How can we get into the fight? Wait. I just had a thought." Lieutenant Hilliard was still talking nonstop. It was after three o'clock and they had already gone over everything associated with the attack at least twice. Winters was feeling lifeless and enervated from lack of sleep but the astonishing Hilliard continued to exude exuberance.

"What a great idea," Randy continued, talking to himself. "But we can do it. You briefed the pilots tonight, didn't you, so you know who's going after what targets?" Vernon nodded his head. "Then that's it. We'll tape a personal 'screw you' to the side of the missile that's going to get Gaddafi. That way part of us will go into battle."

Vernon did not have the energy to dissuade Randy from his crazy plan. As the time for the attack drew closer, Lieutenants Winters and Hilliard went into the hangar on the *Nimitz* and found the airplane assigned to Lieutenant Gibson (Winters never knew why, but he immediately assumed it would be

Gibson who would score a missile on the Gaddafi enclave). Laughingly, Randy explained to the fresh ensign on watch what he and Vernon were going to try to do. It took them almost half an hour to locate the right plane and then identify the missile that would be the first to be launched against the Gaddafi household.

The two lieutenants argued for almost ten minutes about the message they were going to write on the paper that would be taped on the missile. Winters wanted something deep, almost philosophical, like "Such is the just end to the tyranny of terrorism." Hilliard argued persuasively that Winters' concept was too obscure. At length a tired Lieutenant Winters assented to the visceral communication written by his friend. "DIE, MOTHER-FUCKER," was the message the two lieutenants inscribed on the side of the missile.

Winters returned to his bunk exhausted. Tired and still a little unsettled by the magnitude of the coming day's events, he pulled out his personal Bible to read a few verses. There was no comfort in the good book for the Presbyterian from Indiana. He tried praying, generic prayers at first and then more specific, as had been his custom during critical moments in his life. He asked for the Lord to guard his wife and son and to be with him in this moment of travail. And then, quickly and without thinking, Lieutenant Vernon Winters asked God to rain down terror in the form of the missile with the taped message on Colonel Gaddafi and all his family.

Eight years later, sitting in his office at the U.S. Naval Air Station in Key West, Commander Winters would remember that prayer and cringe inside. Even then, in 1986, just after he finished the prayer, he had felt weird and disoriented, almost as if he had somehow committed a blasphemy and dis-pleased the Lord. A brief hour of sleep that followed was torturous, full of dreams of hideous gargoyles and vampires. He watched the planes leave the carrier the next morning at dawn in a dreamlike trance. His mouth had a bitter metal taste when he mechanically shook Gibson's hand and wished him luck.

For all those years Winters had wished that he could have rescinded that prayer. He was convinced that God had permitted that particular missile carried by Gibson to take the life of Gaddafi's infant daughter just to teach Winters a personal lesson. *On that day,* he thought as he sat in his office on a Thursday in March 1994, *I committed sacrilege and violated your trust. I overstepped my bound and lost my privileged position in your sanctuary. I have asked for forgiveness many times since then but it has not been forthcoming. How much longer must I wait?*

VERNON Allen Winters was born on June 25, 1950, the day that the North Koreans invaded South Korea. He was reminded of the significance of his birthdate throughout his life by his father, Martin Winters, a man who was a hardworking, deeply religious corn farmer in Indiana at the time Vernon was born. When Vernon was three years old and his sister Linda was six, the family moved off the farm and into the town of Columbus, a white, middle-class town of thirty thousand or so in south central Indiana. Vernon's mother had felt isolated out on the farm, particularly during the winter, and wanted more company. The Winters' farm provided a nice cash profit. Mr. Winters, by now almost forty, put most of the nest egg aside as security for a rainy day and became a banker.

Martin Winters was proud to be an American. Whenever Mr. Winters would tell Vernon about the day of his birth, the story would inevitably center around the news of the start of the Korean War and how it was explained to the nation by President Harry Truman. "I thought that day," Mr. Winters would say, "that it was surely no coincidence. The good Lord brought you to us that special day because of his purpose for you. And I bet he meant for you to be a protector of this wonderful country we have created . . ." Later banker Winters would always see to it that the Army-Navy football game was one of the key events of the year and he would tell his friends, particularly when it became obvious that young Vernon was a good student, that "the boy is still trying to choose which of the academies to attend." Vernon was never asked.

The Winters family lived a simple Midwestern life. Mr. Winters was moderately successful, eventually becoming the senior vice-president of the largest bank in Columbus. The family's chief social activity was church. They were Presbyterians and spent almost all day Sunday at the church. Mrs. Winters ran the Sunday school. Mr. Winters was a deacon and voluntarily managed the church finances. Vernon and Linda helped supervise the smaller children at Sunday school and were responsible for the special Bible displays on the bulletin boards in the kindergarten and primary school rooms.

During the week Mrs. Winters sewed and watched soap operas and sometimes played bridge with friends. She never worked outside the home. Her husband and her children were her job. She was an attentive, patient parent who deeply cared for her children and tirelessly chauffeured them to their many activities throughout their years of adolescence.

Vernon played all sports in high school, football and basketball because it was expected of him, baseball because he loved it. He was above average at all sports, not outstanding at anything. "Activities are important, particularly sports," banker Winters often told him approvingly. "The academies look at much more than your grades." The only significant decision that Vernon had to make in the first eighteen years of his life was which of the service academies he preferred. (Mr. Winters, being cautious, was prepared politically to secure a nomination for Vernon to any of the academies. He strongly urged Vernon to think about applying to all three just in case.) In his junior year at Columbus High School, Vernon took the Scholastic Aptitude Test (SAT) and made such a high score that it was obvious he would be able to pick his own favorite. He chose Annapolis and was not questioned about the reasons. If he had been, he would have answered that he just liked the idea of himself in a Navy uniform.

Vernon's teenage years were remarkably linear, particularly considering that they occurred at a time of great social turmoil in the United States. The Winters family prayed together for hours after the Kennedy assassination, worried about local boys in the Vietnam War, remarked with concern when three prominent high school seniors refused to cut their hair and were expelled from school, and attended a couple of church-sponsored meetings on the evils of marijuana. But all these anxieties were outside the daily harmony of the Winters family. Music by the Beatles and the Rolling Stones did penetrate the controlled Winters culture, of course, and even some of the protest songs sung by Bob Dylan and Joan Baez were played on Vernon's stereo. But neither Vernon nor his sister Linda paid much serious attention to the lyrics.

It was an easy existence. Vernon's closest friends were all from families like his. Mothers did not work, fathers were bankers or lawyers or businessmen, almost all were Republicans (but a patriotic Democrat was accepted) and believed fervently in God, country, and the entire litany that ends in apple pie. Vernon was a "good kid," even an "exceptional kid," who first drew attention to himself by his performances in the annual church pageants at Christmas and Easter. The pastor of their church was a great believer that reenactment of the birth and crucifixion of Christ, performed by the children of the town, was a powerful way to reconfirm the faith of the local citizenry. And Reverend Pendleton was correct. The Columbus Presbyterian Church pageants were one of the highlights of the local year. When the church congregation and their friends saw their own children acting in the roles of Joseph, Mary, and even Christ, they became involved in the depicted events at an emotional level that was virtually impossible to achieve in any other way.

Reverend Pendleton had two casts for each pageant, so that more children could participate, but Vernon was always the star. When he was eleven years old Vernon first portrayed Christ in the Easter pageant and it was mentioned in the religious column of the Columbus newspaper that his tortured dragging of the cross had "captured all of man's suffering." He was Joseph at Christmas and Jesus at Easter for four years running, before he became too old and therefore no longer eligible for the pageants. The last two years, when Vernon was thirteen and fourteen, the role of the Virgin Mary in the "A" cast was played by the pastor's daughter, Betty. Vernon and Betty were together quite often while rehearsing and both families were delighted. All four parents made no secret of the fact that they would generously approve if, "assuming God wills it," the Vernon-Betty friendship would eventually mature into something more permanent.

Vernon loved the attention he received from the pageants. Although Betty was touched deeply by the religious aspects of their performances (she remained truly devoted to God, without wavering, through everything in her life), Vernon's joy was standing by his proud parents after each performance and soaking up the praise. In high school he gravitated naturally toward the small drama activity and was the lead in the school play every year. His mother supported this over his father's mild objections ("After all, dear," she would say, "I don't think anyone is really going to think Vernon's a sissy when he's playing three sports.") and because she also vicariously enjoyed the applause.

During the summer of 1968, just before he entered Annapolis, Vernon worked in his uncle's cornfields. Only a little more than a hundred miles away there were riots at the Democratic Convention in Chicago, but in Columbus Vernon spent his summer evenings with Betty, talking with chums and drinking root beer at the A & W Drive-in. Mr. and Mrs. Winters played miniature golf or canasta with Vernon and Betty from time to time. They were delighted and proud to have "good clean kids" who were not hippies or drug victims. All in all, Vernon's last summer in Indiana was ordered, constrained, and very pleasant.

As expected, he was a model student at Annapolis. He studied hard, obeyed all the rules, learned what his professors taught him, and dreamed of being the commander of an aircraft carrier or a nuclear submarine. He was not outgoing, for the big-city boys seemed way too sophisticated for him and he did not always feel comfortable when they talked about sex so casually. He was a virgin and he was not ashamed of it. He just didn't feel the need to broadcast it around the U.S. Naval Academy. He had a couple of dates a month, nothing special, just when the occasion called for it. After a blind date early his junior year with Joanna Carr, a cheerleader at the University of Maryland, he took her out several more times. She was vivacious, lovely, fun, and modern. She drew out the best in Vernon, made him laugh and even relax. She was his date for the weekend of the Army-Navy game in Philadelphia.

(During his entire time at the Academy, Vernon went home every summer and every Christmas to Indiana. He always saw Betty Pendleton when he was home. Betty graduated from high school and entered a nearby state college to study education. Once or twice a year, on special occasions such as the anniversary of their first kiss or New Year's Eve, Betty and he would celebrate, in a sense, by doing a little something intimate. Like controlled petting [outside only] or kissing lying down. Neither of them ever suggested any variation in this well-established routine.)

Vernon and Joanna were joined for the weekend by another midshipman, the closest acquaintance that Vernon had at Navy who was still not quite what one would call a friend, Duane Eller, and his date from Columbia, an extremely loud and pushy girl named Edith. Vernon had never spent much time around a New York City girl and he found Edith absolutely obnoxious. Edith was violently anti-Nixon and anti-Vietnam and seemed, despite the fact that her date for the weekend was going to be a military officer, anti-military as well. The original plan for the weekend had been decidedly proper, even backward given that it was 1970 and casual intercourse was not unusual on college campuses. Vernon and Duane were to share one motel room and the two girls were to share another. Over a pizza dinner the night before the game, Edith frequently insulted Joanna and Vernon both ("Miss Betty Crocker— Go-Team-Go" and "Onward Christian Soldiers, God's on Our Side") and Duane did nothing to intercede. Seeing that Edith was annoying Joanna, Vernon suggested to Joanna that it might be easier if the two of them shared a room instead of following the original game plan. She readily agreed.

Vernon had made no sexual moves on Joanna on the four or five dates that they had had together. He had been attentive, had kissed her good night a couple of times, and had held her hand most of the evening on their last date. Everything had always been extremely proper, but there had never actually been any opportunity for intimacy. So Joanna really didn't know what to expect. She liked this handsome Hoosier midshipman and had thought, a couple of times, about the possibility of the involvement developing into something serious. But Vernon was not yet anyone "super special" for her.

Just after they made the room change (which a drunken Edith made more difficult by embarrassing them and herself with lewd comments), Vernon very carefully apologized to Joanna and told her that he would sleep in the car if she were offended. The room was a typical Holiday Inn room with two double beds. Joanna laughed. "I know you didn't plan this," she said. "If I need protection, I can order you to your bed." The first night they enjoyed watching television and drinking more beer in the room. They both felt a little awkward. At bedtime they shared a couple of almost passionate kisses, laughed together, and then went to separate beds.

The next evening, after the postgame dance sponsored by the Naval Academy at a downtown Philadelphia hotel, Joanna and Vernon returned to their room at the Holiday Inn just before midnight. They had already changed into their jeans and Vernon was brushing his teeth when there was a knock on their door. Joanna opened the door and Duane Eller was standing there, a gigantic shit-eating grin on his face and his hand clenched around some small object. "This stuff is fuckin' fantastic," he said, thrusting a joint into Joanna's hand. "You've just got to try it." Duane withdrew quickly with a wild smile.

Joanna was a bright young woman. But it did not occur to her that her date had never even seen a joint, much less smoked one. She herself had smoked marijuana maybe a dozen times over a four-year period, beginning in her junior year in high school. She liked it, if the situation and the company were right; she avoided it when she couldn't have control of her environment. But she had enjoyed the weekend with Vernon and she thought this might be a perfect way to loosen him up a little.

Under almost any circumstances Vernon would have said no to any offer of marijuana, not just because he was against all drugs, but also because he would have been terrified that somehow he would be discovered and eventually thrown out of Annapolis. But here was his lovely date, a mainstream American cheerleader from Maryland, and she had just lit a joint and offered it to him. Joanna quickly saw that he was a grass neophyte. She showed him how to inhale and hold in the smoke, how not to bogart the joint, and eventually how to use a roach clip (one of her hairpins) to finish it off. Vernon had expected to feel as if he were drunk. He was astonished to find that he felt more alert. Much to his own surprise, he began reciting e.e. cummings poems he had been studying in Lit. And then he and Joanna began to laugh. They laughed at everything. At Edith, football, the Naval Academy, their parents, even Vietnam. They laughed until they were almost crying.

An overpowering hunger attacked Vernon and Joanna. They put on their jackets and walked out into the cold December air to find something to eat. Arm in arm they paraded down the suburban parkway, finding a convenience store that was still open about a half mile from their motel. They bought Cokes and potato chips and Fritos and, much to Vernon's astonishment, a package of Ding Dongs. Joanna opened the potato chips while they were still in the store. She put one in Vernon's mouth and they "Mmmed" while the checkout clerk laughed with them.

Vernon could not believe the taste of the chips. He ate the entire bag while they were walking back to their room. When he was finished, Vernon burst spontaneously into song, singing "Maxwell's Silver Hammer" by the Beatles. Joanna joined in vigorously on the "Bang, bang, Maxwell's silver hammer came down upon his head . . ." She reached up with the side of her fist and playfully banged on the top of his head. Vernon felt jaunty, liberated, as if he had known Joanna forever. He put his arm around her and kissed her ostentatiously as they turned into the driveway leading to their motel.

They sat on the floor with all their munchies spread out in front of them. Vernon turned on the radio. It was tuned to a classical station in the middle of a symphony. Vernon was mesmerized by the sound. For the first time in his life, Vernon could actually hear the individual instruments of the orchestra in his head. He visualized a stage and saw the musicians pulling their bows across the violins. He was fascinated and excited. Vernon told Joanna that all his senses were alive.

To Joanna Carr, it seemed that Vernon was finally opening up. When he leaned over to kiss her, she was more than willing. They kissed sweetly but deeply several times while the symphony was playing. During a momentary break for some more munchies, Joanna tuned the radio to a rock and roll station. The music changed the pace in their necking. Driving, jangling sounds increased the tempo and their kisses became more passionate. In his ardor Vernon pushed Joanna down on the floor and they kissed over and over again as they lay side by side, still fully clothed. They became enthralled by the strength of their arousal.

The radio now started playing "Light My Fire" by the Doors. And Vernon Allen Winters of Columbus, Indiana, third-year midshipman at the U.S. Naval Academy, was no longer a virgin by the time the long song was over. "The time to hesitate is through, no time to wallow in the mire, try now you can only lose, and our love become a funeral pyre . . . Come on baby, light my fire . . . Come on baby, light my fire." Vernon had never lost control of himself before in his entire life. But when Joanna stroked the outline of his swollen penis underneath his jeans, it was as if a giant wall of steel and concrete suddenly gave way. Years later, Vernon would still marvel at the raw passion he showed for two, maybe three minutes. The combination of Joanna's insistent kisses, the grass, and the driving rhythms of the music pushed him over the edge. He was an animal. Still on the floor of the motel room, he pulled vigorously on Joanna's slacks several times, nearly tearing them as he managed to free them from her hips. Her underpants half followed the slacks. Vernon grabbed them roughly and pulled them down the rest of the way while he was squirming out of his own jeans.

Joanna tried in a quiet voice to slow Vernon down, to suggest that maybe the bed would be better. Or at least it would be more pleasant if they actually took off their shoes and socks and didn't make love with their pants around their ankles restricting their movement. But Vernon was gone. Years of restraint left him no ability to deal with his own surging desire. He was possessed. He crawled on top of Joanna, a look of frightening seriousness on his face. For the first time she was scared and her sudden fear heightened her sexual excitement. Vernon struggled for a few seconds (the music was now in the frenzied instrumental part of "Light My Fire") to find the right spot and then entered her abruptly and forcefully. Joanna felt him drive once, twice, and then shudder all over. He was done in maybe ten seconds. She intuitively knew that it had been his first time and the pleasure of that knowledge outweighed her bruised feelings about his lack of finesse and gentleness.

Vernon said nothing and quickly fell asleep on the floor next to Joanna. She gamely went to the bed, pulled the bedspread off, cuddled into Vernon's arms on the floor, and wrapped the spread around them. She smiled to herself and drifted off to sleep, still a little puzzled by this Hoosier lying next to her. But she knew that they were now special to each other.

How special Joanna would never really know. When Vernon woke up in the middle of the night, he felt an overpowering sense of guilt. He could not believe that he had smoked dope and then virtually raped a girl he hardly knew. He had lost control. He had been unable to stop what he was doing and had clearly crossed the bounds of propriety. He winced when he thought about what his parents (or worse, Betty and Reverend Pendleton) would think about him if they could have seen what he had done. Then the guilt gave way to fear. Vernon imagined that Joanna was pregnant, that he had to leave Annapolis and marry her (What would he do? What kind of job would he have if he were not a naval officer?), that he had to explain all this to his parents and to the Pendletons. Worse still, he next imagined that at any minute the motel would be raided and the police would find the butt of the joint in the roach clip. He would first be kicked out of the Academy for drug abuse, *then* find out that he had made a girl pregnant.

Vernon Winters was now really scared. Lying on the floor of a motel room on the outskirts of Philadelphia at three o'clock on a Sunday morning, he began to pray in earnest. "Dear God," Vernon Winters prayed, asking for something specific for himself for the first time since he asked God to help him on the day that he took the SATs, "let me get out of this without harm and I will become the most perfectly disciplined naval officer that you have ever seen. I will dedicate my life to defending this country that honors you. Just please help me."

Eventually Vernon managed to fall asleep again. But his sleep was fitful and disturbed by vivid dreams. In one dream Vernon was dressed in his midshipman's uniform but was on stage back at the Columbus Presbyterian Church. It was the Easter pageant and he was again Christ, dragging the cross to Calvary. The sharp edge of the cross on his shoulder was cutting through his uniform shirt and Vernon was aware of anxiety that he might not pass inspection. He stumbled and fell, the cross cut deeper through the uniform as he had feared and he could see some blood running down his arm. "Crucify him," Vernon heard someone shout in the dream. "Crucify him," a group of people in the audience shouted together as Vernon tried vainly to see through the klieg lights. He woke up sweating. For a couple of moments he was disoriented. Then again his emotions went the cycle from disgust to depression to fear as he played through the events of the night before.

Joanna was tender and affectionate after she woke up but Vernon was very distant. He explained his attitude by saying he was worried about his coming exams. A couple of times Joanna started to talk about what had happened the night before, but each time he rapidly changed the subject. Vernon suffered through brunch and the drive back to College Park to Joanna's sorority house. Joanna tried to kiss him meaningfully when they parted but Vernon did not reciprocate. He was in a hurry to forget the entire weekend. Back in the privacy of his own room in Annapolis, he contritely bargained again with God to let him escape unscathed.

Midshipman Vernon Winters was true to his word. He not only never talked to Joanna Carr again (she called and failed to reach him a couple of times, sent two letters that were unanswered, and then gave up), he also gave up dating altogether during his final eighteen months at Annapolis. He worked very hard on his studies and attended chapel, as he had promised God, twice each week.

He graduated with honors and did his initial tour of duty on a large aircraft carrier. Two years later, in June of 1974, after Betty Pendleton had completed college and obtained her teacher's certificate, Vernon married her in the Columbus Presbyterian Church where they had played Joseph and Mary a dozen years earlier. They moved to Norfolk, Virginia, and Vernon believed that the pattern of his life was set. His life would be going out to sea for long stretches and then coming home for short stays with Betty and any children they might have.

Vernon regularly thanked God for keeping up His part of the bargain and he dedicated himself to being the finest officer in the U.S. Navy. All of his fitness reports praised his dependability and thoroughness. His commanding officers openly told him that he was admiral material. Until Libya. Or more specifically, until he returned home after the Libyan action. For the entire world changed for Vernon Allen Winters during the few weeks after the American attack against Gaddafi.

CAROL and Troy were sitting in deck chairs at the front of the *Florida Queen*. They were facing forward in the boat, toward the ocean and the warm afternoon sun. Carol had removed her purple blouse to reveal the top of a one-piece blue bathing suit, but she was still wearing her white cotton slacks. Troy was shirtless in a white surfing outfit that came quite a way down his beautiful black legs. His body was lean and sinewy, clearly fit but not overly muscled. They were talking casually and animatedly, laughing often in an easy way. Behind them underneath the canopy, Nick Williams was reading *A Fan's Notes* by Fred Exley. Every now and then he would look up at the other two for a few moments and then return to his book.

"So why didn't you ever go to college?" Carol was asking Troy. "You clearly had the ability. You would have made a fantastic engineer."

Troy stood up, took off his sunglasses, and walked to the railing. "My brother, Jamie, said the same thing," he said slowly, staring out at the quiet ocean. "But I was just too wild. When I finally did graduate from high school, I was hungry to know what the world was like. So I took off. I wandered all over the U.S. and Canada for a couple of years."

"Was that when you learned about electronics?" Carol asked. She checked her watch to see what time it was.

"That was later, much later," said Troy, remembering. "Those two years of wandering I didn't learn anything except how to survive on my wits. Plus what it was like to be a black boy in a white man's world." He looked at Carol. There was no noticeable reaction.

"I must have had a hundred different jobs," he continued, looking back at the ocean, "I was a cook, a copyboy, a bartender, a construction worker. I even taught swimming lessons in a private club. I was a bellman in a resort hotel, a greenskeeper for a country club . . ." Troy laughed and turned again to see if Carol was paying attention. "But I guess you're not interested in all this . . ."

"Sure I am," Carol said, "it's fascinating to me. I'm trying to imagine what you looked like in a hotel uniform. And if Chief Nick is right, we still have another ten minutes to pass until we reach where we're going." She dropped her voice. "At least you *talk*. The professor is not exactly social."

"Being a black bellhop at a southern Mississippi resort hotel was an amazing learning experience," Troy began, a smile spreading across his face. Troy loved to tell stories about his life. It always placed him center stage. "Imagine, angel, I'm eighteen years old and I luck into a job at the grand old Gulfport Inn, right on the beach. Room and board plus tips. I'm on top of the world. At least until the chief bellman, an impossible little man named Fish, takes me out to the barracks where all the bellhops and kitchen staff live and introduces me to everybody as the 'new nigger bellhop.' From bits of discussion I can tell that the hotel is in some kind of trouble because of possible racial discrimination and hiring me is part of their response.

"My room in the barracks was right behind the twelfth green on the golf course. A small bunk bed, a dresser built into the wall, a desk or table with a portable lamp, a sink to brush my teeth and wash my face—that's where I lived for six weeks. Down at the other end of the building was the great community bathroom that everyone left whenever I showed up.

"In my high school in Miami virtually the entire student body was Cuban or black or both. So I knew almost nothing about white people. From books and television I had this fantasy image of whites as handsome, competent, educated, and rich. Ha. My fantasy quickly vanished. You would not have believed the crew that worked in that hotel. The head bellman Fish smoked dope every night with his sixteen-year-old son Danny and dreamed of the day he would find a million dollars left in somebody's room. His only other goal in life was to continue screwing the chef's wife, Marie, in the supply closet every morning until he died.

"One of the other bellmen was a poor, lonely soul whose real name was Saint John because his brilliant parents thought that 'Saint' was a given name. He had only six teeth, wore thick glasses, and had a giant tumor underneath his left eye. Saint John knew that he was ugly and he worried all the time about losing his job because of his personal appearance. So Fish exploited him unmercifully by giving him all the shittiest assignments and forcing him to pay kickbacks with a portion of his tips. The other bellmen also ridiculed Saint John at every opportunity and made him the butt of their practical jokes.

"One night I was sitting quietly in my room reading a book when there was a soft knock on the door. When I answered it, Saint John was standing there. He looked confused and distracted. He was holding a small game box in one hand and a six-pack of beer in the other. I waited a few moments and then asked him what he wanted. He looked nervously in both directions and then asked me if I knew how to play chess. When I told him yes and added that I would enjoy a game, Saint John grinned from ear to ear and mumbled something about being glad that he had taken a chance. I invited him in and we played and talked and drank beer for almost two hours. He was one of nine children from a poor, rural Mississippi family. While we were playing, Saint John casually let slip that he had been a little reluctant to ask me to play because Fish and Miller had told him that niggers were too dumb to play chess.

"Saint John and I became friends, at least sort of, for the few more weeks that I stayed there. We were united by the deepest of bonds, we were both outsiders in that strange social structure created by the employees of the Gulf-port Inn. It was from Saint John that I learned about the many misconceptions that Southern whites have about blacks." Troy laughed. "You know, one night Saint John actually followed me to the bathroom to verify with his own eyes that I was not significantly larger than he was."

Troy returned to his deck chair and looked at Carol. She was smiling. It was hard not to enjoy Troy's stories. He told them with such enthusiasm and self-involved charm. Under the canopy Nick also had put his book aside and was listening to the conversation.

"Then there was this giant Farrell, early twenties, who looked like Elvis Presley. He supplied liquor to the guests at cut rates, operated an escort service on call, and took excess hotel goods to sell at his sister's market. He rented part of my room to store some of the liquor. What a character. After big convention breakfasts Farrell would pour the leftover orange juice in the pitchers into bottles and keep it for resale. One morning the hotel manager found a case of the juice temporarily sitting in a room off the lobby and demanded to know what was going on. Farrell grabbed me and took me out front. He told me that he wanted to make a deal. If I would acknowledge that I had taken the juice, Farrell would pay me twenty dollars. He explained that if I confessed, nothing would happen to me, because niggers were expected to steal. But if he Farrell were caught, he would lose his job . . ."

Nick came out from under the canopy. "I hate to break this up," he said, a little sarcastic edge in his voice, "but according to our computer navigator, we are now at the south edge of the region on the map." He handed the map back to Carol.

"Thanks, Professor," Troy laughed, "I believe you saved Carol from being talked to death." He walked over to where all the monitoring equipment had been set up on the footlocker next to the canopy. He turned on the power supply. "Hey, angel, you want to tell me now how this all works."

Dale Michaels' ocean telescope was programmed to take three virtually simultaneous pictures at each fixed setting. The first of the pictures was a normal visible image, the second was the same field of view photographed at infrared wavelengths, and the third was a composite sonar image of the same frame. The sonar subsystem did not produce crisp pictures, only outlines of objects. However, it probed to greater depths than either the visible or infrared elements of the telescope and could be used even when the water underneath the boat was murky.

Affixed to the bottom of almost any boat, the compact telescope could be driven thirty degrees back and forth about the vertical by a small internal motor. The observation schedule for the telescope was usually defined by a preprogrammed protocol. The details of this sequence as well as the critical optical parameters for the telescope were all stored in the system microprocessor; however, everything in the software could be changed in realtime by manual input if the operator desired.

Data from the telescope was carried to the rest of the electronic equipment on the boat by means of very thin fiber optics. These cables were bracketed along the edge of the boat. About ten percent of the pictures reconstructed from this data were then displayed (after some very crude enhancements) on the boat's monitor in realtime. But all the data taken by the telescope was automatically recorded in the one hundred gigabit memory unit that adjoined the monitor. Another set of fiber optics connected the same memory unit with the boat's central navigation system and the servomotor actuators controlling the telescopes. These circuits were pulsed every ten milliseconds so that the orientation of the telescope and the boat's location at the time of each telescope image could be stored together in the permanent file.

Next to the monitor on top of the footlocker, but on the other side from the memory unit, was the system control panel. Dr. Dale Michaels and MOI were famous throughout the world for the cleverness of their inventions; however, these ingenious creations were not so easy to operate. Dale had tried to give Carol a crash course on the workings of the system the night before she had driven down to Key West from Miami. It had been almost useless. Eventually frustrated, Dale had simply programmed into the microprocessor an easy sequence that mosaicked the area under the boat in regular patterns. He then set the optical gains at normal default values, and instructed Carol not to change *anything*. "All you have to do," Dr. Michaels had said as he had carefully loaded the system control panel into the station wagon, "is push this GO button. Then cover the panel to make certain that nobody inadvertently hits the wrong command."

So Carol certainly could not explain to Troy how anything worked. She walked over beside him on the boat, put her arm on his shoulder, and grinned sheepishly. "I hate to disappoint you, my inquisitive friend, but I don't know any more about how this thing works than I told you when we were setting up all the equipment. To operate it, all we have to do is turn on the power supply, which you have already done, and then push this button." She pushed the GO button on the panel. A picture of the clear ocean about fifty feet underneath the boat appeared immediately on the color monitor. The picture was amazingly sharp. The threesome watched in wonder as a hammerhead shark swam through a school of small gray fish, swallowing hundreds of them in his awesome rush.

"As I understand it," Carol continued as both men stayed glued in fascination to the monitor, "the telescope system then does the rest, following a planned set of observations stored in its software. Obviously we see what it sees here on this monitor. At least we see the visual image. The simultaneous infrared and sonar pictures are stored on the recorder. My friend at MOI (she didn't want to alert them even more by using Dale's name) tried to explain how I could change between the visual and infrared and sonar images, but it wasn't simple. You'd think it would be as easy as pushing an "I" for infrared or an "S" for sonar. Nope. You have to input as many as a dozen commands just to change which output signal is fed into the monitor."

Troy was impressed. Not just by the ocean telescope system, but also by the way Carol, a woman admittedly not educated in engineering or electronics, had clearly grasped the essentials of it. "The infrared part of the telescope must measure thermal radiation," he said slowly, "if I remember my high school physics correctly. But how would underwater thermal variations tell you anything about whales?"

At this point Nick Williams shook his head and turned away from the screen. He recognized that he was hopelessly out of his intellectual element with all these engineering terms and he was more than a little embarrassed to admit his total ignorance in front of Carol and Troy. Nick also didn't believe for an instant that Carol had brought all this electronic wizardry on board to find whales that had strayed from their migration route. He walked over to the small refrigerator and pulled out another beer. "And what we're going to do for the next two hours, if I understand it correctly, is ride around in the boat while you look for whales on that screen?"

Nick's derisive comment carried with it an unmistakable challenge. It intruded upon the warm and friendly rapport that had been created between Carol and Troy. She allowed herself to become irritated again by Nick's attitude and fired back her own verbal fusillade. "That *was* the plan, Mister Williams, as I told you when we left Key West. But Troy tells me that you're something of a treasure hunter. Or at least *were* some years ago. And since you seem to have convinced yourself that treasure is really what I'm after, perhaps you'd like to sit here next to me and look at the same pictures to make sure I don't miss any whales. Or treasure, as the case may be."

Nick and Carol glared at each other for a few moments. Then Troy stepped between them. "Look, Professor . . . and you too, angel . . . I don't pretend to understand why you two insist on pissing each other off. But it's a pain in the ass for me. Can't you just cool it for a while? After all," Troy added, looking first at Nick and then at Carol, "if you two go for a dive, you're partners. Your lives may depend on one another. So knock it off."

Carol shrugged her shoulders and nodded. "Okay by me," she said. But seeing no immediate response from Nick, she couldn't resist another shot. "Provided that Mr. Williams recognizes his responsibility as a PADI member and stays sober enough to dive."

Nick's eyes flashed angrily. Then he walked over to the deck railing and dramatically poured his new beer into the ocean. "Don't worry about me, sweetheart," he said, forcing a smile, "I can take care of myself. You just worry about what you do."

The ocean telescope microprocessor contained a special alarm subroutine that sounded a noise like a telephone ring whenever the programmed alarm conditions were triggered. At Carol's request, Dale Michaels had personally adapted the normal alarming algorithm just before she left for Key West so that it would react to *either* a large creature moving across the field of view *or* a stationary "unknown" object of significant size. After he had finished the logic design for the small change and sent it to his software department for top priority coding and testing, Dale had smiled to himself. He was amused by his complicity with Carol. This piece of technological subterfuge would certainly convince Carol's companions, whoever they might be, that she was earnest in her search for whales. At the same time, the alarm would also sound if what Carol was really seeking, supposedly an errant (and secret) Navy missile currently under development, appeared on the ocean floor underneath the boat.

The basic structure for both alarm algorithms was easy to understand. To identify a moving animal, it was sufficient to overlay two or three images taken less than a second apart (at any wavelength, although there was greater accuracy in the process with the sharper visual images), and then compare the data using the knowledge that most of the scene should be unchanged. Significant miscompares (connected areas in the overlay that differed from image to image) would suggest the presence of a large moving creature.

To identify foreign objects in the field of view, the alarm algorithm took advantage of the tremendous storage capacity of the memory unit in the telescope data processing system. The near simultaneous infrared and visual images were fed into the memory unit and then crudely analyzed against a data set that contained chains of pattern recognition parameters over both wavelength regions. These pattern parameters had been developed through years of careful research and had been recently expanded by MOI to include virtually everything normal (plants, animals, reef structures, etc.) that might be seen on the ocean floor around the Florida Keys. Any large object that didn't correlate in realtime with this existing data base would be flagged and the alarm would sound.

The alarms made it unnecessary to sit patiently in front of the screen and study the thousands of frames of data as they were received on the boat. Even Troy, a confessed "knowledge junkie" whose interest in everything was almost insatiable, grew tired of staring at the monitor after about ten minutes, particularly when the boat entered into deeper water and very little could be seen in the visual images.

A couple of solitary sharks triggered alarms and created momentary excitement about twenty minutes after the telescope was activated, but a long period void of any discoveries followed. As the afternoon waned Nick became more and more impatient. "I don't know why I allowed myself to be talked into this wild goose chase," he grumbled to nobody in particular. "We could have been preparing the boat for the weekend charter."

Carol ignored Nick's comment and studied the map one more time. They had traversed from south to north the region she and Dale had defined and were now moving slowly east along the northern periphery. Dale had constructed the search area based upon his own inferences from the questions asked him by the Navy. He probably could have pinned down the area of interest with greater certainty with a few more questions of his own, but he hadn't wanted to arouse any suspicions.

Carol knew that the search was a little like finding a needle in a haystack, but she had thought it would be worthwhile because of the potential payoff. If she could somehow find and photograph a secret Navy missile that had crashed near a populated area . . . What a scoop that would be! But now she too was growing a little impatient and it was hard for her to revive her earlier excitement after the long afternoon in the sun. They would have to head back to Key West soon to ensure arrival by nightfall. *Oh well*, she thought to herself with resignation, *at least I gave it a shot. And as my father used to say, nothing ventured, nothing gained.*

She was standing all the way at the prow of the boat when suddenly alarms started coming from the memory unit next to the monitor. One ring, then two, followed by a brief silence. A third ring then sounded and was rapidly joined by a fourth. Carol rushed excitedly toward the monitor. "Stop the boat," she shouted imperiously at Nick. But she was too late. By the time she reached the monitor, the alarms had stopped and she could not see anything on the screen.

"Turn around, turn around," a frustrated Carol hollered immediately, not noticing that Nick was again glaring at her.

"Aye, aye, Cap-i-tan," Nick said, jerking on the wheel with such force that Carol lost her balance. The monitor and other electronic equipment started to slide off their flimsy mountings on the top of the footlocker; they were rescued at the last minute by Troy. The *Florida Queen* veered sharply in the water. Despite the quietness of the ocean, a small wave came over the railing on the low side of the deck, catching Carol from the knees down. The bottom of her cotton slacks were left clinging to her calves. Her white tennis shoes and socks were drenched. Nick made no effort to hide his amusement.

Carol was about to joust with him again when the renewed ringing of the alarms diverted her attention. Regaining her squishy footing as the boat leveled off, she saw in the monitor that they were above a coral reef. And deep beneath the boat, barely discernible on the screen, were three whales of the same kind that she had seen on the beach that morning at Deer Key. They were swimming together in what appeared to be an aimless pattern. But there was more. The special alarm message code indicated that there was also a foreign object in or near to the same field of view as the desultory whales. Carol could not contain her excitement. She clapped her hands. "Anchor, please," she shouted, and then she laughed. She saw that Troy had already thrown the anchor overboard.

A few minutes later Carol was hurriedly putting on her buoyancy vest in the aft portion of the boat behind the canopy. Her mask and her flippers had already been adjusted and were beside her on the deck. Troy was helping her by holding up the air bottle that was built into the back of the bulky vest. "Don't worry about Nick," Troy said. "He may be grumpy today for some reason, maybe because Harvard lost the basketball game, but he's a fabulous diver. And he has the reputation of being the best dive teacher in the Keys." He grinned. "After all, he taught me a couple of months ago and we're not even supposed to be able to swim."

Carol smiled and shook her head at Troy. "Don't you ever stop joking?" she said. She slid her free arm through the second opening and the vest fell into place. "By the way," she continued softly, "for an expert diver your friend certainly uses antiquated equipment." At this moment she regretted her decision to leave her customized diving vest in the station wagon. She always used it when she dove with Dale and it had all the latest advances, such as ABC (Automatic Buoyancy Compensation) and a perfect pocket for her underwater camera. But after all the brouhaha when she came through the marina headquarters with her footlocker of electronic equipment, Carol had decided not to attract further attention by bringing in a state-of-the-art diving vest.

"Nick thinks the new vests make it too easy for the diver. He wants them to have to adjust their buoyancy manually—so that they are more conscious of how far down they are." Troy looked Carol over. "You're pretty light. This belt may be enough by itself. Do you normally use any weights?"

Carol shook her head and pulled the belt around her waist. Nick came around the canopy carrying his mask and flippers. He had already put on his diving vest with air bottle and his weighted belt. "Those whales of yours are still in the same spot down there," he said. "I've never seen whales hang around like that." He handed her a piece of chewing tobacco. She rubbed the tobacco on the inside of her mask (to prevent fogging) while Nick walked around behind her. He looked at her air gauge and checked both her regulator and the secondary mouthpiece that he might have to use to share her air in the event of an emergency.

Nick talked to Carol while he was making her final equipment checks. "This is your charter," he began in what sounded like a friendly tone, "so we can go almost anywhere you want while we are down there. The dive will not be too difficult, since it's only forty-five feet or so to the floor. However," Nick moved around in front of Carol and looked directly in her eyes, "I want one thing thoroughly understood. This is my boat and I am responsible for the safety of the people on it. Including you, whether you like it or not. Before we dive, I want to make certain that you will follow my lead under the water."

Carol recognized that Nick was trying to be diplomatic. It even flashed through her mind that he looked sort of cute standing there in front of her in his diving gear. She decided to be gracious. "Agreed," she said. "But one thing before we descend. Remember that I'm a reporter. I will have a camera with me and may want you to move from time to time. So don't get angry if I motion you out of the way."

Nick smiled. "Okay," he said, "I'll try to remember."

Carol put on her flippers and mask. Then she picked up her underwater camera by the strap and threw it over her neck and shoulder. Troy helped her tighten the strap in the back. Nick was sitting on the side of the boat at a break in the railing, right next to a crude ladder that Troy had just dropped overboard. "I've checked the water already," Nick said, "and there's quite a current up here. Let's go down the anchor rope until we reach the ocean floor. Then you can pick the direction from there."

Nick rolled backward off the boat. In a moment he surfaced, treading water. Carol returned his thumbs-up sign (the signal between divers that everything's all right) and sat down herself on the side of the boat. Troy helped her make one last comfort adjustment to her vest. "Good luck, angel," Troy said. "I hope you find what you're looking for. And be careful."

Carol put the regulator in her mouth, took a breath, and then repeated Nick's backward roll maneuver. The ocean water felt cool against her sunbaked back. In a few seconds she joined Nick over at the anchor rope and the two of them repeated the thumbs up sign. Nick led the way down. He went hand over hand, cautiously, never completely releasing the rope. Carol followed carefully. She could feel the strong current that Nick had mentioned. It pulled at her, trying to take her away from the rope, but she managed to hold on. Every six to eight feet in the descent, Nick stopped to equalize the pressure in his ears and looked up to see both that Carol was following and that she was all right. Then he continued his descent.

There was nothing much to see until they reached the reef beneath them. The telescope pictures had been so sharp that they had been misleading. The reef with its riot of color and its surfeit of plant and animal life had seemed to be right underneath them because of the automatic focusing action of the optical system. But thirty-five feet is a long way down. Any normal three-story building could have been sitting on the ocean floor underneath the *Florida Queen* and it would not have touched her hull.

When they finally reached the top of the reef where the anchor was implanted, Carol realized she had made a mistake. She did not recognize her surroundings and therefore did not know which direction to take to find the whales. She reproached herself briefly for not having spent a few more moments studying the monitor to make sure that she knew where all the landmarks were. *Oh well*, Carol then thought, *It's too late for that now. I'll just pick a direction and go. Besides, I don't have any idea where the alarm object is anyway.*

Visibility in the water was fair to good, maybe fifty to sixty feet in all directions. Carol adjusted her buoyancy slightly and then pointed to a gap between two reef structures, both of which were covered with kelp, sea anemones, and the ubiquitous coral. Nick nodded his head. Tucking her arms to her side to streamline her movement, Carol kicked up and down with her flippers and swam toward the gap.

Behind her, Nick watched Carol swim with appreciation and admiration. She moved through the water as gracefully as the school of yellow and black angelfish beside her. Nick had not interrogated Carol very much about her diving experience and had not known exactly what to expect. He had suspected from her ease and familiarity with the equipment that she was a seasoned diver; but he had not prepared himself for an underwater peer. Except for Greta, Nick had not encountered a woman before who was as comfortable under the water as he was.

Nick absolutely loved the peace and serenity of the rich and vibrant world beneath the ocean surface. The only sound he ever heard down there was his own breathing. All around him the coral reefs teemed with life of unimaginable beauty and complexity. There, underneath him now, was a grouper taking a bath by sitting at the bottom of a natural hole and letting dozens of tiny cleaner fish eat away all the accumulated parasites. A moment earlier, Nick's downward excursion toward the ocean floor had scared up a manta ray hidden in the sand. This large ray, called a devilfish by the cognoscenti, had undulated out of its hiding place at the last moment and just missed Nick with its powerful and dangerous tail.

Nick Williams felt at home down in this watery world at the bottom of the Gulf of Mexico. It was his recreation and his refuge. Whenever he was distressed or disturbed by events on the surface, he knew that he could dive and find relaxation and escape. Except on this particular dive he was aware of an ineffable emotion, a beginning perhaps, a longing that was barely defined, possibly mixed up with a memory of years ago. He was following a beautiful mermaid as she swam along the reef and the sight stirred him. *I have acted like a schoolboy*, he thought, *and a bore. Or worse. And why? Because she is pretty? No. Because she is so alive. So much more alive than I am.*

Carol and Nick made two different excursions, each time starting from the anchor rope, without finding the whales or anything else unusual. When they returned to the anchor after the second unsuccessful foray, Nick pointed at his watch. They had been under the water for almost half an hour already. Carol wagged her head up and down and then held up her index finger, indicating that she would try one more direction.

They found the whales right after they crossed over a big upward bulge in the reef that came within fifteen feet of the surface. Nick saw them first and pointed down. The three whales were about twenty feet below them and maybe thirty yards ahead. They were still swimming slowly, more or less together, in the same directionless, near circular pattern that Nick and Carol had watched on the screen. Carol waved Nick out of the way and pointed at her camera. She then swam toward the whales, taking pictures as she approached them while carefully monitoring her depth and equalizing the pressure in her ears.

Nick swam down beside her. He was certain the whales had seen the two of them, but for some reason they had made no attempt to flee. In all his years as a diver, Nick had only once seen a whale in the open ocean accept the nearby presence of a human. And that had been a calfing mother, in a Pacific Ocean lagoon off of Baja California, whose birth pangs were a more powerful force than her instinctive fear of humans. Here, even when Carol approached to within twenty feet or so, the whales continued their indolent drift. They appeared to be lost, or maybe even drugged.

Carol slowed her approach when the whales made no attempt to get away. She took some more photographs. Close-up pictures of whales in their natural habitat were still uncommon, so her trip had already been a journalistic success. But she too was puzzled by their behavior. Why were they ignoring her presence? And what were they doing hanging around this particular spot? She remembered being surprised by the solitary whale during her morning swim and wondered again if somehow all these strange events were related.

Nick was off to her right, about twenty yards away. He was pointing at something on the other side of the whales and gesturing for Carol to come toward him. She swam away from the great mammals and headed in Nick's direction. She saw immediately what had attracted his attention. Below the whales, just above the ocean floor, there was a large dark hole in the bottom of an imposing reef structure. At first glance it appeared to be the entrance to an underground cave of some kind. But Carol's sharp eyes noticed that the lip-shaped fissure was extremely smooth and symmetric, almost suggesting to her that it was an engineering construction of some kind. She laughed at herself as she swam up beside Nick. The amazing underwater world and the bizarre behavior of these whales were playing tricks with her mind.

Nick pointed down at the hole and then at himself, indicating that he was going down to check it out more closely. When he started to leave, Carol had a sudden impulse to reach for his foot and pull him back. A moment later, as she watched Nick swim away, a powerful fear of unknown origin swept over her. She began to tremble as she struggled gamely with this strange emotion. Goose bumps appeared on her arms and legs and Carol felt an overwhelming desire to get away, to escape before something terrible happened.

An instant later she saw one of the whales move toward Nick. If Carol had been on land she could have yelled, but fifty feet deep in the ocean there was no way to warn someone from afar. As Nick drew near the opening, unaware of any danger, he was brushed to the side by one of the whales with such force that he bounced against the reef and then carromed off. He fell down onto a small spot of sand on the ocean floor. Carol swam toward him quickly while keeping a careful eye on the whales. Nick had lost his regulator and did not seem to be making any attempt to replace it. She drew up beside him and flashed the thumbs-up sign. There was no response. Nick's eyes were closed.

Carol felt a surge of adrenaline as she reached for Nick's regulator and thrust it into his mouth. She beat against his mask with her fist. After a few painfully long seconds, Nick opened his eyes. Carol tried thumbs up again. Nick shook his head, as if he were clearing out the cobwebs, smiled, and then returned the okay signal. He started to move but Carol restrained him. She indicated with gestures for him to sit still while she hurriedly looked him over. From the force with which Nick had hit the reef, Carol feared the worst. Even if his diving gear was all right, certainly his skin would have been ripped and torn by the sharp coral and the impact. But, incredibly, there did not appear to be significant damage to either Nick or the equipment. All she could find were a couple of small scrapes.

The three whales remained in the same area where they had been before. Looking up at them from below, Carol thought that they looked like sentinels guarding a particular piece of ocean territory. Back and forth they swam, inscribing a total composite arc of maybe two hundred yards. Whatever it had been that had caused one of the whales to vary its swimming pattern and run into Nick was certainly unclear. But Carol did not want to risk another encounter. She motioned for Nick to follow her and they swam about thirty yards away, to a sandy trench between the reefs.

Carol planned to return to the surface as soon as it was clear that Nick was not seriously hurt. But while Carol was thoroughly surveying his body to make certain that she had not overlooked any serious lacerations in her hurried check, Nick discovered two parallel indentations in the sand below him. He grabbed Carol's arm to show her what he had found. The indentations were grooved like tank tracks and were about three inches deep. They appeared to be fresh. In one direction the tracks ran toward the reef fissure underneath the three whales. In the other direction the parallel lines extended as far as Nick and Carol could see, running along the sandy trench between the two major reefs in the area.

Nick pointed up the trench and then swam away in that direction, following the tracks with fascination. He did not turn around to see if Carol were following. Carol quickly backtracked as close to the fissure as she dared (was she imagining again or were the three whales watching her as she crept along the ocean floor?) to take some pictures and to verify that the tracks did indeed emanate from the opening in the reef. She thought she saw a network of similar indentations converging just in front of the fissure, but she did not tarry long. She didn't want to be separated from Nick in this spooky place. When she turned around, he was just barely in sight. But he had fortunately stopped when he realized that Carol was not behind him. Nick made an apologetic gesture when she finally caught up with him.

At one point the parallel lines disappeared as the sandy trench turned to rock, but Nick and Carol located the continuation of the same tracks some fifty yards farther along. The trench eventually became so narrow that they were forced to swim six feet or so above it to keep from banging against the rocks and coral on either side. Soon thereafter the tracks and the trench made a left turn and disappeared under an overhang. Carol and Nick stopped and floated in the water facing each other. They carried on a conversation with hand gestures. At length, they decided that Carol would go down first to see if anything was under the overhang, since she wanted a close-up photograph of the disappearance of the tracks anyway.

Carol swam carefully down to the floor of the trench, skillfully avoiding contact with the edges of the reef on both sides. Where it disappeared under the overhang, the trench was just wide enough for her to put one of her flippered feet down lengthwise. The overhang was about eighteen inches above the floor, but there was no way she could bend down and look underneath without scraping her face or hands against the reef. Carol gingerly slid her hand under the overhang in the last direction of the tracks. Nothing. She would have to brace herself against the rocks and coral and stick her hand deeper into the area.

While Carol was trying to move herself into a better position, she momentarily lost her balance and felt the sting of coral on the back of her left thigh. *Ouch*, she thought as she put her right hand back under the overhang, *that's one for me. One physical reminder of an amazing day. Weird even. Bizarre whales. Tank tracks on the bottom of the ocean . . . what is this?* Carol's hand closed around what felt like a metallic rod about an inch thick. It was such a surprising touch, she immediately withdrew her hand and a shudder raced down her spine. Her heart rate accelerated and she tried to breathe slowly to calm herself. Then she purposefully put her hand back and found the object again. Or was it another object? This time she felt something metallic all right, but it seemed to be wider and to have four tines like a fork. Carol slid her hand along the object and refound the rod portion.

From his vantage point above her, Nick could tell that Carol had discovered something. Now it was his turn to be excited. He swam down to her as she struggled unsuccessfully to retrieve the object. They changed positions and Nick reached under the projecting rock. He first touched something that felt like a smooth sphere about the size of the palm of his hand. Nick could tell that the bottom of the sphere rested on the sand and that the rod attached to it was elevated by several inches. Nick steadied himself and jerked on the rod. It moved a little. He moved his grip sideways on the rod and heaved again. Several more pulls and the object was out from under the overhang.

For almost a minute Nick and Carol hovered over the gold-metallic object lying beneath them on the sand. Its surface was smooth to the eye as well as to the touch and altogether it was about eighteen inches long. Nothing but the polished, reflecting surface could be seen, suggesting that the object was indeed made from some kind of metal. The long axis of the object was an inch-thick rod that was, at one end, tapered and worked into a kind of a hook. Four inches back from the hook was the center of a small sphere, symmetrically constructed around the rod, whose radius was a little over two inches. The larger sphere that Nick had felt when he first put his hand under the overhang had a radius of four inches or so and it was right in the middle of the rod. This sphere was also perfectly symmetric around the rod axis. Beyond the two spheres the object was unadorned until the rod broke into four smaller branches, the tines that Carol had felt, at its other end.

Carol carefully took photographs of the object as it lay exposed in front of the overhang. Before she was finished, Nick pointed at his watch. They had been underwater almost an hour. Carol checked her air gauge and found that she was almost into the red. She waved a sign at Nick and he swam down to pick up the object. It was extremely heavy, weighing an astonishing twenty pounds or so in Nick's estimation. *Then it wasn't caught on anything when I was trying to pull it out*, Nick thought, *it's just that heavy.*

The weight of the object only increased Nick's excitement that had begun when he had first seen the gold color. Although he had never seen anything quite like this hook and fork with spheres, he remembered that the heaviest pieces from the wreck of the *Santa Rosa* had all been made of gold. And this piece was far heavier than anything he had ever touched. *Jesus*, he thought to himself as he discarded some of the lead weights in his belt to make it easier for him to carry the object up to the boat, *if there's even ten pounds of pure gold here, at current market value of a thousand dollars an ounce, that's $160,000, and this may just be the beginning. Wherever this thing came from, there must be more. All right, Williams. This may be your lucky day.*

Carol's thoughts raced at a mile a minute as she swam in tandem with Nick toward the anchor rope. She was busy trying to integrate everything she had seen in the last hour. She was already convinced that everything was somehow associated with the errant Navy missile—the behavior of the whales, the golden fork with the hook, the tank tracks on the bottom of the ocean. But at first Carol had no clue about what the connections were.

During the swim back Carol suddenly remembered reading some years before a story about Russian submarine tracks being found on the ocean floor outside a Swedish naval yard. In her journalistic mind she began to concoct a wild but plausible scenario to explain everything that she had seen. *Maybe the missile crashed near here and continued to send out data even when it was underwater,* she thought to herself. *Its electronic signals somehow confused the whales. And maybe those same signals were picked up by Russian submarines. And American.* Her thoughts came to a temporary dead end for a moment. *So there are at least two choices,* Carol thought again after swimming a few more strokes and watching Nick approach the anchor rope with the golden object still firmly in his hand. *Either I've found a Russian plot to locate and steal an American missile. Or the tracks and golden fork are somehow part of an American effort to find the missile without alerting the public. It doesn't matter. Either way it's a big story. But I must take that golden thing to Dale and MOI to analyze.*

Both Nick and Carol were dangerously low on air by the time they reached the surface beside the *Florida Queen.* They called Troy to give them a hand with their prize from the deep. Carol and Nick were exhausted when they finally crawled into the boat. But they were also both on emotional highs, thrilled with the discoveries of the afternoon. Everyone started talking at once. Troy had a story to tell too, for he had seen something unusual on the monitor while Nick and Carol were following the tracks in the trench. Nick pulled some beer and sandwiches out of the refrigerator and Carol tended her coral cuts. The laughing trio sat down on the deck chairs together as the sun was setting. They had much to share during the ninety-minute trip back to Key West.

THE camaraderie lasted most of the way back to the marina. Nick was no longer taciturn. Excited by what he believed was the initial find of a major sunken treasure, he was positively a chatterbox. At least twice he retold his version of the whale encounter. Nick was certain that the collision was accidental, that the whale simply happened to be moving in that direction for some other reason and just paid no attention to the fact that Nick was there.

"Impossible," Nick had scoffed when Carol had initially suggested that the whale might have deliberately hit him because he was heading for the fissure in the reef. "Whoever heard of whales guarding a spot in the ocean. Besides, if your theory's right, then why didn't the whale *really* smack me, and finish me off? You're asking me to accept that the whales were protecting an underground cave? And then that they were warning me to stay away with that gentle push?" He laughed good-naturedly. "Let me ask you something, Miss Dawson," he said, "do you believe in elves and fairies?"

"From where I was watching," Carol replied, "it sure looked as if the whole thing was planned." She did not pursue the subject further. In fact, after her initial outbursts, Carol did not talk very much about anything on the trip back to Key West. She too was excited and she was worried that if she talked too much she might inadvertently give away her thoughts about the possible connection between what they had seen and the lost Navy missile. So she didn't mention either her eerie fear just before the whale hit Nick or the network of tracks she thought she saw converging just under the base of the fissure.

As far as Nick was concerned, the object they had retrieved was definitely part of a treasure. It didn't bother him that it was hidden under an overhang at the end of some strange tracks. He shrugged it off by suggesting that maybe somebody had found the sunken treasure several years earlier and then tried to hide a few of the better pieces. (But why were the tracks fresh? And what had made them? Carol wanted to ask these questions but realized it was in her best interest for Nick to remain convinced that he had found treasure.) Nick was blind to all arguments and even facts that didn't support his treasure theory. It was emotionally vital to Nick for the gold fork thing to be the first piece of a great discovery. And like many people, Nick was capable of suspending his normally sharp critical faculties when he had a vested emotional involvement in an issue.

When Nick and Carol finally quieted down enough to listen, Troy had a chance to tell his own story. "After you guys left the area underneath the boat, I guess to follow your trench, I became worried about you and started watching the screen more often. Now, angel, by this time those three whales had been swimming about in that same dumb pattern for over an hour. So I wasn't checking them real close."

Troy was up out of his deck chair, walking back and forth in front of Carol and Nick. It was a dark night; low clouds had rolled in from the north to block the moon and obscure most of the stars. The spotlight from the top of the canopy occasionally caught Troy's chiseled features as he moved in and out of the shadows. "Because I wanted to find you guys, I lifted the alarm suppression the way you showed me and was regularly serenaded by the ding-dong-ding from the three whales. Now listen to this. After a couple of minutes, I heard a fourth alarm. I looked down at the monitor, expecting to see one of you, and I saw another whale, same species, swimming underneath the other three and in the opposite direction. Within ten seconds the original whales turned, breaking their long pattern, and followed the new whale off the monitor to the left. They never returned."

Troy wound up the story with a dramatic inflection and Nick laughed out loud, "Jesus, Jefferson, you do have a way of telling a story. I suppose you're going to tell me now that these whales were stationed there and the new guy came along with different orders. Or something like that. Christ, between you and Carol, you'll have me believe that the whales are organized into covens or whatever." Nick stopped for a moment. Troy was disappointed that Carol didn't say anything.

"Now," Nick continued, dismissing Troy's story and getting to the subject he had been thinking about for almost an hour, "we have an important issue to discuss. We have brought back something from the ocean that could conceivably be worth a lot of money. If nobody else can prove conclusively that it is theirs, then it will belong to the finders." Nick looked first at Carol and then at Troy. "Even though I'm captain and owner of this boat and I carried the thing up from the ocean floor, I'm prepared to offer that we split the proceeds in thirds. Does that sound fair enough to the two of you?"

There was a moderately long silence before Troy answered. "Sure, Nick, that sounds fine to me." Nick smiled and reached across to shake Troy's hand. He then extended his hand to Carol.

"Just a minute," she said quietly, looking directly at Nick and not taking his hand. "Since you've decided to start this conversation, there are several more items that must be discussed. It's not simply a question of money for this object. There's also the issue of possession. Who keeps the golden trident? Who determines when we've been offered a fair price? What do we agree to say, or not to say, to others? And what if other objects are found down there by one or more of us? Do we all share? There's an entire agreement that must be worked out before we dock."

Nick frowned. "Now I understand why you've been so quiet these last few minutes. You've been thinking about your share. I misjudged you. I thought you might decide not to create any more trouble—"

"Who said anything about trouble?" Carol interrupted him abruptly, her voice rising slightly. "If you must know, I'm not that interested in the damn money. I will gladly take my one-third if any dollars are forthcoming from the trident there, for I certainly deserve it. But if any more such treasures are down there and you and Troy can find them without me, then be my guest. I want something else."

Both men were now listening intently. "First and foremost, I want exclusive rights to this story, and that means *absolute* secrecy about what we have found, when and where we found it, and anything else associated with it—at least until we're certain there's nothing more to learn. Second, I want immediate possession of the object for forty-eight hours, before anyone else knows that it exists. After that you can have it to take to the authorities for evaluation."

Uh oh, Carol thought to herself as she saw the searching looks she had elicited from Nick and Troy. *I overdid it. They suspect something. Better back off just a bit.* "Of course," she smiled disarmingly, "I've just given my initial position. I expect that some negotiations may be necessary."

"Wow, angel," Troy said with a laugh, "that was some speech. For just a minute there, I thought that maybe there was a whole other game going on here and you were the only one playing. Of course the professor and I will be delighted to discuss an agreement with you, won't we, Nick?"

Nick nodded. But he had also been alerted by the careful organization and unmistakable intensity of Carol's response. It seemed out of proportion to the journalistic value of their find. *Is she trying to make this some kind of a contest between us?* he thought to himself. *Or am I missing something altogether?*

They had worked out a compromise agreement by the time the *Florida Queen* reached the dock in Key West. Nick would take the golden trident (both of the men liked Carol's name for the object) with him on Friday morning. There was an elderly woman in Key West who was a compendium of treasure knowledge and she would be able to assess its value and to give its probable place and date of origin. The woman would also be a witness to their find in case the trident were ever misplaced. On Friday afternoon, the three of them would meet on the boat or in the marina parking lot at four o'clock. Nick would give the object to Carol and she would keep it over the weekend. After she returned it to Nick on Monday morning, he would be responsible for its care and eventual sale. The three of them had joint ownership of the trident, but Carol waived any interest in future discoveries. Carol wrote the terms of the simple agreement on the back of a restaurant menu from her purse, they all signed it, and she promised to bring copies back the next day.

Troy was quiet and subdued while he was loading all Carol's equipment back into the footlocker. He lifted the locker onto the cart and then pulled the cart along the jetty. Carol walked beside him. It was about nine o'clock and very quiet at the marina. The tall fluorescent lights created a strange reflection on the wooden jetties. "Well, angel," Troy said as Carol and he approached the marina headquarters, "it's been quite a day. I've really enjoyed your company." He stopped and turned to look at her. Her black hair had dried unevenly and looked a bit disheveled, but her face was beautiful in the reflected light.

Troy looked away, out at the water and the boats. "You know, it's a shame sometimes the way life works. You meet somebody by chance, you strike up a friendship, and then poof, they're gone. It's all so . . . so transient."

Carol came over beside him and stretched to kiss his cheek. "And you know I like you, too," she said, lightening up the conversation with a grin and making certain that Troy understood what kind of a friendship they could have. "But cheer up. All is not lost. You'll see me tomorrow for a while and then maybe when I return the golden thing on Monday."

She hooked her arm through his as they momentarily walked back down the jetty, away from the loaded cart. "And who knows," Carol laughed, "I'm down in the Keys from time to time. We could have a drink together and you could tell me some more stories." They could just barely make out the spotlight above the canopy on the *Florida Queen* some hundred yards in the distance. "I see your friend the professor is still at work. He's not strong on goodbyes. Or any other area of manners as far as I can tell."

She turned, switching locked arms, and they walked back to the loaded cart. They moved through the apparently deserted headquarters without speaking. When the footlocker had been replaced in the station wagon, Carol gave Troy a hug. "You're a good man, Troy Jefferson," she said. "I wish you well."

Nick was almost ready to leave by the time Troy returned to the boat. He was packing a small exercise bag. "Looks innocent enough, doesn't it, Troy? Nobody will ever suspect that one of the great treasures of the ocean is in here." He paused a moment and changed the subject. "You put her safely in her car? Good. She's a strange one, isn't she, all feisty and aggressive but still pretty at the same time. I wonder what makes her tick."

Nick zipped up the bag and walked around to the side of the canopy. "Just finish up with the diving gear tonight. Don't worry about the rest of the boat—we'll fix it up tomorrow. I'm going to go home and dream of riches."

"Speaking of riches, Professor," Troy said with a smile, "how about that hundred-dollar loan I asked you for on Tuesday. You never answered me and just said we'll see."

Nick walked deliberately over to Troy and stood right in front of him. He spoke very slowly. "I should have made my Polonius speech to both of us when you asked me for a loan the first time. But here we are now, borrower and lender, and I don't like it. I will lend you a hundred dollars but, Mister Troy Jefferson, this is positively the last time. Please don't ever ask me again. These loans for your so-called inventions are making it hard for me to work with you."

Troy was a little surprised by the unexpected harshness in Nick's tone. But he was also angered by the connotation of the last sentence. "Are you suggesting," Troy said softly, suppressing his temper, "that I'm not telling the truth, that the money is not being spent on electronics? Or are you telling me that you don't believe an uneducated black man could possibly invent anything worth having?"

Nick faced Troy again. "Spare me your righteous racial indignation. This is not a question of prejudice or lies. It's money, pure and simple. My lending you money is fucking up our friendship." Troy started to speak but Nick waved him off. "Now it's been a long day. And a fascinating one at that. I've said all I want to say on the subject of the loan and I consider the issue finished."

Nick picked up his bag, said good night, and left the *Florida Queen*. Troy went behind the canopy to organize the diving gear. About ten minutes later, just as he was finishing, he heard someone calling his name. "Troy . . . Troy, is that you?" an accented voice said.

Troy leaned around the canopy and saw Greta standing on the jetty under the fluorescent light. Even though there was now a slight chill in the air, she was wearing her usual skimpy bikini that showed off her marvelous physique. Troy broke into a grand smile, "Well, well, if it isn't superkraut! How the hell are you? I can see you're still taking care of that wondrous body."

Greta managed the beginnings of a smile. "Homer and Ellen and I are having a small party tonight. We noticed that you were working late and thought that maybe you'd like to join us when you're done."

"Just might do that," Troy said, nodding his head up and down. "Just might do that."

"OH, God, can't we stop now? Finally? Please let us. It's so quiet here, now." She was speaking to the stars and the sky. The old man's head slumped forward in the wheelchair as he drew his last breath. Hannah Jelkes knelt beside him to see if he was indeed gone and then, after kissing him on the crown of the head, she looked up again with a peaceful smile. The curtain fell and rose again in a few seconds. The cast assembled quickly on stage.

"Okay, that's it for tonight, good job." The director, a man in his early sixties, gray hair thinning on the top, approached the stage with a bounce. "Great performance, Henrietta, try to can that one for the opening tomorrow night. Just the right combination of strength and vulnerability." Melvin Burton nimbly jumped up on the stage. "And you, Jessie, if you make Maxine any lustier they'll close us down." He spun around with a flourish and laughed along with two other people at the front of the theater.

"Okay, gang," Melvin turned back to address the cast, "now go home and get lots of rest. It was better tonight, looked good. Oh, Commander, can you and Tiffani stay around for a moment after you change? I have a couple more pointers for you."

He jumped back down from the stage and walked back to the fourth row of the theater where his two associates were sitting. One was a woman, even older than Melvin but with twinkling green eyes behind her granny glasses. She was wearing a bright print dress full of spring colors. The other person was a man, about forty, with a studious face and a warm, open manner. Melvin fretted as he sat down beside them. "I worried when we picked *Night of the Iguana* that it might be too difficult for Key West. It's not as well known as *Streetcar* or *Glass Menagerie*. And in some ways the characters are just as foreign as those in *Suddenly, Last Summer*. But it looks almost okay. If we can just fix the scenes between Shannon and Charlotte."

"Are you sorry now you added the prologue?" the woman asked. Amanda Winchester was an institution in Key West. Among other things, she was the doyenne of the theatrical entrepreneurs in the revitalized city. She owned two of the new theaters near the marina and had been responsible for the formation of at least three different local repertory groups. She loved plays and theater people. And Melvin Burton was her favorite director.

"No, I'm not, Amanda. It clearly adds to the play to get some kind of initial feeling for how frustrating it would be to lead a group of Baptist women on a tour of Mexico in the summer. And without the sex scene between Charlotte and Shannon in that small, stuffy hotel room, I'm not sure their affair is believable to the audience." He paused a moment, reflecting. "Huston did the same thing with the movie."

"Right now that sex scene doesn't play at all," the other man said. "In fact it's almost comical. The hugs they exchange are like the ones my brother gives his daughters."

"Patience, Marc," Melvin answered.

"Something has to be done or we should take the prologue out altogether," Amanda agreed. "Marc's right, the scene tonight was almost comical. Part of the problem is that Charlotte looks like a child in that scene." She paused a moment before continuing. "You know, the girl has gorgeous long hair and we have it stacked on top of her head to look prim and proper. Clearly she wouldn't wear it down all day in the heat of a Mexican summer. But what if she *took* it down when she went to Shannon's room?"

"That's a great idea, Amanda. As I have often said, you would have made a fabulous director." Melvin looked at Marc and they exchanged a warm smile. Then the director settled back in his seat and started thinking about what he was going to tell his two cast members in a few moments.

Melvin Burton was a happy man. He lived with his roommate of fifteen years, Marc Adler, in a beach house on Sugarloaf Key, about ten miles east of Key West. Melvin had directed plays on Broadway for almost a decade and had been associated with the theater in one capacity or another since the mid-fifties. Always careful with his money, Melvin had managed to save an impressive amount by 1979. Worried about the impact of inflation on his savings, Melvin had sought advice from an accountant who was a friend of a close associate. It was almost love at first sight. Marc was twenty-eight at the time, shy, lonely, unsure of himself in the maelstrom of New York City. Melvin's savoir faire and theatrical panache opened Marc up to aspects of life that he had never known.

As the stock market ratcheted upward in the mid-eighties, Melvin watched his net worth near a million dollars. But other factors in his life were not so bullish. The AIDS epidemic hit the theatrical community in New York with a vengeance and both Melvin and Marc lost many of their lifelong friends. And Melvin's career seemed to have peaked; he was no longer in demand as one of the premier directors.

One night on his way home from the theater, Marc was mugged by a group of teenagers. They beat him up, stole his watch and wallet, and left him bleeding in the street. As a saddened Melvin ministered to his friend's wounds, he made a major decision. They would leave New York. He would sell his stocks and convert his fortune to fixed income investments. They would buy a home where it was warm and safe, where they could relax and read and swim together. Maybe they would do some community theater work if it was available, but that was not the most important thing. What *was* important was that they share Melvin's remaining years.

Melvin ran into Amanda Winchester one day while he and Marc were on vacation in Key West. They had worked together briefly on a project that had never panned out twenty years before. Amanda told him that she had just formed a local amateur repertory group to do two Tennessee Williams plays a year. Would he be interested in directing them?

Melvin and Marc moved to Key West and started to build their house on Sugarloaf Key. Both of them thoroughly enjoyed their work with the Key West Players. The actors were everyday people, dedicated and earnest. Some had had a little acting experience. But for the most part, the secretaries, housewives, and retail clerks, plus officers and enlisted men from the U.S. Naval Air Station, were all novices with one thing in common. Each of them viewed his few days on the stage as his moment of glory, and he wanted to make the best of it.

Commander Winters came out of the dressing room first. He was wearing his uniform (he had come right over to rehearsal from the base) and looked a bit stiff and uncertain. He sat down in one of the theater chairs next to Amanda Winchester. "I was really glad to see you back again," said Amanda, taking his hand. "I thought your Goober last fall was just right."

Winters thanked her politely. Amanda changed the subject. "So how are things out at the base? I read an article the other day in the *Miami Herald* about all the modern weapons the Navy has these days, pilotless submarines and vertical takeoff fighters and search and destroy torpedoes. There seems to be no limit to our ability to build more powerful and dangerous toys for war. Are you involved with all that?"

"Only in a limited way," Commander Winters answered pleasantly. Then, anticipating the discussion with the director, he leaned forward so that he could see Melvin and Marc as well as Amanda. "I apologize if I was a little flat tonight," he began. "We have a couple of big problems out at the base and I may have been a bit distracted, but I'll be ready tomorrow—"

"Oh, no," said Melvin, interrupting him, "that's not what I wanted to talk to you about. It's your first scene with Tiffani . . . Ah, here she comes. Let's go up on the stage."

Tiffani Thomas was almost seventeen years old and a junior at Key West High School. A Navy brat all her life, Tiffani had gone to seven different schools in her eleven years since kindergarten. Her father was a noncommissioned officer who had been assigned to Key West about three months before. She had been recommended to Melvin Burton by the high school drama teacher when it became apparent that Denise Wright simply could not play the role of Charlotte Goodall.

"She hasn't done anything for me yet except rehearse," the teacher had said of Tiffani, "but she learns her lines quickly and has a quality, an intensity I guess, that sets her apart from the others. And she's clearly been in plays before. I don't know if she can get ready in three weeks, but she's my first choice by far."

Tiffani probably would not have been called beautiful by her Florida classmates. Her features were too much out of the ordinary to be be properly appreciated by most high school boys. Her assets were olive eyes, quiet and brooding, light freckles on a pale complexion, long red eyelashes tinged with brown, and a magnificent head of thick auburn hair. Her carriage was proper and erect, not slumped like most teenagers, so she probably seemed aloof to her peers. "Striking," Amanda called her, accurately, when she first saw Tiffani.

She was standing on the stage alone in her short-sleeved blouse and jeans as the two men approached. Her hair was pulled back in a ponytail the way her father liked it. Tiffani was very nervous. She was worried about what Mr. Burton was going to say to her. She had overheard the buyer who was playing Hannah Jelkes say that Melvin might do away with the part of Charlotte altogether if "the new girl can't hack it." *I have worked so hard for this part,* Tiffani thought. *Oh please, please, don't let it be bad news.*

Tiffani was looking down at her feet when Melvin Burton and Commander Winters joined her on the stage. "Well, now," Melvin began, "let's get straight to the point. The first scene with you two in the hotel room is not working. In fact, it's a disaster. We must make some changes."

Melvin saw that Tiffani was not looking at him. Gently he put his hand under her chin and lifted it until her eyes met his. "You must look at me, child, for I'm trying to tell you some very important things." He noticed that her eyes were brimming with water and his years of experience told him immediately what was wrong. He leaned forward and whispered so that nobody else could hear, "I said we would make some changes, not do away with the scene. Now get yourself together and listen up."

Burton regained his director's voice and turned toward Winters. "In this scene, Commander, your character Shannon and young Miss Goodall engage in foreplay that leads to intercourse later that night. In the following scene they are discovered, in flagrante delicto, by the confused Miss Fellowes. And that establishes the desperate situation causing Shannon to run to Maxine and Fred at the Costa Verde.

"But our scene does not work right now because nobody watching it will recognize what you two are doing as foreplay. Now I can change the movement to make it easier—putting Shannon already on the bed when he discovers Charlotte behind the door would be one way—and I can change Charlotte's clothing so that she looks less like a little girl, *but* there's one thing that I cannot do . . ." Melvin stopped and looked back and forth from Tiffani to Winters. They were both staring blankly at him.

"Come here, come here, both of you," Melvin said, gesturing impatiently with his right hand. He dropped his voice again. He took Tiffani's hand with his left and Commander Winters' with his right. "You two are lovers for one night in this play. It is essential that the audience believe this or they will not understand completely why Shannon is at the end of his rope, like the iguana. Shannon is desperate because he was originally locked out of his church for giving in to the same lust . . ."

They were both listening but Melvin's director's intuition told him he was still not reaching them. He had another idea. He took Tiffani's hand and put it into the commander's, closing his own hand over theirs for emphasis. "Look at each other for a moment. That's right." He turned to Winters. "She's a beautiful young woman, isn't she, Commander?"

Their eyes were in contact. "And he's a handsome man, isn't he, Tiffani? I want you to imagine that you have an uncontrollable desire to touch him, to kiss him, to be naked with him." Tiffani blushed. Winters fidgeted. Melvin was fairly certain that he saw a spark, albeit a fleeting one.

"Now tomorrow night," he continued, looking at Tiffani and taking his hand off theirs, "I want you to capture *that* feeling when you're hiding in his room. I want it to explode out of you when he notices that you are there. And you, Commander," he looked back at the middle-aged naval officer, "you are torn between an overpowering passion to possess this young girl physically and the almost certain knowledge that it will be the final ruination of both your life and your soul. You are hopelessly trapped. Remember, you fear that God has already forsaken you for your past sins. But, despite that, you finally relinquish yourself to your lust and commit another unpardonable sin."

Tiffani and Commander Winters both realized at virtually the same time that their hands were still intertwined. They looked at each other for a moment and then, embarrassed, awkwardly separated them. Melvin Burton slipped between his players and put his arms around their shoulders. "So go on home now and think about what I've said. And come back tomorrow and really break a leg."

Vernon Winters drove the Pontiac into his driveway in suburban Key West just before eleven o'clock. The house was quiet, the only lights were in the garage and the kitchen. *As regular as the stars,* Vernon thought, *Hap to bed at ten, Betty to bed at ten-thirty.* In his mind's eye he saw his wife go into his son's bedroom, as she did every night, and fiddle momentarily with his sheets and coverlet. "Did you say your prayers?"

"Yes, ma'am," Hap always answered.

Then she would kiss him good night on the forehead, turn out his light as she left the room, and go into her bedroom. Within ten minutes she would have changed into her pajamas, brushed her teeth, and washed her face. She would then kneel beside her bed, her elbows on the top of the blanket and her hands clasped right in front of her face. "Dear God," she would say aloud, and then she would pray until exactly ten-thirty, moving her lips silently with her eyes closed. Five minutes later she would be asleep.

Vernon was aware of a vague disquiet as he walked through the living room toward the three bedrooms on the opposite side of the house from the garage. There was something stirring in him, something that he could not identify exactly, but he assumed it was associated with either the nervousness of opening night or the sudden return of Randy Hilliard to his life. He wanted to talk to someone.

He stopped at Hap's bedroom first. Commander Winters walked in quietly in the dark and sat on the side of his son's bed. Hap was fast asleep, lying on his side. A tiny nightlight beside his bed illuminated his profile. *How like your mother you look,* Winters thought. *And act. You two are so close. I'm almost a trespasser in my own home.* He put his hand gently against Hap's cheek. The boy did not stir. *How can I make up for all the time I was gone?*

Winters gently nudged his son awake. "Hap," he said softly, "it's your dad." Henry Allen Pendleton Winters rubbed his eyes and then sat up quickly in bed. "Yes, sir," he said, "is anything wrong? Is Mom all right?"

"No," his father answered, and then laughed. "I mean yes. Mom's all right. Nothing's wrong. I just wanted to talk."

Hap looked at the clock beside his bed. "Ummm, well, okay, Dad. What do you want to talk about?"

Winters was quiet for a moment. "Hap, did you ever read the copy of the script that I got for you and your mother, the one from my play?"

"No, sir. Not much," Hap replied. "I'm sorry, but I just couldn't get into it. I think maybe it's above my head." He brightened. "But I'm looking forward to seeing you in it tomorrow night." There was a long pause. "Umm, what's it about anyway?"

Winters stood up and looked out the open window. Beyond the screen he could hear the gentle susurration of the crickets. "It's about a man who loses his place with God because he can't or won't control his actions. It's about . . ." Winters turned his head around quickly and caught his son eyeing the clock. A sharp emotional pain raced through him. He waited until it had abated and then drew a breath. "Well, we can talk about it some other time, son. I just realized how late it is."

He walked to the door. "Good night, Hap," he said.

"Good night, sir."

Vernon Winters walked past his wife's room to the third bedroom at the end of the hall. He undressed slowly, now even more aware than before of an unfulfilled longing. He thought for a fleeting second about waking Betty up to talk and maybe . . . But he knew better. *That's not her style,* he said to himself, *never was. Even before when we slept together. And after Libya and the dreams and tears at night who could blame her for wanting her own bedroom.*

He slipped into his bed in his undershorts. The soothing melody of the crickets enveloped him. *And besides. She has her God and I have my despair. There is nothing left between us except Hap. We couple as strangers, both fearing any discovery.*

"THE communication room will close in five minutes. The communication room will close in five minutes." The disembodied, recorded voice sounded tired. Carol Dawson was weary herself. She was talking to Dale Michaels on the videophone. Photographs were strewn all over the desk underneath the screen and the video camera.

"All right," Carol was saying, "I guess I agree with you. The only possible way for me to decipher this puzzle is to bring all the photos and the telescope recording unit back to Miami." She sighed and then yawned. "I'll come up there first thing in the morning, on the flight that arrives at seven-thirty, so that IPL can get an early shot at the recorded data. But remember, I must be back here in time to pick up the golden trident at four. Can the lab process all the data in a couple of hours?"

"That's not the hard part. Trying to analyze the data and piece together a coherent story in an hour or two will be the tough job." Dr. Dale was sitting on the couch in the living room of his spacious condominium in Key Biscayne. In front of him, on the coffee table, was a magnificent jade chess board with green and white squares. Six carved chess pieces were still on the board, the two opposing queens and four pawns, two from each side. Dale Michaels paused and looked meaningfully at the camera. "I know how important this is to you. I've cancelled my eleven o'clock meeting so I can help you."

"Thanks," Carol said automatically. She felt a trickle of irritation. *Why is it*, she thought while Dale talked about one of his new projects at MOI, *that men always demand gratitude for every little sacrifice. If a woman changes her schedule to accommodate a man, it's expected. But if a man revises his precious schedule it's a big fucking deal.*

Dale droned on. Now he was enthusiastically telling her about a new Institute effort to survey the underwater volcanoes around Papua, New Guinea. *Whew*, Carol smiled to herself when she realized that Dale's self-centered focus was bothering her, *I must really be beat. I believe I'm on the verge of being bitchy.*

"Hey," Carol interrupted him. She stood up and started to pick up the scattered photographs. "Sorry to bring a halt to this party, but they're closing the room and I'm exhausted. I'll see you in the morning."

"Aren't you going to make a move?" Dale replied, pointing at the chess board.

"No, I'm not," Carol said, showing just a trace of anger. "And I may not ever. Any reasonable player would have accepted the draw that I offered you last weekend and gone on to more important things. Your damn ego just can't deal with the idea that one game out of five I can battle you to a tie."

"People have been known to make mistakes in the endgame," Dale answered, avoiding altogether the emotional content in her remark. "But I know you're tired. I'll meet you at the airport and take you to breakfast."

"Okay. Good night." Carol hung up the videophone a little brusquely and packed all the photographs in her briefcase. As soon as she had left the marina, she had taken her camera and film straight to the darkroom at the *Key West Independent*, where she had spent an hour developing and studying the prints. The results were intriguing, particularly a couple of the blowups. In one of them she could clearly see four separate tracks converging to a spot just under the fissure. In another photo the bodies of the three whales were caught in a pose that looked as if they were in the middle of a deep conversation.

Carol walked through the spacious lobby in the Marriott Hotel. The piano bar was almost deserted. The lithe black pianist was playing an old Karen Carpenter song, "Goodbye to Love." A handsome man in his late thirties or early forties was kissing a flashy young blonde in a nook off to the right. Carol bridled. *The bimbo must be all of twenty-three*, she said to herself, *probably his secretary or something equally important.*

As she wound her way down the long corridor toward her room, Carol thought about her conversation with Dale. He had told her that the Navy had small robot vehicles, some of them derived from original MOI designs, that could easily have made the tracks. So it was virtually certain that the

Russians had similar vehicles. He had dismissed the whales' behavior as irrelevant but had thought that her failure to find out if anything else was under the overhang had been a serious mistake. *Of course*, Carol had realized when he had said it, *I should have spent another minute looking. Nuts. I hope I didn't blow it.* In her mind's eye she then had carefully revisited the entire scenario at the overhang to see if there were any clues that something else may have been hidden there.

The biggest surprise in the discussion with Dale had come when Carol, in passing, had praised the way the new alarm algorithm had worked. Dale suddenly had become very interested. "So the alert code definitely read 101?" he had said.

"Yes," she had answered, "that's why I wasn't that astonished when we found the object."

"No way," he had said emphatically. "The trident could not have caused the alert code. Even if it was at the edge of the field of view of the telescope, and that seems unlikely given how far you followed the trench, it's too small to trigger the foreign object alarm. And how could it have been seen under the overhang anyway?" Dale had paused for a few seconds. "You didn't look at any of the infrared images in realtime, did you? Well, we can process them tomorrow and see if we can figure out what triggered the alarm."

Carol felt strangely defeated as she opened the door to her motel room. *It's just fatigue*, she said to herself, not wanting to admit that her conversation with Dale had made her feel inadequate. She put her briefcase on a chair and walked wearily to the bathroom to wash her face. Two minutes later she was asleep on the bed in her underclothes. Her slacks, blouse, shoes, and socks were all stacked together in the corner.

She is a little girl again in her dream, wearing the blue-and-yellow striped dress that her parents gave her for her seventh birthday. Carol is walking around with her father in the Northridge Mall on a busy Saturday morning. They pass a large candy store. She lets go of his hand and runs into the store and stares through the glass case at all the chocolates. Carol points at some milk chocolate turtles when the big man behind the display case asks her what she wants.

In the dream Carol cannot reach the counter and doesn't have any money. "Where is your mother, little girl?" the candy store man asks. Carol shakes her head and the man repeats the question. She stands on her tiptoes and tells the man in a confidential whisper that her mother drinks too much, but that her father always buys her candy.

The man smiles, but he still won't give her the chocolates. "And where is your father, little girl?" the candy store man now asks. In the case Carol can see the reflection of a kindly, smiling man standing behind her, framed between two piles of chocolates. She wheels around, expecting to see her father. But the man behind her is not her father. This man's face is grotesque, disfigured. Frightened, she turns back around to the chocolates. The man in the store is now taking the candy away. It is closing time. Carol starts to cry.

"Where is your father, little girl? Where is your father?" The little girl in the dream is sobbing. She is surrounded by big people, all of them asking questions. She puts her hands over her ears.

"He's gone," Carol finally shouts. "He's gone. He left us and went away and now I'm all alone."

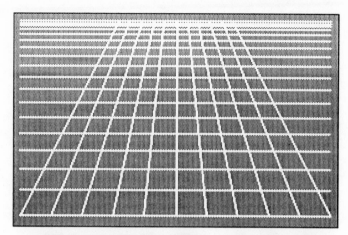

CYCLE 447

GAINST the deep black background of scattered stars, the filaments of the Milky Way Galaxy seem like thin wisps of light added by a master artist. Here, at the far edge of the Outer Shell, near the beginning of what the Colonists call the Gap, there is no suggestion of the teeming activity of the Colony, some twenty-four light millicycles away. An awesome, unbroken quiet is the background for the breathtaking beauty of a black sky studded with twinkling stars.

Suddenly out of the void comes a small interstellar messenger robot. It seeks and finally finds a dark spherical satellite about three miles in diameter that is easily overlooked in the great panorama of the celestial sky. Time passes. A close-up reveals activity on the satellite. Soft artificial lights now illuminate portions of the surface. Automated vehicles are working on the periphery of the object, apparently changing its shape. External structures are dismantled and taken off to a temporary storage area in the distance. At length the original satellite disappears altogether and what is left are two long parallel rails of metal alloy, built in sections of about two hundred yards apiece from the spare parts of the now vanished satellite. Each rail is ten yards across and separated from its matched partner by about a hundred yards.

Regular sorties to the storage area continue until the useful supplies of material are depleted and the tracks extend for a distance of almost ten miles. Then activity stops. The rails from nowhere to nowhere in space stand as mute reminders of some major engineering activity suddenly abandoned. Or was it? From just below a prominent binary pair, the two brightest lights in the eastern sky, a speck emerges. The speck grows until it dominates the eastern quadrant of the sky. A dozen, no, sixteen great interstellar cargo ships with bright, flashing red lights lead a procession of robot vehicles into the region. The ghostly rails to nowhere are surrounded by the new arrivals. The first cargo ship opens and eight small shuttles emerge, each one moving back down the line toward another of the great cargo containers. The shuttles wait silently outside the huge ships while the entourage completes its arrival.

The final vehicle to arrive is a tiny space tug pulling a long, slender object that looks like two folded Japanese fans joined together end to end. It is encased in a transparent and protective sheath of very thin material. Eight small, darting vehicles dance like hummingbirds along its entire length, as if they were somehow guiding it, guarding it, and checking out its health all at the same time.

The large cargo ships shaped like ancient blimps now open and reveal their contents. Most of them are carrying rail sections stacked in enormous piles. The small shuttles unload the sections, leaving them stacked, and set them in groups stretching for miles in both directions from the existing rails. When the rail sections are almost all unloaded, four of the shuttles approach the side of one of the remaining giant cargo ships and wait for the bay doors to swing open. From the inside of this cargo ship come eight machines that attack each of the four shuttles in pairs, breaking them carefully into pieces and taking the parts back into the dark of the cargo bay. A few moments later, an elongated complex of articulating machinery emerges from this great ship. Once released from the confines of the cargo carrier, it stretches itself into a long bench reaching almost a mile in length. Every hundred yards or so along the central platform of this bench, a smaller set of coordinated components form into highly organized local groups.

This is the automated, multipurpose construction system, one of the technological treasures of the Colonists. The entire system moves into place at the end of the tracks and its many remote manipulators begin to pull rail sections from the various stacks. Its sophisticated local hands and fingers deftly put the new sections in place and attach them with atomic welds. The speed is astonishing. An entire mile of new track is finished within minutes and the great builder moves to another group of rail section piles. The completed tracks extend for almost a hundred miles in space.

Having finished with one task, the construction system undergoes its next metamorphosis. Tearing itself into pieces starting from the two ends of the long bench, the monolithic structure disappears and is reorganized into thousands of separate but similar components. These little antlike contraptions attach themselves in groups to individual rail sections. They measure carefully all the dimensions and check all the welds between adjacent sections. Then, as if on cue, the rails on the four ends of the track segments begin to bend and elevate, lifted by the antlike components. The rails twist upward, upward, bringing the rest of the track with them. The two long parallel lines are eventually transformed into a giant double hoop, over ten miles in radius, that looks like an amusement park ferris wheel suspended in space.

With the completion of the double hoop, the construction system again reconfigures itself. Some of the new elements of the system pick up the long slender object shaped like end-to-end Japanese fans. They erect it near the hoop (it is, not surprisingly, almost the exact length as the diameter of the hoops) under the careful surveillance of its hummingbird protectors. Then the object is hoist into place as a north-south spoke in the double hoop structure. Some of the hummingbirds produce unseen thin cables and anchor the spoke to the hoop structure at both ends. The rest of the tiny mechanical speedsters create a web that winds around the center section and connects the great antenna with the east-west axis of the hoops.

The antenna, now connected to its supporting structure, opens slowly at both the north and south pole positions on the hoop. Closer inspection reveals that the hummingbirds are actually pulling the delicate individual folds apart. The folds spread out until the entire interior of the hoops is covered with a mixture of mesh, ribbing, and amazingly complex local arrays. The initial deployment is complete.

The communication complex next goes through an elaborate self-test while its construction minions stand by in case any problems are encountered. The tests are successful and the station is declared operational. Within hours the phalanx of robot emissaries from the inhabited universe picks up all the stray metal lying around and packs it into one of the large cargo ships. Then, as swiftly as they came, the robot vehicles disappear into the blackness around the station, leaving the imposing hoop structure alone as a reminder of the presence of intelligence in the universe.

Around the vast Outer Shell, whose two hundred and fifty-six sections each contain more volume than the Colony, over one thousand similar upgrades have been made during Cycle 446 in an attempt to extend advanced communications capabilities to new locales. This is the last upgrade of a very difficult group in a region near the Gap. This group was delayed several times because of an unacceptably high number of manufacturing deficiencies at the nearest major factory over two light millicycles away. After several attempts to diagnose and repair the problems, eventually the plant had to be closed and virtually rebuilt from scratch. The total delay to the completion of the project was fourteen millicycles, just about what the Council of Engineers had predicted in their worst-case analysis that accompanied the Cycle 446 Proclamation.

As the big moment approaches, all normal activity in the heart of the Colony ceases. In the last nanocycle, there is no business activity, no entertainment. The spaceports are even empty. At precisely 446.9, after two hundred millicycles of debate and discussion by the Council of Leaders, the governmental blueprint for the next era will be delivered and all intelligence in the Colony will be listening.

The giant transmitter is activated on schedule and the Cycle 447 Proclamation pours out at an information rate of a hundred trillion bits of information per picocycle. The actual data rate from the powerful source is much higher, but the information rate is reduced to accommodate requirements for both sophisticated enc..ding and error checks internal to the data. With the coding, only Colony receivers equipped with special decryption algorithms can unscramble the message at any level. And the internal consistency checks on each packet of data in the transmission reduce the probability of receiving an erroneous piece of information, even at an enormous distance, to practically zero.

Following the organization and agenda for The Proclamation established in the Era of Genius, between Cycles 371 and 406, the first microcycle of the transmission is a complete summary of the entire plan. Two hundred nanocycles of this summary are devoted to each of the five divisions governed by the Council of Leaders: administration, information, communication, transportation, and exploration. After a planned break of four hundred nanocycles, to allow receiver adjustments along the path of the signal, the transmission of the actual Cycle 447 Proclamation begins. On and on it goes. It does not stop until twenty microcycles later. Four complete microcycles are used for in-depth explanations of the major projects to be undertaken in each of the five disciplines. Of particular interest to the Committee for the Outer Shell, the group that governs the huge concentric region defining the most distant reach where the Colonists claim jurisdiction, is a plan from the Division of Exploration announcing the repatriation to the Outer Shell of almost a million species from Zoo System #3.

(The transmission of The Proclamation, a wealth of information that can be translated into language, pictures, sounds, and other sensory impressions depending on the receiving beings and the sophistication of their decryption equipment, is the beginning of the governmental process for each cycle. Based upon The Proclamation, regional bodies or administrative agencies with subordinate jurisdictions then adjust their plans for the cycle to be consistent with those announced by the Council of Leaders. This procedure is defined in detail in the Articles of Colonial Confederation.)

The Proclamation is relayed throughout the Colony and the near reaches of the Inner Shell by means of giant communication stations along the developed transportation routes. These stations, actually information centers that store *all* Colony messages in their extensive libraries for as long as a hundred cycles, amplify and retransmit the signal to the next station in the pattern some ten light microcycles away. The edge of the Colony (and hence the beginning of the Inner Shell) was expanded by the Boundary Decree in the Cycle 416 Proclamation to include all points up to three light millicycles from the administrative center. Thus, by the time the Proclamation reaches the mammoth Zoo Complex, a combination of three stars and nineteen planets (four of them artificial) just across the edge of the Colony, the message has been relayed through three hundred stations.

The Committee of Zookeepers eagerly awaits the proclamation to find out the response to their recommended expansion of the Zoo Complex. They are surprised to find their proposal replaced by another repatriation plan. Once before, in Cycle 429, they had proposed an expansion of the zoo to handle the explosion of successful progeny created by the breakthroughs in adaptive genetic engineering during Cycles 426–428. At that time also their request had been denied and the Council of Leaders had recommended repatriation to solve the population problem. During Cycles 430–436 the population of the Zoo Complex was kept approximately constant by these regular transfers of common species back to their original homes.

But starting with Cycle 437, there was a rapid increase in interest in comparative biology. It was triggered by the discovery of a fifth class of life form, called Type E by the Council of Biologists, in Section 28 of the Outer Shell. Subsequent expeditions to the same area showed not only that the dominant life type throughout Sections 28–33 was Type E, but also that Type A was surprisingly present as well in those sections. This was the first time that natural evolution in any region had shown a predilection for any kind of life form other than the Type A of the Colonists and its developed hybrids. The quest to understand these unusual creatures led to the endangered species expeditions in the Outer Shell in Cycles 440 and 441 and the creation, in Cycle 442, of several worlds specifically to study the new Type E life forms.

Many of these new species flourished in Zoo System #3, causing population and space problems again for the Committee of Zookeepers. The space shortage was especially severe and it was exacerbated both by the need to segregate all the Type E life forms and by their rapid reproduction. Therefore, at the beginning of the planning process for this Cycle 447, the Committee of Zookeepers had proposed their small expansion of the Zoo Complex, suggesting not only a fourth zoo system completely dedicated to Type E life forms, but also a vigorous campaign for completing the repatriation of all Colony and Inner Shell species with aggression coefficients below 14.

The Committee of Zookeepers are stunned by the scale of the Outer Shell repatriation plan contained in the Cycle 447 Proclamation. In a lively technical discussion catalyzed by the unexpected proposal, the dangers of returning the Outer Shell life forms to their original planets are vigorously reasserted. The Committee decides tentatively to take an unusual step—to submit a Proclamation Variance to the Council of Leaders. In the draft variance the Zookeepers point out that many genetic experiments have been conducted with the new Type E forms, that the evolutionary possibilities for the new species are therefore uncertain, that the monitoring frequencies and test facilities in the Outer Shell are inadequate, and that the aggression coefficients for many of the group are not yet accurately tabulated.

Before they actually submit the variance, however, the Committee of Zookeepers realizes that someone must have pointed out all these factors in the original debates. So why was the repatriation policy promulgated? Was this part of some new overarching design that downgrades the importance of zoological information altogether? Or is the policy strictly political and possibly connected with the Message from Power #2?

I N keeping with the laws of the Colony governing the dissemination and preservation of important historical information, the official commentary of key Council-level organizations accompanies the transmission of the Cycle 447 Proclamation. Of particular interest to those involved in the Outer Shell repatriation project are the following excerpts from the report of the Council of Engineers:

... The earliest repatriation to the Inner Shell was done on almost an ad hoc basis, simply transporting the life forms, en masse, to their original region or another of similar environment in a nearby sector. This was accomplished by conducting a roundup of the tranquilized creatures at their zoo habitats, loading them into huge cargo vessels maintaining internal conditions equivalent to the habitat, and then dispersing them at their new home. This process worked adequately for small transfers over short distances. It was also cheap. However, it had many severe deficiences that rendered it almost useless for sustained operations.

First and foremost, the ontogenetic development of the creatures was completely interrupted by the repatriation procedure. They were frightened by their removal, disturbed by their necessarily reduced locus of movement during transit, and, once situated in their new locales, bothered by even minute differences from their earlier homes. Their memories, even if electronically cleansed, retained an intense sense of loss that undermined their adjustment. All these conditions taken together led to a marked phylogenetic increase in aggression coefficient, across the board, that did not significantly damp in some of the species for ten to fifteen generations....

... From the point of view of spacecraft design, both the size and distance of the proposed transfers precluded using mature specimens long before the biological and developmental problems were thoroughly understood. When the Cycle 432 Proclamation called for increased repatriation within the Colony and the Inner Shell, there was some panic at the Council of Engineers because it was thought that transportation vehicles on a near planetary scale might be required. Fortunately, the Committees on Biological Engineering and Advanced Robotics proposed that future transfers be accomplished using suspended zygotes together with new versions of the superintelligent robots serving as zoo monitors.

After a few early problems with the zygote technique, it was more or less perfected, at least for the Types A and B life forms so prevalent in the Colony. Repatriation success ratios for the last ten cycles are very high, even for the more difficult Types C and D. However, such success ratios should not be expected in the implementation of the Cycle 447 Proclamation. Not only are some of the target life forms the newest and least understood in the Zoo Complex, but also they will be repatriated, in many cases, to a distant, poorly documented biological environment where monitoring is as infrequent as every three or four hundred millicycles. Some of the more advanced Type E forms have amazingly short life spans for intelligence, as little as five or six millicycles, which means that fifty to a hundred generations may elapse between progress checks. . . .

. . . But all in all it is a magnificent challenge for engineering. Many transfer vehicles will fly well outside the standard transportation infrastructure and therefore must be able to forage raw materials on their own. Conditions at the target worlds may have changed, so adaptability and the processing of new information will play a critical role in the design. The electronic components will have more failures due to the long flight times, meaning that extraordinary fault correction systems must be developed and tested. . . .

And from the Council of Historians:

It is useful to begin our mostly negative comment on the Outer Shell repatriation plan by reminding all Colonists that our Council includes the longest continuously active intelligence pool of any Council in the Directory. Two of our groups have direct memories of the Era of Genius through many generations of biological refresh. Thus it is natural that our approach to any proposed project is to assess its merit in terms of its role in the overall evolution and/or strategy of our society. It is not our desire to dampen the youthful zeal that thrills at the acquisition of new knowledge or the prospect of great adventure; rather, we would like to place a sense of perspective on all Colony endeavors and measure the future impact of any perceived changes in basic policy. . . .

. . . The proposed repatriation scheme is still another step in the dangerous folly of unbridled frontierism that began, in our opinion, with the Boundary Decree of Cycle 416. Instead of discussing the details of the proposed plan without reference to its historical context (there are excellent descriptions of the elements of the plan in the report by the Council of Engineers—some of the significant short-term risks are listed in the report by the Council of Biologists), we wish to delineate its dangers by including it in our broad indictment of the entire genus of adventures spawned by the Boundary Decree. . . .

. . . The justifications advanced for frontierism always sound good on the surface. Its proponents point out that societal change is produced by new information outside the ordinary sweep of events, that frontierism is essentially aimed at producing this kind of new knowledge, and that the resulting change in perspective that comes from a 'new view of the universe' forces the proper and regular reassessment of our culture.

History is usually in general agreement with the advocates of frontierism and that is doubtless why this repatriation proposal and similar other previous exploration activities have been so enthusiastically supported. However, there are limitations to the benefits redounding from new information, especially when frontier investigations reveal knowledge that is either inimical to the fundamental structure of the society or beyond the comprehension of its most learned groups. In these cases the diffusion through the society of the new information is unsettling, instead of being enriching and uplifting, and actually undermines the security of the established institutions.

A perfect example of what happens when frontierism is embraced without constraint can be seen in the events of the last thirty cycles that led to the receipt of the Message from Power #2 in the middle of Cycle 444. The Boundary Decree initiated the process by establishing, in effect, a new jurisdictional domain for the Colonists. The old central Colony had no rigorous boundary. Significant development extended out to only two light millicycles distance from the administrative center. The outermost permanently maintained station was at that time a mere ten light millicycles away. The Decree of Cycle 416 regularized the nearby universe, creating four concentric worlds and expanding the central Colony itself to a radius of three light millicycles. Three specific Shells were also created, with the Outer Shell defined to be the entire region between twelve and twenty-four light millicycles away from the administrative center.

This Outer Shell contained fifty thousand unexplored star systems in a volume a thousand times greater than that of the old central Colony. During the period between Cycles 425 and 430, almost half of the major initiatives identified in the cyclical proclamations were involved, in one way or another, with the exploration of the Outer Shell. (It should be pointed out that during those five cycles there was also documented speculation that such a rapid expansion in our knowledge base might have unforeseen ramifications, but the negativists, as they were called, were drowned out by the collective fascination with the exploratory binge.) Then, in Cycle 433, our new class of interstellar drones, specifically designed to study and categorize the many worlds of the Outer Shell, encountered a large, quiescent spacecraft of unknown origin. Careful in situ investigations were unsuccessful in their attempts to correlate the engineering components of the spaceship with any known technological base for a spacefaring species.

Eschewing the caution suggested by many of the Committees, the Council of Leaders had the enigmatic spaceship towed back to one of the developed cities of the Inner Shell. There it was placed on display and analyzed in detail. The initial conclusion of the drones was validated. The spacecraft had not come from anywhere inside the domain of the Colony. The Council of Engineers concluded that the technological capability of the builders was roughly equivalent to that of the Colonists in the early Era of Genius. But when had it been made? And where did it come from? And most importantly, who had made it?

By deciding to bring the dead spaceship back to civilization, the Council of Leaders basically guaranteed that the unsettling question of its origin would remain uppermost in the minds of the Colonists. This unbridled quest for any and all information again worked to destabilize the culture. The entire society was rife with rumored explanations to the unanswered and disquieting questions raised by the spaceship. The dominant opinion was that the craft had been a Colonial prototype, never put into production, that had somehow been omitted from the official *Encyclopedia of Space Vehicles*. This opinion was consistent with the general tendency of the Colonists to believe they were innately superior to all other life forms.

It might have been possible to let the doubts and fears about the unknown spacecraft diminish to nothing, but the Council of Leaders resuscitated the collective anxieties by announcing, in the Cycle 434 Proclamation, that the largest new project of the Colony would be the design and eventual deployment of a new generation of receiver arrays in the Outer Shell. The purpose of these arrays would be to intercept and decode any coherent radio messages that might be emanating from inside the Gap. It was a clear indication that the leadership believed the silent spaceship to be of extracolonial origin.

In Cycles 435 and 436 wave after wave of disturbing information staggered the Colony. First there was the premature announcement that many extracolonial messages had been decoded. This disclosure supported the widespread rumor of multiple Powers in the galaxy, some of them far more evolved than the Colony. This frightening concept lingered for half a cycle before the Council of Astronomers, responding to these proliferating half-truths, finally announced that all but a handful of the messages could be ascribed to a single power, Power #2, whose center of activity appeared to be about two hundred light millicycles away. Shortly thereafter their next astonishing announcement unambiguously identified Power #2 transmissions coming from sources as far as one hundred and fifty light millicycles apart, or more than three times the diameter across the entire Colony jurisdiction!

Between Cycle 438 and the receipt of the Message, the Council of Leaders ignored advice that the Colony should carefully husband its resources while analyzing the impact of the discovery of the strange spaceship.

Crash programs were instituted in advanced encryption, it is true, primarily to allay concerns that Power #2 might be monitoring all our transmissions. This action was widely hailed as a step in the right direction. However, at the same time the exploration of the Outer Shell was intensified, leading to the identification of the new Type E life forms and the subsequent, thinly disguised endangered species roundup. All suggestions to retrench and slow down the exploration program were ignored. In Cycle 442, in fact, the Zoo Complex created several artificial planets just for the conduct of genetic capabilities experiments with the Type E species.

Then came the Message from Power #2. So simple, so straightforward, so terrifying. It was coded in our most advanced encryption algorithm. It acknowledged our mutual awareness of one another and suggested opening up bilateral communications. Nothing else. End of Message....

...It is not fear of hostility from Power #2 that motivates our objection to continued exploration in the Outer Shell. On the contrary. We as historians think the nascent concern about the possible aggressiveness of Power #2 is unfounded. Study after study has shown that there is a significant positive correlation between high aggression coefficient and inability to evolve into a society with a purview greater than a single solar system. In fact, the probability that a society as advanced as ours could have retained aggression and territoriality as constituents in their overall psychological makeup is vanishingly small.

Nevertheless, such monumental events as the receipt of the Message from Power #2 call for reflection and synthesis, not additional exploratory activities. We should be using our resources to study and understand the entire range of impacts that the Message will have on our society, not squandering them on bold repatriation schemes. It is a question of priorities and once again the advocates of frontierism, exalting new information and technological development over the stability of the society, are blind to the downside risks of their endeavors....

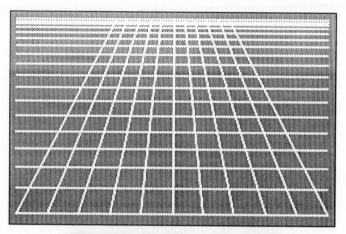

FRIDAY

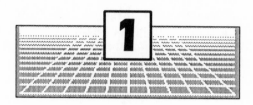

N ICK Williams woke up at five o'clock in the morning and could not go back to sleep. His mind was too active, racing over and over the events of the day before and the possible outcomes of the day ahead. The same phenomenon had occurred often when he was in high school in Virginia and then a few times later, at Harvard, usually just before big swimming meets. If he had too much excitement running through his system, his brain would not turn off enough to let him sleep.

He lay in bed for almost another hour, alternately trying to coax himself back to sleep and indulging his fantasy that what he had found the day before was just the first item in a vast cache of valuable treasure. Nick loved to fantasize. It was always easy for him to see, in his mind's eye, all the scenes in the novels that he loved so much to read. Now for a moment he imagined headlines in the *Miami Herald* announcing his discovery of a hoard of sunken gold off the coast of Key West.

Around six o'clock Nick gave up trying to sleep and climbed out of bed. The little exercise bag was next to the dresser. He pulled the golden trident out to look at it, as he had done four or five times the night before. *What was this thing?* he asked himself. *It must have had some practical use for it's too damn ugly to be ornamental.* He shook his head. *Amanda will know. If anyone can tell me where this thing came from, she can.*

Nick walked across his bedroom to the sliding glass doors and opened the curtains. It was almost sunrise. Beyond the small balcony outside he could see the beach and the ocean. His condominium was on the third floor and had an unspoiled view of the quiet surf. Above the water a couple of brown pelicans soared in graceful formation, waiting for a chance to descend into the water and catch some unsuspecting fish swimming too close to the surface. Nick watched a couple in their seventies walking slowly along the beach. They were holding hands and talking quietly; a couple of times the woman broke away to pick up a shell or two and put it in a small Ziploc bag.

Nick turned away from the door and grabbed the jeans that he had dropped on the floor the night before. He pulled them on over his undershorts and walked into the living room carrying the bag with the trident. He put the golden object carefully on the table where he could study it, and then went back into the open kitchen to start the coffee maker and turn on the radio.

Except for the books, Nick's living room was decorated just like hundreds of Florida seaside condominiums. The couch and easy chair were comfortable and bright, cream in color, with a couple of light green ferns in the pattern for decoration. Two small paintings of water birds standing on an empty beach adorned the otherwise empty walls. Light beige drapes that matched the carpet framed the long sliding glass doors that led to the balcony with the rattan patio furniture.

It was the books that gave the apartment some individuality. Along the wall opposite the couch, between the living room and the bedroom, was the large wood bookcase. It stretched almost all the way from the sliding glass doors in front of the balcony to the bedroom door. Although the general appearance of the apartment was one of disarray (newspapers and sports magazines strewn about here and there on the coffee table, clothes and towels on the floor in the bedroom and the bathroom, dirty dishes in the sink, the dishwasher standing open half full of dishes), the bookcase area was clearly well maintained. Altogether there must have been four or five hundred books on the four shelves of the long bookcase, all paperbacks, virtually all novels, and all carefully filed according to category.

In front of each group of books, Scotch-taped to the outside of the bookshelf, was a sheet of paper identifying the category. Nick had finished A Fan's Notes on the boat on Thursday and had already put it back in its proper place on the shelf (in the category of "American, 20th Century, A–G") right next to a dozen or more books by William Faulkner. He had then selected for his bedtime reading a nineteenth-century French novel, Madame Bovary, by Gustave Flaubert. Nick had read the book once before, during his sophomore year at Harvard, and had not thought that much about it. However, he had been recently surprised to find the book on several lists of the ten finest novels of all time, ranking right up there with such masterpieces as Crime and Punishment by Dostoevsky. Hmm. Perhaps I missed something the first time, he had told himself the previous night before deciding to read it again.

But Nick had not been able to focus on the magnificently detailed descriptions of life in provincial France a hundred and fifty years earlier. As he had followed the story of the lovely Emma Bovary, a woman for whom the stultifying sameness of her life was cause enough to have affairs that would eventually scandalize her village, the excitement of Nick's own life, for once, kept intruding. He was unable to suspend himself in the novel. His mind kept returning to the possibilities offered by the golden object in the exercise bag.

Nick turned the object over and over in his hands while he drank his morning coffee. Then he had an idea. He walked back to the second bedroom, just opposite the kitchen and next to the laundry room, and opened the closet door. Nick used most of this closet as a storage area. In the corner of the closet were four huge cardboard boxes of junk that he had brought with him when he had bought the condominium seven years earlier. He had never opened them even once in the intervening time. But he did remember that in one of those boxes were a bunch of photographs of the objects they had brought up from the *Santa Rosa. Maybe if I look at those pictures,* he thought to himself as he struggled to find the right container in the dimly lit closet, *I will see something that looks like that thing.*

He finally located the correct box and dragged it out into the middle of the living room. At one time its contents might have been well organized, for there were manila folders with filing labels inside. But almost all of the papers and photos and newspaper clippings had fallen out of their original places and were now scattered around the box in a loose jumble. Nick reached in and pulled out a clipping from the *Miami Herald.* It was yellow from age and had been crammed down into one of the corners. Five people, including Nick, were featured in a big photograph on the front page.

Nick stopped for a moment and looked at the photo and the caption. *Has it really been that long?* he wondered, *Almost eight years since we found the* Santa Rosa. The caption identified the five individuals in the photograph as the crew of the *Neptune,* a dive and salvage boat that had found an old Spanish ship named the *Santa Rosa* sunk in the Gulf of Mexico about fifteen miles north of the Dry Tortugas. Gold and silver objects worth more than two million dollars had been retrieved from the vessel and were piled in front of the happy, smiling crew. From left to right they were Greta Erhard, Jake Lewis, Homer Ashford, Ellen Ashford, and Nick Williams.

That was before they started eating, Nick thought to himself. *Ellen ate because of Greta, because it gave her an excuse in her own mind for what was happening with Homer. And Homer ate because he could afford it. Just like he does everything else. For some people constraints are the only thing that saves them. Give them freedom and they go berserk.*

Nick dug deeper into the box, looking for a set of twenty or so photographs that showed most of the large gold items they had retrieved from the *Santa Rosa.* Eventually he started finding some of the pictures, in groups of four or five, in different parts of what was now becoming a hopeless pile at the bottom of the box. Each time he would find some more photos, he would pull them out, look at them carefully, and then shake his head to acknowledge that the golden trident did not look a thing like any of the objects from the *Santa Rosa.*

At the bottom of the box Nick encountered a yellow manila folder with a rubber band wrapped carefully around it. Thinking at first that this folder might contain the rest of the pictures from the *Santa Rosa,* Nick pulled out the folder and opened it hastily. An 8 × 11 picture of a beautiful woman in her early thirties slid out and fell on the living room floor. It was followed by handwritten notes, cards, a few letters in envelopes, and then about twenty sheets of bond paper covered with double-spaced typing. Nick sighed. How was it possible that he hadn't recognized this folder?

The woman in the portrait had long black hair, lightly frosted in the front. She was wearing a dark red cotton blouse, slightly open at the top to show a triple strand of pearls just under the neck. In blue ink that contrasted with the red of the blouse, someone with magnificent, clearly artistic hand- writing had written, "Mon Cher—Je t'aime, Monique," across the lower right portion of the photograph.

Nick bent down on his knees to pick up the scattered contents of the folder. He looked at the portrait carefully, his heart skipping a few beats as he remembered how beautiful she had been. He started to sort the typed pages together. At the top of one of the pages was written, in all capital letters, "MONIQUE," and then underneath it, "by Nicholas C. Williams." He started to read.

"The wonder of life lies in its unpredictability. Each of our lives is ir- revocably changed by the things we cannot have possibly forecast. We walk out of the door every morning to go to work or to class or even to the grocery store, and ninety-nine times out of a hundred we return without anything having happened that we will remember even a month in the future. On those days our lives are swept up in the banality of living, in the basic humdrum cadence of everyday existence. It is the other day, the magic day, for which we live.

"On this magic day our character becomes defined, our growth is accel- erated, our emotional transitions are made. Sometimes, maybe once in a lifetime, there will be a string of these magic days, one after another, so full of life and change and challenge that we are completely transformed by the experience and our souls become suffused with a boundless joy. During that time we are often overcome by the simple and incredible miracle of just being alive. This is the story of one such magic period.

"It was spring break in Fort Lauderdale. Our swimming season had just finished at Harvard and my uncle, as a present for my twenty-first birthday, offered to let me use his condominium in Florida for a couple of weeks so I could unwind from the twin rigors of studying and swimming practice . . ."

Nick had not looked at these pages for almost ten years. As he read the first few paragraphs he remembered, vividly, the ecstasy in which they were written. *It was two nights before the party. She was at some social function that night, would be too late, would come by first thing in the morning. I couldn't sleep. It was the first night in a week I had been away from her.* He stopped for a moment, old emotions twisting around inside him, making him feel dizzy and slightly nauseous. He read the first paragraph again. *It was also before the pain. Before the incredible goddamn pain.*

For almost thirty minutes music had been playing on the radio. Nick had heard it, he knew it was there, but he could not have identified any of the songs. It had been background music. Now, just at the moment when his memories of Monique were the most poignant, the Miami "classic rock and roll station, WMIM, 99.9 on your FM dial," played Cyndi Lauper's haunting 1984 hit "Time After Time." The music seemed to increase markedly in amplitude. Nick had to sit down and grab a breath. Until the song, he had been able to deal with his memories of Monique. But somehow that song, the one he had played on the cassette player in his car almost every night as he had made the drive from Fort Lauderdale to Palm Beach to see her, carried with it all the youthful love, joy, fear, and anger that had marked the entire affair. Nick was overwhelmed. As he sat on the couch and listened to the song, hot tears welled up in his eyes and then ran softly down his cheeks.

". . . Lying in my bed, I hear the clock tick, and think of you . . . Caught up in circles, confusion is nothing new . . . Flashback, warm nights, almost left behind . . . Suitcase of memories . . . Time after Time."

"YOU say, go slow, I fall behind. . . . The second hand unwinds . . ." Brenda leaned over and turned the volume down on the cassette player. "It's me, Mr. Stubbs, honest. Brenda Goldfine. Don't you recognize me?" She was shouting at an old man in a blue uniform who was sitting on a stool in a small circular tower in the middle of the road. "And that's Teresa Silver in the back. She's not feeling too well. Come on, open the gate and let us through."

The security guard climbed down from his stool and slowly walked out in front of Nick's old Pontiac. He wrote the license number down on a note pad and then came around to Brenda's window. "All right this time, Brenda, but this is not according to the rules. All visitors coming into Windsor Cove after ten o'clock at night must be cleared *ahead* of time."

At length the guard raised the gate and Nick moved his car forward again. "The guy's really a pain in the ass," Brenda said to Nick, smacking her gum as she talked, "Christ, you'd think he owned one of the places or something." Nick had heard about Windsor Cove. Or rather had read about it. Once when he was over at his uncle's home in Potomac, Maryland, there had been a copy of *Town and Country* magazine on the table and he had read about the "gracious life of Windsor Cove." Now, as he drove past the estates in the most prestigious section of Palm Beach, he was awed by the personal wealth displayed.

"Over there. That's Teresa's house." Brenda pointed at a colonial house set back about a hundred yards from the road. Nick drove into the long semicircular driveway and eventually stopped in front of a walkway leading to the front of the house. It was an imposing place. Two full floors, six white columns over twenty feet high, an opulent door whose top half was an arched, stained glass window of a white heron in flight against a blue sky filled with fleecy clouds.

Brenda looked in the back of the car where her friend was passed out. "Look, I'd better handle this. I'll go up and talk to Mrs. Silver and explain what happened and everything. Otherwise you could be in deep shit. Sometimes she jumps to conclusions."

By the time Brenda reached the front door to ring the bell, it had already opened. An attractive woman in a red silk blouse and a pair of chic black slacks was waiting. Nick guessed that she had probably been called by the security guard. He couldn't tell much about the conversation, but he could see that Teresa's mother was asking questions. After a couple of minutes, Brenda and the woman came back to the car. "You didn't tell me she was *still* passed out," Nick heard a surprisingly husky voice say. There was also some kind of accent, European perhaps. "You know, Brenda, this is absolutely the last time she can go anywhere with you. You just can't control her. I'm not even sure that you try." The voice was angry but not strident.

Nick opened his door and climbed out of the car. "This is the guy I was telling you about, Mrs. Silver," Brenda said. "Without him Teresa might still be lying on the beach."

Mrs. Silver extended her hand. Nick took it, feeling a little awkward. He didn't know how to shake hands with a woman. "I understand that I'm in your debt, young man," Mrs. Silver said graciously. "Brenda tells me that you rescued Teresa from all sorts of horrors." The light from the street lamps played about her sculptured face. Her hand was soft, sensual. Nick smelled just a trace of perfume, something exotic. Her eyes were fixed on his, unwavering, inquisitive.

"Yes, Ma'am," Nick said clumsily. "I mean, well, she had had too much to drink and I thought the crowd of teenagers she was with were a little bit out of control." He stopped. She was still watching him, measuring him. He was becoming agitated and didn't understand why. "Somebody had to help her and I just happened to be there . . ." He trailed off weakly.

Mrs. Silver thanked him again and turned to Brenda. "Your mother's expecting you, dear. We'll stay out front until you get home. Flash your lights to let us know you're there." Brenda looked happy to be dismissed. She scampered off into the night in the direction of the nearest house about a hundred yards away.

There was a momentary pause as they watched the sixteen-year-old disappear into the night. Nick found himself stealing furtive looks at Mrs. Silver's profile. An inchoate awareness of what he was feeling made him more nervous. *Jesus, she's beautiful. And young. How could she be the girl's mother?* He was wrestling with a jumble of thoughts as he saw the lights flicker in the distance.

"Good," she said, turning to Nick with a smile, "Brenda's home. Now we can worry about Teresa." She stopped for a moment and laughed. "Oh, I almost forgot. We haven't been formally introduced. I'm Teresa's mother, Monica Silver."

"I'm Nick Williams," he said in response. Her dark eyes were fixed on him again. In the reflected light the expression in her eyes seemed to vary. One moment she was a pixie, then a seductress, then a very proper Palm Beach society woman. Or was Nick imagining it? He couldn't return her gaze anymore. He felt his cheeks flush as he averted his eyes.

"I had to carry her from the beach to the parking lot," Nick said abruptly, as he went around to the back door of his car and opened it. The teenager had been leaning against the door and nearly fell out. She didn't stir. He picked Teresa up and threw her over his shoulder. "So it's no problem for me to carry her for you now. I'm used to it."

They walked quietly down the path toward the house, Monica Silver leading by a few steps. Nick watched her walk in front of him. She moved effortlessly, like a dancer, with almost perfect posture. Her dark hair was wrapped up at the back in a chignon. *It must be very long*, he thought to himself with delight, imagining her hair flowing down her beautiful back.

It was a warm and humid Palm Beach evening. Nick was sweating by the time they reached the entrance. "Could you do me one more favor, Nick?" Mrs. Silver asked. "Could you carry her up to her room? My husband's not here and the help has all gone to bed. And I doubt seriously if she's going to get herself together well enough to climb the stairs, even with my help, in the near future."

Nick followed Mrs. Silver's instructions and carried Teresa through the atrium, into the living room, up the entry steps onto the platform, up the left flight to the second floor, and then into her bedroom. It was huge. In her room Teresa had a king-size bed with four posters, a giant television, an entire cabinet of movies for the VCR, and a sound system that would have been a credit to any rock and roll band. Bruce Springsteen posters and photos were all over the room. Nick laid Teresa gently on her bed. She murmured "Thank you," indicating to him that at least she was semiconscious. Her mother bent over her and gave her a kiss.

Nick left the two of them alone and went back down the stairs into the living room. He could not believe that somebody really could live in a house like this. Why the living room alone was bigger than the house in Falls Church where he grew up. He wandered around the room after he came down the stairs. There were original paintings on the walls, crystal glass chandeliers hanging from the ceiling, and art objects and bric-a-brac both on the tables and in every nook and cranny. It was all too much for him. He was overwhelmed.

He felt a hand on his shoulder and involuntarily recoiled. Monica Silver chided him, "Goodness, you're jumpy. It's only me." He turned around to look at her. Was he imagining it or had she somehow combed her hair and put on fresh makeup in the few seconds they had been separated? For the first time he saw her in the full light. She was the most beautiful woman that he had ever seen. His breath was taken away and he felt giddy. Outside he had not been able to see her skin clearly. Now he found himself staring at her bare arms, following the elegant contours of her neck. Her skin had the smoothness of ivory. It called to him to touch it. *Watch yourself, Williams,* he heard a voice inside him say, *Or you are going to be outrageous.* He tried to calm himself.

But it was useless. He could not take his eyes off her. She was saying something. She had asked him a question. He had not even heard it, so dumbfounded was he by what was happening, by where he was. She was leading him somewhere in the house. His imagination was running wild. She took him into a small room with a table and told him to sit down.

"It's the least I can do," she was saying, "to repay you for what you did for Teresa. I know you must be hungry. And we still have some great food left over from the party tonight."

Nick was in a breakfast nook just off the kitchen. To his left a door led to the patio and then outside, into the back yard. The lights around the huge swimming pool were still on. He could see manicured gardens with roses in bloom, chaise longues, colorful umbrellas, white iron tables with twisted, lacy legs—he could not believe that it was all real. He felt transported to another world, a world that existed only in books and movies.

Monica Silver laid out some food on the table. Smoked salmon, onions, capers, cream cheese, two different kinds of bread, plus a dish of some other kind of fish that Nick did not recognize. "That's marinated herring," she said with a smile, noticing Nick's quizzical expression. She handed him a wine glass. He took it and unconsciously looked her straight in the eyes. He was transfixed. He felt weak and powerless, as if he were being drawn into her deep brown, bewitching eyes, into her world of richness and luxury and beauty. His knees were weak, his heart was racing, he could feel his fingers tingling.

She poured some white wine in his glass and then in her own. "This is a brilliant Burgundy, Clos des Mouches," she said, touching her glass to his with a light tinkle. "Let's make a toast."

She was radiant. He was enthralled. "To happiness," she said.

They talked for over three hours. Nick learned that Monica Silver had grown up in France, that her father had been a small, struggling fur merchant in Paris, and that she had met her husband, Aaron (the biggest of the big Montreal furriers), while helping her father at the shop. She had been seventeen at the time of the whirlwind courtship. Mr. Silver had proposed just seven days after they had met and she had accepted immediately even though her husband-to-be was twenty years older. She moved to Montreal and married him before she was eighteen. Teresa was born nine months later.

Nick told her that he was in his junior year at Harvard, majoring in English and French to get a good liberal arts education and prepare himself for either law school or graduate school. As soon as she found out that he was in his third year of French, she switched and spoke to him in her native language. Her name became Monique. He missed some of what she said, but it didn't matter. He understood the gist of it. And her dramatic voice plus the sound of the foreign language only increased the power of the spell already cast by the wine and her beauty.

Nick also tried to speak French from time to time. Whatever self-consciousness he might have ordinarily felt was swept away by the magic of the setting and their growing rapport. They laughed together easily at his mistakes. She was gracious and charming when she corrected him, always adding "mais vous parlez français très bien" in the early part of the evening. Later, as their conversation became more personal (Nick talked about his problems with his father; Monique wondered aloud if there was anything a mother could do with a teenage daughter except hope that some basic values had been learned), Monique changed to the more personal "tu" form in talking to him. This established an additional intimacy between them that deepened in the wee hours of the morning.

Monique talked about Paris, about the romance of the streets, the bistros, the museums, the history. Nick visualized it all and felt transported with her to the city of lights. She told about her dreams when she was growing up, about walking in the sixteenth arrondissement among the wealthy and promising herself that someday . . . He listened closely, enraptured, an almost beatific smile upon his face. In the end, Monique had to tell him that it was time to go because she had an early tennis lesson in the morning. It was after three o'clock. He apologized as they walked together to the door. She laughed and said that it had been fun. At the door she reached up and kissed him on the cheek. His heart soared out of his body at the touch of her lips. "Call me sometime," she said with a playful smile, as she closed the door behind him.

For over thirty hours Nick thought of nothing but Monique. He talked to her in his mind during the day; she was his lover in dreams at night. He called her once, twice, three times, each time talking to her answering machine. The third time he left her his phone number and address and suggested that she try to get in touch with him when her schedule would permit.

By noon on the second day after his evening at the Silvers' Palm Beach mansion, he started to calm down, to realize that there was no sense in his continuing to worship the image of a woman he had met for a single evening. Especially a woman who was married to someone else. In the late afternoon he went out on the beach to play volleyball with some of the other college students he had met during his first days in Florida. He had just served an ace when he thought he heard his name being called by a husky, accented voice that was absolutely unmistakable.

He thought for a moment he was dreaming. Standing in the sand not ten yards away was Monique. She was wearing a bright red and white striped bikini and her long black hair hung down her back to just above her waist. The volleyball game stopped. His friends whistled. He walked over to her, his heart pounding in his temples and his breath struggling to find its way out of his constricted chest. Monique smiled and slid her arm through his. She explained that she had brought Teresa into Lauderdale for a small high school party and since it was so hot . . .

They walked along the beach and talked as the sun set behind the condominiums. They were oblivious to the young people all around them. The gentle waves washed their feet with warm water as they walked. Monique insisted that they eat in Nick's condo, so they stopped for tuna fish, tomatoes, onions, and mayonnaise to put on their sandwiches. Cold beer, potato chips, and sandwiches on a bare formica table was the dinner. Lovemaking was the dessert. Nick almost had an orgasm on their first kiss and his passion made him klutzy and funny in trying to remove her bikini. Monique slowed him down, smiled softly, neatly folded her bikini and his bathing suit (while he of course was going wild), and then came to join him on the bed. After two kisses naked on the bed, Nick was seized by a paroxysm of lust. He rolled roughly on top of Monique and began gyrating with his hips. At first a bit alarmed, Monique slowed him just a bit and guided him gently into her.

Monique's body was nearly perfect. Nice, full, upright breasts (they had been reconstructed of course after she had nursed Teresa but how could Nick have known or cared?), slim waist, rounded, feminine ass (not one of those boyish asses that really skinny women have), taut muscled legs kept in shape with lots of exercise. But it was her skin, that magnificent ivory skin, that sent Nick into ecstasy. It was so soft and easy to the touch.

Her mouth seemed to fit his perfectly. Nick had been with two women before, a high-priced call girl given to him as a Christmas present after the Harvard swimming team had discovered he was still a virgin at the end of his freshman year and Jennifer Barnes from Radcliffe, his sometimes steady date during most of his sophomore year. Jennifer's teeth always clanged against his when they kissed. But that had not been the only difficulty in his relationship with Jennifer. She was a physicist and her approach to sex had been almost clinical. She measured sizes and durations and frequencies and even quantities of ejaculant. After three "scheduled performances" with Jenny, Nick had decided it wasn't worth it.

Nick gasped as he slid into Monique. Both of them knew it would be over soon. Ten seconds later Nick finished his climax and started to withdraw. But Monique held his rear firmly in her hands, keeping him in place, and deftly (how did she do it?) rolled over so that she was on top. Nick was now out of his element. In his limited experience, withdrawal was the next step after orgasm. He didn't know what Monique was doing. Ever so slowly, her eyes half closed as she hummed a piece of classical music to herself, Monique rocked back and forth on top of him, her vaginal walls holding tightly to his now flaccid penis. After a couple of minutes she began to grind her pelvis forward as she rocked and, much to Nick's amazement, as her breath shortened he found himself becoming aroused again. Now her eyes closed altogether and her rhythm became stronger, the thrusts of her forward motion grinding with a little pain into his bones. Nick was now definitely erect and he started following her motion, lightly gyrating in pattern with her.

Monique leaned forward, concentrating but smiling with her eyes closed, preparing for her own orgasm. She was acutely aware and delighted that Nick was up again. Timing her own progress perfectly (and in complete control of the situation), she adroitly and softly reached down and began titillating Nick's nipples in rhythm with her forward thrusts. Nick had never had his breasts touched in lovemaking before and was shocked. But the raw excitement was overwhelming. She increased her play, even pinching him when she saw (and felt) his response. As wave after wave of delightful release coursed through her body, Nick uttered a loud, wailing scream and had his second orgasm in fifteen minutes. At the end of the climax he was completely given over to pleasure and made animal sounds and shook involuntarily from exhausted satiety.

Nick was a little embarrassed by his noisy and uncontrolled response, but Monique's playful and friendly afterplay assured him that everything was all right. She went to his closet, pulled out one of his three dress shirts, and put it on. The tails came almost down to her knees (Monique was only five feet five and Nick was a shade less than six two) and she looked positively gamine with her pixie smile, long hair, and man's shirt. Nick began to declare his love but Monique came forward and put her finger to his lips. Then she kissed him lovingly, told him that she needed to pick up Teresa, jumped in the shower for what could not have been more than a minute, dressed, kissed him again, and walked out the door. Nick did not move during this entire time. After she left he fell asleep contentedly. He did not dream.

For the next eight days Nick was on top of the world. He saw Monique every day, most of the time at her Palm Beach mansion, but sometimes at his uncle's condominium. They made love at every opportunity and it was always different. Monique was full of surprises. The second time Nick went to her house, for example, he found her in the back, swimming naked in the pool. She told him that she had given all the servants the day off. Within minutes they were frolicking and laughing on the grass between the garden and the pool.

Their affair was conducted in French. Monique taught him about food and wine. They shared their knowledge of French literature. One passionate night they argued about André Gide's *La Symphonie Pastorale* both before and after lovemaking. Monique defended the pastor and laughed at Nick's insistence that the blind Gertrude was "an innocent." Another evening, when Monique demanded that Nick wear a black Halloween mask and a pair of white leotards throughout their long French dinner, they read Jean Genet's *Le Balcon* together as a prelude to sex.

The days raced by relentlessly, clothed in the magic of love and intimacy. Once Nick showed up at the mansion and Monique greeted him dressed in an incredible coat, a full-length Alaskan seal fur with indigo fox trim around the collars as well as down the lapels and framing the sleeves from the shoulders to the wrists. The coat was the softest thing Nick had ever touched, even softer than her tantalizing skin. His playful paramour had turned the air conditioning up as high as it would go so that she could wear her favorite coat. She was wearing nothing underneath it. After lovemaking that evening she dressed Nick's naked body in one of her husband's beaver coats, explaining the presence of half a dozen fur coats in Palm Beach with a simple "it's our business and we like to have some things to show our friends and acquaintances in case they are interested."

Nick professed his love with increasing zeal each time they met anew. Monique responded with her usual "je t'aime," but would not reply to Nick's insistent questions about the future. She avoided all questions about her relationship with Mr. Silver, except to say that he was a workaholic and that he stayed in Montreal most of the year. He had bought the place in Palm Beach primarily because Monique did not like the cold and wanted a more active social life than the one they had in Montreal. Monique usually spent the period from Christmas to Easter in Palm Beach; Teresa, who had just finished her spring break from her exclusive private school and had returned to Canada, came down as often as possible so that she could be with her mother.

Monique gave short, terse answers about her present life. But she waxed rhapsodic about her childhood in Paris. She never criticized her husband or complained about her married life. Yet she did tell Nick that her days with him had been the happiest time of her life. She also talked about some of her friends, but Nick never met any of them. They were always alone.

One day she picked him up in her Cadillac and they headed toward Key Largo so that he could do some diving at the Pennekamp Recreation Area. As always, she was wearing her wedding ring. On this particular day Nick had vowed to himself that he would get some answers about the future, and the constant presence of her wedding ring pissed him off. He asked her to remove it. She politely refused, then grew angry when he pressed her. She pulled the car off the highway in the marshland north of the Keys and stopped the engine.

"It is a fact that I am married," she said resolutely, "and taking the ring off is not going to change anything. I am in love with you, without doubt, but you have understood my situation from the beginning. If you cannot deal with it anymore, then perhaps we should just call it quits."

Nick was shocked by her response. The thought of being without her terrified him. He apologized and professed his love. He began kissing her passionately and then jumped in the back seat. He told her that he needed her right then, that moment. She somewhat reluctantly joined him and they had intercourse on the back seat of her Cadillac. Monique was quiet and pensive most of the rest of the day.

On Friday, exactly a week after they had met, Monique took Nick to a tuxedo shop to have him fitted for a black tie dinner with some friends that she was having on Saturday night in her home. So finally he was going to be seen with her. "And," Nick thought, "*now* she will talk about our future." Nick was supposed to be in Boston on Monday morning and his parents were expecting him Saturday night in Falls Church, but he assured himself that he could drive all day (and all night if necessary, so pumped up was he in his love for Monique) to get to classes on Monday morning.

Nick was full of hope and dreams when he showed up at the Silver mansion on Saturday night. He looked elegant in his summer tux, and the smile with which he greeted Monique at the door could have won a prize. Even with the doorman standing by, he handed her a dozen red roses, gave her a kiss, and told her that he loved her. "Of course you do," she said lightly, "doesn't everybody?" She took him inside and introduced him to the four other people who had also come early as the "young man who saved our Teresa one day in Lauderdale." Then Monique excused herself. It was her fashion, Nick later learned, to ask a few select friends to come early to a party, to greet them in casual attire, and then to return an hour or so later, when everyone had arrived, with a grand entrance. As Monique gracefully walked up the stairs of the mansion, Nick's eyes followed her with an unmistakable look of adoration.

"Isn't she magnificent?" Nick was asked by a relaxed, tanned man of about fifty who offered him a martini. His name was Clayton. "Once I was with her all weekend on their yacht, while Aaron was in Montreal. I thought she had invited me for a little diversion." He laughed. "But I was wrong. She just wanted some company and I could talk about France and Europe. Come with me (he slipped his arm through Nick's) and I'll introduce you to the select group that was invited early today."

Nick was treated with extreme courtesy by the other favored guests, but he was wary of their questions about Monique. He was, after all, a Southern boy, and if there was something to say about their relationship, it was her place to say it. So he answered politely but modestly and didn't elaborate at all.

One of the two women at the bar, who introduced herself as Jane Somebody, said that she was Monica's oldest friend in Palm Beach. (They all called her Monica. It was impossible for Nick to call her anything but Monique. Nick wondered if they could guess what was going on or if Monique had told them.) Jane was in her late thirties, plump and raucous, a heavy drinker and a chain smoker. She had once been fairly attractive but had lived too hard too soon. She was one of those people who touch everybody during a conversation. She made Nick nervous.

The other guests began to arrive. Jane and Clayton (as in Clayton Poindexter III of Newport and Palm Beach. Clayton, when asked by Nick what he did, answered, "NVMS." Nick of course had absolutely no idea what that meant. Clayton laughed. "NVMS—No visible means of support—a term used to cover all bums.") seemed to be acting as hostess and host in Monique's absence. They introduced him to everybody. Nick had three or four martinis and told the Teresa story at least seven times during the first hour that he was in the Silver mansion.

Nick was becoming fairly spiffed by this time. He sang to himself as he took another martini off the cocktail tray being proffered by one of the servants. The alcohol had buoyed his spirits and made him feel somehow temporarily suave and debonair. Nick was on the patio talking to Monique's "riding partner," a lovely woman in her mid-twenties named Anne, when he heard scattered applause from the living room. "It's Monica," Anne said. "Let's go see."

The grand stairway in the Silvers' colonial mansion rose to a platform maybe six feet above the living room floor and then split, with two different sets of stairs then continuing up to the second floor. Monique was standing on the platform, acknowledging the applause, dressed in a simple navy blue knit dress that seemed form-fitted to her perfect body. The back was cut way down, almost to the bottom of her spectacular hair (she turned around to please the forty or so guests), and, in the front, two thin pieces of cloth ran from her shoulders to her waist, covering each breast adequately but leaving plenty of cleavage to be admired. Entranced by the vision of his queen, Nick cheered lustily, a little too loud, "Bravo. Bravo." Monique seemed not to hear his cheer. She had turned and was looking up the stairs.

It probably took an entire minute for Nick to comprehend the sight he was seeing. A man, a distinguished-looking man in his early fifties, wearing a custom-made tan tuxedo and sporting an amazing sapphire ring on his little finger, came down the staircase and put his arms around Monique's waist. She reached up and kissed him. He smiled and waved at the crowd as they politely applauded. They walked down the stairs together to the living room.

Who is that? Nick thought to himself and even through the gin and the vermouth and all the incredible feelings the answer came back, *That is her husband, Aaron. What is he doing here? Why didn't she tell me?* And then, following very swiftly, *How could she do this to me? I love her and she loves me and there is something very very wrong. This cannot be happening.*

Nick tried to breathe but felt as if a large piece of earth-moving machinery were pressed against his chest. Instinctively he turned away from the sight of Monique and Aaron walking down the stairs arm in arm. As he did he spilled part of a martini on Anne's shoulder. His apology was very clumsy. Now completely discombobulated, he stumbled over to the bar, trying desperately to breathe and to stop the pounding in his chest. *No. No. She can't be doing this. There must be some mistake.* His mind could not read the message that his eyes were transmitting. He drank another martini swiftly, barely aware of his surroundings or the jumbled feelings torturing his soul.

"There he is." He heard her voice behind him, the voice that had come to signify everything that was valuable and important in life, the voice of love. But this time he was terrified. Nick turned and Monique and Aaron were standing right in front of him.

"So finally I get to meet this young man I've heard so much about," he said. Aaron was pleasant, friendly, without a trace of anything but gratitude in his voice. Aaron Silver was holding out his hand. Monique was smiling. *God, she's so beautiful. Even now, when I should hate her.* Nick mechanically shook Aaron's hand and quietly accepted his thanks for "helping Teresa at a difficult time." Nick said nothing. He turned to look at Monique. She reached up and kissed him on the cheek. *Oh those lips. How I long still for those lips. Why? Why? What happens to us now?*

Nick suddenly realized that there were tears in his eyes. *Ohmygod. I'm going to cry.* Embarrassed beyond measure, Nick abruptly excused himself and walked out onto the patio. Now the tears were running down his cheeks. He was afraid he was going to sit down on the grass and start bawling like a baby. Confused, puzzled, he walked around the garden with his head down and tried, without success, to draw a regular breath.

He felt a hand on his elbow. It was Jane, the last person on Earth that Nick wanted to see at this moment. "She'll be out to see you in a few minutes. First she and Aaron have to make the rounds, you know how it is at parties when you're the hostess." Jane lit a cigarette. Nick was certain he was going to puke. He turned quickly to ask her to put out the cigarette and he lost his equilibrium.

Maybe it was the drink, maybe the adrenaline, maybe it was just too much. Nick's head was spinning around and around. He inadvertently leaned against Jane for support. She misunderstood, and then pulled his head to her shoulder. "There, there," she said. "Don't take it so hard. You and Monique will still be able to have some time together. Aaron will only be here for a couple of days and then he'll go back to Montreal to work. Besides," she said with gusto, "if you're anywhere near as good as Monica says you are, I'd be delighted to take care of you when she's with Aaron."

Nick pushed her away and staggered back. He felt as if he had just been hit in the face with a sledgehammer. The full impact of Jane's comment sunk in slowly and an uncontrollable mixture of anger and hurt surged to the surface. *What? What? She knows. This cloying bitch knows. Maybe they all know. What? Fuck. Fuck this altogether.* And then, almost immediately, as his mind began to take the measure of the evening's events, *How do I get out of here? Where is the exit?* As he walked around the house to the front (he was not about to go inside again), from deep inside Nick there now came a sound, a sound that welled up to the surface and could not be contained. This was the wail of pain, the unmitigated and ineluctable cry of the animal in total despair. Millennia of acculturation have made it rare to hear such cries from human beings. But this loud and untoward scream, which rose into the Palm Beach night like a siren from a police car, gave Nick his first comfort. While the partygoers were trying to decide what they had heard, Nick climbed into his 1977 Pontiac and drove away.

He drove south toward Fort Lauderdale, his heart still pumping like crazy and his body trembling from adrenaline. He didn't think about anything coherently. The pictures in his mind seemed to come at random, without any clear connection between them. Monique was the focus of all the pictures in the montage. Monique in her Alaskan seal coat, Monique in her red and white bathing suit, Monique in her dress tonight (Nick winced, for just off-screen left in his mind's eye, he could see Aaron coming down the stairs). Had it all been meaningless? Was it just a game? Nick was too young to know about the grays of life. For him it was a simple question of black or white. It was either wonderful or it was shit. Monique either loved him passionately and wanted to give up her luxurious life to marry him, or she was just using him to satisfy her sexual needs and her ego. *So*, he concluded, as he arrived at his uncle's condominium in Fort Lauderdale, *I was another of her toys. I was like her furs and horses and yachts and clothes. I made her feel good.*

Disgusted with himself, depressed beyond belief, a headache starting to tear his brain apart from the martinis, Nick rapidly packed his clothes. He didn't bathe or eat. He took his two suitcases down to the car, left the rented tuxedo with the managers of the complex, and drove out toward Interstate 95. A couple of miles before he reached the freeway, Nick pulled the car off on the shoulder and allowed himself a few tears. That was all. The external hardness that would characterize the next ten years of his life began at that moment. *Never again*, he said to himself. *I will never again let some bitch make a fool of me. No way, José.*

Ten years later, early on a March morning in his condominium in Key West, Nick Williams would idly play with a metallic golden object sitting on his coffee table and experience again the terrible pain of seeing Monique with her husband at that party. Wistfully, with some mature chagrin, he would remember also how, when he reached I-95, he turned left and south toward Miami and the Keys instead of right and north toward Boston. He couldn't have explained why at the time. He might have said that Harvard was trivial after Monique or that he wanted to study life and not books. He didn't understand that his need to start *absolutely* fresh came from the fact that he could not face himself.

He had not played the memory of Monique through from start to finish for five years. This morning, for the first time, Nick had been able to distance himself from the recalled emotions, ever so slightly, and to see the entire affair with a tiny bit of perspective. He recognized that his blind youthful passion had set him up for the anguish, but he was still reluctant to find Monique faultless. At least the memory no longer destroyed him. He picked up the trident and walked to the window. *Maybe it's all coming together now*, he said to himself. *A new treasure. A final molting of the last adolescent angst.* He thought about Carol Dawson. She was vexing but her intensity fascinated him. Always the dreamer, Nick visualized Carol in his arms and imagined the warmth and softness of her kiss.

CAROL watched in fascination as the octopus captured its prey with its long tentacles. "Imagine what it would be like to have eight arms," Oscar Burcham said. "Just think of the brain architecture necessary to separate all the inputs, to identify which stimulus was coming from which limb, to coordinate all the tentacles in defense or acquisition of food."

Carol laughed and turned to her companion. They were standing in front of a large, translucent glass window inside a dimly lit building. "Oh, Oscar," she said to the old man with the bright eyes, "you never change. Only you can think of all these living creatures as biological systems with architectures. Don't you ever wonder about their feelings, their dreams while they are sleeping, their concepts of death?"

"Aye, well I do," Oscar replied with a twinkle in his eye. "But it's virtually impossible for human beings, even with a common language and developed communications skills, to truly describe their feelings. How could we even know or appreciate, for example, a dolphin's sense of loneliness? In our maudlin way we ascribe to them human emotions, which is ridiculous." He paused for a moment to think. "No," he continued, "it's more fruitful to conduct scientific inquiry at levels where we can understand the answers. In the long run, I believe that knowing how these creatures function, in the scientific sense, is more likely to lead us to their emotional quotients than conducting psychological experiments whose outcomes cannot be interpreted."

Carol reached over and kissed him fondly. "You take everything I say so seriously, Oscar. Even when I'm kidding, you always pay attention to my comments." She stopped and looked away. "You're the only one who does."

Oscar pulled back dramatically and put both his hands on Carol's right shoulder. "Somewhere here there's a chip . . . I know it for a fact . . . It's almost always here . . . Ah, I found it." He looked at her knowingly. "It's not becoming, you know. Here you are, a successful, even celebrated reporter, still suffering from what could only be described as terminal insecurity. What's this about? Did you and the boss have a big fight this morning?"

"No," Carol replied, as they walked across the room to another part of the aquarium. "Well, sort of I guess. You know how he is. He takes over everything. I'm working on this big story down in Key West. Dale comes to the airport to pick me up, takes me out to breakfast, and proceeds to tell me exactly what I should be doing to cover my assignment. His suggestions are almost all good, and I appreciate his help on the technical issues, but it's the *way* he talks to me. As if he thinks I'm stupid or something."

Oscar looked at her intently. "Carol, my dear, he talks to everybody that way, including me. He doesn't mean anything by it. He is absolutely convinced of his own superiority and nothing has ever happened in his life to change his mind. He was a millionaire from his own patents before he graduated from MIT."

Carol was impatient and frustrated. "I know all that, Oscar, believe me, I know. But you're protecting him again. Dale and I have been lovers for almost a year. He tells everybody how proud of me he is, how much he enjoys being stimulated by my mind. But when we're together, he treats me like a fool. This morning he even argued with me about what I was having for breakfast. For Christ's sake, I've been nominated for a Pulitzer Prize but the guy who wants to marry me doesn't think I can order my own breakfast."

They were standing in front of a large tank with crystal-clear water. About half a dozen small whales were swimming in circles around the tank, occasionally going to the surface for air. "You came and asked my opinion in the beginning, my young friend," he said quietly. "And I told you that I thought your souls were not compatible. Do you remember what you said to me?"

"Yes," she answered with a rueful smile. "I asked you what the chief scientist of MOI could possibly know about souls. I'm sorry, Oscar. I was sorry at the time. I was so headstrong. Dale looked great on paper and I wanted your approval—"

"Forget it," he interrupted her. "You know how I feel about you. But never underestimate a scientist. Some of them," he said abstractedly, "want to know facts and concepts so that ultimately they can understand the overall nature of everything. Including the putative soul.

"Now take these whales," Oscar continued, increasing the tempo and adroitly changing the subject. "We have been mapping their brains for almost a decade now, isolating various kinds of functions in specific locations, and trying to correlate their brain structure with that of a human being. We have been reasonably successful. The language function that governs their singing has been separated and the location of the physical controls for all parts of the body have been identified. In fact, we have found an area in the whale brain that corresponds to the equivalent function for every major capability in the human brain. But there's still a problem, a mystery if you will."

One of the whales stopped in its normal circuit about the tank. It seemed to be watching them. "There's a large section of their brain that we have been unable to allocate to any specific function. A brilliant scientist years ago, after listening to the whales' songs while they were migrating and correlating those songs with the rest of their behavior, postulated that this large, unmapped portion of their brain was a multidimensional memory array. His hypothesis was that the whales store entire incidents in that array, including sights, sounds, and even feelings, and that they relive these incidents during migration to alleviate the boredom. Our tests are starting to confirm his theory."

Carol was intrigued. "You mean, they might put in that array the entire set of sensory impressions from something important, like calving, and then have, in a sense, a full instant replay during a particularly boring part of the migration route? Wow. That's fascinating. My memory irritates me all the time. It would be great if somehow I could go in there, in a directed sense, and pull out anything I want. Complete with feelings." She laughed. "There have been times in the summers when I couldn't remember exactly how great it felt to ski and I have almost panicked, worrying about whether or not that feeling might be gone the next winter."

Oscar waved at the whale and it swam away. "Be careful," he said. "Other people have also thought that it would be fantastic if our memories were more complete, like a computer's. But suppose we did have a perfect, multidimensional memory like that hypothesized for the whale. And suppose we had the same lack of entry control that is characteristic of human memory as it now exists. You know, where *what* we remember and *when* we remember it are not under our individual control. Then there would be problems. We might even be nonfunctional as a species. A song, a picture, a smell, even the taste of a cake might suddenly force us to confront anew the full emotions associated with the death of a loved one. We might have to see again a painful fight between our parents. Or even the trauma of our own birth."

Oscar was quiet for a moment. "No," he said finally, "evolution has served us in good stead. It couldn't develop an entry control mechanism for our memories. So to protect us, to keep us from being demolished by mistakes or past events, evolution built a natural fade process into our memories—"

"Carol Dawson. Carol Dawson. Report immediately to the audiovisual conference room adjacent to the director's office."

The loudspeaker interrupted the quiet in the MOI aquarium. Carol gave Oscar a hug. "It's been great, Ozzie, as always," she said, watching him wince as she used her pet name for him. "But it looks like they've finished developing the pictures. Incidentally, I think the whole business about the whales' memories is fascinating. I want to come back and do a feature on it. Maybe next week sometime. Give my love to your daughter and grandson."

Carol had become so engrossed in the discussion with Oscar that she had momentarily forgotten why she had flown to Miami early that morning. Now she felt anew a keen sense of excitement as she drove back to the main MOI administrative building from the aquarium. Dale had been confident at breakfast that processing the infrared images would reveal something of interest. "After all," he had said logically, "the foreign object alarm was triggered repeatedly. And nothing could be seen in the visual images. Therefore, either the infrared observations caused the alarm or the algorithm did not work properly. The second possibility is very unlikely, since I designed the data flow myself and my best programmers tested it after it was coded."

Dale was uncharacteristically excited when she walked into the conference room. Carol started to ask him a question but was silenced by a vigorous negative motion of the head that followed his smile of greeting. Dale was talking to two of the image-processing technicians. "Okay, then, we're squared away? Display the images in this sequence. I'll call for each one by using the pickle." The technicians left the room.

Dale came over and grabbed Carol. "You are not going to believe this," he said, "what a bonanza. What a fucking bonanza!" He settled down a little. "But first things first. I promised myself that I would not spoil it for you." He showed her to a seat at the conference table in front of the large screen and then sat down beside her.

He pushed the remote-control switch. Up on the large screen came a still frame of the three whales in the reef area under the boat. The fissure could clearly be seen to the right and beneath the whales. Dale looked at Carol. "I see," she shrugged, "but what's the deal? I took pictures with my underwater camera that are just as good."

Dale turned back to the screen and pushed the remote several more times. The successive scenes zoomed in on the hole in the coral reef, eventually isolating and centering on a small glint in the lower left side of the fissure. Again Dale looked at Carol. "I have a similar blowup," she said pensively. "But it's impossible to tell if something is really there or if it's an artifact of the photographic process." She stopped herself. "Although the fact that two distinctly different techniques found the light in essentially the same place suggests that it might not be a processing distortion." She leaned forward, interested. "So what's next?"

There was no way he could contain himself. Dale jumped up and started pacing around the room. "What's next," he began, "could be your ticket to the Pulitzer dinner in New York. Now I am going to show you exactly the same sequence of images, only these were taken in the infrared a fraction of a second later. Watch closely, especially in the center of the fissure."

The first processed infrared image covered the same area underneath the boat that the first visual image had shown. In the infrared picture, however, what was shown were thermal variations in the scene. In the processing, each pixel (an individual picture element in the image) was given a specific temperature based on the infrared radiation observed from that portion of the frame. Similar temperatures were then grouped together by the computer processing and assigned the same color. This process created isothermal regions, or regions of roughly the same temperature, that were visually connected by color. The result was that in the first picture the whales stood out in red, most of the reef plants were blue, and the normalized water temperature formed a dusky gray background. It took Carol a moment to adjust to the display. Dale was smiling triumphantly. Before Carol had a chance to focus on two small regions, one red and another brown, down in the center of the hole in the reef, the zoom process had begun. In a few seconds an infrared close-up of the fissure clearly demonstrated why Dale was so excited.

"I told you there was something under the boat," he said, walking to the screen and pointing at a brown, elongated object. The object was cylindrical at one end and tapered to a point at the other. The fissure had been blown up by the zoom process so that it almost completely filled the screen. Even with all the magnification, the quality of the infrared image was superb. Inside the opening three or four different colors could be seen; however, only two, the brown and the red, were continuous over a significant number of pixels.

"Holy shit," said Carol, involuntarily rising from her seat and walking over to join Dale, "that brown thing must be the lost missile. It was underneath us all the time." She picked up the pointer and waved it at the screen. "But what's this red area? It looks like the Cheshire cat from *Alice in Wonderland*."

"I'm not absolutely certain," Dale replied, "and it's probably not anything of major significance. But I do have a crazy idea. Actually it's based on what you told me about the strange behavior of the whales down there. It *may* be the head of another whale, back away from the light, looking out of the cave. Or whatever the opening is. Here, look at this. By zooming out a little we obtain one single picture that shows both of the red isothermal regions. Look how the red region in the middle of the fissure and the red from your sentinel whales look the same. Even with additional stretching, the two regions remain comparable in temperature. Not a proof of any kind, but it certainly supports my proposition."

Carol's mind was racing ahead. She was already planning her next move. It was essential that she retrieve that missile before anybody knew it was there. She needed to return to Key West as soon as possible. She picked up her purse and her briefcase. "Can someone drive me to the airport, please, Dale? Right now. I want to call that Lieutenant Todd again and scare him a bit. You know, make him a little more cautious and buy some time for us."

She paused, thinking of a million things at once. "But I can't call him from here without making him suspicious . . . And I must make some arrangements for a boat for tomorrow . . . Oh, incidentally, I assume you have hard copy of those pictures available for me."

Dale nodded his head. "I do," he said. "But first sit down and relax for a second. I want to show you something else. I don't yet know if it's a real phenomenon, but if it is . . ." Carol started to protest but there was something in his manner that told her to acquiesce. She sat down. He launched into a discussion of enhancement algorithms, explaining how the information in pictures could be stretched to highlight special features and allow easier interpretation.

"Okay, Okay," she said at length. "The bottom line is what I need. I know already how clever you and your engineers are."

Dale put the first infrared image back on the screen, the one that showed the full view of the three whales underneath the boat. "This picture does not have much thermal granularity. Every pixel in the region colored red, for example, does not correspond to exactly the same temperature. In reality, the spread in temperatures for the same color is roughly five degrees. Now if we stretch the image, and make the isothermal regions only cover a total spread of *two* degrees each, we obtain this picture."

In the new image there were ten different colors. It was much harder to see individual features, and spurious data points made the picture extremely difficult to interpret. A portion of the front of one of the whales was now a different color from the rest of the animal.

"The limit of accuracy of the equipment, by the time the raw spectral data is converted to temperatures, is about one degree. If we show another stretch of the same picture, with the connected isothermal regions now only covering a total range of one degree each, then the picture almost becomes gibberish. Now there are twenty different colors for the isothermal regions and, because the noise or error in each data point is of the same magnitude as the spread in the isothermal region, it is virtually impossible to see the figures of known objects like the three whales. I tell you all this up front to make certain you realize that what I am about to show you may be completely wrong. It is, nevertheless, absolutely fascinating."

The next image projected on the screen was a close-up down on the floor of the ocean, just above the trench that Carol had followed when backtracking to find the origin of the tracks. The familiar parallel lines just barely showed up in the infrared image. The fissure was almost off the left side of the image. On either side of the trench, blue color broken with some occasional green marked the two reefs. Carol looked at Dale with a puzzled expression on her face.

"This close-up has the same five-degree granularity as the big reference image. There is nothing of note here." He flashed another picture. "Nor here, where we have increased the number of colors to ten again. But look at this." One more image went up on the screen. The picture was very difficult to follow, much less interpret. As many as twenty different colors connected odd regions in what appeared to be random patterns. About the only thing that was regular in the picture were the background rocks on which the coral and other sea life were living. And it was those background rocks that had Dale so excited.

"This is what I wanted you to see," he said, waving his hand at the rocks on the two sides of the trench. "The two reef structures do not have the same color. For some unknown and absolutely inexplicable reason, every background rock area on *this* reef is coded chartreuse. On the opposite reef, just across the trench a few feet away, all the background rock is yellow. A one-degree difference. Now if some of the yellow pieces were interspersed with the chartreuse, and vice versa, then I would say that the data clearly has no significance and that what we are seeing are noise signatures. But this pattern is compelling."

Carol was lost. She could see that the rocks on one reef structure were all chartreuse and that the opposite reef was yellow. But it didn't mean anything to her. She shook her head. She needed more explanation.

"Don't you understand?" Dale said with a final dramatic flourish. "If this data is right, then we have found something else of great importance. Either there is some source *inside* one of the reef structures that is making its surface uniformly warmer, or, and I admit this sounds truly incredible, one of the two is *not a reef at all* and is something else masquerading as a reef."

I T was almost always impossible to find a parking place in the middle of the working day near Amanda Winchester's house in Key West. The Hemingway Marina had revitalized the old part of the city where she lived, but as usual everyone had underestimated the need for parking. All the repainted and renovated nineteenth-century mansions along Eaton and Caroline streets had signs on the street saying such things as DON'T EVEN THINK ABOUT PARKING HERE IF YOU'RE NOT A RESIDENT, but it was no use. People who worked in the retail shops around the marina parked where it was convenient for them and avoided the heavy parking fee at the marina lot.

After searching fruitlessly for a parking place for fifteen minutes, Nick Williams decided to park outside of a convenience store and walk the block or so to Amanda's house. He was strangely anxious. Part of his nervousness was due to his excitement, but he was also feeling a little guilty. Amanda had been the major sponsor of the original *Santa Rosa* expedition and Nick had spent considerable time with her after they had found the treasure. Amanda and Nick and Jake Lewis had all three believed that Homer Ashford and his menage à trois had somehow hidden part of the treasure and then cheated them out of their proper shares. Nick and Amanda worked together trying to find evidence that Homer had stolen from them, but they were never able to prove anything conclusively.

During this period Amanda and Nick had become quite close. They had seen each other virtually every week and for a while he had thought of her as an aunt or grandmother. But after a year or so, Nick had stopped going by to visit her. He hadn't understood it at the time, but the real reason he began to avoid her was that Amanda was too intense for him. And she was always too personal. She asked him too many hard questions about what he was doing with his life.

On this particular morning he had no real options. Amanda was widely recognized as *the* expert on sunken treasure in the Keys. There were two components in her life, treasure and the theater, and her knowledge of each was encyclopedic. Nick had not called first because he didn't want to discuss the trident unless she was willing to see him. So it was with some trepidation that he rang the doorbell on the front porch of her magnificent home.

A young woman in her early twenties came to the door and opened it just a bit. "Yes?" she said, her face wedging into the crack, her expression wary.

"My name's Nick Williams," he said. "I would like to see Mrs. Winchester if possible. Is she in?" There was a pause. "I'm an old—"

"My grandmother is very busy this morning," the girl curtly interrupted him. "Perhaps you can call and make an appointment." She started to close the door and leave Nick standing on the porch next to his exercise bag. Then Nick heard another voice, a muffled exchange, and the door swung open.

"Well, for goodness sake," Amanda said with her arms outstretched, "I have a young gentleman caller. Come here, Nikki, and give me a kiss." Nick was embarrassed. He walked forward and gave the elderly woman a perfunctory hug.

As he withdrew from the embrace, he started to apologize. "I'm sorry I haven't been by to see you. I mean to, but somehow my schedule—"

"It's all right, Nikki, I understand." Amanda interrupted him pleasantly. Her eyes were so sharp they belied her age. "Come in and tell me what you've been up to. I haven't seen you since, goodness, has it been a couple of years already since we shared that cognac after *Streetcar?*" She led him into a combination study and living room and sat him down next to her on the couch. "You know, Nikki, I thought your comments about the actress playing Blanche DuBois were the most observant ones I heard during the entire run. You were right about her. She couldn't have played Blanche except as a total mental case. The woman simply had no concept of a feminine sexual appetite."

Nick looked around him. The room had hardly changed in the eight years since he had last visited it. The ceiling was very high, maybe fifteen feet. The walls were lined with bookcases whose full shelves extended all the way to the ceiling. Opposite the door a huge canvas painting of Amanda and her husband standing outside their home on Cape Cod dominated the room. A new 1955 Ford was partially visible in the background of the painting. She was radiantly beautiful in the picture, in her early thirties, dressed in a white evening gown with daring red trim both around the wrists and along the collar of the neck. Her husband was in a black tux. He was mostly bald, with short blond hair graying at the temples. His eyes were warm and kindly.

Amanda asked Nick if he wanted tea and he nodded. The granddaughter Jennifer disappeared into the hallway. Amanda turned and took Nick's hands in hers. "I am glad you came, Nikki, I have missed you. From time to time I hear a snippet here or there about you or your boat, but often second-hand information is altogether wrong. What have you been doing? Still reading all the time? Do you have a girlfriend?"

Nick laughed. Amanda had not changed. She had never been one for small talk. "No girlfriend," Nick said, "same problem as always. The ones that are intelligent turn out to be either arrogant or emotionally inept or both; the ones that are sensitive and affectionate have never read a book." For some reason Carol Dawson jumped into Nick's mind and he almost said, without thinking, "except for, *maybe*," but he stopped himself. "What I need," he said instead, "is someone like you."

"No, Nikki," Amanda replied, suddenly serious. She folded her hands in her lap and stared momentarily across the room. "No," she repeated softly, her voice then gathering intensity as she turned back to look at him, "even I am not perfect enough for you. I remember well all your fantasy visions of gracious young goddesses. Somehow you had mixed the best parts of all the women in your favorite novels together with your teenage dreams. It always seemed to me that you had put women up on a pedestal; they had to be queens or princesses. But in the girls you actually dated, you looked for weaknesses, signs of ordinariness, and indications of common behavior. It was almost as if you were hoping to find them imperfect, to detect chinks in their armor so that you could justify your lack of interest."

Jennifer arrived with the tea. Nick was uncomfortable. He had forgotten what it was like to talk to Amanda. Her emotional probing and her unsolicited observations were both extremely disquieting to him this morning. Nick had not come to see her to dissect his attitude toward women. He changed the subject.

"Speaking of treasure," he said, bending down to pick up his bag, "I found something very interesting yesterday while I was out diving. I thought maybe you might have seen something like it before." He pulled the trident out and handed it to Amanda. She almost dropped it because she was not prepared for its weight.

"Goodness," she said, her skinny arm trembling under the strain of holding the golden trident out in front of her. "What could it possibly be made from? It's too heavy to be gold!"

Nick leaned forward and took the object. He held it for her as she ran her fingers over its exceptionally smooth exterior. "I've never seen anything like this, Nikki. I don't need to get out all the books and the photographs for comparison. The smoothness of the finish is inconsistent with the processing techniques in Europe during or after the galleon days. This must be modern. But I can't tell you anything else. Where in the world did you find it?"

He told her just the outline of the story, careful as always not to give away key bits of information. It was not just the agreement he had made with Carol and Troy; treasure hunters never really trust anybody. But he did share with Amanda his idea that perhaps someone had cached this particular piece, as well as some others, for later retrieval. Nick insisted that this idea of his was a perfectly plausible explanation for the tracks on the ocean floor.

"Your scenario seems very unlikely to me," Amanda said, "although I must admit that I am baffled and have no better explanation. Maybe Miss Dawson has some sources that can shed some light on the origin of this thing. But there is almost no chance that I am mistaken. I have personally seen or viewed close-up photographs of every significant piece of treasure recovered from the Keys in the past century. You could show me a new piece today and I could probably tell you in what European country it was made and in what decade. If this object comes from a sunken ship, it is a modern ship, almost certainly after World War II. Beyond that I can't help you."

Nick put the trident back in the bag and started to leave. "Wait just a minute before you go, Nikki," Amanda said as he stood up. "Come over here for a minute." She took him by the arm and led him over to a spot just in front of the large painting. "You would have liked Walter, Nikki. He was a dreamer also. He loved to look for treasure. Every year we would spend a week or two in the Caribbean on a yacht, ostensibly looking for treasure but just generally sharing each other's dreams. From time to time we would find objects on the bottom of the ocean that we couldn't understand and we would create fanciful conjectures to explain them. Almost always there was some prosaic explanation that was inferior to our fantasies."

Nick was standing beside her with his bag in his right hand. Amanda turned to him and put her hand softly on his left forearm. "But it didn't matter. It didn't even matter that most of the years we came up empty-handed altogether. For we always found the real treasure, our love for each other. We always returned home renewed and laughing and thankful that life had allowed us to share another week or ten days in which we had imagined and fantasized and hunted for treasure together."

Her eyes were soft and loving. Her voice was low but full of passion. "I do not know when or if you will come again, Nikki, but there are some things that I have been wanting to say to you for some time. If you like, you can dismiss them as the ravings of a sententious old woman, but I may never have a chance to tell you these things again. You have all the attributes I loved in Walter, intelligence, imagination, sensitivity. But something is wrong. You are alone. By choice. Your dreams of treasure, your zest for life—you do not share these things. It is very sad for me to see this." She stopped for a second and looked back at the painting. Then she completed her thought, almost as if she were talking to herself. "For when you are seventy years old and look back at what your life has meant, you will not focus on your solo activities. What you will remember are the incidents of touching, those times when your life was enriched by a moment of sharing with a friend or loved one. It is our mutual awareness of this miracle called life that allows us to accept our mortality."

Nick had not been prepared for an emotional encounter with Amanda. He had thought that he would stop by to see her for a few moments, ask her about the trident, and then depart. In retrospect he realized that he had treated Amanda very callously over the years. She had offered genuine friendship and he had spurned it, taking her out of his life altogether when their interaction no longer suited him. He winced as he recognized how selfish he had been.

As he walked slowly down the street, idly looking at the gracious old houses built over a hundred years ago, Nick took a deep breath. He had experienced too many emotions for one morning. *First Monique, then Amanda. And it looks as if the trident is not going to solve all my problems. Funny how things always come in groups.*

He found himself musing that maybe there had been a lot of truth in what Amanda had said. He acknowledged that he had been feeling lonely lately. And he wondered if the vague loneliness was indeed coupled to a creeping awareness of his own mortality, to the passage of that phase of life enshrined by Thomas Wolfe with the phrase, "For we were young, and we knew that we could never die." Nick was feeling very tired when he came to the end of the sidewalk and turned onto the pavement of the convenience store parking lot.

He saw her before she saw him. She was standing next to the driver's side of her brand-new red Mercedes sports coupé. She had a small brown paper bag in her arm and was looking in the window of the car next to hers, Nick's 1990 Pontiac. Nick felt a quick rush of adrenaline followed by anger and distrust. She finally saw him just as he started to speak. "Why, Greta, what a surprise! I guess we just happened to be in this part of Key West today at exactly the same time."

"Ya, Nick, I thought it was your car. How are you?" Greta put the paper bag on the hood of her car and approached him in a friendly manner. She had either missed or was ignoring the sarcasm in his greeting. She was wearing a sleeveless yellow tank top and a pair of tight blue shorts. Her blonde hair was pulled back in two short pigtails.

"Don't play innocent with me, fräulein," Nick overreacted. "I know you didn't come here to shop." He was nearly shouting. He used his free arm to accentuate his comments and block Greta's approach. "This is not one of the stops on your circuit. You came here to find me. Now what do you want?" Nick dropped his arm. A couple of passersby had stopped to watch the exchange.

Greta stared at him for a moment with those crystal-clear eyes. She was wearing no makeup. She looked like a little girl except for the wrinkles on her face. "Are you still so angry, Nick? After all these years?" She came up next to him and smiled knowingly into his eyes. "I remember one night, almost five years ago," she said playfully, "when you were not so angry. You were glad to see me. You asked me if I would have you for one night, no questions asked, and I agreed. You were great."

In a momentary flash Nick remembered the rainy night when he had stopped Greta just as she was leaving the pier. He recalled also how desperately he had needed to touch someone, anyone, on that particular night. "That was the day after my father's funeral," he said roughly, "and didn't mean shit anyway." He looked away. He did not want to return her piercing gaze.

"That wasn't the impression I had," Greta continued in the same playful but otherwise emotionless tone. "I felt you inside me, I tasted your kisses. You can't tell me—"

"Look," interrupted Nick, clearly irritated. "What do you want? I don't want to stand here all morning arguing with you about some stupid night five years ago. Now I know that you're here for a reason. What is it?"

Greta backed off a step and her face hardened. "You are a very difficult man, Nick. It could be such fun doing business together if you weren't such a, how do you say, pain in the ass." She stopped for a moment. "I *have* come from Homer. He has a proposition for you. He wants to see what you found yesterday in the ocean and maybe discuss a partnership."

Nick laughed triumphantly. "So I was right all along. You were sent to find me. And now that bastard wants to discuss a partnership. Hah. Not a fucking chance. You won't steal from me again. Tell your employer or lover or whatever he is to cram his proposition up his ass. Now if you'll excuse me . . ."

He started to walk around Greta and open his car door. Her strong hand grabbed his forearm. "You're making a mistake, Nick." Her eyes bored into his again. "A big mistake. You can't afford to do it on your own. What you found is probably worthless. If it is, let *him* spend the money." Her chameleon eyes shifted one more time. "And it would be such fun to work together again."

Nick climbed into his car and turned on the engine. "No dice, Greta. You're wasting your time. Now I've got to go." He backed out of the parking place and then drove into the narrow street. The treasure was front and center in his mind again. He had been momentarily depressed by what Amanda had told him about the trident, but the fact that Homer wanted to see it gave Nick a feeling of power. *But,* he asked himself, *how does he know already? Who talked? Or could someone have seen us?*

WHEN Commander Winters returned to his office after a scheduled meeting with the public relations department, his secretary, Dora, was conspicuously reading the Key West newspaper. "Ahem," she said, deliberately attracting his attention. "Is the Vernon Winters starring in *The Night of the Iguana* at the Key West Playhouse tonight anyone I know? Or are there two of them in this town?"

He laughed. He liked Dora. She was almost sixty, black, a grandmother more than a dozen times, and one of the few secretaries on the base who actually had some pride in her work. She treated everybody, including Commander Winters, like one of her children. "So why didn't you tell me?" she said with feigned outrage. "After all, what if I had missed it altogether? I told you last year to make certain that you always told us when you were performing."

He took her hand and gave it a little squeeze. "I had intended to tell you, Dora, but somehow it just slipped my mind. And you know that my thespian activities are not exactly embraced by the Navy, so I don't ballyhoo them about so much. But I'll have some tickets for you and your husband in a couple of weeks." He looked at the stack of message notes on her desk. "That many, huh? And I was only gone a little over two hours. It never rains but it pours."

"Two of these are supposedly urgent." Dora looked at her watch. "A Miss Dawson from the *Miami Herald* will call back in about five minutes and that Lieutenant Todd has been calling all morning. He insists that he must see you *before* lunch or he can't be properly prepared for the meeting this afternoon. Apparently he left a long message on your Top Secret telemail sometime this morning. Right now he's furious with me because I wouldn't interrupt your meetings to tell you about his message. Is it really that important?"

Commander Winters shrugged his shoulders and opened the door to his office. *I wonder what Todd wants,* he thought. *I guess I should have checked my telemail before running off to the meeting with the chief.* "Did you put all the rest of the messages on the computer?" he asked Dora before he closed the door. She nodded. "Okay, I'll talk to Miss Dawson when she calls. Tell Todd that I will see him in fifteen minutes." He sat down at his desk and turned on his computer. He activated his telemail subdirectory and saw that he had three new entries already this morning, one in the TOP SECRET queue. Commander Winters identified himself, entered the top secret code word, and started to read Lieutenant Todd's transmission.

The phone rang. After a few seconds Dora buzzed him and told him that it was Miss Dawson. Before they started, Commander Winters agreed that the interview could be on the videophone and that it could be taped. He recognized Carol immediately from her occasional appearances on television. She explained to him that she was using the communications facility at the Miami International Airport.

"Commander Winters," she said, wasting no time, "we have an uncorroborated report that the Navy is engaged in a search for something important, and secret, in the Gulf of Mexico between Key West and the Everglades. Your press people and a Lieutenant Todd have both denied the report and referred all questions to you. Our source also told us, and we have subsequently verified both of these facts, that there are today a large number of technology ships sailing in the Gulf and that you have been trying to rent sophisticated ocean telescopes from the Miami Oceanographic Institute. Do you have any comment?"

"Certainly, Miss Dawson." The commander wore his best acting smile. He had carefully rehearsed the response in his morning meeting with the admiral. "It's really amazing how rumors fly, particularly when someone suspects the Navy of nefarious deeds." He chuckled. "All the activity is just preparation for some routine maneuvers next week. A few of the sailors who man the technology ships are a little rusty and wanted some practice this week. As for the MOI telescopes, we intended to use them in our maneuvers to check their value in assessing underwater threats." He looked directly at the camera. "That's it, Miss Dawson. There's nothing special going on."

Carol watched the commander on the monitor at the airport. She had expected someone with an imposing air of authority. This man had a softness in his eyes, some kind of sensitivity that was unusual in a career military officer. Carol had a sudden idea. She walked up close to her own camera. "Commander Winters," she said pleasantly, "let me ask you a hypothetical question. If the Navy were testing a new kind of missile and one test flight went astray, possibly even threatening population centers, wouldn't it be likely that the Navy, claiming national security reasons as its defense, would deny that such a thing had happened?"

For a fleeting fraction of a second the expression in the eyes of Commander Winters wavered. He looked shocked. Then he regained control. "It is difficult to answer such a hypothetical question," he intoned formally, "but I can tell you that it is Navy policy to keep the public informed about its activities. Only when the flow of information to the public could significantly undermine our national security would any kind of censorship take place."

The interview wound up quickly. Carol had accomplished her objective. *Damn*, said Commander Winters to himself as Dora announced that Lieutenant Todd was waiting to see him. *I should have expected that question. But how did she know that? Did she somehow trick Todd or one of the other officers? Or did someone in Washington spill the beans?*

Winters opened the door to his office and Lieutenant Todd nearly stormed into the room. With him was another tall young lieutenant, thick shouldered with a bushy mustache, whom Todd introduced as Lieutenant Ramirez of the Naval Intelligence Division. "Did you read my telemail message? What did you think? My God, it's almost unbelievable what those Russians have done. I had no idea they could be so clever." Todd was almost shouting as he paced excitedly around the office.

Winters watched Todd jumping around the room. *This young lieutentant, he thought, is in a big hurry to get somewhere. His impatience is oozing out of every pore. But what in the world is he saying about the Russians? And why is this Mexican muscleman here with him?*

"Sit down, please," the commander replied, motioning at the two chairs opposite his desk. He looked sternly at Lieutenant Todd. "And start by explaining why Lieutenant Ramirez is here. You know the regulations; we were all briefed on them again last week. Only officers at the rank of commander or higher can authorize sharing information on a need-to-know basis."

Todd immediately defended himself against the reproach. "Commander Winters, sir," he replied, "I believe that what we have here is a major international incident, far too big to be handled by special projects and systems engineering alone. I left word on your telemail interrupt at 0830 this morning for you to contact me ASAP, that there was a significant new development in the Broken Arrow project. When I had not heard from you by 1000, even though I had tried several additional times to reach you by telephone, I became worried that we might be losing valuable time. I then contacted Ramirez so that he and his men could start their work."

Todd stood up from his chair. "Sir," he began again, the excitement rising in his voice, "maybe I didn't make it clear enough in my telemail message. We have hard evidence that someone *commanded* the Panther to go astray, right after the APRS was activated. We have confirmed from a special manual search of the intermittent telemetry data that the command receipt counters went *crazy* during a two-second period just before the missile veered off course."

"Calm down, Lieutenant Todd, and sit down again." Winters was irritated, not just by Todd's nonchalant dismissal of the regulations issue, but also by his undisguised accusation that Winters had been delinquent in responding to his messages. The commander's day had begun with a meeting with the admiral who ran the air station. He had wanted a briefing on all this Broken Arrow business. So Winters had not even been in his office, except for a couple of minutes, until after he came back from the public relations department.

When Todd was again seated, Winters continued carefully, "Now spare me the hysteria *and* your personal conclusions. I want you to give me the facts, only the facts, slowly and without prejudice. The accusations you made a few moments ago are very very serious. In my eyes, if you have jumped to unsubstantiated conclusions too quickly, your fitness as an officer may be in doubt. So start at the beginning."

There was a flash of anger in the lieutenant's eyes and then he opened his notebook. When he spoke, his voice was a monotone, carefully modulated to be free of all emotion. "At precisely 0345 this morning," he began, "I was awakened by Ensign Andrews, who had been working most of the night on the telemetry dumps that we recalled both from the Canaveral station and the tracking ship near Bimini. His assignment had been to go through the scheduled sequence of events onboard the Panther missile and determine, from the scattered telemetry if possible, if any anomalous events had occurred onboard just before the missile went off course. We thought that this way we might have a chance to isolate the cause of the problem.

"Basically Ensign Andrews was a detective. As you know, the data system is quite constrained by the limited downlink bandwidth. So the packets of telemetry data come out in a somewhat artificial way, meaning that many of the data values governing the behavior of the bird at the time it changed direction would not have been sent to the Earth until several minutes later, *after* the missile had gone awry and the tracking stations had already dropped and regained lock a couple of times.

"Ensign Andrews showed me that in the intermittent data there were four discrete measurements taken from the command receipt counter, a simple buffer in the software that increments by one every time a new command message is correctly received by the missile. At first we did not believe what we were seeing. We thought perhaps someone had made an error or that the decommutation maps were wrong. But by 0700 we had both checked the values from the two tracking sites and verified that we were indeed looking at the correct channel. Commander, in the 1.7 seconds after the APRS was activated, the command receipt counter registered over three *hundred* new messages. And then the missile swerved away from its intended target."

The commander was writing in a small spiral notebook while Todd was talking. It took him almost half a minute to finish his notes. Then he looked up at Todd and Ramirez. "Am I to believe then," he said, his voice heavy with sarcasm, "that this is the *entire* data set upon which you wish to base your indictment of the Soviet Union and put our Navy intelligence community on alert? Or is there something else?"

Todd looked confused. "You think it's more likely," Commander Winters continued, his voice now rising, "that the Russians knew the code for the command test set and transmitted three hundred messages in less than two seconds, exactly at the right time and from somewhere off the Florida coast, than it is that somewhere in the 4.2 software system there is an error that is improperly incrementing the command receipt counter? My God, Lieutenant, use your head. Are you seeing bogeymen at night? This is 1994. There is virtually no tension on the international scene. You believe that the Russians are so colossally stupid that they would risk detente to command a Navy cruise missile off course while it is still under test? Even if they could somehow command the missile to a specific location and then recover it and understand it thoroughly by reverse engineering, why would they take such a horrendous chance for such a comparatively small return?"

Todd and Ramirez said nothing during the commander's harangue. Ramirez was starting to look uncomfortably embarrassed toward the end. Todd's boyish self-confidence had faded as well and he began to wring his hands and pop his knuckles absentmindedly. After a long pause Winters continued, firmly but without some of the exasperation of his initial speech.

"We assigned some specific work items yesterday, Lieutenant. They were supposed to be addressed by today. Look again at the 4.2 software, particularly to see if there were any errors in the interface with the command test set that showed up during module or integration testing. Maybe there was a bug in the command receipt counter subroutine that did not get corrected in the new release. And for the meeting this afternoon, I want you to show me a list of possible failure modes that would explain the telemetry data, *other than* commands being sent from a foreign power. And then show what you are planning to do to analyze each failure mode and reduce the length of the list."

Ramirez stood up to leave. "Under the circumstances, Commander, I feel that my presence here is a little, uh, improper. I have briefed a couple of my men already and have kicked off some investigative work to see if there is now or has been recently any Russian military or civilian activity in the area. I had put a top priority on the effort. In view of this conversation, I feel I should suspend—"

"Not necessarily," Commander Winters interrupted him. "It might be very difficult for you to explain at this juncture." He looked at both of the squirming young lieutenants. "And it is not my wish to be vindictive and put you both on report, although I think you both acted hastily and outside regulations. No, Lieutenant, continue with the intelligence gathering, it may eventually be of some importance. Just don't make a big deal out of it. I'll accept the responsibility."

Ramirez walked toward the door. He was clearly grateful. "Thank you, Commander," he said sincerely, "for a minute there I thought maybe I had crapped in my mess kit. I've learned a very valuable lesson."

Winters saluted the intelligence officer and motioned Todd, who was apparently also preparing to leave, back to his seat. The commander walked over in front of the Renoir painting and appeared to be studying it. He spoke quietly, without turning to face the junior lieutenant. "Did you say anything to that reporter Miss Dawson about a missile, or did she mention a missile to you while you were talking to her?"

"No, sir, there was nothing like that," Todd asserted. "She was even vague when I asked her what she had heard."

"She either has some inside information or is very very lucky," the commander said abstractedly, almost to himself. He walked over closer to the painting and imagined that he could hear the piano being played by the younger of the two sisters. Today he heard a Mozart sonata. But it was not the right time to listen. *This young man needs a good lesson out of all this,* Winters thought as he turned around.

"Do you smoke, Lieutenant?" he asked, offering Todd a cigarette and placing one in his own mouth. The younger man shook his head. "I do," said Winters, lighting his Pall Mall, "even though there are a thousand reasons why I shouldn't. But I almost never smoke around people who don't. It's a question of consideration."

Winters walked over to look out the window and blew the smoke slowly out his mouth. Todd looked puzzled. "And right now," Winters continued, "I'm smoking, strangely enough, also out of consideration. For you. You see, Lieutenant Todd," he said, wheeling around dramatically, "I'm calmer after I smoke. That means I can deal better with my anger."

He walked directly over in front of the lieutenant. "Because I'm *goddamn mad* about this, young man. Make no mistake about that. There's a part of me that wants to make an example of you, maybe even court martial you for not following regulations. You're too cocky, too sure of your own conclusions. You're dangerous. If you had slipped and made some of the comments you made in here to that woman reporter, then it would be Katie bar the door. But"—Winters walked around behind his desk and stubbed out his cigarette,—"it has always been my belief that people should not be crucified for a single mistake."

The commander sat down and leaned back in his chair. "Just between us guys, Lieutenant, you're on probation with me. I don't want to hear any more nonsense about an international incident. This is a simple case of a malfunctioning test missile. Do your job thoroughly and carefully. Don't worry, you'll be noticed if the work is done properly. The system is not blind to your ambition or your talent. But if you run off half-cocked one more time on this problem, I will personally see to it that your personnel file is ruined."

Todd could tell that he was being dismissed. He was still angry, now at himself mostly, but he knew better than to let any of it show. He considered Commander Winters to be a marginally competent old fart, and he hated being lectured by him. *As of now, however, I have no choice but to accept it,* he said to himself as he left the commander's office.

ICK'S message light was blinking when he walked into his town-
house after the meeting with Amanda and the encounter with Greta.
He put the bag with the trident back in the closet and turned on
the answering machine. Julianne appeared on the small three-inch
monitor. Nick smiled to himself. She always left all of his messages, no matter
how small, in video.

"Sorry to tell you this, Nick, but your Tampa charter for tomorrow and
Sunday just called up to cancel. They said they heard a weather forecast calling
for thunderstorms. Anyway, all is not completely lost 'cause you get to keep
their deposit." She paused a couple of seconds. "By the way, Linda and Corinne
and I are going to Sloppy Joe's tonight to hear Angie Leatherwood. Why don't
you stop by and say hello? I might even buy you a drink."

Shit, said Nick to himself. *I needed the money. And Troy did too.* He
automatically entered Troy's name on the small keyboard near the phone and
waited for Troy to pick up the receiver and turn on the video switch.

"Why hello, Professor. What are you doing on such a beautiful day in
the tropics?" Troy was in a good humor as usual. Nick could not understand
how anyone could be in such a perpetually good mood.

"I have bad news and bad news, my friend," Nick replied. "First, Amanda
Winchester says our trident is modern and almost certainly not a part of any
ancient treasure. For my part, I'm not completely convinced. But it doesn't
look promising. Second, and probably more important for the short term, our
charter has cancelled. We have no work for the weekend."

"Ouch," Troy said, a frown sweeping over his face. "That *do* present
some problems." For a moment it seemed that Troy couldn't figure out what
to say. Then the normal Troy was back, smiling cheerfully, "Hey, Professor,
I have an idea. Since we now both have nothing to do this afternoon, why
don't you come over here to the Jefferson sanitarium for some chips and beer?
I want to show you something anyway." His eyes were twinkling.

Under almost any circumstances Nick would have declined Troy's offer
and spent the afternoon reading *Madame Bovary*. But the morning had already
been heavy with emotion and Nick was acutely aware that he needed some
levity. He smiled to himself. Troy was a very funny man. An afternoon of
booze and mirth sounded appealing. Besides, Troy had been working for him
for four months and they had not yet taken any time to socialize. Even though
they had spent many hours working together on the boat, Nick had never
once visited Troy's apartment. "All right," Nick heard himself respond, "you're

on. I'll bring the food and you get the beer. I'll see you in twenty to thirty minutes."

When Nick stopped his car in front of the small frame duplex in one of Key West's oldest sections, Troy was just arriving himself. He had apparently walked to a nearby store, for he was carrying a large brown paper bag containing three six-packs of beer. "This ought to hold us for the afternoon." He winked as he greeted Nick and led him up the walkway to his front door. A paper sign was taped to the door. It said, PROF—BE BACK IN A JIFF—TROY. Troy took the sign down and reached up to a small ledge above the door to find a key.

Nick had never wondered what Troy's apartment would be like. But he certainly would not have imagined the living room that he found when he followed Troy inside. The room was laid out neatly and furnished in what could only be called early grandmother style. The motley array of old couches and easy chairs purchased at neighborhood garage sales (none of which was the same color, which was of no importance to Troy—he thought of furniture in terms of functional units, not as pieces of decoration) were arranged in a rectangle with a long wooden coffee table in the middle. An assortment of electronics and video magazines were neatly stacked upon the table. Dominating the room was a state-of-the-art sound system whose four tall speakers were carefully placed in the corners so that all the sound was focused toward the center of the room. As soon as the two men were inside, Troy went over to the compact disc player on the top of the stereo equipment rack and turned it on. A wonderfully rich, black, female voice backed by a piano and a guitar filled the room.

"This is Angie's new album," Troy said, handing Nick an open beer. He had been to the kitchen and the refrigerator while Nick was looking around the room. "Her agent thinks this one will go gold. *Love Letters* just barely missed, but she made more than a quarter of a million off it anyway. Not counting the money from the concert tour."

"I remember your telling me that you knew her," Nick said, taking a long drink from his beer. He had walked across the room to a box next to the stereo rack where sixty or seventy discs were neatly arranged. On the front of an open disc jacket on the top of the box was a beautiful young black woman, softly backlit. She was wearing a long dark cocktail dress. *Memories of Enchanting Nights* was the title of the album. "Is there more to the story of Miss Leatherwood?" Nick said, looking up at Troy. "This is one magnificent lady, if you ask me."

Troy came over beside him. He programmed the disc player to cut eight on the album. "Thought you'd never ask," he grinned expansively. "This song probably says it best." Nick sat down in one of the strange easy chairs and listened to a soft ballad with an easy beat in the background. The title of the song was "Let Me Take Care of You, Baby." It told the story of a gifted lover who made the songstress laugh at home or in bed. They were compatible, they were friends. But he couldn't talk commitment because he hadn't made it yet. So in the last stanza the woman singing the song appeals to him to swallow his pride and let her make it easy for him.

Nick looked at Troy and rolled his eyes while he shook his head. "Jefferson," he said, "you're too much. I never know when you're telling the truth and when you're slinging bullshit with both arms."

Troy laughed and stood up from the couch. "But, Professor," he protested, "that's what makes it more interesting." He came over and took Nick's empty beer can. "It's hard for you to believe, isn't it?" he said, still smiling while he looked directly at Nick, "that maybe your funny black first mate has a few dimensions you haven't seen."

Troy turned and walked toward the kitchen. Nick could hear him opening beer cans and putting the chips in a bowl. "So," Nick hollered, "I'm waiting. What's the scoop?"

"Angie and I have known each other for five years," Troy said from the kitchen. "When we were first dating she was only nineteen and completely naive about life. One night we were over here, right after I first moved in, and we were listening to a Whitney Houston album. Angie started singing."

Troy came back in the living room. He put the bowl of assorted chips on the little wood coffee table and sat down in a chair next to Nick. "The rest, as they say in Hollywood, is history." He waved his arms. "I introduced her to the owner of a local night club. Within a year she had a recording contract and I had a problem. She was my woman. But I couldn't afford to keep up with her." Troy was uncharacteristically quiet for a few seconds. "It's really shit when your pride stands in the way of your feelings for the only woman you've ever loved."

Nick was surprised to discover that Troy's intimate revelation had touched him. Nick leaned forward in his chair and dropped his hand lightly on Troy's shoulder in a gesture of understanding. Troy changed the subject quickly. "And what about you, Professor? How many broken hearts are hanging in your closet? I've seen the way Julianne and Corinne and even Greta look at you. Why haven't you ever married?"

Nick laughed and guzzled his beer. "Christ, this must be my lucky day. Do you know, Jefferson, that you're the second person today to ask me about my love life? And the first one was a seventy-year-old woman."

Nick took another drink. "Speaking of Greta," he continued, "I ran into her this morning—and it wasn't an accident. She was waiting for me while I was talking to Amanda. She knew that we found something yesterday and wanted to talk about a partnership deal. Do you know anything about this?"

"Sure do," Troy answered easily. "Homer must have had her spying on us. When I finished up with the boat last night, she was waiting to pump me for information. She had watched you leave with your exercise bag and either guessed or knew that we had found something. I didn't tell her anything, although I didn't deny it either. Remember, Ellen saw Carol and me in the marina office with all that snazzy equipment."

"Yeah, I know," said Nick, "and I really didn't expect to keep it entirely under wraps forever. I just wish we could find more of the treasure, if it exists, before those snoops start to follow our every move."

The two men sat in silence, drinking their beer. "But you've managed to avoid my question," Troy said at length with a mischievous smile. "The subject was women. How come a guy like you, handsome, educated, apparently not gay, does not have a steady woman?"

Nick thought for a moment. He studied Troy's friendly, guileless face and decided to take the plunge. "I'm not sure, Troy," he said seriously, "but I think maybe I push them all away. I find something wrong with them so I have an excuse." A new idea crept into Nick's mind. "Maybe I'm getting even in a way. You asked about broken hearts? The biggest one in the closet is my own. Mine was torn to shreds when I was a kid by a woman who probably doesn't even remember me."

Troy rose from his chair and walked over to the disc player to change the music. "Listen to us," he said lightly, "both struggling with the infinite complexity of the female species. May they remain forever crazy and mysterious and wonderful. And by the way, Professor"—Troy's characteristic grin had returned,—"I brought this subject up to warn you. Unless I miss my guess, that reporter lady has her sights set on you. She likes challenges. And so far you have given off nothing but negative signals. To say the least."

Nick jumped up from his chair with a spurt of energy. "I'm going for another beer, my good man. Until just this moment I had thought that I was talking to someone with insight and understanding. Now I find that I'm talking instead to some stupid black man who thinks 'asshole' is a term of endearment." He paused briefly on his way to the kitchen to pick up some potato chips. "By the way," he shouted at Troy between crunches on his chips, "you said on the phone that you wanted to show me something. Was that the Angie Leatherwood album or was it something else?"

Troy met him in the hall as Nick was returning with the beer. "No," he said earnestly, "it was something else. But I wanted to talk to you for a little first to make sure . . . well, I'm not sure why, maybe to give me some confidence that you wouldn't put me down."

"What are you talking about?" Nick said, a little confused.

"It's in here," Troy replied, knocking on a closed door off the hall in the opposite direction from the living room. "It's my baby. I've been working on it for over two years now, alone most of the time—although Angie's artistic kid brother Lanny has helped me with some of it—and now I want you to try it out." He smiled. "You will be my first alpha tester."

"What the hell . . . I'm lost. What's an alpha tester?" Nick's brow furrowed as he tried to follow the conversation. The two quick beers on an empty stomach had already given him a small and unexpected buzz.

"My invention," Troy said slowly, letting each word sink in, "is a computer game. I've been working on it for almost two years. And you are going to be the first outsider to play it."

Nick screwed up his face as if he had just eaten a particularly tart piece of grapefruit. "Moi?" he exclaimed. "You want me to play a computer game? You want me, whose hand-eye coordination is almost nonexistent even when completely sober, to sit down and shoot aliens, or dodge bombs, or roll marbles at a frenzied pace that only neo-adolescents can enjoy? Jefferson, have you lost your mind? This is Nick Williams, the guy you call the Professor, the man who sits and reads *books* for entertainment."

"Very, very good," Troy replied, laughing heartily at Nick's outburst. "You're perfect as an alpha tester. My game is not one of those arcade games that test your reflexes, although there are a few places in the game where the pace is fairly fast. My creation is an adventure game. It's a little like a novel, except that the player defines the outcome of the game. I'm aiming at a wide audience and I'm including a lot of unusual technological wrinkles. I would love to see how you respond."

Troy took Nick's shrug as grudging assent and opened the door to what should have been the master bedroom in the duplex unit. Instead, what greeted Nick's eyes was an almost phantasmagoric collection of electronic equipment filling every nook and cranny of a fairly large room. His first impression was one of total chaos. But after shaking his head and blinking a couple of times, Nick could make out some order in the jumble of scopes, monitors, cables, computers, and sundry unattached parts. On one side of the room was a chair about ten feet in front of a giant screen. Between this chair and the screen was a low table with a keyboard on it. Troy motioned to Nick to sit down.

"My game is called *Alien Adventure*," Troy said excitedly, "and it will start as soon as I boot the discs and you are ready at the keyboard. But there are some things that I must tell you first, before you start." He knelt beside Nick and pointed at the keyboard. "There are three critical keys for you to remember while you are playing the game. First, the X key stops the clock. From the moment you start the game, the clock continues to run. While the clock is running you are consuming vital resources. There is only this one way to stop the clock and gather your wits without paying a penalty. Hitting the X key allows you to stop and think.

"Even more important than the X is the S key. The S allows you to checkpoint or, as you would say, save the game. Right now you can't understand what I'm telling you, because you haven't played complicated computer games before, but believe me, you must learn regularly to save the game. When you hit the S key, all the parameters of the game you are playing are written into a special data base that has a unique identifier. Then, at any time in the future, you can call that identifier and the game will restart in exactly the place where you saved it. This feature can be a life saver. If you take a risky route in the game and your character ends up dying, it's the save game feature that keeps you from having to start all over again."

Nick was amazed. This was a different Troy than he had ever seen before. True, he had been a little surprised and considerably impressed by his first mate's ability to fix virtually any piece of electronic gear on the boat, but never in his wildest dreams had he imagined that Troy left the boat and went home to work with similar parts in a much more creative way. Now this same smiling black man had him sitting in a chair in front of a giant screen and was lecturing him patiently like a child. Nick could hardly wait to see what would happen next.

"Finally," Troy said, asking with his eyes if Nick was still following him, "there's the H or help key. When you simply have run out of imagination and don't know what to do, you can push H. The game will then give you some hints on how you might proceed. But I must warn you of one thing. The clock continues to run while you are being helped. And, there are some places in the game, during a battle for instance, where pushing the H key can be disastrous, because you are essentially defenseless during the time that the game processes your request for help. H is most useful when you are in a benign spot and trying to figure out your overall strategy."

Still squatting beside him, Troy handed Nick a small spiral notebook and motioned for him to open it. The first page said "Command Dictionary." On each page was a separate entry, legibly written by hand, that explained the game command that would result from hitting the key listed at the top of the page. "Here are the rest of your commands, fifty in all," Troy said. "But you don't need to memorize them. I'll help you. You'll learn some of them yourself after you play the game for a while. Most of the important commands are activated by a single stroke on the keyboard, but some of the commands require two entries."

Nick flipped through the notebook. He noted that the key L prompted the command "Look." But another entry was necessary to identify *what* instrument was being used to look. L followed by a 1, for example, meant to look with your eyes. L8 meant to look with an ultraviolet spectrometer, whatever that was. Nick was already overwhelmed. He looked over at his friend, who was busy making final checks on some equipment.

Troy came back to the chair and looked down at Nick. "Now," he said, "I think you're ready. Any questions?"

"Just one, my lord and guide," Nick replied with mock meekness. "May I please have another beer before I risk my manhood in some weird world of your creation?"

Actually Nick was not yet ready to play the game. Even after Troy booted three compact discs, there were more preliminary activities before Nick could begin the game itself. He had to enter his name, race, age, and sex in response to questions that appeared on the giant screen. Nick looked at Troy with a curious tilt of his head and a weird expression on his face. "Don't ask questions at this point," Troy told him, "it will all be clear soon enough."

The screen next was filled with a beautiful ringed planet that looked like what an artist who favored purple might make out of Saturn. The perspective was from the pole of the planet; the rings were all displayed like the different sections of a dart target. Little flecks of light gleamed intermittently from the rings, indicating that the sun or star or whatever was the source for the reflected light was in the vicinity of the viewer. It was a lovely picture. A simple credit in block titles, *Alien Adventure* by Troy Jefferson, was superimposed on the ringed planet for three or four seconds and the sound of soft classical music could be heard in the room. Nick resisted an urge to chuckle when he heard Troy's voice, clearly serious and self-conscious, coming from one of the speakers.

Troy's recorded voice explained the initial conditions for the game. The adventurer was on a space station in polar orbit around Gunna, the largest planet belonging to another solar system whose central body was the G-type star that we call Tau Ceti, only ten light years or so away from the Earth. "Tau Ceti has eight primary bodies in its system," Troy's voice said, "including six planets and two moons.

"Maps of the system are available at the commissary on the space station," Troy's voice continued, "although some of the regions have been incompletely mapped. When your adventure begins, you are sleeping in your cabin onboard the station. An alarm sounds on your personal receiver . . ."

The voice faded and the sound of an alarm could be heard. The picture on the giant screen was the inside of a space cabin, almost certainly taken from one of the many successful science fiction movies. In the upper right hand corner of the screen was a game digital clock that was changing by one unit every four seconds or so. Nick looked helplessly at Troy. Troy suggested that he hit the L key. In a few seconds Nick learned that he could use the direction keys on the board to look at specific items in his cabin. Each time he hit a direction key, the picture on the screen changed to correspond to a different point of view. Nick noticed that there was a fuzzy picture on his small television and followed Troy's suggestion to watch until it became clear.

When the focus on his cabin television sharpened, Nick could see a young woman wearing a long, full, richly red dress that dropped almost all the way to the floor. She was standing, somewhat incongruously, in a small, stark room furnished with a single bed, a little desk, and a straight chair. Some light was entering the room through the solitary window near the ceiling and behind the desk. Thick vertical bars were imbedded in the window glass.

The camera zoomed in on her face. Nick leaned forward in his chair in Troy's apartment. "Why . . . why it's Julianne," Nick said in astonishment, just as the woman began to speak.

"Captain Nick Williams," she said, much to his surprise, "you and I have never met, but your reputation for valor and justice is unequaled in the Federation. I am Princess Heather of Othen. While attending the great ball at the inauguration of the Viceroy of Toom, I was kidnapped by willens and taken to their stronghold on the planet Accutar. They have told my father, King Merson, that they will not release me unless he cedes to them all the ore-rich asteroids in the Endelva region.

"He must not do that, Nick," the princess continued earnestly as the camera zoomed in on her face, "or he will deprive our people of their only source of hanna, the key to our immortality. My sources tell me that already my father wastes away, brooding over his impossible predicament. My sister Samantha has fled from Othen with a key division of our best soldiers and a huge store of hanna. It is not clear whether she intends to try to free me or to revolt against my father's rule in the event that he should decide to give up the Endelva asteroids in exchange for my life. She has always been completely unpredictable.

"Yesterday the willens delivered an ultimatum to my father. He must make his decision in one month, or they will behead me. Captain Williams, please help me. I do not want to die. If you come and rescue me, I will share with you the Othen throne and the secret of our immortality. We can live forever as king and queen."

The transmission stopped suddenly and the picture was gone. The screen again showed a picture of the inside of Nick's cabin onboard the space station. Nick resisted an impulse to applaud and sat without moving. Somehow Troy had made Julianne into a very believable Princess Heather. *But how did my name get into the script?* he wondered. He wanted to ask questions but a warning message flashed on the giant screen, indicating that time was passing and the adventurer was not taking any action. Nick found the X key and the digital clock on the screen stopped. He turned to Troy. "So what do I do now?"

With Troy's occasional help, Nick equipped himself for a journey, found his way to the spaceport, and climbed in a small shuttle craft. Despite Troy's hints that his chances for survival in "open space" were small unless he spent more time examining the other facilities on the space station, Nick blasted off anyway. It was great fun. He used the commands on the keyboard to control his speed and direction. What he saw on the screen was perfectly matched with his commands, giving him the illusion that he was actually flying a vehicle through space. He saw many other vehicles on the monitor as he maneuvered toward his target, a planet named Gunna, but none of them approached his shuttle. Just outside the Gunna sphere of influence, however, a needle-nosed craft approached him quickly and then, without warning, blasted him with a battery of missiles. Nick was unable to escape. The screen filled with fire from the explosion that ripped through his shuttle. Then the monitor went blank and black except for the simple message "Game Over" in white letters in the middle of the screen.

"Time for another beer?" Nick asked, surprised to discover that he was actually disappointed by the death of his character.

"Right on, Captain," Troy replied.

They walked into the kitchen together. Troy opened the refrigerator and pulled out two more beers. He handed one to Nick. The professor was still absorbed in thinking about the game. "If I remember correctly, there were four sections marked on that map of the space station," Nick said aloud. "And I only went in two of them. Would you mind telling me about the other two sections?"

"You missed the cafeteria and the library," Troy said, delighted that Nick was still interested. "The cafeteria is not all that important," he added, laughing, "although I've never known you to go anywhere before without eating first. But the library—"

"Don't tell me," Nick said, interrupting him. "Let me figure it out. In the library I can learn about willens and the Otheners, or whatever they're called, who can live forever and what exactly is a Viceroy of Toom." He shook his head. "My, my, Troy. I must say that I am more than a little impressed. I have no idea how anyone could create something like this. And I have a feeling that I've just scratched the surface."

"I take it you're ready to continue, Professor?" Troy replied, acknowledging the praise with a huge grin. "One piece of advice. While you're in the library, look in the *Encyclopedia of Space Vehicles* so you can at least tell a hostile ship when it appears. Otherwise you're never going to reach the exciting parts of the game."

The afternoon passed quickly. Nick found that escape into the imaginative world of Troy's game was magnificently relaxing, just the tonic that he needed after the morning memories of Monique. Troy knew that Nick was enjoying the playing and he was thrilled. He felt a surge of creative pride and his belief that *Alien Adventure* would be his ticket to success was reborn.

In his vain search for Princess Heather, Nick died a couple more times. Once, when he landed on the unmapped planet Thenia, a black man with a lizard head approached him and told him to leave, that there was nothing but trouble on Thenia. Nick ignored the warning and moved away from his shuttle in a land rover. He narrowly escaped a volcanic eruption only to be trapped and eaten by a gigantic slime mold that oozed out of the ground in the vicinity of his shuttle landing site.

In another reincarnation Nick encountered Samantha, Princess Heather's sister, played for a couple of scenes by Julianne's buxom friend Corinne. Actually, Troy had made Corinne up to look like Susie Q, the famous porn queen of the early nineties, and most of the actual pictures that appeared on the game screen were taken from her ribald classic, *Pleasure Until Pain*. Deft interleaving of new footage with the borrowed shots gave the illusion of being in the movie with Susie Q while she offered sexual delights beyond refusal.

Samantha alias Susie Q alias Corinne seduced Nick and then stabbed him to death with a small dagger while he was lying naked and expectant on the bed. By this point the two men were drinking their final six-pack of beer and the combination of the pornographic scenes and the alcohol had made their conversation coarse and degenerate. "Shit," exclaimed Nick, entreating Troy to replay the scene where a naked Samantha/Susie Q comes up to the camera to take his erect penis in her mouth. "I have never, no never, even heard of a computer game where you almost get a blow job. Man, you are twisted. A genius, yes, I'll agree. But absolutely fucking twisted. What on God's earth induced you to put sex scenes in this game?"

"Hey, man," Troy laughed, putting his arm around Nick as they half staggered into the living room, "the name of the game is sales. And right here, in *Entertainment Software* (he picked up a magazine from the table), it says that seventy-two percent, seventy-two fucking percent, my friend, of all the people who buy computer games are 16- to 24-year-old males. And do you know what that group likes *in addition to* computer games and science fiction? *Sex*, my man. Can't you just see some teenage nerd retreating into his room to play this game and whack off? *Eeee yaaa!*" Troy fell down on one of the easy chairs and beat his chest.

"You're crazy, Jefferson," Nick said, watching Troy's display. "I don't know if I can ever again be alone with you on a boat. You are a certified nut case. I mean, just imagine the reviews. *Alien Adventure* features an encounter with Susie Q, the queen of pornography, in an underground castle on the asteroid Vitt. Which reminds me, how in the world did you get all those movie pieces in there?"

"Lots of research and hard work, Professor," Troy answered, starting to calm down a little. "Lanny and three of his friends have spent maybe a thousand hours watching film for me, trying to find exactly the right clips. And none of this would be possible, of course, without the new data storage methods. We can now store an excellent digital version of every movie ever made in the United States in a warehouse not much larger than this duplex. I've just used data base capabilities to the fullest."

Nick crushed a beer can in his hands. "It's fabulous. Really. But I don't know about the sex business. And why do you have the player register his race at the beginning of the game? Don't you think that will offend some people? I never saw anything in the game that was based on the racial information."

Even though he was drunk, Troy became momentarily serious and almost somber. "Look, man," he said firmly, "sex and race are both a part of life. It may be true that people play computer games primarily for entertainment, and that they would prefer not to be confronted by some topics when they are amusing themselves, but I must be allowed some creative license. Race is with us every day and ignoring it, it seems to me, only contributes to the problem."

Troy brightened up. "Hey, Professor. That lizard-man who warned you on Thenia was black. You went ahead anyway despite his warning. What if he had been white? Would you have turned around and gone back to the shuttle? A black man playing the game encounters a *white* lizard-man on

Thenia. It's part of the show, man. There are twenty or so changes in the scenario that are based on racial input."

Nick's expression was clearly disbelieving. "Really," Troy said, standing up to return to the room where they had played his game, "I'll show you. Watch how the game starts if you register that you are a black male."

Nick followed Troy back into the computer room. His curiosity was clearly piqued. Troy turned the game on and Nick entered the biographical data, changing his race to black. This time, when the television picture in his space station cabin came into focus, Princess Heather was black! The princess this time was, in fact, Angie Leatherwood. "Well, I'll be damned," Nick said, looking over at a beaming Troy. "You are one clever dude, Mr. Jefferson." Nick walked out of the room whistling and shaking his head again. Troy turned off the game and followed.

"Okay," Nick began, once they were back in Troy's living room and seated on the couch, "one last question and then let's forget the game for the time being. How did you get my name into it? I thought that was very impressive."

"It was originally Lanny's idea, based on a movie he watched about a speech therapist. Lanny had all the minor characters spend a day mouthing all the vowel and consonant sounds in a test session. Then we just put the sounds together with what are called audio analytic continuation techniques." Troy laughed. He was feeling ebullient and basking in the compliments. "But it does have its drawbacks. Our interpreter only knows how to read simple English words. We may have to suppress that feature if we sell the game abroad."

Nick stood up. "Well, I've run out of superlatives. By the way, are there more of you, brothers, sisters, anything? I guess I'd like to warn the rest of the world."

"Only me now," Troy replied, a faraway look fleetingly crossing his face. "I had a brother, Jamie, six years older than me. We were very close. He died in an automobile accident when I was fourteen."

There was an awkward silence. "I'm sorry," Nick said, again touched by Troy's openness. Troy shrugged his shoulders and struggled with the sudden memory.

Nick changed the subject. They talked about the boat and then about Homer and his crew for several minutes. Suddenly Nick looked at his watch. "Jesus Christ," he said. "It's after four o'clock. Weren't we supposed to meet Carol Dawson at four?"

Troy jumped out of his chair. "We sure were. Some partners we turned out to be," he was grinning again, "spending the entire afternoon drinking beer and playing games." The two men shared a small hug, threw the empty beer cans in the trash, and went out the door toward Nick's car.

AROL was clearly irritated as she sat in the communications room at the Marriott. She was drumming her fingers on the desk while she listened to the telephone ring. There was a click and then Nick's voice said, "I am not at home at the present time. But if—" She flipped the switch off hastily and completed the sentence, her sardonic mimicry releasing some of her frustration, "But if you'll leave your name, your number, and the time that you called, I'll get back to you as soon as I return. S-h-i-t. Shit. I knew I should have called before I left Miami."

She dialed another number. Bernice answered and put her right through (on video) to Dr. Dale Michaels. Carol did not bother with a greeting. "Can you believe that I can't even find the stupid bastard? He's not on his boat, he's not at home. Nobody knows where he is. I could have stayed in Miami and taken a nap."

Carol had not told Dr. Dale much about Nick and Troy. And what she had said about Nick had not been flattering. "Well, what did you expect?" Dale responded. "You wanted to go out with amateurs as a cover. Why would you think that he would be easy to find before your appointment? That kind usually stays in bed with his dame of the day until he has some reason to greet the world." Dale chuckled to himself.

Carol found herself strangely annoyed by Dale's disdainful comment about Nick's love life. She started to say something but decided against it. "Say, Dale," she said instead, "is this phone line absolutely secure? I have a couple of sensitive items to discuss with you."

He smiled. "Nothing to worry about. I have sensors that flash if there is the slightest unexplained break anywhere in the line. Even on your end."

"Good," Carol replied. She pulled out her notebook and scanned a hand-written list. "As far as Arnie Webber knows," she said, looking up at the video camera, "there are no legal prohibitions against salvaging any U.S. government property, provided it is returned to its rightful owner very soon after its retrieval. So I wouldn't technically be committing a crime if I pull the missile up." She checked the first item off her list.

"But, Dale, I thought about something else on the flight down here from Miami. This thing is, after all, some kind of guided missile. What if it blows up? Am I crazy to worry about such a thing? Or is it somehow incapacitated or whatever by sitting down there in the sand and salt water for several days?"

Dale laughed. "Sometimes, Carol, you're divine. I am fairly confident that the new missile is designed to operate either in the air or in water. And

I don't think that the sand would be able to foul up its critical parts in a short period of time. However, the fact that it hasn't exploded yet suggests to me that it probably wasn't armed in the first place, except possibly for a small destruct device that may or may not have already failed. You are taking a calculated risk in retrieving that missile. I still strongly suggest that you make your dive, obtain the photographs, and then go public with the story. Dredging the missile up for display purposes seems to me to be more of a stunt than journalism. Besides, it's dangerous."

Carol was curt. "As I said in the car, you are entitled to your opinion. The Navy could make a case that I faked the pictures somehow. But they cannot argue with a missile that has physical presence and can clearly be seen by a nationwide television audience. I want maximum impact for the story."

She checked another item off the list in her notebook. "Oh, yes, I forgot to mention this morning that I met another boat captain down here, a bit of a creep actually, an older fat man named Homer. He seemed to recognize me almost immediately. Wealthy, big yacht and all that. Strange crew—"

"Was his last name Ashford? Homer Ashford?" Dale interrupted her.

Carol nodded. "So you know him?" she asked.

"Certainly," Dale replied. "He was the leader of the expedition that found the *Santa Rosa* treasure in 1986. You've met him too, although it's obvious you've forgotten. He and his wife were guests at the MOI awards banquet early in 1993." Dale stopped to think. "That's right. I remember now, you were real late coming to the party because of that threat made against you by Juan Salvador. But I'm surprised you forgot them, the wife especially. She was a great big fat woman and she thought you were the cat's pajamas."

Slowly but surely it all clicked in Carol's memory. She recalled a bizarre evening right after she first started going with Dale. She had run a piece in the *Herald* on cocaine trafficking and had suggested that the Cuban city councilman, Juan Salvador, was deliberately inhibiting the police investigations. At noon that day, a usually reliable source had called her editor at the paper and told him that Señor Salvador had just purchased a contract on Carol's life. The *Herald* had assigned her a bodyguard and recommended that she alter her normal schedule so that her whereabouts would always be uncertain.

The evening of the MOI banquet Carol was in a fog. The bodyguard had been with her for only three hours and already she felt confined and restricted. But Carol had been genuinely frightened by the threat. At the banquet she had scrutinized every face, looking for an assassin, waiting for someone to make a move. As she sat in the hotel communications room fourteen months later, she did vaguely remember meeting Homer (he had been dressed in a tux) and some jolly fat woman who had followed her around for twenty minutes or so. *Damnit*, Carol thought. *It's my memory again. I should have recognized him immediately. How stupid of me.*

"Okay," Carol said to Dale, "I remember them now. But why were they at the MOI awards banquet?"

"We were honoring our leading benefactors that night," Dale replied. "Homer and Ellen have been big supporters of our underwater sentry effort. In fact, he has field tested many of our prototypes at his facility there in Key West. Real solid test data too. Best compilation of sentry/intruder responses that anybody has catalogued. Why, it was Ashford who showed us how the MQ-6 could be fooled—"

"Okay, Okay," Carol said, realizing that her tolerance threshold was still extremely low. "Thanks for the information. It's now a quarter till four. I'm going to go down to the marina to meet Nick Williams and make arrangements for tomorrow. If anything new comes up, I'll call you at home tonight."

"Ciao," said Dale Michaels, trying without success to sound sophisticated, "and please be careful."

Carol hung up the phone with a sigh. She wondered if she should spend a minute or two figuring out where she and Dale were going. *Or not going. As the case may be.* She thought about all the things she needed to do. She closed her notebook and rose from her chair. *Not right now,* she thought. *I don't have time now to think about Dale. But as soon as I have a break in this crazy life of mine.*

Carol was really fuming when she walked back into the marina head-quarters the second time. She approached the information desk with fire in her eyes. "Miss," she said nastily to Julianne, "as I told you fifteen minutes ago, I had an appointment here at four o'clock with Nick Williams and Troy Jefferson. It is now, as you can see, after four-thirty."

Carol pointed at the digital clock with an impatient, sweeping gesture that commanded Julianne to look. "We have both established independently that Mr. Williams is not home," Carol continued. "Now are you going to give me Mr. Jefferson's phone number, or should I make a scene?"

Julianne did not like Carol or her obvious attitude of superiority. She held her ground. "As I told you, Miss Dawson," she said politely but with a biting overtone, "marina policy prohibits our giving out the phone numbers of the independent boat owners or their crew members. It's a question of privacy. Now if you had a formal charter through the marina," Julianne continued, enjoying her moment of glory, "then it would be our job to assist you. But as I said earlier, we have no record—"

"Goddamn it, I know that," replied Carol furiously. She slammed the envelope of photos that she was carrying down on Julianne's counter. "I'm not an imbecile. We've been through this before. I told you I was supposed to meet them here at four o'clock. Now if you won't help me, I want to talk to your superior, the assistant manager or whatever."

"Fine," said Julianne, her eyes firing darts of contempt at Carol. "If you will just take a seat over there, I will see if I can locate—"

"I will *not* take a seat," shouted Carol in exasperation. "I want to see him now. This is an issue of extreme urgency. Now pick up the phone and—"

"Is something wrong here? Perhaps I can help." Carol spun around. Homer Ashford was standing right behind her. Just to the right, toward the gate in the direction of the jetties, Greta and a big heavy woman (*That's Ellen. Now I remember her,* Carol thought) were talking quietly. Ellen smiled at Carol. Greta looked right through her.

"Well, hello, Captain Homer," Julianne said sweetly, "it's nice of you to ask. But I think everything's under control. Miss Dawson here has just indicated that she does not accept my explanation of marina policy. She is going to wait for—"

"Maybe you *can* help," Carol interrupted Julianne defiantly. "I had an appointment here at four o'clock with Nick Williams and Troy Jefferson. They have not shown up. Do you by any chance happen to know Troy's phone number?"

Captain Homer gave Carol a suspicious look and exchanged a knowing glance with Ellen and Greta. He turned back to Carol. "Well, it is certainly a surprise, Miss Dawson, to see you back here again. Why we were just talking about you this morning, saying that we hoped you had a good time on your free day in Key West." He paused for effect. "Now I wonder why you've come back here again, the very next day. And did I hear correctly, you need to see Williams and Jefferson on an issue of extreme urgency? It couldn't possibly have anything to do with all that equipment you brought in here yesterday, could it? Or the little gray bag that Williams has been guarding since last night?"

Uh oh, thought Carol, as Greta and Ellen moved in around her. *I'm surrounded.* Captain Homer started to pick up the sealed envelope on Julianne's counter but Carol stopped him.

"If you don't mind, Captain Ashford," she said firmly, taking his hand off the envelope and putting the photos under her arm. She lowered her voice. "I would like to talk to you privately." Carol nodded her head at the two women. "Can we go out in the parking lot together for a minute?"

Homer's beady eyes squinted at her. Then his face broke into the same obnoxious, lecherous smile that Carol had seen on the *Ambrosia.* "Certainly, my dear," he said. He shouted to Greta and Ellen as he walked out the door with Carol, "Wait here. I'll only be a minute."

Necessity is the mother of invention, Carol thought to herself as she led Homer Ashford out the door. *So invent, bitch. And now. As in this moment.*

They walked up the steps to the parking lot. Carol turned to Captain Homer at the top of the steps with a conspiratorial look on her face. "I can tell that you've figured out why I'm here," she said. "I didn't want it this way, I thought it would make a better story if nobody knew what I was doing. But you're obviously too clever for me." Homer grinned foolishly. "But I would ask you to tell as few people as possible. You can tell your wife and Greta, but please nobody else. The *Herald* wants it to be a surprise."

Homer looked puzzled. Carol leaned over and almost whispered in his ear. "The *entire* Sunday magazine section the fourth week in April. Isn't that unbelievable? Working title, 'Dreams of Being Rich,' stories about people like you, like Mel Fisher, like the four Floridians who have won over a million dollars each in the lottery. On how sudden income changes your life. I'm doing the whole piece. I'm starting with the treasure angle because of its general interest."

Carol could see that Captain Homer was reeling. She knew she had him off guard. "Yesterday I just wanted to check your boat quickly, see how you lived, see how it would photograph. I freaked out a little when you recognized me so fast. But I had always planned to go out with Williams first." Carol laughed. "My treasure-finding equipment from MOI faked him out. He still thinks I am a genuine treasure seeker. I almost completed my whole interview with him yesterday. I only came back today to finish a couple of small items."

An alert went off in Homer Ashford's system when Carol talked about faking out Nick Williams. Homer wasn't certain he believed this smooth reporter's story even now. He mused to himself that her story was plausible, but there was still one big unanswered question. "But what is Williams carrying around in that bag?" he asked.

"That," said Carol, sensing his distrust, "is nothing." She raised her eyebrows and laughed again. "Or almost, anyway. We pulled up a worthless old trinket yesterday afternoon so I could photograph the salvage process for the story. I told him to have it appraised today. He thinks I'm an eccentric. He must be keeping it hidden in the bag because he's embarrassed and doesn't want anybody to see him with it."

Carol lightly hit Captain Homer in the ribs with her elbow. He shook his head. Part of him realized he was being told a very clever lie. But somehow enough of it made sense that Homer couldn't pierce the deception. His brow furrowed for a moment. "So I guess you'll want to talk to us when you're through with the other two . . ."

At just that moment, unbeknownst to Carol, Nick and Troy drove into the marina parking lot. They were still slightly drunk and silly. "Lawdy, lawdy," said Troy, spotting Carol and Captain Homer in conversation, "I believe my eyes have screwed up. They're sending a picture of a beauty and a beast to my brain. It's Miss Carol Dawson together with our favorite fat captain. Now what do you suppose they're talking about?"

"I don't know," said Nick, bridling instantly, "but I'm damn sure going to find out. If she's double-crossing us . . ." He pulled the car quickly into a parking place and started to jump out. Troy reached across and restrained him.

"Now why don't you let me handle this one?" Troy said. "Humor may be just the right ticket here."

Nick thought for a moment. "Maybe you're right," he said. "I'll let you go first."

* * *

Troy walked into view just as Carol and Captain Homer were finishing their conversation. "Helloooo, angel," he said from forty yards away, "what's happening?"

Carol held her hand up in acknowledgment but didn't turn around to greet Troy. "So that's 2748 Columbia, just beyond the Pelican Resort, at eight-thirty tomorrow night?"

"Right," replied Homer Ashford. He nodded his head in Troy's direction and started to leave. "We'll be ready for you. Bring plenty of tape, for it's a long story." He made a peculiar clucking sound with his mouth. "And plan to stay for a little party afterward."

Homer was already halfway down the steps when Troy walked up beside Carol. "Hello, Captain Homer. Goodbye, Captain Homer," he said quietly, still playing the comic. He leaned over to kiss Carol on the cheek. "Hi there, angel . . ."

"Yuch," Carol pulled her cheek away. "You smell like a brewery. No wonder I've had to look all over town for you two." She saw Nick coming toward them across the parking lot. He was carrying the exercise bag. She raised her voice. "Well, Mr. Williams, what a pleasant surprise. How nice that you and your brother here could climb down from your bar stools long enough to keep our appointment." She looked at her watch. "My, my," she said in her most sarcastic voice, "we are certainly fashionably late. Let's see, if one waits fifteen minutes for a full professor, how long does one wait for a fake professor?"

"Knock off the bullshit, Miss High and Mighty," Nick said, responding angrily to her barbs. He joined Carol and Troy and then caught his breath. "We have a few bones to pick with you as well," he continued. "Just what were you doing talking to that asshole Ashford?"

Nick sounded threatening. Carol recoiled. "Listen to him," she said, "the typical macho male. Always shifts the blame to the woman. 'Hey bitch,' he says, 'forget I'm late, forget I'm an arrogant bastard, it was your fault anyway . . .' "

"Hey, hey . . . *hey*," Troy interceded. Carol and Nick were glowering at each other. They both started to speak but Troy interrupted them again. "Children, children, please," he continued, "I have something important to say." They both looked at him. Troy raised his arms for quiet. Then he adopted a stiff pose and pretended to be reading. " 'Fourscore and seven years ago, our forefathers brought forth upon this continent a new nation . . .' "

Carol cracked up first. "Troy," she said, smiling despite her anger, "you are something else. You are also ridiculous."

A grinning Troy punched Nick on the shoulder. "How did I do, Professor? Would I make a good Lincoln? Could a nice young black boy play Lincoln for the white folks?"

Nick smiled reluctantly and looked down at the macadam while Troy jabbered. When Troy was finished, Nick's tone to Carol was conciliatory. "I'm sorry we were late," he said in measured tones, "we forgot what time it was. Here's the trident."

Carol recognized how difficult it had been for Nick to apologize. She accepted gracefully with a short smile and a gesture with her hands. "You keep the trident for a little while longer," she said after a brief silence. "We have a lot of other things to talk about." She looked around. "But this may be the wrong place and the wrong time."

Both Nick and Troy were giving her questioning looks. "I have some very exciting news," she explained, "some of which is here in your copy of the pictures that I developed this morning. Bottom line is that the telescope picked up an infrared signal coming out of the fissure from some kind of large object or objects." She turned to Nick. "It may be more treasure. We can't be certain what it is based on the images."

Nick reached for the envelope. Carol pulled it away. "Not here, not now. Too many eyes and ears. Take my word for it. What we have to do now is make plans. Can you two take me out again tomorrow morning early and be prepared to salvage objects possibly as big as two hundred pounds? Of course, I intend to pay for chartering the boat again."

"Wow," whistled Nick, "two hundred pounds! I can hardly wait to see the pictures." He was sobering up rapidly. "We'll need to borrow a dredger and—"

"I still have the telescope so we can use it again," Carol added. She looked at her watch. "It's almost five o'clock now, how much preparation time do you need?"

"Three hours, four hours at the most," Nick said, calculating swiftly. "With Troy's help, of course," he added.

"Gladly, my friends," Troy replied. "And since Angie has reserved a special table for me at Sloppy Joe's for her ten-thirty show tonight, why don't we meet there and go over the details for tomorrow?"

"Angie Leatherwood is a friend of yours?" Carol said, obviously impressed. "I haven't seen her since she made the big time." She paused for a second and handed the envelope to Nick. "Look at these images in private. The whole set was taken just under the boat where we were diving. Some are obviously blowups of others. It may take a little time for your eyes to adjust to all the colors. But it's the brown object or objects that we're after." Carol could tell that both of the men were eager to see the pictures. She walked with them toward Nick's car. "So I'll see both of you tonight at Sloppy Joe's about ten-fifteen." She turned to head for her own parking place.

"Uh, Carol, just a minute," Nick stopped her. Carol waited while Nick, suddenly awkward, tried to figure out a nice way to ask his question. "Would you mind telling us why you were talking to Captain Homer?" he at last said tactfully.

Carol looked at Nick and Troy for a minute and then laughed. "I ran into him while I was in the office trying to call you guys. He wanted to know about the piece we retrieved yesterday. I put him off the track by telling him I was doing a feature article on all members of the crew that found the *Santa Rosa* treasure eight years ago."

Nick glanced at Troy with mock disgust. "You see, Jefferson," he said with exaggerated emphasis. "I told you there was a legitimate explanation." The two men waved at Carol as she headed for her car.

" L IEUTENANT Todd," the commander said with exasperation, "I am beginning to think that the U.S. Navy has overestimated your intelligence or experience or both. It is beyond me how you can continue even to consider the possibility that the Panther was *commanded* off course by the Russians, particularly in light of the new information you presented this afternoon."

"But, sir," the younger man answered stubbornly, "it is still a viable hypothesis. And you yourself said in the meeting that a good failure analysis does not exclude any reasonable possibility."

The two men were in Commander Winters' office. The commander walked over to look out the window. It was almost dark outside. The air was heavy, still, and humid. Thunderstorms were building over the ocean to the south. The base was nearly empty. At length Winters looked at his watch, heaved a sigh, and came back across the room towards Lieutenant Todd. He was smiling only slightly.

"You listened well, Lieutenant. But the operative word here is 'reasonable.' Let's review the facts. Did I or did I not hear correctly that your telemetry analysis unit found this afternoon that the commands rejected counter on the bird also incremented during the flight, beginning as early as off the coast of New Brunswick? And that, apparently, over one *thousand* command messages were rejected as the missile made its way down the Atlantic Coast? How do you propose to explain all this in terms of your scenario? Did the Russians deploy an entire fleet of ships along the flight path, just to confuse and capture one solitary Navy test missile?"

Commander Winters was now standing directly in front of the taller young lieutenant. "Or maybe you believe," he continued sarcastically, before Todd could respond, "that the Russians have a new secret weapon that flies alongside a missile going at Mach 6 and talks to it en route. Come on, Lieutenant, on what reasonable grounds do you consider this bizarre Russian hypothesis of yours still viable?"

Lieutenant Todd did not yield. "Sir," he answered, "none of the other possible explanations for the missile's behavior makes any more sense at this stage. You now say that you believe it's a software problem; however, our very brightest programmers cannot imagine how the only external indication of a major, system-level software malfunction could be that two, and only two, command counters go haywire. They have checked all the internal software diagnostic data that was telemetered to the ground and they can find no problems. Besides, the pre-release checkout indicates that all the software was working fine just seconds before the flight began.

"And we know something else. Ramirez has learned from Washington that there have been peculiar movements in the Russian submarine fleet off the Florida coast in the last forty-eight hours. I'm not saying that the Russian hypothesis, as you call it, is the answer. Just that until we have a more satisfactory explanation of a failure mechanism that could cause both command counters to increment, it makes sense to carry one option that assumes maybe the Panther was actually commanded."

Winters shook his head. "All right, Lieutenant," he said finally. "I will not order you to take it off the list. But I will order you to concentrate this weekend on finding the missile in the ocean somewhere and identifying a hardware and/or software problem that could have caused either the command counter anomaly or the change in the flight path or both. There must be an explanation that does not involve operations on a massive scale by the Russians."

Todd started to walk around Winters and leave. "Just a minute," the commander said, his eyes narrowing. "I don't believe it's necessary, is it Lieutenant, to remind you of who will be held responsible if the outside world gets wind of this Russian business?"

"No, Commander . . . sir," was the answer.

"Then carry on," said Winters, "and let me know if there are any significant new developments."

Commander Winters was in a hurry. He had called the theater right after Todd had left and told Melvin Burton that he was going to be late. He drove quickly into a hamburger stand, wolfed down a burger and fries, and headed for the marina area.

He arrived at the theater when most of the rest of the cast was already dressed. Melvin met him at the door. "Quickly now, Commander, we have no time to spare. The makeup must be correct the first time." He looked nervously at his watch. "You're in the pulpit in exactly forty-two minutes." The commander entered the men's dressing room, took off his Navy uniform, and put on the dour black and white regalia of an Episcopal priest. Outside the door to the dressing room, Melvin paced back and forth, going through a final checklist in his mind.

Commander Winters was in the pulpit when the curtain rose. He had a strong case of normal opening-night jitters. He looked across the three rows of his stage congregation to the full audience in the theater. He saw his wife Betty and son Hap on the second row. Winters smiled at them quickly before the applause died down. Then his nervousness disappeared as he launched into Shannon's sermon.

The short prologue sped by quickly. The lights dimmed another time for fifteen seconds, the set changed automatically, and he was in the final scene, walking into his hotel room in Mexico and still mumbling to himself phrases from his letter. Shannon/Winters sat down on his bed. He heard a noise in the corner of the room and looked up. It was Charlotte/Tiffani. Her gorgeous auburn hair was down over her shoulders. She was wearing a light blue silk nightshirt, cut low in the middle, which her ample and upright breasts filled completely. He heard her say, "Larry, oh Larry, finally we're alone together," and she came to sit beside him on the bed. Her perfume filled his nostrils. Her hand was behind his head. Her lips pressed against his, insistent, hard, searching. He pulled back. Her lips followed, then her body. He fell back on the bed. She crawled on top, her kisses continuing, her breasts pushed against his pounding chest. He put his arms around her, slowly at first, and then, lying on his back, he enveloped her with a deep embrace.

The lights flashed off and on for several seconds. Charlotte/Tiffani slid off of Winters and lay beside him on the bed. He could hear her labored breathing. A voice was heard, "Charlotte." Then again, with a loud knock on the door, "Charlotte, I know you're in there." The door sprang open. The two lovers half sat up in bed. The lights went off and the curtain came down. The applause was loud and sustained.

Commander Vernon Winters pushed open the door and stumbled outside. He was at the alley entrance to the theater. The door, over which was a single light bulb covered with insects, opened onto a small wooden platform a few steps above the pavement. Winters walked down the three steps and stood beside the red brick wall of the theater. He pulled out a cigarette and lit it.

He watched the smoke curl upward against the red brick. In the distance there was a burst of lightning, then a pause before the sound of rolling thunder. He inhaled deeply again and tried to understand what he had been feeling during those five or ten seconds with Tiffani. *I wonder if they could tell*, he thought. *I wonder if it was obvious to everyone.* When he had changed clothes for the first full act of the play, he had noticed the telltale tracks on his undershorts. He expelled some more smoke and winced. *And that little girl. My God. She knows for sure. She must have felt it when she was on top of me.*

Despite himself, he recaptured for an instant his excitement when Tiffani had pressed herself against him. His breath shortened. A first tinge of guilt began to manifest itself. *My God,* he thought again. *What am I? I'm a dirty old man.* For some reason he found himself thinking of Joanna Carr, of a night almost twenty-five years ago. He remembered the moment when he took her . . .

"Commander," he heard a voice say. He turned around. Tiffani was standing on the platform in her T-shirt and jeans, her long hair down over her shoulders. Now she was walking down the steps toward him. "Commander," she said again with a mysterious smile, "may I have a cigarette?"

He was dumbfounded, stupefied. He said nothing. Winters automatically reached into his pocket and pulled out his pack of Pall Malls. The girl took one, packed it against her fingernail, and slid it into her mouth. She waited a second, maybe two. Then she gave him another smile. Winters at last woke up and produced his cheap supermarket lighter. She cupped his trembling hand and inhaled vigorously on the cigarette.

Winters watched her, fascinated, as she pulled the smoke into her lungs. He studied her mouth, her white neck, her uplifted chest as she caressed the smoke. With the same rapt attention, he watched her diaphragm subside and the smoke curl out of her pursed lips.

They stood there together, quietly smoking, neither speaking. Over the ocean there was another flash of lightning, another roll of thunder. Each time that Tiffani would put the cigarette in her mouth, the mesmerized Winters would follow her every move. She would inhale deeply, intently, pulling hard on the cigarette for the nicotine her body cherished. He was only vaguely aware of his jumbled thoughts.

She's beautiful, so beautiful. Young and fresh and full of life. And that hair. How I would love to wrap it around my neck . . . but she's not a little girl. She's a young woman. She must sense what I'm feeling, my fascination for her . . . she smokes as I do. With complete concentration. She caresses . . .

"I love stormy nights," Tiffani broke the silence as still another distant flash of lightning lit up the sky. She moved closer to him and then craned her neck to see around a group of trees that was blocking her view of the cloud formation where the lightning was occurring. She brushed against Commander Winters ever so slightly. He was electrified.

His mouth was dry. His body was suffused with desire, a desire he barely recognized. He could not answer her comment. Instead he stared off at the growing storm and took the final drag from his cigarette.

She too finished her cigarette and dropped it on the pavement. As she turned to face him and their eyes met, the last wisps of smoke were playfully wandering across her lips. She gave a quick, flirtatious blow with her mouth and Winters felt a burst of lust in his groin. He retained his self-control and they entered the theater in silence.

The applause continued. Commander Winters brought the women who had played Maxine and Hannah, one on either side of him, forward for their final bow, just as they had planned before the performance began. The applause intensified. Again he stared at the empty seats where Betty and Hap had been before the intermission. He heard a voice from the audience shout "Charlotte Goodall" and Winters improvised. He took the two ladies back to the line of the assembled cast and walked down the line to Tiffani. For a moment she did not understand. Then her face broke into a radiant smile and she took his hand.

He walked forward with her to the front of the stage, their hands wrapped together in a tight hold. This was her special moment. She was near tears as she heard the applause grow again. He stood aside and she bowed gracefully to the audience. She finished her bow, took his hand again with a delightful squeeze, and backed up into the line with the cast.

Melvin, Marc, and Amanda were all backstage while they were dressing. Enthusiastic congratulations were everywhere. Melvin particularly seemed ecstatic. He admitted that he had had some misgivings during rehearsals, but that everyone had been wonderful. The director confided to Winters that the bedroom scene with Tiffani had been "superb—couldn't have been better," as Melvin literally danced out the dressing room door.

Winters was overwhelmed with a myriad of emotions. He was pleased with his performance in the play and the audience reception, but other more personal things were on his mind. What had happened to Betty and Hap? Why had they left at intermission? In his mind's eye, Winters imagined Betty watching his love scene with Tiffani. He had a momentary panic as he convinced himself that she had known, from out in the audience, that her husband was not acting at all, that he was every bit as aroused as the character he was playing.

What had occurred with Tiffani he could not begin to understand and could not even think about without starting to feel guilty. While he was putting back on his Navy uniform, he allowed himself to taste again her kisses on the bed in the play and to feel the sexual tension while they smoked together in the alley. But beyond his awareness of his arousal he would not go. Guilt was a depressing emotion, and on his successful opening night he did not want to be depressed.

When Commander Winters walked out of the men's communal dressing room, Tiffani was waiting for him. Her hair was back in pigtails, her face scrubbed free of makeup. She looked again like a little girl. "Commander," she said, almost with servility, "would you do me a favor, please?" He smiled his assent. She beckoned to him and he followed her out in the hall that was adjacent to the backstage quarters.

A red-haired man about the commander's age was standing in the hall, nervously smoking a cigarette and pacing. It was obvious that he felt uncomfortable and out of place. Next to him was a tawdry brunette, early thirties perhaps, chewing gum and talking to the man in a whisper. The man noticeably relaxed when he saw the commander in his uniform.

"Well, sir," he said to Winters when Tiffani introduced him as her father, "it's good to meet you. I don't know much about this acting business, but I worry that it's unhealthy for my daughter sometimes." He winked at his wife, Tiffani's stepmother, and lowered his voice. "You know, sir, with all the wimps and fags and other weirdo actors, a man can't be too careful. But Tiff told me there was a real Navy officer, a bona fide commander, as part of the cast. At first I didn't believe her."

Mr. Thomas was definitely getting signals both from Tiffani and his wife. He was talking too much. "I'm regular Navy myself," he blurted out as Winters remained silent, "almost twenty-five years. Signed up when I was just a boy of eighteen. Met Tiff's mother two years later—"

"Daddy," Tiffani interrupted him, "you promised that you wouldn't embarrass me. Please just ask him. He probably has things that he needs to do."

The commander had certainly not been prepared to meet Tiffani's father and stepmother. In fact, he had never for a moment even thought about her parents, although as he stood there, listening to Mr. Thomas, it all made sense. Tiffani was, after all, only a junior in high school. *So of course she lives at home,* he thought. *With her parents.* Mr. Thomas was looking very serious. For about a second Winters felt fear and the beginning of panic. *No. No,* he thought quickly, *she can't have told them anything. It's all much too soon.*

"My wife and I play bridge," Mr. Thomas was saying, "duplicate bridge, in tournaments. And this weekend there's a big sectional in Miami. We'll be leaving tomorrow morning and coming back very late on Sunday night."

Winters was puzzled. He was lost in this conversation. Why should he care about what the Thomases did with their free time? At length Mr. Thomas came to the point. "So we had called Mae's cousin in Marathon and asked her if she would pick my daughter up after the show tomorrow night. But that would mean Tiff would have to miss the cast party. Tiff suggested that maybe you would be willing to see her home safely from the party and," Mr. Thomas smiled pleasantly, "keep a fatherly eye on her while I'm off playing bridge."

Winters instinctively glanced at Tiffani. For just a few milliseconds he saw a worldly look in her eyes that tore through him like a fireball. Then she was a little girl again, entreating her father to let her go to the party.

The commander played his role well. "All right, Mr. Thomas," he replied, "I'll be glad to help you out." He patted Tiffani fondly. "She deserves to go to the party, she's worked hard." He paused for a moment. "But I have a couple of questions. There will certainly be champagne at the party and it will probably go real late. Does she have a curfew? How do you feel about—"

"Just use your own judgment, Commander," Mr. Thomas cut him short. "Mae and I trust you completely." The man reached over and shook Winters' hand. "And thank you very much. By the way," he added, as he turned around to leave, "you were great, although I must admit I was worried when you were necking with my daughter. The fag that wrote the play must have been one weird dude."

Tiffani's stepmother mumbled thanks over her chewing gum and the girl herself said "See ya tomorrow" as the three of them walked away. The commander reached in his pocket for another cigarette.

Betty and Hap were both asleep, as Commander Winters knew they would be, when he finally arrived home around eleven o'clock. He walked softly past his son's room but then stopped outside of Betty's. Basically a considerate man, Winters spent a few seconds weighing Betty's sleep against his need for an explanation. He decided to go in and wake her up. He was surprised to find that he was nervous when he sat down on the side of her bed in the dark.

She was sleeping on her back with a sheet and a very thin blanket both pulled up neatly to within about two inches of her shoulders. He shook her lightly. "Betty, dear," he said. "I'm home. I'd like to talk to you." She stirred. He shook her again. "It's Vernon," he said softly.

His wife sat up in bed and turned on the light on the end table. Underneath the light was a small picture of the face of Jesus, a man wise beyond his thirty or so years, with a full beard, a serious look, and a glow approximating a halo behind his head. "Goodness," she said, frowning and rubbing her eyes, "What's going on? Is everything all right?" Betty had never been particularly pretty. But in the last ten years she had ignored her looks altogether and had even put on twenty pounds of ungainly weight.

"Yes," he answered. "I just wanted to talk. And to find out why you and Hap left the show just after the intermission."

Betty looked him directly in the eyes. This was a woman without guile, even without nuance. Life was simple and straightforward for her. If you truly believed in God and Jesus Christ, then you had no doubts. About anything. "Vernon," she began, "I have often wondered why you choose to perform in such strange plays. But I have never complained about it, particularly since it seems to be the only thing that has excited you in a good way since Libya and that awful beach incident."

She frowned and a cloud seemed to cross her face momentarily. Then she continued in her matter-of-fact way. "But Hap is no longer a child. He is becoming a young man. And hearing his father, even in a play, refer to God as a 'petulant old man' and a 'senile delinquent' is not likely to strengthen his faith." She looked away. "And I thought it was equally disturbing for him to watch you groping with that young girl. All in all," she said, glancing back at her husband and summarizing the entire issue, "I thought the play had no values, no morals, and nothing worth staying for."

Winters felt his anger building but struggled with it, as he always did. He envied Betty her steadfast faith, her ability to see God clearly in every daily activity. He himself felt disjoint from the God of his childhood and his fruitless personal searches had not yet resulted in a clearer perception of Him. But a couple of things Winters did know for certain. His God would laugh with and have compassion for Tennessee Williams' characters. And He would not be pleased by bombs falling on little children.

The commander did not argue with Betty. He gave her a brotherly kiss on the cheek and she turned off the light. For just a moment he wondered. *How long has it been? Three weeks?* But he couldn't remember the exact time. Or even whether or not it had been good. They "fooled around," as Betty called it, whenever her awareness of his need overcame her general lack of interest. *Probably about normal for couples our age,* Winters thought, somewhat defensively, as he undressed in his room.

But he was not able to sleep as he lay quietly in the dark underneath the sheet. The feeling of arousal that had been so intense first during the play and then again out in the alley continued to call to him. With pictures. When he closed his eyes he could again see Tiffani's soft and flirtatious lips blowing out the last of the smoke that had been deep within her lungs. His mouth could still taste those passionate kisses that she had forced upon him during the bedroom scene. And then there was that special look when her father had asked him to take care of her at the party. Had he imagined it?

Several times Commander Winters changed positions in his bed, trying to dispel the images in his mind and the nervousness that was keeping him awake. He was unsuccessful. Eventually, while he was lying on his back, he realized there was one possible release from this kind of tension. At first he felt guilty, even embarrassed, but the waves of images of Tiffani continued to flood into his brain.

He touched himself. The images from the day sharpened and began to expand into fantasies. She was lying on top of him on the bed, as she had been in the play, and he was responding to her kisses. For a brief second Winters became frightened and held himself in check. But a desperate surge of longing removed his last inhibition. He was again an adolescent, alone in his rich imagination.

The scene in his mind changed. He was lying naked on a huge king-size bed in an opulent room with high ceilings. Tiffani approached him from the lighted bathroom, also naked, her long auburn hair cascading over her shoulders and hiding the nipples of her breasts. She took a last languorous pull from her cigarette and put it out in the ashtray beside the bed, her eyes never leaving his as she slowly, almost lovingly, expelled the last of the smoke from her mouth. She climbed into the bed beside him. He could feel the softness of her skin, the tingle of her long hair against his neck and chest.

She kissed him gently but passionately, with her hands behind his head. He felt her tongue playing enticingly across his lips. She moved her body into position next to him and pressed her pelvis into his. He felt himself rising. She took his penis in his hand and squeezed lightly. He was completely erect. She squeezed again, then gracefully raised her body up and inserted him deep inside her. He felt a magical moist warmth and then exploded almost immediately.

Commander Winters was staggered by the power and the intensity of his fantasy. Somewhere inside him a voice cried for caution and warned of dire consequences if he let this fantasy become too real. But as he lay spent and alone in his suburban home, he pushed his guilt and fears aside and allowed himself the unrivaled bliss of post-orgasmic sleep.

SLOPPY Joe's was an institution in Key West. The favorite bar of Hemingway and his motley crew had managed to adapt quickly to the multifaceted evolution of the city that it had come to symbolize. Many denizens of the old city had been almost apoplectic when the bar had forsaken its historic location downtown and moved into the vast shopping complex surrounding the new marina. But even they grudgingly admitted, after the club reopened in a well-ventilated large room complete with sound stage and excellent acoustics, that the Tiffany lamps, long wooden bars, narrow mirrors from ceiling to floor, and memorabilia from a hundred years in Key West had been tastefully rearranged in a way that retained the spirit of the old bar.

It was altogether fitting that Angie Leatherwood should perform as the headliner at Sloppy Joe's during her brief and infrequent returns to the city of her birth. Troy's glib tongue had originally talked the owner, a transplanted fifty-year-old New Yorker named Tony Palazzo, into giving her an audition when she was still nineteen. Tony had heard her sing for five minutes and then had exclaimed, punctuating his comments with wild hand gestures, "It's not enough that you bring me a black girl who's so beautiful she takes your breath away. No, you bring me one who also sings like a nightingale. Mama mia. Life is not fair. My daughter Carla would kill to sound like that." Tony had become Angie's biggest fan and had unselfishly promoted her career. Angie never forgot what Tony had done for her and always sang at Sloppy Joe's when she was in town. She was like that.

Troy's table was front and center, about ten feet away from the edge of the stage. Nick and Troy were already seated at the small round table and had finished their first drinks when Carol arrived about five minutes before ten-thirty. She apologized and mumbled something about parking in Siberia. As soon as she arrived, Nick pulled out the envelope of images and both men told her that they had found the pictures fascinating. Nick began asking questions about the photographs while Troy summoned a waiter. Nick and Carol were involved in an earnest conversation about the objects in the fissure when the new drinks reached the table. Nick had just mentioned that one of them looked like a modern missile. It was ten thirty-five. The lights flashed off and on to announce that the show was beginning.

Angie Leatherwood was a consummate performer. Like many of the very best entertainers, she never forgot that it was the audience that was the customer, that it was they who both created her image and enhanced her mystique. She began with the title song from her new album, "Memories of Enchanting Nights," and then sang a medley of Whitney Houston songs, according a tribute to that brilliant songstress whose talent had sparked Angie's own desire to sing. Next she showed her versatility by blending a quartet of songs with different beats, a Jamaican reggae, a soft ballad from her first album, *Love Letters*, a nearly perfect Diana Ross imitation from an old Supremes song, "Where Did Our Love Go?" and an emotionally powerful, lilting encomium to her blind father entitled "The Man with Vision."

Thunderous applause greeted the conclusion of each song. Sloppy Joe's was sold out, including all the standing room along the hundred-foot bar. Seven different huge video screens scattered throughout the spacious club brought Angie home to those who were not close to the stage. This was her crowd, these were her friends. A couple of times Angie was almost embarrassed because the clapping and the bravos would not stop. At Troy's table, very little was said during the show. The threesome pointed out songs they particularly liked (Carol's favorite was the Whitney Houston song, "The Greatest Love of All"), but there was no time for conversation. Angie dedicated her penultimate song, "Let Me Take Care of You, Baby," to her "dearest friend" (Nick kicked Troy under the table) and then finished with her most popular cut from *Love Letters*. The audience gave her a standing ovation and hooted noisily for an encore. Nick noticed while he was standing that he was a little woozy from the two strong drinks and was also feeling strangely emotional, possibly because of the subliminal associations created by the love songs that Angie was singing.

Angie returned to the stage. As the noise subsided, her soft and caressing voice could be heard. "You all know that Key West is a very special place for me. It was here that I was raised and went to school. Most of my memories bring me back here." She paused and her eyes scanned the audience. "There are many songs that bring back memories and the emotions that go with them. But of all of them, my favorite is the theme song from the musical *Cats*. So, Key West, this is for you."

There was scattered clapping as the music synthesizers accompanying her played the introduction to "Memories." The audience remained standing as Angie's mellifluous voice launched into the beautiful song. As soon as she began, Nick was instantly transported to the Kennedy Center in Washington,

D.C., in June of 1984, where he was watching a production of *Cats* with his mother and father. He had finally come home to explain to them why he had been unable to return to Harvard after his spring break in Florida. But try as he might, he could not begin to tell the story to his disappointed father and brokenhearted mother. All he could say was, "It was a woman . . ." and then he would fall silent.

It had been a sad reunion. While he was visiting his home in Falls Church, the first malignant polyps had been discovered and removed from his father's colon. The doctors had been optimistic about several more years of life, but they had stressed that colon cancer often recurred and metastasized to other parts of the body. In a long talk with his suddenly frail father, Nick had promised to finish his degree in Miami. But that was little solace to the older man; he had dreamed of seeing his son graduate from Harvard.

The performance of *Cats* at the Kennedy Center had been only mildly entertaining for Nick. In the middle he had found himself wondering how many people in the audience really knew the author of the source material for the songs, this poet T.S. Eliot, who not only admired and enjoyed feline idiosyncrasies, but also once began a poem by describing the evening "spread out against the sky, like a patient aetherized upon a table." But when the old female cat walked to center stage, her beauty faded into wrinkles, and began her song of her "days in the sun," Nick had been moved right along with the entire audience. For reasons he never understood, he had seen Monique singing the song, years in the future. And in Washington he had wept, silent tears hidden quickly from his parents, when the achingly pure soprano voice had reached the climax of the song.

"Touch me . . . It's so easy to leave me . . . all alone with my memories . . . of my days in the sun . . . If you touch me . . . you'll understand what happiness is . . ."

Angie's voice at Sloppy Joe's was not nearly as piercing as that soprano in Washington. But she sang with the same intensity, evoking all the sadness of someone for whom all the joys of life are in the past. The corners of Nick's eyes filled with tears and one of them brimmed out to run down his cheek.

From where Carol was standing, the lights from the stage reflected off Nick's cheek. She saw the tear, the window of vulnerability, and was herself moved in return. For the first time she felt a deep stirring, almost an affection for this distant, solitary, but strangely attractive man.

Ah Carol, how different it might have been if, for once in your life, you had not acted impulsively. If you had just let the man have his moment of loneliness or heartbreak or tenderness or whatever he was feeling, then you might have mentioned it later, at a quieter time, to some advantage. The sharing of this moment might even have eventually been part of the bonding between you. But you had to tap Nick on the shoulder, before the song was through, before he even realized himself that he was tearful, and break his precious communion with his inner self. You were an interloper. Worse, as so often happens, he interpreted your smile as derision, not sympathy, and like a frightened turtle withdrew completely from the evening. It was guaranteed that he would reject as insincere any subsequent overtures of friendship.

Troy missed the interplay between Carol and Nick. So he was quite surprised, when he turned around and sat down after the final applause, to find Nick's shoulders set in an unmistakable pose of hostility. "Wasn't she wonderful, angel?" Troy said to Carol. "And how about you, Professor? Was this the first time you heard her sing?"

Nick nodded. "She was great," he said, almost grudgingly. "And I am thirsty. Can a man get a drink in this place?"

Troy was slightly offended. "Well, pardon us," he said. "So sorry that the entertainment lasted so long." He tried to signal for the waiter. "What's eating him, angel?" he said conversationally to Carol.

Carol shrugged her shoulders. Then, trying to lighten the atmosphere, she leaned toward Nick and tapped him on the forearm on top of the table. "Hey, Nick," she said, "have you been taking angry pills?"

Nick quickly withdrew his arm and grumbled something inaudible as a reply. He turned away from the conversation and saw that Angie was approaching the table. He stood up automatically and both Carol and Troy joined him. "You were fantastic," said Carol, a little too loud, just as soon as Angie was within earshot.

"Thanks . . . Hi," replied Angie, as she walked up to the table and took the chair that Troy had pulled out for her. She spent a few moments graciously acknowledging the praise from people at the nearby tables. Then she sat down and smiled. "You must be Carol Dawson," she said easily, leaning across the table toward the reporter.

Angie was even more beautiful in person than she had been in the picture on the disc jacket. Her coloring was a dark brown, not quite black. Her makeup, including the light pink lipstick, was muted to permit her natural assets, including virtually perfect white teeth on prominent display when she smiled, to draw the attention. But beyond the beauty was the woman herself. No still photograph could do justice to the natural warmth that radiated from Angie. You liked her immediately.

"And you must be Nick Williams," Angie said, extending her hand to Nick. He was still standing, looking uncomfortable and uncertain, although Troy had already seated himself. "Troy has told me so many things about you in the past few days, I feel as if we're already friends. He claims that you've read every novel ever written that's worth reading."

"That's an exaggeration, of course," Nick replied, obviously pleased to be recognized. He seemed to loosen up a little and finally sat down. He started to add another comment but Carol jumped into the conversation and cut him off.

"Did you write that beautiful song about the blind man yourself?" she asked, before Angie had really had time to sit down and collect herself. "It seemed to be a very personal statement."

"Yes," Angie answered Carol pleasantly, without a trace of irritation at Carol's aggressive behavior. "Most of my material comes from other sources, but occasionally I write a song myself. When it is a very special subject for me." She smiled briefly at Troy before continuing. "My father is a remarkable, loving man, blind from birth but with an uncanny comprehension of the world at all levels. Without his patience and guidance, I probably would never have had the courage to sing as a little girl. I was too shy and self-conscious. But my father convinced all of us when we were small that we were somehow special. He told us that God had given each of us something unusual, something uniquely ours, and that one of the great joys of life was discovering and then developing that special talent."

"And that song, 'Let Me Take Care of You, Baby,' did you really write that for Troy?" Nick blurted out his question before Angie had finished her sentence. He thereby destroyed the soft mood created by Angie's loving description of her father. Nick was on the edge of his chair and for some reason seemed agitated and unsettled. Troy wondered again what he had missed in the interaction between Carol and Nick that had caused his friend to become so tense.

Angie looked at Troy. "I guess so," she said with a wistful smile, "although it was originally meant to be a playful tune, a light commentary on the game of love." She stopped for a moment. "But it does talk about a real problem. It's very hard sometimes being a successful women. It interferes—"

"Amen. Amen," Carol interrupted while Angie was still developing her thought. This was one of Carol's favorite subjects and she was ready to pounce on the opportunity. "Most men cannot deal with a woman who is the least bit successful, much less in the spotlight." She looked directly at Nick and then continued, "Even now, in 1994, there are still unwritten rules that must be followed. If you want to have a permanent relationship with a man, there are three don'ts: Don't let him think you're smarter than he is, don't suggest sex first, and, above all, don't make more money than he does. These are the three key areas where their egos are extremely fragile. And if you undermine the ego of any man, even when you're just kidding with him, then it's a lost cause."

"Sounds like you're an expert," Nick replied sarcastically. His hostility was obvious. "I wonder if it ever occurred to any of you liberated females that men are not put off by your success, but rather by the way you handle it. What you accomplish in life does not mean shit at the personal level. Most ambitious, aggressive women I have met (and now he was looking directly at Carol) go out of their way to make male-female relationships into some kind of competition. They will not let the man, even for a moment, have the illusion that he lives in a patriarchal society. I think some of them purposely emasculate—"

"There it is," Carol jumped in triumphantly. She nudged Angie, who was smiling but still a little embarrassed at the rancor in this exchange. "That's the magic word. Whenever a woman wants to argue and not accept as gospel some profound male truth, she is trying to 'castrate' or 'emasculate'—"

"Okay, you guys," Troy interjected firmly, shaking his head. "That's enough. Let's change the subject. I had thought that maybe you two could enjoy an evening together, but not if we're going to start this way."

"The problem," Carol continued, now looking at Angie and ignoring Troy's request, "is that men are frightened. Their hegemony in the Western world is threatened by the emergence of women who aren't willing to be just barefoot and pregnant. Why, when I was at Stanford—"

She stopped and turned when she heard the legs of a chair scraping across the floor. "With all due respect, Miss Leatherwood," Nick was standing up again, holding the chair in his hand, "I believe I will excuse myself. I thoroughly enjoyed your music, but I do not wish to subject you to any more bad manners. I wish you continued good fortune in your career and I hope that someday you can spend some time on the boat with Troy and me." Nick turned to Troy. "I'll see you at the marina at eight o'clock in the morning." Finally he looked at Carol. "You, too, if you still want to go. You can tell us about the wimps at Stanford while we're out in the middle of the Gulf."

Nick did not wait for a reply. He picked up the envelope and walked back through the crowd toward the exit. As he was approaching the door he heard a voice calling him, "Nick. Oh, Nick. Over here." It was Julianne, waving to him from a nearby table full of glasses and ashtrays. She and Corinne and Linda were surrounded by half a dozen men but Julianne was moving them all around and pulling up an empty chair. Nick walked over to her table.

Thirty minutes later Nick was very drunk. The combination of Julianne's occasionally brushing his leg, Corinne's gigantic breasts (they were covered now but he could remember them from Troy's game in the afternoon), and intermittent glimpses of Carol through the cigarette smoke had made him very horny as well. *God damn it, Williams,* he had thought to himself when he first sat down with Julianne's group. *You blew it again. Here you had this perfect chance to charm her. Maybe even score.* But half an hour later, after the drinks, his thoughts were more reminiscent of Aesop's fox. *She's too aggressive for me anyway. Famous. Pushy. Probably too hard underneath. And cold in bed. Another ballbuster.* Yet still he watched her from across the room.

The extra chairs that had been brought in for Angie's performance were cleared away to make room for dancing. A disc jockey orchestrated the rest of the evening from a booth next to the stage; one could dance to a variety of modern musical selections, watch the outrageously overproduced music videos on the big screens, or just talk, for the music was not overwhelmingly loud. Most of the people around Nick were from the marina. During a break in the music, just after Nick had downed another fast tequila, Linda Quinlan leaned across the table. "Come on, Nick," she said, "let us in on your secret. What did you and Troy find yesterday?"

"Nothing special," said Nick, remembering his agreement but surprised to discover that he did indeed want to talk about it.

"Rumor says different," jumped in one of the men at the table. "Everybody knows that you took something to Amanda Winchester this morning. Come on, tell us what it was. Have you found a new treasure ship?"

"Maybe," said Nick, a drunken grin on his face, "just maybe." Another strong impulse pushed him to tell the story and show the pictures, but he stopped himself. "I can't talk about it," was all he would say.

At this moment two burly young men, short-haired Navy types wearing officer's uniforms, were making a beeline for Nick's table from the other side of the floor. One of them was dark, Hispanic. Their approach was confident, even arrogant, and their arrival at the table stopped all the conversation. The white lieutenant put his hand on Julianne's shoulder. "All right, gorgeous," he said boldly, "the Navy is here. Why don't you and your friend there (he nodded at Corinne—Ramirez was standing behind her), come and dance with us?"

Julianne said, "No, thank you," very politely and smiled. Todd looked down at her. He was weaving just a little and it was clear from his eyes that he had been drinking heavily.

"You mean to tell me," he said, "that you would prefer to sit here with these local geeks rather than dance with future admirals?" Julianne felt his hand tighten on her shoulder. She looked around the table and tried to ignore him.

Todd did not like rejection. He took his hand off Julianne's shoulder and pointed at Corinne's breasts. "Christ, Ramirez, you were right. They *are* monsters. Wouldn't you like to snarf one of those?" The two lieutenants laughed crudely. Corinne squirmed self-consciously.

Linda Quinlan's steady boyfriend rose from his chair. Other than Nick, he was the only one of the men at the table who was approximately the same size as Todd and Ramirez. "Look, guys," he said reasonably, "the lady said no very nicely. There is no need to insult her or her friends—"

"Listen to him, Ramirez," Todd interrupted, "this character said we insulted someone. Since when is admiring the size of someone's cachungas an insult?" He chuckled to himself at his cleverness. Ramirez made a sign to leave but Todd waved him off.

The drunken Nick had been ready to explode all night. "Get out of here, asshole," he said, quietly but firmly. He was still sitting down next to Julianne.

"Who are you calling asshole, cocksucker?" the truculent Lieutenant Todd replied. He turned to Ramirez. "I do believe that I am going to be forced to strum the head of this impertinent bastard."

But Nick was ahead of him. Rising swiftly, he uncoiled a vicious punch that struck Todd full in the face and sent him tumbling backwards, into another table covered with drinks. Todd and the table crashed to the floor and Nick went after him. Ramirez pulled Nick off his fellow officer and, when Nick turned and swung at him as well, Ramirez gave Nick a push that caused his unsteady legs to give way. Nick fell back over Julianne and another full table collapsed upon the floor.

From across the room Carol and Angie and Troy could see the fracas and recognize Nick in the middle of it. "Uh oh," Troy said, jumping up to go to his friend's aid. Carol was right behind him. When they reached the opposite side of the room, both club bouncers were already on top of the action. Meanwhile, Nick and Julianne were still trying to get unscrambled on the floor and Todd was slowly rising to his feet.

In the fight, the envelope of photos had been knocked free and a couple of them had fallen partially out. Ramirez had picked the envelope up off the floor and, because of the bright colors, was looking at the pictures. The close-up of the brown missile in the fissure was clearly visible in the top photo. "Hey," he said to the shaken Todd, "look at this. What do you think this is all about?"

Carol acted instantly. She walked past Ramirez, grabbed the envelope and pictures, and before he could say anything, she screamed, "Not again, Nick, no, I don't believe it. How could you be drunk again?" She knelt down beside Nick on the floor and cradled his head in her free hand. "Oh, darling," she said, as he stared at her in complete disbelief, "you promised that you'd stop."

The astonished crowd watched as Carol kissed Nick full on the mouth to prevent his saying anything. Troy was amazed. "Troy," she shouted a moment later, while Nick was trying to gather his wits. "Troy, where are you? Here, give me a hand." Troy rushed up and helped Nick to his feet. "We're taking him home now," she announced to the onlookers. She and Troy each took one arm and the three of them stumbled toward the door of the nightclub. They passed the manager in the doorway. Carol told him that she would come by the next day to settle accounts. She and Troy half carried Nick into the street.

As they walked away from Sloppy Joe's, Carol turned around and saw that part of the crowd had followed them to the door. Ramirez and Todd, the latter still rubbing his cheek, were standing in front of the group with puzzled expressions on their faces. "Where are we taking him, angel?" Troy asked when they were out of earshot. "We don't even know where he parked his car.

"It doesn't matter," Carol replied, "just as long as we are out of sight of the club."

The awkward threesome turned right, down the same alley that ran behind the theater where The Night of the Iguana had finished an hour before. Just past the theater there was a small vacant lot on the left. Carol stopped the trio at the edge of the lot, opposite a grove of trees, and looked back to make certain they were not being followed. She heaved a sigh and loosened her grip on Nick. She unconsciously fanned her sweating face with the envelope she had recovered from Ramirez.

Nick was now almost coherent. "I had no idea," he mumbled to Carol, pulling his arm free from Troy and trying to embrace her, "that you felt that way about me."

"I don't," Carol said emphatically. She pushed his arms away and back-pedaled toward the vacant lot. Nick didn't understand and continued his approach. "Stop," she shouted angrily at him. "Stop, you drunken bastard."

She tried to fend off his advance with her hands. But he kept coming. Just before Troy moved up to restrain him, Carol slapped Nick hard in the face with the hand that was not holding the envelope. Momentarily startled, Nick lost his footing and fell into the grass on his stomach.

Still fuming, Carol bent down beside him and forcefully rolled him over on his back. "Don't you ever, *ever*, use physical force with me," she shouted at Nick. "Not under *any* circumstances." She dropped the envelope on Nick's stomach and stood up quickly. She looked at Troy, shook her head in disgust, and stalked off down the alley.

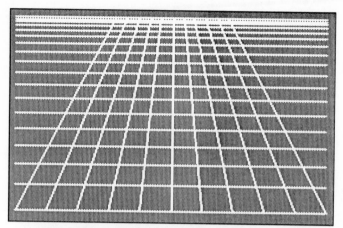

ASSEMBLY
AND TEST

UNDER the scanning electron microscope they look like tightly coiled springs with a small tail. When they are placed in water or some other liquid, the springs seem to stretch out and cilialike appendages extend a few angstroms out from the tail to provide motility.

There are millions of them concentrated in a mixture the size of a tiny drop of water and they are being carefully checked by a laser device that is also counting and sorting them as it illuminates microscopic portions of the mixture. When the count is completed, the smaller division of the separated mixture is sluiced out of the metal receptacle and down a channel into another liquid, this one emerald green in color, that is contained in a bottle-shaped beaker. The springs spread out and follow random paths in wandering around the beaker.

External mechanisms regularly churn the emerald green liquid. Around the inside of the beaker, tiny sensors register the temperature, pressure, and exact chemical and electrical characteristics of the fluid. Some parameter is not absolutely perfect. A small valve opens a port in the base of the beaker and a new chemical is injected into the green solution. Continuous measurements monitor the diffusion of this additional material. At length the fluid is properly altered and a new equilibrium is reached.

Everything is now ready. From above several thousand small pellets are dropped into the container. Some of these pellets float on the surface but most sink to variable depths in the liquid. Embedded in each of the pellets is a complicated engineering construction on an amazingly miniaturized scale. The external surface of the pellets contains sensors that scan the nearby region of the liquid for the springlike objects. A high-frequency transmitter housed next to the sensors directs a call to the springs and attracts them to the neighborhood. Clusters of springs develop around each pellet.

Now, one at a time, these springs are harvested by small instruments inside the spongy outer section of the pellet and then loaded in carriers that are electrically fired toward the central cavity of the pellet. Within that cavity sits a single black, amorphous spot, its exterior constantly changing shape as its opaque material shifts around to follow unknown stimuli. This spot is surrounded by a yellow goo that fills the remainder of the cavity.

The first spring slips out of its carrier, then locates and penetrates the spot. The spring can be seen for an instant moving toward the center. However, it is broken up and destroyed within milliseconds. Other springs are fired into the cavity at regular intervals and all try, after penetration, to reach some special region in the spot. Finally one of the procession succeeds and the spot changes color to bright red. In rapid succession, some enzyme in the spongy outer section of the pellet is dumped into the yellow goo, turning its color a little toward green, and all the rest of the springs disappear, apparently absorbed by the pellet structure. The entire pellet itself next elongates and extends a miniature propulsion system into the emerald liquid. After carefully steering around the many hazards, it then joins the queue of fertilized pellets moving, one by one, through a round diaphanous membrane in the bottom of the beaker.

The fluid dense with pellets speeds along a narrow tube until it reaches a partially closed container approximately the size of the beaker. Inside this translucent jar, a mechanical, spoonlike object digs into the stream of liquid flowing through and plucks out the pellets. They are lifted up and then suspended momentarily around the passing fluid in a heavy gas enclosed by the jar. Within moments each of the pellets splits and their carapaces apparently dissolve, leaving visible inside the jar an array of the little red spots surrounded by the off-yellow goo and suspended in an invisible gas.

The goo extends itself slowly throughout the jar above the flowing fluid until all the open areas between the red spots are filled. When the emerald stream below drops to a trickle and then disappears altogether, the goo hardens into a gelatin and fills the ports where the fluid once entered and departed. Within the jar are several thousand red spots embedded in the yellow-green gelatin. The spots undergo no visible change throughout this process.

Time passes. Activity in the jar ceases. Occasionally mechanical probes to test the stability of the gelatin are inserted into the jar at the old fluid ports. At last the translucent jar is removed from its storage location by what looks like a robotic forklift. It is placed on a moving belt that now carries it, along with several dozen other jars containing different kinds of objects (blue pencils, purple stars, and red boxes can all be seen) also suspended in yellow-green gelatin, to a vast circular oven almost an inch in diameter. Here all the jars are carefully baked together. Inside the oven, the molecules of the jar material immediately evaporate. Next a pair of disembodied manipulator hands wrap an incredibly thin blanket of connective filaments around all the gelatinous structures. After some time this ensemble unit is then pulled automatically out of the oven and packaged inside a gold metallic envelope whose several layers are designed to provide all the remaining environmental protection.

* * *

The hypergolic propellants mix and burst instantly into flame, pouring fire out the rocket nozzle. The slender vehicle rises, slowly at first, but later with astonishing speed. Before reaching the zenith of its flight, the rocket stage underneath the strange paraboloid payload falls away and tiny motors ignite on the underside of the flying boomerang. At the apex of the trajectory, the entire package suddenly explodes and apparently disintegrates. Hundreds of pieces of the original payload fall toward the surface of the planet in seemingly random directions.

Closer inspection reveals that each individual piece resulting from the explosion is made of a gold metallic material encased in plastic. A small sensor/propulsion package is attached to the plastic; it supplies needed vernier corrections during the descent after the controlled explosion. The plastic debris falls upon a strange, hybrid planet, obviously artificial judging by the wide variety of incongruous surfaces and cloud groupings that can be recognized from an altitude of tens of miles. There are scattered liquid lakes of different hues plus discontinuous surface topography with regions of desert and grasslands as well as barren mountains and canyons. A connected quarter of the planet is covered with clouds. The clouds are here white and fleecy, there brown and thick. Some of the clouds are active, building and changing with hints of turbulence. Other parts of the cloudy region are static, small wisps of white stretching without change across the sky.

One of the plastic vehicles plunges through a misty blue cloudbank into an emerald sea. The plastic is left on the surface, but the encased gold metallic object sinks thirty feet to the floor of the ocean. For a day or two there is no discernible change in its appearance. Then a protrusion begins to form in its north polar region, on the top of the golden sphere as it sits on the ocean floor. The growth expands slowly, until the spherical shape appears to have a large carbuncle on its top. A metamorphsis now takes place. On the outside of the protrusion, the hard metal surface softens and begins to resemble an organic membrane. Although the membrane is thick and dense, it occasionally bulges, suggesting some motion on the other side of its golden barrier.

Eventually a thin black rod, a probe of some kind, thrusts through the surface into the emerald ocean. A second probe becomes visible, then a third, both long black rods like the first one, but each equipped with strikingly different apparatus scattered along the length of the rod. Something larger pushes against the membrane, once, twice, then finally breaking through. What a strange contraption! It's an aerodynamic shape about three inches long, in two separate segments with a joint between them. The forebody is a nosecone; the afterbody is long and slender and tapers to a point. In addition to the three probes on the front of its forebody, it has four other furlable appendages or arms, two connected to the side of each segment.

It swims over to a nearby underwater plant with its arms stored next to its smooth body. There it unfurls the multifaceted appendages and begins to examine the plant. An astonishing array of tiny instruments studies the plant for a few moments and then the entity moves away. The same procedure is repeated with each plant encountered. Eventually the thing finds a plant that it "likes" and its pincers remove a major leaf. The leaf is neatly folded into a smaller volume and is then carried back to the object with the golden membrane.

The strange forager is joined by a partner, a carbon copy of itself, and by two fat fish with multiple arms and legs. The latter pair scuttle off to the side and begin modifying the ocean floor. Days pass. The things with the probes work ceaselessly, bringing more and more varieties of plant and animal life back to the home base. The legged fish meanwhile have constructed, out of available sand, rocks, shells, and living creatures, almost a thousand tiny, sealed rectangular homes on the ocean floor. These fish entities too work without break. Their next task is to transport each of the red spots, one at a time, from the golden cradle to their new houses.

If a microscope were available, it would show that some structure was already developing inside the red spots, giving them definition and distinction, by the time of their initial transport. But they are still very, very small. Once the red spots and their gelatin protection are carefully implanted inside their tiny houses, the foragers make routine stops on each trip to deposit a portion of their harvest. At the same time, the fish with legs, the architects and builders of the rectangular houses, begin working on transparent, igloolike homes for the embryos of another species.

A year later moonlight falls on the emerald lake. Several hundred eager, excited, wriggling necks, some royal blue and some pale blue, struggle upward to find the moon. Their heads pivot to face all directions and maybe two dozen separate indentations and orifices can be seen in each face. The necks crane this way, then that way. The silent serpents are searching for something.

From the direction of the moon a bizarre ship approaches on the water. It is large compared to the young serpents, its twin towers standing about eight feet out of the water and about six feet above, on the average, a squarish platform fifteen feet on a side that forms the bottom of the boat. The top surface of this platform is irregular, undulating, and cratered. The platform floats smoothly upon the water.

The ship comes into the middle of the serpents and stops. The serpents divide into two groups according to the color of their necks and then line up on either side of the ship in very orderly rows and columns. A single musical note, a B-flat with a flautish timbre, comes from the ship. Quickly the note is repeated up and down the rows and columns by each of the serpents on the two sides of the boat. Then a second note issues forth from the ship, also sounding like a flute, and the process repeats itself. For hours the music lesson continues, covering a range of both notes and chords, until some of the serpents on each side lose their voices. The exercise concludes with an attempted ensemble performance by the royal bluenecked serpents, but the result is a painful cacophony.

Inside the ship, every note, every movement, every response by the juvenile serpents to the music lesson is carefully monitored and recorded. The ingenious engineering design of the boat is based upon the key controlling elements of the original cradle. However, although segments of gold metallic material (as well as the long black rods and even portions of the fat fish with legs) appear in the computer that runs the ship, the primary constituents of its mass are derived from great quantities of local rock and organic matter taken from the floor of the emerald lake. The ship is the quintessential music teacher, a virtually perfect synthesizer equipped with microprocessors that not only store all the responses of the pupils, but also contain software that will allow experimentation with a range of individualized methods of teaching.

But this sophisticated robot, engineered by the artificial intelligence packed around the serpent zygotes and made almost entirely of chemical compounds extracted from material found in the neighborhood of the landing point, is itself being watched and studied from afar by test engineers. The current test is in its earliest stages and is progressing splendidly. This is the third different configuration tried for the music teacher, the hardest part of the design of the cradle that will carry the serpent zygotes back to Canthor. The first was an abysmal failure; the embryos developed into adolescents all right, but the teacher was never able to instruct them well enough that they could sing the mating song and reproduce. The second design was better; it was able to teach the serpents to perform the courtship symphony and a new generation of the species was produced. However, this next group of adult serpents was not able subsequently to teach their progeny to sing.

The best of the bioengineering personnel in the Colony were brought in to study this problem. After pouring over quadrillions of bits of accumulated data associated with the development of the serpents and other related species, they found a curious correlation between the degree of nurturing provided by the parent and the resulting ability of that infant, upon reaching maturity, to teach its own offspring. The artificial intelligence package responsible for the first six months of serpent life was then redesigned to include a surrogate mother whose only purpose was to hold and cuddle the fledgling serpents at regular intervals. Subsystem tests proved successful; this slight alteration of the early nurturing protocol produced adult serpents that were able to teach their children to sing.

This demonstration test lasts for more than four millicycles. At the end of the period, the test is declared an unqualified success. A strong, creative serpent population nearing twenty-five thousand fills the artificial lake. Limitations to future growth are only test related. Eventually the test survivors are transported to another locale in the Zoo Complex and the Canthorean serpents are added to the list of species ready for zygote repatriation.

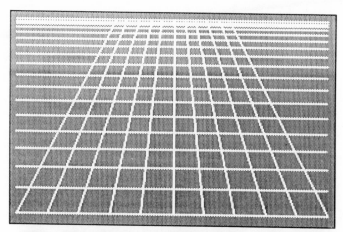

SATURDAY

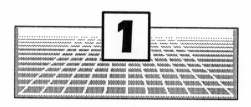

THE full moon rises over the placid ocean. Troy stares at the moon-
beams, watching them shimmer on the quiet water. Angie appears and
stands in the water in front of him. She is wearing a skintight white
bathing suit, one piece, and is submerged from the waist down.

She beckons to him and he walks across the damp sand toward the water.
He is barefoot and is also wearing a white bathing suit. The water is surprisingly
warm. Angie begins to sing. Her magnificent voice enfolds him as Troy draws
nearer to her in the light surf.

They touch and kiss. She pulls away and gives him a smile of encour-
agement. Troy feels himself becoming aroused. Suddenly a siren pierces the
air, destroying the calm of the night. Instantly the sea becomes choppy, agitated, full of whitecaps. Troy turns around, alarmed, and glances at the shore.
He sees nothing special. He looks back at the ocean. Angie has disappeared.
Out in the distance, near the horizon, Troy thinks he sees the beginning of
a tidal wave. The siren shrieks again and Troy sees a large shapeless mass
riding a nearby wave in the moonlight.

He goes toward the object. The tidal wave is now defined in the distance,
filling half his dream screen. The bulky object nearby is a black body dressed
in a red muscle shirt and bluejeans. The siren grows louder. Troy rolls the
body over and looks at the face. It is his brother, Jamie.

Troy Jefferson bolted upright in bed, his heart pounding furiously, his
mind making the transition from the dream world to reality. Outside his duplex
apartment a siren raged. He could tell from the frequency change that the
police car or ambulance had just sped past his front door. He shook himself
and crawled out of bed. The digital clock on the end table read 3:03.

Troy walked to the kitchen. He went to the refrigerator and poured himself
a glass of grapefruit juice. He listened to the siren in the distance until it faded
away altogether. Then he started back to the small second bedroom where he

slept. In the hallway he was stopped by the sound of another siren, this one even louder, that seemed to be coming toward him. For a few seconds he thought the siren was just outside his front door and he recalled, vividly, another siren in the middle of another night. His heart began to pound anew. "Jamie," Troy said to himself almost involuntarily, "Jamie. Why did you have to die?"

Troy could still see the events of that evening with perfect clarity. Nothing in the first tableau had faded even a little. The beginning memory was the three of them, Jamie, Troy, and their mother, sitting silently at the dinner table, eating fried chicken and mashed potatoes. Jamie had just arrived home from Gainesville for spring break that afternoon and had spent almost an hour, before they had sat down to eat, regaling his fifteen-year-old brother with stories of football and university life. Jamie had been Troy's idol throughout his childhood. Handsome, intelligent, and articulate, Jamie had also been blessed with incredible physical gifts. As a result, he had been the starting halfback for the Florida Gators in his sophomore year and was being touted as a potential All-American for the following season. Troy had bitterly missed Jamie when he had first gone away to the university, but in the intervening eighteen months he had learned to accept his absence and to look forward to his brother's holiday visits.

"So, bro," Jamie had said with a smile, when he finished his dinner and pushed his plate away, "what about you? You've finished another quarter already. Did you make the grades of a future astronaut?"

"I did okay," Troy had replied, hiding his pride. "I made a B plus in Social Studies because my teacher thought I had taken an anti-American position in my paper on the Panama Canal."

"I guess an occasional B plus is acceptable," Jamie had laughed, his affection for his younger brother clearly showing. "But I bet Burford didn't make many B's when he was in the ninth grade."

Whenever Troy recalled the fateful evening that his brother was killed, he always remembered the mention of Guion Burford, the first American black astronaut. Most of the time his memory, because it was so painful to proceed immediately to the terrible recollection of his dying brother in his arms, would choose to digress to a happier time, to a remembrance of his brother Jamie that was almost as vivid as the death scene, but was happy and reinforcing instead of being gut wrenching and depressing.

During the summer before his death, on a hot, humid day in late August, Jamie Jefferson had arranged a third personal meeting with his football coach at Florida to request permission to skip practice for two days. He wanted to take his little brother, Troy, to see the launch of the space shuttle. In the first two meetings, the coach had vigorously opposed Jamie's taking the time away from the important workouts, but he had stopped short of denying the request.

"You still don't understand, coach," Jamie had said firmly at the start of their third and final meeting on the subject. "My little brother has no father. And he's a genius at math and science. He blows the top off those standardized aptitude tests. He needs a role model. He needs to know that blacks can do something significant other than sports." The coach had eventually relented and given Jamie permission, but only because he had figured out that Jamie was going to go under any circumstances.

Jamie had driven his battered Chevrolet nonstop across Florida, picked up his brother in Miami, and continued northward without sleeping for another four hours to Cocoa Beach. They had arrived in the middle of the night. Jamie, by now exhausted, parked the car in a beach access zone next to a seven-story condominium along the nicest part of the beach. "All right, little brother," he had said, "now get some sleep."

But Troy had not been able to sleep. He had been too excited thinking about the launch scheduled the next evening, the eighth shuttle launch in all, the first one that had ever occurred at night. He had been reading everything he could find about astronaut Burford and the plans for the mission. He kept imagining that it was the future and that he, Troy Jefferson, was an astronaut about to be launched into space. After all, Burford was living proof that it could indeed be done, that a black American could attain the upper echelons of society and become a popular hero on the basis of his intelligence, personality, and hard work.

At sunrise Troy had crawled out of the car and walked the few yards to the beach. It was very quiet. Troy's company was limited to a few walkers and joggers plus a couple of those bizarre sand crabs, whose eyes wavered back and forth at the end of peculiar stalks as they raced sideways into their holes in the sand. To the north Troy could see some of the launch pads for the unmanned rockets at Cape Canaveral Air Force Base, but in his mind's eye he saw them as the launching apparatus for the shuttle. He wondered what astronaut Burford was doing at that very moment. What was he eating for breakfast? Was he with his family or with the astronaut crew?

Jamie had awakened around noon and the brothers had spent the early afternoon on the beach together, laughing and playing in the surf. Then they picked up some hamburgers and drove the final half hour to the Kennedy Space Center. Jamie had strongarmed an avid Gator booster, an aerospace executive who lived in Melbourne, for tickets to the VIP viewing area. They arrived there just before nightfall. Four miles away, the impressive shuttle launch configuration, consisting of the orbiter mounted on top of an orange external tank with two solid rocket boosters on the side, stood erect against its launching tower as the final countdown began.

No observing experience in Troy's life would ever come close to rivaling his watching the space shuttle blast off that night. As he listened to the countdown being announced over the loudspeakers in the VIP area, he was eager and anticipant, but not yet in awe. The moment the engines ignited, however, filling the Florida night with reddish-orange flame and thick white clouds of billowing smoke, Troy's eyes nearly popped out of his head. But it was the combination of his seeing the giant spaceship, slowly and majestically lifting itself into the heavens riding a long slender flame, and his hearing the astonishing sound, a constant roar punctuated with unexplained pops (which at only four miles away still arrived twenty or so seconds behind the sight of the engine ignition), that really caused the goose bumps to break out on his skin, the tears to come to his eyes, and the tingle to spread through his body. Troy's intense emotional excitement lasted well over a minute. He stood beside his brother Jamie, tightly holding his hand, his back arched as he strained to follow the flame rising higher and higher and then finally disappearing in the night sky above him.

After the launch they slept again in the car. Jamie then dropped Troy at the bus station in Orlando and headed back to Gainesville for football practice. Young Troy felt that he was a new person, that he had been transformed by his experience. In the week that followed he obsessively followed the flight. Burford became his hero, his new idol. During the first two quarters of the following year, he applied himself avidly to his schoolwork. He had a goal. He was going to be an astronaut.

Little did Troy know that on a March night only seven months later he would have another experience, this one devastating and deeply disturbing, that would completely overshadow the thrill he had felt at the shuttle launch. On that later March evening, his brother Jamie would stop by his room before leaving the house around eight o'clock. "I'm going over to Maria's, bro," Jamie would say. "We'll probably take in a movie."

Maria Alvarez was eighteen and still a senior in high school. She had been Jamie's steady girl for a couple of years. She lived in Little Havana together with her Cuban family and eight siblings.

Troy had given his brother a hug. "I'm glad you're here, Jamie. There are so many things that I want to show you. I made you a set of headphones in school—"

"I want to see everything," his brother had interrupted him. "But tomorrow, first thing in the morning. Now don't stay up too late. Astronauts need plenty of sleep so they can be alert." Jamie had smiled and walked out of Troy's room. It was the last thing Troy would ever hear him say.

Troy never could remember what he had heard first when he had awakened in the middle of that night. His mother's wild wail had mixed with the screech of the nearby sirens to create an imbroglio of sound that was unforgettable and terrifying. Troy had raced to the door and into the front yard wearing only his pajama bottoms. The sound of the ambulance siren was drawing closer. His mother was at the end of the short walkway in front of the house, bending down over a dark body spread partly in the street in front of Jamie's Chevrolet and partly in their yard. Three policemen and half a dozen curious bystanders were huddled around his distraught mother.

"Somehow," he heard one of the policemen say as Troy, in a panic, tried to figure out what was happening, "he managed to drive home. It's incredible after all the blood he lost. He must have been hit four times in the stomach . . ."

His mother's cry intensified again and, at that moment, Troy put all the pieces together and recognized the body lying on its back. A chill went through him, he gasped, and then Troy fell on his knees beside his brother's head.

Jamie was struggling for breath. His eyes were open but they did not seem to be focusing on anything.

Troy cradled Jamie's head in his hands. He looked down at his brother's stomach. His red shirt was awash in blood that seemed to be flowing in a continuous stream from an area just above the genitals. Blood was on Jamie's jeans, on the ground, everywhere. Troy felt himself gag, then retch involuntarily. Nothing came up. Hot tears filled his eyes.

"We think it was a gang shooting, Mrs. Jefferson," the policeman droned on. "Probably some kind of a mistake. Everybody knows that Jamie wasn't mixed up with that kind of crowd." Reporters had arrived. Lights were flashing from cameras. More sirens approached.

Jamie's eyes went blank. There was no sign of breathing. Troy pulled his brother's head to his chest. He instinctively knew that Jamie was dead. He began to sob uncontrollably. "No," he mumbled. "No. Not my brother. Not Jamie. He never hurt anybody."

Someone tried to comfort him, to pat him on the shoulder. Troy shrugged them off violently. "Leave me alone," he shouted between sobs. "He was my brother. He was my only brother." After a couple of moments, Troy tenderly placed Jamie's head back down on the ground. He then collapsed in total despair beside him.

At almost three-thirty in the morning some ten years later, in March of 1994, Troy Jefferson would be at home, alone in his duplex, awake with the memory of that terrible moment when Jamie had died. He would feel anew the heartbreak of that loss. And he would realize again, very clearly, that most of his adolescent dreams had died with his brother, that he had forsaken his dreams of college and being an astronaut because they were inextricably coupled with his memory of Jamie.

Somehow he had stumbled through high school in the three years that had followed Jamie's death. But it had taken the combined efforts of his mother and the school and the city authorities to keep Troy from abandoning school altogether. Then, as soon as he had graduated, he had left Miami. Or rather, ran away. Away from what had happened and what might have been. For over two years he then wandered in a desultory manner throughout North America, a young, solitary black man, bereft of love and friendship, looking for something to overcome the feeling of emptiness that was his constant companion.

So I finally came to Key West, Troy would think, years later, as he settled back in his bed in the middle of the morning for a couple more hours of sleep. *And for some reason made myself a home. Maybe it was just time. Or maybe I had learned enough to know that life goes on. But somehow, although the wound has never healed, I got past Jamie. And found the lost Troy. Or so I hope.*

The dream that had been interrupted by the siren suddenly came back into his mind. Angie was beautiful in the moonlight in her white bathing suit. *And now for some unfinished business,* Troy laughed to himself, concentrating on the image of Angie as he returned to sleep.

"**G**OOD morning, angel," Troy said with a grand smile as Carol approached the *Florida Queen*. "Ready to do some fishing?" He hopped out of the boat and shouted at Nick, who was around at the back on the other side of the canopy. "She's here, Professor," he hollered. "I'm going out to the parking lot to get her stuff." Carol gave Troy the keys to her car and he took off in the direction of the marina office.

Carol paced for a few moments on the jetty before Nick emerged from behind the canopy. "Come on down on the boat," he said, scowling a little as he wiped some heavy dredging chain with a dark cloth. Nick felt terrible. He had a nasty hangover. And he was still bothered by the events of the night before. Carol didn't say anything at first. Nick stopped cleaning the chain and waited for her to speak.

"I don't know exactly how to say this," she began in a firm but pleasant voice, "but it's important to me that I say it before I get on the boat." Carol cleared her throat. "Nick," she said deliberately, "I don't want to dive with you today. I want to dive with Troy."

Nick gave her a quizzical look. He was standing in the sun and his head was aching. "But Troy—" he began.

"I know what you're going to say," she interrupted him. "He doesn't have much experience and it could be a dangerous dive." She stared directly at Nick. "That doesn't matter to me. I have enough diving experience for both of us. I prefer to dive with Troy." She waited a few seconds. "Now if you're not willing—"

This time it was Nick who interrupted Carol. "All right, all right," he said, turning away. He was surprised to find that he was both hurt and angry. *This woman is still pissed,* he said to himself. *And I thought maybe . . .* Nick walked away from Carol and went back on the other side of the canopy to finish preparing the small rented salvage crane he and Troy had installed the night before. Since they had used this old equipment several times on other excursions, the installation had been straightforward and without major problems.

Carol climbed onto the boat and put her copy of the photos on top of the counter next to the steering wheel. "Where's the trident?" she called to Nick. "I thought I'd take another look at it this morning."

"Bottom left drawer, under the nav equipment," was his swift and sharp reply. She took the gray bag out of the drawer, opened it, and pulled out the golden trident. She held it by the long middle rod. It felt funny for some reason. Carol put the object back in the bag and pulled it out a second time. Again she held the heavy trident in her hands. It still didn't feel right. Carol remembered grasping the rod underneath the overhang in the water and wrapping her hand slowly around the central rod. *That's it,* she said to herself. *It's thicker.*

She turned the object over in her hands. *What's the matter with me?* she thought. *Have I lost my mind? How could it be thicker?* She examined it one more time with great care. This time she thought that the individual tines of the fork had lengthened and that she could detect a perceptible increase in the overall weight. *Good grief. Can this be possible?* she wondered.

Carol pulled out the photos she had brought along. All the images of the trident that she had with her had been taken underwater. But she was certain that she could discern two subtle changes since it was first photographed. The axis rod did appear to be thicker and the tines of the fork did indeed look longer.

"Nick," she said in a loud voice. "Nick, can you come here?"

"I'm right in the middle of something," an unfriendly voice responded from the other side of the canopy. "Is it important?"

"No. I mean yes," Carol answered. "But it can wait until your first available moment."

Carol's mind was racing. *There are only two possibilites,* she said to herself with logical precision, *either it has changed or it hasn't. If it hasn't changed, then I must be spooked. For it definitely seems thicker. But how could it change? Either on its own or someone changed it. But who? Nick? But how could* he . . . ?

Nick came up to her. "Yes?" he said in a distant, almost hostile tone. He was obviously annoyed.

Carol handed him the trident. "Well?" she said, smiling and looking at him expectantly.

"Well, what?" he answered, totally confused by what was happening and still angry about the earlier interaction.

"Can you tell the difference?" Carol continued, nodding at the trident in his hand.

Nick turned it upside down as she had done. The sunlight glinted off the golden surface and hurt his eyes. He squinted. Then he switched the object from hand to hand and looked at it from many different angles. "I think I'm lost," Nick said at length. "Are you trying to tell me that there's some change in this thing?"

He held it out between them. "Yes," she said. "Can't you feel it? The central rod's thicker than it was on Thursday and the tines or individual elements of that fork on one end are a little longer. And don't you think the whole thing is heavier?"

Nick's headache continued to throb. He looked back and forth between the trident and Carol. As far as he could tell, the object had not changed. "No, I don't," he said. "It seems the same to me."

"You're just being difficult," Carol persisted, grabbing the trident back. "Here, look at the pictures. Check out the length of the fork there compared to the overall rod and then look at it now. It's different."

There was something in Carol's general attitude that really irritated Nick. She always seemed to assume that she was right and everyone else was wrong. "This is absurd," Nick nearly shouted in reply, "and I have a lot of work to do." He paused for a moment and then continued. "How the hell could it change? It's a metal object, for Christ's sake. What do you think? That somehow it *grew*? Shit."

He shook his head and started to walk away. After a couple of steps, he turned around. "You can't trust the pictures anyway," he said in more measured tones. "Underwater photos always distort the objects . . ."

Troy was approaching with both the cart and Carol's equipment. He could tell from the body positions, even without hearing the words, that his two boatmates were at it again. "My, my," he said as he walked up, "I can't leave you two alone for a minute. What are you fighting about this morning, Professor?"

"This supposedly intelligent reporter friend of yours," Nick replied, looking at Carol and speaking in a patronizing manner, "insists that our trident has changed shape. Overnight I guess. Although she has not yet begun to explain how. Will you please, since she won't believe me, explain to her about the index of refraction or whatever it is that fouls up underwater pictures."

Carol appealed to Troy. "But it has changed. Honest. I remember clearly what it felt like at first and now it feels different."

Troy was unloading the cart and putting the ocean telescope system on the *Florida Queen*. "Angel," Troy said, stopping to check the trident that she was extending toward him with both hands, "I can't tell whether it has changed or not, but I can tell you one thing. You were very excited when you found it the first time and you were also underwater. With that combination I wouldn't trust my own memory of how something felt."

Carol looked at the two men. She was going to pursue the discussion but Nick abruptly changed the subject. "Did you know, Mr. Jefferson, that our client Miss Dawson has requested your services as a diving partner today? She doesn't want to dive with me." His tone was now acerbic.

Troy looked at Carol with surprise. "That's real nice, angel," he said quietly, "but Nick is really the expert. I'm just a little more than a beginner."

"I know that," Carol responded brusquely, still chafing from the outcome of the previous conversation. "But I want to dive with someone I can trust. Someone who behaves responsibly. I know enough about diving for both of us."

Nick gave Carol an angry look and then turned and walked away. He was pissed. "Come on, Jefferson," he said. "I've already agreed to let Miss High and Mighty have her way. *This* time. Let's get the boat ready and finish setting up that telescope thing of hers again."

"My father finally divorced my mother when I was ten," Carol was saying to Troy. They were sitting together in the deck chairs at the front of the boat. After they had gone over the procedures for the dive a couple of times, Carol had mentioned something about her first boating experience, a birthday on a fishing boat with her father when she was six, and the two of them had moved comfortably into a discussion of their childhood. "The breakup was awful." She handed the can of Coke back to Troy. "I think you might have been luckier, in some ways, never to have known your father."

"I doubt it," Troy replied seriously. "From my earliest days, I resented the fact that some of the kids had two parents. My brother, Jamie, tried to help, of course, but there was only so much he could do. I purposely chose friends who had fathers living at home." He laughed. "I remember one dark black kid named Willie Adams. His dad was at home all right, but he was an embarrassment to the family. He was an older man, nearing sixty at the time, and he didn't work. He just sat on the front porch in his rocking chair all day and drank beer.

"Whenever I went over to Willie's house to play, I would always find some excuse to spend a little time on the porch sitting next to Mr. Adams. Willie would fidget uncomfortably, unable to understand why I wanted to listen to his father tell his old, supposedly boring stories. Mr. Adams had been in the Korean War and he loved to tell about his friends and the battles and, particularly, the Korean women and what he called their tricks.

"Anyway, you could always tell when Mr. Adams was about to start one of his stories. His eyes would begin to stare in front of him, as if he were looking intently at something far off in the distance, and he would say, as much to himself as anybody, 'Tell the truth, Baby Ruth.' Then he would recite the story, almost as if he were quoting from a written book, 'We had driven the North Koreans back to the Yalu and our battalion commander told us they were ready to surrender,' he would say. 'We were feeling good, talking about what we were all going to do when we got back to the States. But then the great yellow horde poured out of China . . .' "

Troy stopped. He stared out at the ocean. It was easy for Carol to see him as a young boy, sitting on a porch with his embarrassed friend Willie and listening to stories told by a man who lived hopelessly in the past but who, nevertheless, represented the father that Troy had never had. She leaned over to Troy and touched his forearm. "It makes a pretty picture," she said. "You probably never knew how happy you made that man by listening to his stories."

Around on the other side of the canopy, Nick Williams was sitting by himself in another deck chair. He was reading *Madame Bovary* and trying without success to ignore both his residual hangover and the scattered tidbits of conversation he was overhearing. He had programmed the navigation system to return automatically to the dive site from Thursday, so there was nothing else he really needed to do to pilot the boat. Nick almost certainly would have enjoyed sharing the conversation with Carol and Troy, but after his earlier confrontation with her, in which he felt she had made it clear that she didn't want to associate with him, he was not about to join them. It was now necessary that he ignore her. Otherwise she would conclude that he was just another wimp.

And besides, he liked his book. He was reading the part where Emma Bovary gives herself over completely to the affair with Rudolph Boulanger. Nick could see Emma sneaking away from her house in the small French provincial village and racing across the fields into the arms of her lover. Most of the time in the past, whenever Nick had read a novel about a beautiful, dark heroine, he had pictured Monique. But interestingly enough, the Emma Bovary that he was envisioning while he was reading on the boat was Carol Dawson. And more than once that morning, when Nick had read Flaubert's descriptions of the passions of Emma and Rudolph, he had imagined himself in the role of the bachelor from the French landed gentry making love to Emma/Carol.

The automatic navigation system that guided the boat while Nick was reading consisted of a simple transmitter/receiver combination and a small miniprocessor. Taking advantage of a worldwide set of synchronous satellites, software in the processor established the boat's location very precisely and then followed a preprogrammed steering algorithm to the desired final site. Along the way, the two-way link with the satellite overhead provided the necessary information to update the path through the ocean.

When the *Florida Queen* was within a mile of the dive site, the nav system sounded a tone. Nick then went to the controls and changed to manual guidance. Carol and Troy rose from their chairs. "Remember," she said, "the primary purpose of our dive is to photograph and salvage whatever it was that we saw down in that fissure on Thursday. If we have enough time afterward, we will go back to the overhang where we found the trident."

Carol walked over and switched on the monitor attached to the ocean telescope. She was standing only a few feet away from Nick. They had not exchanged any words since right after the boat left Key West. "Good luck," he said quietly.

She looked at him to see whether he was serious or was being sarcastic. She couldn't tell. "Thank you," she said evenly.

Troy joined Carol at the monitor. She pulled the photographs out of the envelope so they could be used to define the exact spot to anchor. For a couple of minutes she issued instructions to Nick, based on what she was seeing from the telescope, commanding small corrections to the boat's position. At last the ocean floor underneath them looked almost exactly as it had on Thursday when they had seen the whales. With one major difference.

"Now where's that hole in the reef?" Troy said innocently. "I don't seem to be able to find it on the monitor."

Carol's heart was speeding as she glanced back and forth from the telescope screen to the photographs. *Where is that fissure?* she thought, *It can't have disappeared.* The boat drifted away from the dive site and Nick steered it back. This time Troy dropped the anchor overboard. But Carol still could not see any sign of the fissure. She could not understand it.

"Nick," she said finally, "could you give us a hand? We were down there together and we both saw the hole. Are Troy and I just confused in some way?"

Nick came over from the steering wheel under the canopy and stared into the monitor. He too was puzzled. But he thought he saw other things on the bottom of ocean that also looked a little different. "I don't see the hole either," he said, "but maybe it's just the lighting. We were here in the afternoon last time and now it's ten in the morning."

Troy turned to Carol. "Maybe Nick ought to dive with you. He was there before, has seen the fissure, and knows how to find the overhang. Everything I know is from the pictures."

"No," said Carol quickly. "I want to dive with you. Nick's probably right. We just can't see the fissure because of the different lighting." She picked up her underwater camera and walked around the canopy toward the back of the boat. "Let's get going," she said. "We'll do just fine."

Troy gave Nick a silent shrug, as if to say "I tried," and followed her a few moments later.

" **B** UT Richard," Ramirez said, "we could get into big trouble."

"I don't see how," Lieutenant Todd replied. "Or why anybody ever has to know. The Navy built the system, after all, primarily for its own ships. We just allow everyone else to use it. All we have to do is interrogate the master register and get the Doppler and ranging time history for their particular identification code. Then we can figure out where they are. It's easy. We do it all the time for our own vessels."

"But we signed a maritime convention restricting our access to the private registers except in life-or-death or national security cases," Ramirez continued.

"I can't just tap into the satellite files because you and I suspect a certain boat of being on an illegal mission. We need more authority."

"Look, Roberto," Todd argued vehemently, "who do you think is going to give us permission? We don't have the photographs. We only have your word for it. No. We must act on our own. If we're wrong, then nobody ever has to know about it. If we're right, we'll nail that bastard, we'll both be heroes, and nobody will give us a hard time about what we've done."

Ramirez was silent for a few seconds. "Don't you at least think we should inform Commander Winters? He is, after all, the officer in charge of this Panther investigation."

"Absolutely not," said Lieutenant Todd quickly. "You heard him at the meeting yesterday. He thinks we're out of line already. He'd like nothing better than to shit all over us. He's jealous." Todd saw that Ramirez was still undecided. "I'll tell you what," he said, "we'll call him *after* we find out where the vessel is."

Lieutenant Ramirez shook his head. "That won't make any difference. We still will have exceeded our authority."

"Shit," said Todd in exasperation. "Tell me what has to be done and I'll do it. Without you. I'll take all the risk." He stopped and looked directly at Ramirez. "I can't fucking understand it. I guess you Mexicans really are gutless. You're the one who actually saw the missile in the photograph, but . . ."

Ramirez's eyes narrowed. His voice became hard. "That's enough, Todd. We'll get the data. But if this turns out to be a disaster, I will personally break your neck with my own hands."

"I knew you'd see it my way," Lieutenant Todd replied, smiling as he followed Ramirez to a command console.

Commander Winters put the extra six-pack of Coke on the top of the ice and then closed the cooler. "Anything else," he shouted out the door at his wife and son, "before I haul this thing out to the car?"

"No, sir," was the reply from the driveway. The commander picked up the cooler and carried it through the screen door. "Whew," he said, as he loaded it in the open trunk of the car, "you have enough food and drink in here for a dozen people."

"I wish you were coming, sir," said Hap. "Most of the rest of the fathers will be there."

"I know. I know," answered Winters. "But your mother's going. And I need to do some private rehearsing for tonight." He gave his son a brief hug. "Besides, Hap, we've talked about this before. Lately I haven't felt comfortable at organized church activities. I believe that religion is between God and the individual."

"You haven't always felt that way," Betty interjected from the other side of the car. "In fact, you used to love church picnics. You'd play softball and swim and we would laugh all evening." There was just a trace of bitterness in her voice. "Come on, Hap," she said after a momentary pause. "We don't want to be late. Thank your father for helping us pack."

"Thanks, Dad." Hap climbed into the car and Winters' closed the door behind him. They waved to each other as the Pontiac backed out of the driveway into the street. As they drove away, Winters mused to himself, *I must spend more time with him. He needs me now. If I don't it will soon be too late.*

He turned around and walked back into the house. At the refrigerator he stopped and opened the door. He poured himself a glass of orange juice. While he was drinking it, he looked idly around the kitchen. Already Betty had cleaned up the breakfast dishes and put them in the dishwasher. The counters were scrubbed. The morning paper was neatly folded on the breakfast table. The kitchen was tidy, orderly. Like his wife. She abhorred messes of all kinds. Winters remembered one morning, back when Hap was still in diapers and they were living in Norfolk, Virginia. The little boy had been exuberantly pounding the kitchen table and suddenly his arms had flailed out, knocking Betty's cup of coffee and the creamer onto the floor. They both broke and made quite a mess all over the kitchen. Betty had stopped her meal abruptly. By the time she had returned to her cold scrambled eggs, there was not the slightest indication anywhere, not on the floors, the lower cupboard, or even in the wastebasket (she packed all the broken pieces neatly in the basket liner and then removed the entire bag to the outside cans), that there had been an accident.

Just to the right of the refrigerator in the Winterses' kitchen, hanging on the wall, there was a small plaque with simple lettering. "For God so loved the world," it said, "that He gave His only begotten son, that whosoever shall believe in Him shall have everlasting life . . . John 3:16." Vernon Winters saw this kitchen plaque every day, but he had not actually read the words for months, maybe even years. On this particular Saturday morning he read them and was moved. He thought about Betty's God, a God very similar to the one he had worshipped in his childhood and adolescence in Indiana, a quiet, calm, wise old man who sat up in heaven somewhere, watching everything, knowing everything, waiting to receive and answer our prayers. It was such a simple, beautiful image. "Our Father, Who art in Heaven," he said, recalling the hundreds maybe thousands of times that he had prayed in church, "Hallowed be thy name. Thy kingdom come. Thy will be done. On Earth as it is in Heaven . . ."

And what is thy will for me, old man, Winters thought, a little taken aback by his own irreverence. *For eight years you have let me drift. Ignored me. Tested me like Job. Or maybe punished me.* He walked over to the kitchen table and sat down. He took another sip from his orange juice. *But have I been Forgiven? I don't yet know. Never once in all that time have You given me a definite sign. Despite my prayers and my tears. One time,* he thought, *Right after Libya, I wondered if maybe . . .*

He remembered being half asleep on the beach, lying on his back with his eyes closed on a big comfortable towel. In the distance he could hear the surf and children's voices, occasionally he could even distinguish Hap's voice or Betty's. The summer sun was warm, relaxing. A light began to dart about on the inside of his eyelids. Winters opened his eyes. He couldn't see much because the sunlight was too bright and there was also a glare, a metal glint of some kind, in his eyes. He shaded his forehead with his hand. A little girl with long hair, a year old perhaps, was standing just above him, staring at him. The glint was coming from the long metal comb in her hair.

Winters closed his eyes and opened them again. Now he could see her better. She had shifted her head just a little so the glare was gone. But she was still staring fixedly at him, with absolutely no expression on her face. She was wearing only diapers. He could tell that she was foreign. *Arab perhaps*, he had thought at the time, looking back into her deep brown, almond-shaped eyes. She didn't move or say anything. She just watched him, curious, relentless, without seeming to notice anything that he did.

"Hello," Winters said quietly. "Who are you?"

The little Arab girl gave no sign that she had heard anything. After a few seconds, however, she suddenly pointed her finger at him and her face looked angry. Winters shuddered and sat up abruptly. His quick action frightened her and she began to cry. He reached for her but she pulled away, slipped, lost her balance, and fell on the sand. Her head hit something sharp when she fell and blood started running down her scalp and onto her shoulder. Terrified, first by the fall and then by the sight of her own blood, the little girl began to wail.

Winters hovered over her, struggling with his own panic as he watched the blood splatter the sand. Something unrecognized flashed through his mind and he decided to pick the little Arab girl up to comfort her. She fought him violently, with the reckless abandon and surprising strength of the toddler, and struggled free. She fell again on the sand, on her side, the blood from her scalp injury scattering drops of red around the light brown sand. She was now completely hysterical, crying so hard she often could not catch her breath, her face suffused with fear and anger. She pointed again at Winters.

Within seconds a pair of dark brown arms swooped out of the sky and picked her up. For the first time Winters noticed that there were other people around, lots of them in fact. The little girl had been picked up by a man who must have been her father, a short, squat Arab man in his mid-twenties wearing a bright blue bathing suit. He was holding his daughter protectively, looking as if he were expecting a fight, and consoling his distraught young wife whose sobs intermingled with the little girl's frantic cries. Both the parents were looking at Winters accusingly. The mother daubed at the little girl's bleeding head with a towel.

"I didn't mean to hurt her," Winters said, recognizing as he spoke that what he said would be misinterpreted. "She fell and hit her head on something and I . . ." The Arab couple were backing away slowly. Winters turned to the others, maybe a dozen people who had come over in response to the little girl's cries. They also were looking at him strangely. "I didn't mean to hurt her," he repeated in a loud voice. "I was just . . ." He stopped himself. Big tears were falling off his face and onto the sand. *My God*, he thought, *I'm crying. No wonder these people . . .*

He heard another cry. Betty and Hap had apparently just walked up behind him as the Arab couple had backed away with their bleeding daughter. Now, having seen the blood on his father's hands, five-year-old Hap had broken into tears and buried his face in his mother's hip. He sobbed and sobbed. Winters looked at his hands, then at the people standing around him. Impulsively he bent down and tried to clean his hands in the sand. The sound of his son's sobbing punctuated his vain attempt to wipe his hands free of the blood.

As he was kneeling in the sand, Commander Winters glanced at his wife Betty for the first time since the incident had started. What he saw on her face was abject horror. He entreated her for support with his eyes, but instead her eyes glazed over and she too fell to her knees, careful not to disturb her tearful son who was clinging to her side. And Betty began to pray. "Dear God," she said with her eyes closed.

The crowd dispersed slowly, several of them going over to the Arab family to see if they could be of any help. Winters stayed on his knees in the sand, shaken by his own actions. At length Betty stood up. "There, there," she consoled her son Hap, "everything will be all right." Without saying another word, she carefully picked up the beach bag and towels and started walking toward the parking lot. The commander followed.

They left the beach and drove back to Norfolk where they were living. *And she never asked about it*, Winters thought, as he sat at his kitchen table eight years later. *She wouldn't even let me talk about it. For at least three years. It was as if it had never happened. Now she mentions it once in a blue moon. But we still have never discussed it.*

He finished his orange juice and lit a cigarette. As he did so, he thought immediately of Tiffani and the night before. Fear and arousal simultaneously stirred in Winters when he thought of the coming evening. He also found that he had a curious desire to pray. *And now dear God*, he said tentatively, *are you testing me again?* He was suddenly aware of his own anger. *Or are You laughing at me? Maybe it wasn't enough for You to forsake me, to leave me adrift. Maybe You won't be satisfied until I am humiliated.*

Again he felt like crying. But he resisted. Winters crushed out his cigarette and stood up from the table. He walked over to the side of the refrigerator and pulled the plaque containing the Bible verse off the wall. He started to throw it in the trash but, after hesitating for a second, he changed his mind and put it in one of the kitchen drawers.

CAROL was swimming rapidly about six feet above the trench as they approached the final turn. She took a few photographs while she waited for Troy to catch up, pointed down below her to where the tracks turned to the left, and then started swimming again, more slowly this time, following the tracks in the narrow crevice toward the overhang. Nothing here had changed. She motioned for Troy to stay back and swam down into the trench, carefully, as she had done before when she was with Nick. Her search of the area under the overhang was very thorough. She did not find anything.

She gestured to Troy that nothing was there, and then, after another quick sequence of photographs, the two divers began retracing their path, going back along the tracks toward the area under the boat where they had already spent fifteen minutes earlier searching fruitlessly for the fissure they had seen on Thursday. It had mysteriously vanished. All the tracks, although somewhat eroded, still converged in front of the reef structure where the hole had been just two days before. Carol had poked and prodded, even damaged the reef in several places (which, as an environmentalist, she hated to do, but she was certain the hole *had* to be there), but had not found the fissure. If Troy had not seen it so clearly, first on the ocean telescope monitor and then in the pictures, he would have thought that it was just a figment of Nick and Carol's collective imagination.

As Carol, deep in her thoughts, turned right over the main trench after leaving the side path that had led to the overhang, she was careless and brushed ever so slightly against a crop of coral that was extending outward from the reef. She felt a sting on her hand. She looked down and saw that she was bleeding. *That's funny,* she thought, *I just barely touched it.* Her mind flashed back to ten minutes before, when she had been roughly pushing the coral and kelp aside in search of the fissure. *And I wasn't even scratched . . .*

A wild, inchoate idea started forming in her mind. Excited now, she intensified her swimming down the long trench where the fissure had been. Troy could not keep up with her. It was a long swim but Carol completed it in about four or five minutes. She checked her regulator pressure as she waited for her diving partner. They exchanged the thumbs-up sign when he arrived and Carol tried, without success, to explain her idea to Troy using hand signals. Finally, she bravely reached out and grabbed a piece of coral with her hand. Carol saw Troy's eyes open wide and his face grimace behind his mask. She opened her hand. There were no cuts, no scrapes, no blood. Astounded, Troy swam over beside her to look at the coral colony she had just disturbed. He too could touch and even hold this strange coral without cutting his hand. What was going on?

Carol was now pulling the coral and kelp away from the reef. Troy watched in amazement as a huge segment of the reef structure seemed to peel off, almost like a blanket . . .

They heard the great WHOOSH only milliseconds before they felt the pull. A giant chasm opened in the reef behind them and everything in the area, Troy, Carol, schools of fish, plants of all kinds, and an enormous volume of water, was swept into the hole. The current was very swift but the channel was not too large, for Carol and Troy bounced against what felt like metallic sides a couple of times. There was no time to think. They were carried along, as if on a water slide, and simply had to wait for the ride to be over.

The dark gave way to a deep dusk and the current slowed markedly. Separated by about twenty feet, Carol and Troy each tried to gather his wits and figure out what was happening. They appeared to be in the outer annulus of a large circular tank and were going around and around, passing gates of some kind after every ninety degrees of revolution. The water in the tank was about ten feet deep. Carol rolled on her back and looked up. She could see a lot of large structures above her, some of them moving, that seemed to be made out of metal or plastic. She could not see Troy anywhere. She tried to grab the sides of the tank so she could stop and look for him. It was useless. She could not resist the motion of the current.

They made three or four trips around the circle without seeing each other. Troy noticed that all the fish and plants had slowly disappeared from their annulus, suggesting that some kind of sorting process was underway. Suddenly the current increased and he was pitched forward and down, under the water and then through a half-open gate, into darkness again. Just as a trace of light appeared above the water and the rate of flow again slowed, he felt something clamp on to his right arm.

Troy was lifted out of the water a foot or so. In the dim light he couldn't see exactly what it was that had caught him, but it felt very strong. It held him without additional movement. Troy looked behind him in the current, where he had been, and he saw Carol's tumbling body approaching. With his free left arm he grabbed at her. She felt his arm and immediately wrapped herself around it. She composed herself, lifted her head out of the water, and struggled to reach the trunk of Troy's body. She succeeded in holding tight to him as the current rushed past. She caught her breath and for just a moment their eyes met behind their diving masks.

Then, inexplicably, the clamp released. When they were back in the water, the current did not seem so strong. They were able to hold on to each other without much difficulty. After about fifteen seconds, the flow of the water slowed down altogether. They had been deposited in a pool in what appeared to be a large room and the water was draining out, running into some unseen orifice at the far end of the room. The last of the water disappeared. Shaken and exhausted, Carol and Troy started to stand up in their diving gear.

Carol had great difficulty getting to her feet. Troy helped her up and then pointed to his regulator. Ever so slowly, he slipped out of his mouthpiece and sampled the ambient environment. One breath, then another. As far as he could tell, he was breathing normal air. He shrugged his shoulders at Carol and, in a fit of bravado, took off his mask as well. "Hellooo," he shouted nervously, "Anybody there? You have guests out here."

Carol slowly removed both her mask and her regulator. She had a dazed look on her face. The two of them looked around. The ceiling was about ten feet above them. Overall the dimensions of the chamber were roughly equivalent to a large living room in a nice suburban home. The walls, however, were quite unusual. Instead of being flat and forming nice right-angle joints at each of the intersections, the walls were made of large, curved surfaces, some concave and some convex, that were alternately colored red and blue. Without thinking, Carol began walking around, slowly of course because of the bulky diving gear, and taking photographs.

"Uh, just a moment, Miss Dawson," Troy said with a hesitant smile. He pulled off his flippers and followed her. "Before you take any more pictures, angel, would you kindly tell this unsophisticated black boy just where in the fuck he is? I mean, last I knew, I was going down under the boat to look for a hole. I think I found it, but I must say it's a trifle unnerving to be visiting someone and not know just who it is. So could you stop with the journalism bit for just a minute and tell me why you are so calm."

Carol was right in front of one of the concave blue wall panels. There were two or three indentations in the wall structure, at about eye level, that formed circles or ellipses. "Now what do you suppose this is?" Carol wondered aloud. Her voice sounded flat, as if she were far away.

"Carol," Troy almost shouted. "Stop it. Stop right now. We can't just blissfully walk around here as if this is a typical afternoon stroll through a model house. We have to talk. Where are we? How are we going to get out and go home? Home, remember the place? I guarantee you it's not under the ocean two hours away from shore." He grabbed her by the shoulders and shook her.

She started to snap out of her daze. She looked slowly around the entire room and then back at Troy. "Jesus," she said. "And shit." He saw her tremble a little and stepped forward to hug her. She indicated for him to leave her alone. "I'm all right. At least almost." Carol took a couple of deep breaths and then smiled. "Anyway, I've sure got one hell of a story here." She looked around the room again. "Uh, Troy," she said with her brow wrinkled, "how did we get in here? I don't see a doorway or an opening or anything."

"Good question," Troy replied. "A very good question, to which I might have the answer. I think these crazy colored walls move around. I believe I saw the walls rolling into place when I was under the water. So all we have to do is push them aside and find our way out." He tried to wedge his hands into a crack that was a connection between a red and a blue piece of the wall structure. He was unsuccessful.

Carol left Troy and started to pace around the perimeter of the room in her ungainly diving apparatus. She quickly stopped and took off everything except her bathing suit. She seemed intent on both examining and photographing every single panel in the wall. Troy took off his own air tanks and buoyancy vest as well, dropping them on the light metal floor with a clank. He watched her for a minute.

"Carol, oh Carol," he said from across the room, a big fake grin spreading across his face. "Would you like to tell me what you're doing now? I mean, after all, angel, I may be able to help."

"I'm looking for something that says 'Eat Me' or 'Drink Me,' " she replied with a nervous laugh.

"Of course," Troy mumbled to himself, "that was absolutely obvious."

"Do you remember *Alice in Wonderland?*" Carol asked from the opposite side of the room. She had found a long, thin protruberance that looked like a handle sticking out from the center of one of the red panels. She waved and he came over. The two of them tried to twist and turn the handle. Nothing happened. Carol became frustrated struggling with it.

Troy thought he saw a first sign of panic in Carol as her eyes frantically scanned the rest of the room. He pulled himself up and stood at attention, military style. "Speak roughly to your little boy . . . And beat him when he sneezes . . . He only does it to annoy . . . Because he knows it teases."

The deep furrows in Carol's face showed that she thought Troy had temporarily lost his mind. "That was the Queen of Hearts, I think." Troy laughed. "I'm not sure exactly. But I had to learn it for a play when I was in the fifth grade." Carol had relaxed and was also laughing in spite of her fear. She reached up and gave Troy a kiss on the cheek. "Careful, now, careful," he said with a twinkle in his eye. "We black men are easily aroused."

Carol slid her arm through Troy's as they finished walking around the rest of the room, searching the walls for any sign of an exit. Troy's banter made Carol feel comfortable. "When I was in the eighth grade a black teacher of mine told me that *Alice* was a racist story. He contended that it was very significant that it was a *white* rabbit that Alice followed. He said that no nice little white girl would ever have pursued a *black* rabbit down a hole." He stopped in front of another red panel. "Well, well," he said. "What have we here?"

This red panel looked just like the rest of the wall from a distance. But up close, within a range of a couple of feet or so, all kinds of patterns, made with small white dots, could be seen stippled on top of the red paint. An array of consecutive rectangular sections outlined by the white dots highlighted the center of the panel. "Hey, angel," Troy said, pushing on the sections at random, "don't you think this looks suspiciously like a keyboard?" Troy began to push on the keys at random. Carol joined him. It became a game. The two of them stood at the red panel for almost a minute, putting their fingers into every outlined section and pushing hard.

Suddenly Carol backed away from the panel, turned around, and started walking directly across the room. "Where are you going?" yelled Troy, as Carol, spinning around to answer, nearly stumbled over her diving gear on the floor.

"I have a crazy idea," called Carol. "Call it feminine intuition. Call it psychic if you will." She had reached the red panel where they had struggled with the handle. Now she pulled it down easily and immediately heard a creak. She jumped back, startled, as the entire panel folded back and away from her, revealing a dark opening large enough for a truck to enter. Troy came over beside her and the two of them stared into the void.

"Holy shit," he said. "Are we supposed to go in there?"

Carol nodded. "I'm certain we are."

Troy looked at her with a curious expression. "And just how do you know that?"

"Because it's the only way out of here," Carol replied.

Troy cast one final glance around the strange room with the curved and colored walls. There was an indisputable logic to what Carol had said. He took a deep breath, held Carol's hand, and walked into the black tunnel.

Behind them they could barely see the small shaft of light coming from the room where they had left their diving gear. Inside the pitch-black hallway they moved very slowly, cautiously. Troy kept one hand on the wall and the other clenched around Carol's. The sound of their labored breathing, heightened by the constant fear and apprehension, reverberated off the rounded walls. They didn't talk. Twice Troy had started to sing a few lines from a popular song, to assuage his own disquiet, but both times Carol stopped him. She wanted to be able to hear in case there were any other noises.

At one point she squeezed his hand and stopped. "Listen," she said in a whisper. Troy held his breath. There was utter silence, except for something very soft that he couldn't quite identify, way off in the distance. "Music," Carol said. "I think I hear music."

Troy strained to identify the sound just below the threshold of his hearing. It was useless. He pulled on Carol's hand. "It's probably inside your head," he said. "Let's go."

They had made a turn and the light behind them had disappeared. Altogether they had been in the tunnel for about ten minutes. Carol was becoming despondent. "What if this doesn't go anywhere?" she asked Troy.

"That doesn't make any sense," he replied quickly. "Somebody built it for some purpose. It's obviously a connecting passageway." He fell silent.

"Who built it?" Carol asked the question that had been troubling both of them during the long tense walk down the dark hallway.

"Another good question," Troy replied. He hesitated just a minute before continuing with his answer. "My guess is the United States Navy. I think we're in some kind of top-secret underwater laboratory that nobody knows about." *Of course,* he thought, not saying it out loud because he didn't want to disturb Carol, *it could also be Russian. In which case we are in deep shit. If the Russians have a large, secret laboratory this close to Key West, they are not going to be happy . . .*

"Look, Troy," Carol said excitedly. "I see a light. There is somebody here after all." The tunnel was about to split into two parts. At the end of one of the two forks, the one sharply to the left, a patch of illumination could clearly be seen. Still holding hands, Troy and Carol walked briskly toward the light. Troy was aware that his heart was beating very rapidly.

Carol almost raced into the new room. She had expected that they were about to be found, that this mysterious adventure was now going to end and everything would be explained. Instead, as she looked around her in a small, oval chamber with the same bizarre panels for walls (except these were colored brown and white, instead of red and blue as in the previous room), she felt a tremendous confusion. "What is this place?" she asked Troy. "And how are we going to get out?"

Troy was standing in the center of the room with his head tilted back as far as it would go. He was staring up at a vast arched ceiling some thirty to thirty-five feet above them. "Wow," he exclaimed, "this is one huge place." The muted light illuminating the room was coming from slabs of partially translucent material, possibly glass crystals, that were embedded in the ceiling.

The brown and white panels forming the walls for the particular room they had entered were only ten feet high, but they were high enough to prevent Carol and Troy from seeing out. They had a strange sense of both freedom and confinement. On the one hand, first the tunnel and now this small room, the size of a child's bedroom in a small house, had made them feel claustrophobic; however, the sense of space conveyed by the cathedral ceilings was liberating.

"Well?" asked Carol, somewhat impatiently, after waiting a few moments while Troy walked around and surveyed the room. He was observing that the brown and white wall panels were only slightly curved and were thus much closer to normal walls than those in the initial room had been.

"I'm sorry, angel," he replied, "I forgot the question."

She shook her head. "There is only one question, Mr. Jefferson. I believe that you asked it of me on our last tour stop." She looked at her watch. "In about fifteen minutes, we will have exceeded the maximum time for our air supply. Unless I miss my guess, our friend Nick is probably starting to worry right now. But we still have no idea . . . What are you doing?"

She interrupted herself when Troy bent down to pull a small knob on one of the brown panels in the corner of the room. "These are drawers, angel," he said, as the bottom part of the panel came out several inches from the wall.

"Like a dresser." He opened a second drawer above the first. "And they have something in them."

Carol came over to see. She reached into the second drawer that Troy had opened and pulled out a rust-colored sphere about the size of a tennis ball. The surface of the ball was very curious. Instead of being smooth and regular, it had grooves cut into it, mostly on one side, and tiny bumps, like those on the surface of a pickle, around and next to the grooves. In other places there were poorly defined indentations as well. Carol examined the sphere in the weak light. "I've seen something like this before," she said. "But where?" She thought for a few seconds. "I've got it," she announced, pleased that her memory had come through, "this looks exactly like the model of Mars in the National Air and Space Museum."

"Then I must have the Earth," Troy replied, showing her a mostly blue sphere the size of a softball that he had removed from the top drawer. The two of them stood together in the dim light, looking back and forth at the spheres they were holding in their hands. "Shit," Troy shouted eventually, spinning around and looking at the ceiling. "And double shit. Whoever you are, we've had enough. Come out now and identify yourself."

A partial echo of his voice came back to them. Otherwise they heard nothing. Anxious to be doing something, Carol continued her search of the room. She found another group of three drawers in a nearby brown panel. While she was opening the first of these, Troy playfully hurled his blue ball at what appeared to be an exit, a dark opening between panels on the other side of the room. The sphere hit a white panel near the exit with a thunk and started to fall to the floor. However, just before it touched the ground, the sphere lifted up, as if pulled somehow from above, and stopped in the center of the room about five feet above the floor. It began to spin.

Troy's eyes opened wide. He walked over to the sphere and placed his hand between the ball and high ceiling, trying to find the strings. Nothing happened. The Earth sphere continued to spin slowly and inscribe a circle in the air in the middle of the room. Troy pushed the ball lightly. It moved in response to his push, but after his applied force was removed and the effect had dissipated, the sphere returned to its previous location and continued its earlier movement. Troy turned around. Carol had her back to him and was searching unsuccessfully for another set of drawers. The Mars ball was still in her left hand.

"Uh, Carol," Troy said slowly. "Would you mind coming over here a moment?"

"Certainly," she replied without looking. "Jesus, Troy, these drawers are full of all kinds . . ." She had turned around and now noticed the Earth sphere hovering in the air near the center of the room. Her brow knitted. "That's cute," she said tentatively, "real cute. I didn't know you were a magician as well." Her voice trailed off. She could see the perplexed expression on Troy's face. She walked over next to him to have a closer look.

The two of them stood silently for at least ten seconds as they watched the blue softball slowly spin in the air. Next Troy took the Mars sphere from Carol and tossed it, underhanded, up toward the high ceiling. It arched up and fell down normally, until it was just above the floor. Then, like the blue sphere before it, the Mars ball developed its own sense of direction and momentum. It floated up about five feet off the floor, began to spin slowly, and hovered in the air next to the blue sphere representing the Earth.

Carol grabbed Troy's hand. She shivered and then regained her composure. "There's something about this that gives me the willies," she said. "All in all, I would deal better with a caterpillar asking me, 'Who are you?' At least in that case I would have some idea what I'm up against."

Troy turned around and led Carol back over to the partially opened drawers. "I ran into this old bearded dude once when I was hitchhiking," he began, as he pulled out a basketball that was covered with latitudinal belts and bands in shades of red and orange. He aimlessly tossed the big Jupiter ball over his shoulder, using both hands. Carol watched it, still fascinated, as it joined the other two spheres orbiting around an empty focus in the middle of the room.

"He was driving an old run-down pickup truck and smoking a joint. At first we talked a little. He would ask me questions and I would start to give an answer. But after a sentence or two, he would interrupt me and say, 'You don't know shit, man.' That was his response to everything."

Troy methodically emptied all six of the drawers while he was telling his story. He threw all the objects he found into the center of the room. A few of them he watched, casually, as if he were witnessing an everyday occurrence. Each of the new spheres repeated the earlier pattern. A nearly complete working model of the solar system was forming about five feet above the floor.

"Finally I grew tired of his game and was quiet. We drove along for miles in silence. It was a clear and beautiful night and he kept hanging his head out the window to look at the stars. Once, when he pulled his head back in, he lit another joint, handed it to me, and pointed back out the window at the stars. '*They* know, man, *they* know,' he said. Miles later, when he let me out of the truck, he leaned over and I could see the wildness in his eyes. 'Remember, man,' he whispered, 'you don't know shit. But *they* know.' "

As Troy finished the tale, Carol came over beside him and pulled out two handfuls of tiny fragments from the final drawer. They were a little sticky to the touch. She shook them off her hands and they miraculously flew around the room and coalesced into the ring systems of Saturn and Uranus. She looked at Troy in awe.

"Does that bizarre story have a point?" Carol asked. "I must admit that I am amazed at how nonchalant you are about this whole damn thing. For myself, I'm just about ready to freak out. Completely."

Troy pointed at the miniature planets floating in the air. "What we are seeing has no explanation in terms of our experience. We've either died together or transferred to a new dimension or someone is playing mind games with us." He smiled at Carol. "If you must know, angel, I'm scared absolutely shitless. But like that old stoned hippie, I keep telling myself, 'They know.' Somehow it gives me comfort."

They heard a soft sliding sound and a shaft of bright light burst into the room from an opening that was forming between two panels, one brown and one white, just to the right of the exit. Carol recoiled automatically and covered her eyes for an instant. Troy also jumped back at first, but then shaded his eyes with his hands and watched. The panels continued to slide until an opening about two feet wide had developed. The room was beginning to fill with light. Troy saw a great illuminated ball coming slowly through the opening. "Here comes the Sun . . . Doot-un-Doo-Doo, Doo . . . Here comes the Sun," he sang anxiously, "And I say . . . it's all right . . ." He hummed a few more bars of the song as Carol opened her eyes.

"Jesus," she said. The bright orb, the size of a giant beach ball, lifted itself into its proper place in the orrery and flooded the entire room with its radiance. The spinning, orbiting planets shone with reflected light from their sides facing the Sun. Carol stood transfixed, silent tears running down her face. She could not speak or move. She was completely overwhelmed.

Troy was also frightened, but not yet so much that his ability to function was impaired. However, a moment later he saw something in the exit that sent a bolt of terror through his system. His heart surged into overdrive as he blinked and then squinted, making certain his mind was not playing tricks on him as he looked just around the bright light of the model Sun. Instinctively, he turned to protect Carol and shielded her from what he had just seen.

"Don't look now," he whispered, "but we have a visitor."

"What?" said Carol, confused and still stunned.

Troy held her by the arms and they moved together several steps to the right. He looked over his own shoulder and saw the thing again.

"Over by the exit," he said, turning around, unable any longer to hide his panic.

Carol's eyes indicated that she had found the source of Troy's terror. She had no idea what it was, but she could see that it was large, clearly threatening, and absolutely different from anything that she had ever seen or imagined. It had also moved into the room. She heard Troy's frantic, incoherent shouts, but their meaning didn't register. She looked at the thing again and her mind balked. She opened her mouth to scream. Nothing came out at first. She dropped to her knees on the floor. She heard the sound of screams in her ear, but they seemed far, far away. Her brain was sending a message that said, 'You're screaming,' but for some reason it didn't seem possible. It had to be someone else.

The thing was coming toward her. Its main body was about eight feet tall at that moment, but it was continually changing its shape and size as it undulated across the room. Whatever it was, Troy and Carol could see into it and even through parts of its structure. A transparent external boundary membrane was wrapped around a permanently seething set of mostly clear fluid matter that ebbed and flowed with each movement. The thing moved like an amoeba, matter simply heading in the right direction, but with astonishing speed. Tiny black dots were scattered just behind all its external surfaces, darting in all directions, apparently supervising the continuous reconfigurations that gave it motion. A half dozen chunks of grayish, opaque matter, objects a foot or so square, were also embedded near the center of the primary body.

But it was not the main body of the thing that was so terrifying. Protruding from its upper portions was a frightening array of a dozen appendages, mostly long and slender in shape, that appeared to be stuck into the main body like sharp objects in a pin cushion. It looked as if the large, clear, amoebalike structure was a versatile transportation system that could carry virtually anything and that the payload, at least for this usage, was this family of constantly active rods, all of which were threatening because their end effectors resembled needles, hands, brushes, teeth, and even swords and guns. In Carol's mind, she was being attacked by a heavily armored tank that could change size in an instant and move on invisible treads in any direction.

Troy moved to the side, trying to calm his fear and catch his breath, as he watched the thing zero in on Carol. Its longest attachment, a reddish plastic implement which split into two short tines about a foot away from the primary body, suddenly extended itself outward an additional three feet and stopped just six inches in front of Carol's eyes. She screamed and pushed it away, forcefully, but it popped right back into position. Troy plucked the Jupiter ball out of the air and, with all his might, hurled the sphere at the center of the thing. The shapeless mass fell back on impact and immediately retracted its extended appendages. But in an instant the thing reconfigured itself somehow and adjusted its matter to let the ball pass completely through. Before it hit the floor on the other side, Jupiter rose into the air and came back to take its proper position in the solar system model.

The thing had now stopped advancing toward Carol. It was sitting in the middle of the room, its spindly appendages flailing around in all directions. It seemed to be making a decision. Troy bravely grabbed a rod with an end effector like a brush and tried to pull it away from the main structure. Instantly, core clear material flowed into the joint where that particular rod was attached, strengthening the connection. But Troy's action definitely caused a change in its pattern. The thing started after him. Ever so carefully, making sure it would follow him while watching out for another quick extension of the red implement with the two tines, Troy edged toward the exit. As the thing continued to move toward him, Troy motioned for Carol to get back. Then he broke for the door, tripping slightly over an extended rod on his way out.

It hardly hesitated. With surprising celerity the thing made itself short and squat. A maximum amount of exposed surface was now on the floor and it could move more quickly and efficiently. The deployed group of attachments were placed into some kind of compact traveling configuration and the thing hustled out the door.

Carol was left alone on her knees on the floor. The solar system model was above her and to the right. For over a minute she didn't move. She just watched the spinning planets abstractedly and listened for the occasional sound of Troy's footfalls in the distance. At length there was a long period of silence and Carol rose to her feet. She took several small, slow steps, reassuring herself that she was all right, and then walked over to the exit opening between the panels. The exit opened onto a corridor that ran in both directions.

Troy had gone to the right when he had left the room. After remembering her camera and going back to take a few quick photographs of the suspended planets, Carol followed Troy's path, also taking the corridor to the right. She walked slowly down the black hall, turning around frequently to locate the light coming from the room that she had just left. There was now a close ceiling over her head. The hall next split into two forks; both directions were dark. Carol listened for sounds. Again she thought she heard music, but she couldn't begin to identify where it was coming from.

This time she chose the left fork in the hallway. Soon it narrowed and seemed to be circling back in the direction from which she had just come. She was just about to turn around and retrace her steps when she distinctly heard two noises, something like a thud followed by a scraping sound, off to the right in front of her. Drawing her breath slowly and struggling to conquer her fear, Carol moved forward in the dark. After about twenty more feet she came upon a low door that opened to the right. She bent down slightly and peered in. In the dusky light she saw unusual shapes and structures in another small room with walls made of the now familiar curved and colored panels. She crawled through the doorway and stood up.

Soft local lights located in a few of the wall panels came on as soon as Carol's feet contacted the floor in the room. Her arrival also triggered two or three notes from some kind of musical instrument. It sounded like an organ and was apparently way off in the distance in another part of the cathedral area enclosed by the vast arched ceilings that were again above her. She stopped, surprised. She stood still for several seconds. Then, without moving, Carol carefully surveyed her new surroundings.

In this room the wall panels were very bright, alternating between purple and gold, and they were extremely curved. Along with Carol in the room there were three objects of unknown purpose. One looked like a writing table, a second like a long, low bench that was wide at one end and tapered to a point at the other, and the third resembled a very tall telephone pole whose top and bottom were connected by sixteen thin strings stretched out and around a broad ring about one third of the way down the pole.

Carol could walk between the thin strings. The ring, made out of a gold metallic material, was a couple of feet above her head, almost at the level of the top of the wall panels. She grabbed one of the strings and felt it vibrate.

It made a muffled, flat sound. She backed away from the string and tried to pluck it. A note sounded, very lyrical, like a heavy harp. Carol realized she was standing inside a musical instrument. But how to play it? She spent a few minutes wandering around the room, trying without success to find the equivalent of a bow. She knew it would be impossible to play the harp if she had to run around and pluck each individual string herself.

She walked over to the writing table. She quickly figured out that it was also a musical instrument. It looked much more promising. There were indentations in the table, sixty-four altogether, set up in eight rows and eight columns. Pressing each key produced a different sound. Although Carol had taken five years of piano lessons as a small child, it was a difficult chore, at first, for her even to play "Silent Night" on the strange writing table. She had to correlate the sounds made by pressing the individual keys with the notes and chords that she remembered from her childhood. While she was teaching herself to play the instrument, she stopped often to listen to the delicate, crystal sound that it made. It reminded her mostly of a xylophone.

Carol stood at the table for several minutes. Eventually she played an entire verse of "Silent Night" without making a single mistake. Carol smiled, pleased with herself, and relaxed momentarily. During this interlude the great organ in the distance (which she had heard briefly when she had entered the room and could now pinpoint as being somewhere in the upper reaches of the cathedral area) suddenly began to play. Carol felt goose bumps rise on her arms, partially due to the beauty of the music and partially because it reminded her again of what a bizarre world she had entered. *What is that organ playing?* she thought to herself. *It sounds like an overture.* She listened for a few seconds. *Why . . . that's an introduction. To "Silent Night"! It's very creative.*

The organ sound was joined by several others, each emanating from somewhere in the ceiling. All the instruments together played a complex version of the "Silent Night" that Carol had so painstakingly pounded out on the writing table a few moments before. The beautiful music swelled throughout the cathedral. Carol looked up and then closed her eyes. She spun her body around and around in a little dance. When she opened her eyes again, each of them confronted what appeared to be a tiny optical instrument no more than an inch away. Carol froze in terror.

The thing had noiselessly come up behind her while she was playing music at the writing table and had waited patiently, while deploying its appendages, until she was ready to turn around. It was about her height now and the closest part of the translucent main body was only an arm's length away. As Carol stood there motionless, barely daring to breathe, five or six of the thing's attachments came forward to touch her. A small digging instrument scraped some skin off her bare shoulder. The sword cut off some of her hair. A tiny cord attached to one of the long rods wrapped around her wrist. A set of bristles the size of the head of a toothbrush traveled across her chest, tickling her nipples through her bathing suit and crossing over the camera that was draped around her neck. She was having so many feelings simultaneously that she had lost track of all the stimuli. Carol closed her eyes and tried to concentrate on something else. She felt a needle prick her forehead.

It was over very fast, less than a minute altogether. The thing retracted its appendages, backed up a couple of feet, and stood there, observing her from a distance. Carol waited. After another twenty seconds, the attachments were stowed, as they had been when the thing had gone after Troy, and it left the room.

Carol listened for sounds. It was totally quiet again. She backed up from the writing table and tried to organize her thoughts. After about a minute, the purple and gold wall panels began to move to the side on their own accord. They folded upon themselves and formed small stacks. Then the corridors around the music room collapsed and automatically organized their partitions into neat piles. Carol found herself standing in one huge room under the cathedral ceilings. In the distance her weird antagonist with the flailing appendages passed through a side door about twenty-five yards away and disappeared quickly from view.

She looked around. There was no sign of Troy. The walls were creamy white and nondescript, somewhat boring after the colored panels in the earlier rooms. There were two doors, opposite each other in the middle of the room. Except for the musical instruments, which now seemed completely out of place clustered together at one end of such a vast room, the only other object she could see was a small piece of carpet against the wall to the left. In front of her against the far wall, about fifty yards away, there was what appeared to be a large window on the ocean. Even from a distance she could see and identify some of the fish swimming by.

At first Carol hurried toward the window. When she was about halfway there and even with the doors, she stopped a few seconds and took a few photographs of the rather bland room. Curiously, the small carpet was not where she remembered it. It had somehow been moved while she was walking. She approached the carpet very slowly. Her weird experiences since she and Troy had been sucked out of the ocean had made Carol understandably wary. As she drew closer, she saw that the flat object lying on the floor was definitely not a carpet. From above she could see an intricate internal design, like a complex network of sophisticated electronic chips. There were strange whorls and geometric patterns on its surface; they had no specific meaning to Carol but they reminded her of the fractal designs Dr. Dale had shown her one night in his apartment. The symmetries of the object were readily apparent. In fact, each of the four quadrants of the carpet was identical.

It was about six feet long, three feet wide, and two inches thick. The dominant color was slate gray, although there were some significant color variations. Some of the larger individual components must have been color-coded according to some master plan. Carol could identify groupings of similar elements in red, yellow, blue, and white within the design. The overall harmony of the colors was striking, suggesting that some effort had been made by the designers to include aesthetic considerations.

Carol bent down on her knees beside the carpet and studied it more intently. Its surface was densely packed. The closer she looked, the more detail she found. *Extraordinary*, she thought. *But what in the world is it? And how did it move? Or could I possibly have imagined it?* She put her hand on the exposed top surface. She felt a soft tingle, like a gentle electric shock. She slid one hand under the edge and lifted slightly. It was heavy. She removed her hand.

Her desire to escape from this strange world now overruled her curiosity. Carol took a photograph of the carpet from the top and started walking away in the direction of the window. After several strides, she turned quickly to her left to look at the carpet one more time. It had moved again and was still even with her in the room. Carol continued walking toward the window, now watching the carpet out of the corner of her eye. When she had walked another ten feet, her peripheral vision saw it arch up quickly along a line through its center, pulling the rear of its body in a forward direction. Half a second later the front end of the carpet scooted forward and the center fell flat against the floor again. This maneuver was repeated six or eight times in rapid succession as the carpet zipped up to a position even with Carol in the room.

Despite her situation, Carol laughed. She was still full of adrenaline and uptight, but there was definitely something humorous about a multicolored carpet that could crawl like an inchworm. "Ha," Carol said out loud, "I caught you. Now you owe me an explanation."

Carol certainly did not expect a reply to her comment. Nevertheless, after just a short delay, the behavior of the carpet was altered. First it began to generate small wave pulses along its surface, with four or five crests from front to back. After smartly reversing the direction of motion of the waves several times, the carpet's next trick was to keep its front end fixed on the floor, as if there were suction cups holding it down, and raise its back side entirely off the floor. In that mode it was about six feet tall. It seemed to be looking at Carol.

She was flabbergasted. "Well, I asked for it," she said out loud, still amused by the antics of the carpet. Now it seemed to be motioning for her to go toward the window. *I have lost my mind*, she thought to herself. *Completely. Troy was right. Maybe we're dead.* The carpet arched over on the floor and began to scamper toward the window, tumbling in somersaults like a slinky toy. Carol followed. *This is nuts*, she thought as she watched the carpet move somehow through the window and into the ocean. *And Alice thought she was in Wonderland.*

The carpet was playing in the water, dodging fish as they swam by in schools and teasing a sea urchin stuck fast against the reef. At length it came back into the room and stood upright. A little water dripped on the floor when the carpet set in motion a series of fast simultaneous waves, both latitudinal and longitudinal, that effectively shook the residual liquid from its surface. It then faced Carol and clearly beckoned for her to go through the window into the ocean.

"Look here, flat guy," she said, chuckling to herself as she tried to figure out what to say. *Now I know I'm insane*, she thought in a flash. *I'm standing here talking to a carpet. Next thing I know it will talk back.* "Now I'm not stupid," she continued. "I recognize that you're trying to get me to go into the ocean. But there are a few things that you don't—"

The carpet interrupted the conversation by going quickly through the window into the ocean again. It performed a couple of flips and came back into the room with Carol. Once more it shook itself and then stood rigidly, upright as before, as if to say, "See, it's easy."

"As I was saying," Carol began again, "I have perhaps gone crazy, but I'm willing to trust that I can indeed go through that window in some magical way. My problem is that there is water out there. I can't breathe in water. Without my diving gear, which I left somewhere in this labyrinth, I will die."

The carpet didn't move. Carol repeated her statement, using elaborate hand gestures to make her key points. Then she fell silent. After a short wait the carpet began to move about actively. It then approached her carefully and amazingly stretched itself out in all directions so that it was almost double its original size. Carol wasn't significantly fazed. At this point she was almost incapable of being astonished again. Even by an elastic carpet that pulled its two top sides together, over her head, to form a cone.

Carol backed away a couple of steps from the now giant carpet. "Oh ho," she said, "I think I understand. You are going to form an air pocket for me so that I can breathe." She stood still for a moment, thinking and shaking her head. "Why not," she said at last, "it's no weirder than anything else that's happened."

With the carpet hovering over and around her head, Carol closed her eyes and walked directly toward the window. She took a deep breath when she felt a soft plastic touch on different parts of her body. Suddenly the water was all around her except for the small air pocket from the neck up. It was hard for Carol to keep her diving discipline, but she managed to equalize the pressure every six to eight feet during her ascent. She took one final breath and zoomed up to the surface. The carpet peeled off in the last foot before she broke water.

The *Florida Queen* was about fifty yards away. "Nick," she shouted with all her might, "Nick, over here." She swam furiously toward the boat. A wave broke over her head. The boat was again visible, she could see a figure in profile. He was looking over the side of the boat. "Nick," Carol cried again when she had gathered her strength. This time he heard her and turned around. She waved her arms.

NICK had followed Carol and Troy on the monitor right after their initial descent, when they were still directly under the boat searching for the fissure. But he had quickly tired of watching them swim around in circles and had returned to his deck chair to read his novel. Afterward he had walked over to the screen several more times to look for them and had seen nothing; Carol and Troy had already left to investigate the area under the overhang.

Nick had checked the monitor again after he had finished *Madame Bovary*. He had been a little surprised to discover that the fissure was again clearly visible underneath the *Florida Queen*. He next assumed that he must have been correct, that it had just been a case of bad lighting, since with the sun directly overhead, the hole in the reef looked much smaller to him than it had two days before. He had then busied himself about the boat until his wrist alarm went off, indicating that Carol and Troy had about five more minutes of air remaining.

Nick walked over and looked at the images being taken by the ocean telescope and placed in realtime on the screen. There was no sign of Carol and Troy under the boat. Nick started becoming restive. *I hope they're paying attention*, he thought. He realized that they had been gone from view for a long time and that he had never seen them actually explore the fissure, their primary goal. A creeping disquiet began to spread through him as the clock continued to run out.

There's only one explanation, he thought, fighting against the negative ideas that were filtering into his mind. *They have been gone a long time, so they must have found something interesting at the overhang. Or somewhere else.* For just a moment Nick imagined that Carol and Troy had found a lode of treasure, full of objects that looked like the strange trident they had retrieved on Thursday.

The second hand seemed to be racing on his watch. It was now one minute until they should run out of air. Nick nervously checked the monitor again. Nothing. He felt his heart speed up. *They must be in the red*, he thought. *Even if they have carefully conserved the air, they must be in the red.* Nick worried for a second about a gauge failure, but he quickly remembered checking both of them himself when he arrived at the boat that morning. *Besides, it's terribly unlikely they would both fail . . . so there must be trouble.*

Another minute passed and Nick realized that he had not formulated a plan as to what he would do if they didn't show up. His mind raced swiftly through his options. There were two distinctly different action patterns he could follow. He could put on his diving gear and go look for them along the trench between the fissure and the overhang. Or he could assume that, in their excitement, Carol and Troy had simply neglected to check their air gauges regularly and as a result had been forced to surface wherever they were when they ran out of air.

If I go down after them, he thought, *I probably won't reach them in time.* Nick had a moment of self-recrimination because he had not properly prepared for this contingency. It would take him several valuable minutes to put on and check out his own diving apparatus. *That settles it. I must assume they're around here somewhere. Floating on the surface.* He looked briefly at the screen one more time and then walked over to the side of the boat. He scanned the ocean. It was a little choppy now. He didn't see any sign of them.

Nick turned on the engine and pulled in the anchor. He made a quick mental assessment of the general direction to the overhang and started steering with the engine at very low throttle. Unfortunately, he could not see the telescope monitor from the steering wheel, and the canopy blocked his vision behind him. Nick was in perpetual motion, back and forth from the wheel to the screen to the sides of the boat. As his fear and frustration began to build, so did his anger. It was now five minutes after the nominal time that their air supply would have been depleted.

Damnit, Nick thought, still not allowing his brain to nurture images of disaster, *How could they be so careless? I knew I shouldn't have let them go as a pair.* He continued to castigate himself and then turned on Carol. *I let that woman push me around. I will sure as hell straighten her out when I find them.* Nick turned the boat sharply to the left.

He thought he heard a voice. Nick ran to the side of the boat. He had no sense of what direction the shout had come from. After two or three more seconds he heard it again. He turned and saw a figure wave. Nick waved back and went over to the steering wheel to change the direction of the boat. He pulled out a strong rope from the equipment drawer and tied it around one of the stanchions next to the ladder. He threw the line to Carol as the boat pulled up alongside her and then he cut the motor back to idle.

She had no trouble catching the line. As he was reeling her in, Nick's eyes searched the surrounding water for Troy. He could not see him. Carol had now reached the ladder. "You would not believe . . ." she started, trying to catch her breath as she put her first foot on the ladder.

"Where's Troy?" interrupted Nick, gesturing out at the ocean.

Carol took another step up the ladder. It was clear that she was exhausted. Nick took her hand and she came into the boat. She stood up on her wobbly legs.

"Where's Troy?" Nick asked again forcefully. He looked at Carol. "And what happened to all your gear?"

Carol took a deep breath. "I . . . don't know . . . where Troy is," she stammered. "We were sucked down—"

"You don't *know!*" shouted Nick, now frantically looking around on the ocean surface. "You go on a dive, come up without your gear, and don't know where your partner is. What kind—"

A small wave hit the boat. Carol had raised her hand to protest Nick's diatribe, but the motion of the boat knocked her feet out from under her. She fell hard on her knees and winced at the pain. Nick was hovering over her, still shouting. "Well, Miss Perfect, you better come up with some fucking answers fast. If we don't find Troy soon, he'll be dead. And if he's dead, it will be your goddamn fault."

Carol instinctively cowered at the anger of the large man. Her knees hurt, she was exhausted, and this man was yelling in her face. Suddenly her emotions gave way. "Shut up," she shouted. "Shut up, you asshole. And get away from me." She was flailing with her arms, hitting Nick on the legs and in the stomach. "You don't know anything," she said after taking a quick breath. "You don't know shit."

Carol put her head in her hands and began to cry. In that instant, a long-buried memory burst upon her mind. Her five-year-old brother was sobbing hysterically and attacking her, pummeling her with his fists. She had her hands up to protect herself. "It's your fault, Carol," he was screaming, "he left because of you." She remembered the hot tears in her eyes. "It's not true, Richie, it's not true. It wasn't my fault."

On the boat Carol glanced up through her tears at Nick. He had backed away and was looking sheepish. She wiped her eyes and took a deep breath. "It was *not* my fault," Carol said deliberately and emphatically. Nick stuck out his hand to help her up and she smacked it away. He mumbled "I'm sorry" as she rose to her feet. "Now if you'll just shut up and listen," she continued, "I'll tell you what happened. The reef under the boat wasn't a reef at all . . . Oh, my God . . . It's here."

Nick saw a look of consternation break on Carol's face. She pointed over behind him, on the other side of the boat. He turned around to look. At first he didn't notice anything. Then he saw a strange flat object that looked like a piece of carpet inching along the boat toward the telescope monitor. He screwed up his face and turned back to Carol with a puzzled expression.

While Carol had been talking, the carpet had somehow crawled up the side and then flopped into the boat. By the time she started to explain, it was already standing in front of the television monitor, looking at the images the telescope was taking of the ocean floor beneath the boat. There was no time for lengthy explanations. "What the fuck?" Nick said, and walked over to apprehend the peculiar visitor. When his hand was about an inch away from touching the carpet, he felt a strong electrical discharge in the end of his fingers. "Ow!" he said, jumping back. He shook his hand and watched with amazement. The carpet continued to stand in front of the screen.

Nick looked at Carol as if he expected some assistance. But she was finding the whole scene amusing. *"That* thing is just one of the reasons the dive was strange," she said, making no effort to provide any help. "But I don't think it will hurt you. It probably saved my life."

Nick grabbed a small fishnet hanging on the side of the structure holding up the canopy and slowly approached the carpet. As he drew near, it seemed to turn and look at him. Nick lunged forward with the net. The carpet dodged deftly and Nick lost his balance. He fell against the monitor with his arms akimbo. Carol laughed out loud, remembering the first time they met. The carpet flipped over to the telescope data system and wrapped itself tightly around the entire set of electronic equipment.

From the floor of the boat Nick watched the carpet investigating the data system and shook his head in disbelief. "What the hell is that thing anyway?" he shouted to Carol.

She came over and graciously offered a hand to help him up. It was her way of apologizing for her earlier outburst. "I have no earthly idea," Carol replied. "At first I thought it might be a sophisticated Navy robot. But it is much too advanced, too intelligent." She pointed at the sky with her free left hand. *"They* know," she said with a smile.

The comment reminded Carol of Troy and she became solemn. She walked over to the side of the boat and stared at the ocean. Nick was now standing up next to the monitor within an arm's length of the carpet and the data system. It looked as if the carpet had somehow extended part of itself into the internal electronics. Nick watched for a few seconds, fascinated, as the various digital diagnostic readouts on the top of the data system went crazy. "Hey, Carol," he said. "Come here and look at this. That damn thing is plastic or something."

She did not turn around at first. "Nick," Carol asked softly, finally facing him, "what are we going to do about Troy?"

"As soon as we get this damn invader out of here," Nick replied from underneath the canopy, where he was now looking through his kitchen implements, "we'll do a systematic search of the area. I may even dive and see if I can find him."

Nick had picked up a large cooking fork with a plastic handle and was about to attempt to pry the carpet off the data system. "I wouldn't do that if I were you," admonished Carol. "He'll leave when he's ready."

But it was too late. Nick stuck the fork into and through the carpet and up against the uppermost rack of electronic parts. There was a popping sound and a tiny blue arc zapped down the fork, driving Nick backward with a powerful kick. Alarms went off, the digital readout from the data system went blank, and the ocean telescope monitor began to smoke. The carpet dropped down on the floor and began making the little waves that it had showed to Carol in the large room with the window on the ocean. A moment later, two alarms from the navigation system sounded, indicating not only that the boat's current location had been lost, but also that the nonvolatile memory, where all the parameters that permitted satellite communication were stored, had been erased.

In the middle of the noise and smoke, Nick stood with a puzzled expression on his face. He was rubbing his right arm from his wrist to his shoulder. "I'm numb," he said in astonishment. "I can't feel anything in my arm."

The carpet continued with its wave patterns on the floor of the boat while Carol picked up a pail, leaned overboard for some water, and doused the monitor. Nick had not moved. He was still standing there, looking helpless and pinching his arm. Carol threw the rest of the water on Nick. "Shit," he sputtered, backing up involuntarily, "why did you do that?"

"Because we have to find Troy," she said, walking over to the boat's controls. "And we can't wait all day. Ignore the damn carpet . . . and your arm. A man's life is at stake."

She increased the speed of the boat. As she did, the carpet stood up again, twisted around, and hustled to the side. Nick tried to stop it but it was out of the boat and into the water in a flash. As Carol steered the boat through circles of larger and larger radius, Nick stood on the side of the *Florida Queen* and searched for Troy.

An hour later they both agreed there was no reason for them to continue the search. Carol and Nick had been over the entire region of the ocean in the boat several times (with some care and difficulty, because they no longer had a working navigation system) and had found no trace of Troy. After he had convinced himself that his arm was all right, Nick had even donned his diving equipment, as a last resort, and had retraced the path from the fissure to the overhang and back. Still no sign of Troy. Nick had been just slightly tempted to investigate the fissure, but Carol's wild story seemed remotely plausible, and Nick did not like the idea of being sucked into some bizarre underground laboratory. And he knew that if he were to disappear, it would be virtually impossible for Carol to guide the boat back to Key West without an active navigation system.

Carol recounted the whole story of her dive while she and Nick were canvassing the area. He was certain she was liberally embellishing the details, but he could see no overarching logical flaws in her tale. And he himself had, after all, confronted the carpet on the *Florida Queen*. So he acknowledged, in his own mind, that Carol and Troy had indeed had hair-raising experiences in an underwater building of some type and that the technology they had encountered was definitely more advanced than anything they had ever seen before.

But Nick was reluctant to accept Carol's blithe explanation that the trio had met some extraterrestrials. It didn't seem likely to Nick that a first contact would be made under such mundane circumstances. Although he readily admitted that the carpet was a marvel of capability far beyond his ken, he did not think of himself as being technologically sophisticated and therefore he could not state, categorically, that human beings could not have created it.

In fact, Nick thought to himself as he was carefully searching the horizon with his binoculars for reference landmarks before beginning the trip back to Key West, *what a perfect deception. Suppose the Russians or even our own Navy wanted to mislead* . . . He stopped himself in mid-thought and realized that if he were right, and their encounter had been with a human creation, then they could very well still be in danger. *But why was Carol allowed to leave? And why didn't they confiscate my boat?* Nick found a small island that he recognized off in the distance and changed the orientation of the boat. He shook his head. It was all very confusing.

"You don't agree with me that we've just met some ETs?" Carol came up beside Nick and slightly teased him with her question.

"I don't know," he answered slowly. "It seems like quite a leap to make. After all, if there is an extraterrestrial infestation in the waters of the Gulf of Mexico, it should have been found before now. Submarines and other boats with active sonar must cross this region at least once or twice a year." He smiled at her. "You've been reading too much science fiction."

"On the contrary," she responded, fixing him with her gaze, "my experience with state-of-the-art technology is almost certainly more extensive than yours. I have done a series of features on the Miami Oceanographic Institute and have seen what kind of ingenious new concepts are being developed. And nothing, absolutely nothing, comes close to the carpet or the giant amoeba thing. The likelihood that there is some nonfantastic explanation for all this is very very small." She paused for a moment. "Besides," she continued, "maybe the laboratory hasn't been there for long. Maybe it was just recently finished or even transported here."

Nick had felt himself bridle when Carol had started her comment. *There she goes again*, he had thought. *So sure of herself. So cocky and competitive. Almost like a man.* He admitted to himself that he had also been known to make arguments from authority. And she was certainly right in one respect. She had had much more exposure to high technology than he had. Nick decided not to argue with her. This time.

There was a momentary pause in the conversation. Carol was also becoming more sensitive to the dynamic of their interaction. She had noticed in realtime that Nick's face had tightened when she had suggested that she knew more about technology than he did. *Uh oh*, had flashed through her mind. *Come on, Carol. Be a little more tactful and considerate.* She decided to change the subject.

"How long will it take us to reach the marina?" she asked. In her excitement on Thursday afternoon, she had not paid much attention to time during their return trip.

"A little less than two hours," Nick replied. He laughed. "Unless I get lost. I haven't used manual guidance in these waters for over five years."

"And what are you going to say when we get there?"

Nick looked at her. "To whom . . . about what?" he asked.

"You know. About our dive. About Troy."

They stared at each other. Nick finally broke the silence. "My vote would be to say nothing about it . . . until . . . until we know for certain," he said quietly. "Then if Troy shows up, there's no problem."

"And if he doesn't ever show up . . ." Carol's voice trailed off, "then we, Mr. Williams, are both in very deep shit." The gravity of their situation was becoming clear to both of them.

"But who do you think will ever believe such an incredible tale?" Nick said after a moment. "Even with your pictures, there's no really hard evidence to corroborate our story. These days people can create any kind of photo they want on a computer. Remember that murder case in Miami last year, where an alibi photograph was produced and admitted as official evidence? And then later that data processor showed up and blew the whistle?" He paused. Carol was listening intently. "And whoever built that place may be dismantling it at this very moment," he continued. "Otherwise, why did they let us get away? No. I say we wait awhile. Twenty-four hours or so anyway. And think carefully about what we're going to do."

Carol nodded her head affirmatively. "I think I agree with you, although not exactly for the same reasons." She was aware there was still a journalistic voice inside her that wanted to guard the information for her sensational scoop. She hoped her ambition wasn't somehow standing in the way of making the right decision for Troy. "But Nick," Carol said reflectively, "you don't think we're endangering Troy in any way by not contacting the authorities?"

"No," Nick replied immediately. "I suspect that if they were going to kill him, they would have done so already. Or will soon."

This part of the conversation was too casual for Carol. She walked over to the edge of the boat and stared out at the sea again. She thought of Troy and their wild adventure after they were sucked into the fissure. He had helped her hang together. No question about it. His humor and wit had kept her from falling apart. And he may have well saved her life by deflecting the attention of that thing.

He was a warm, sensitive man underneath that funny exterior, she thought. *Very aware. He also seemed to be covering lots of pain. From somewhere.* For a moment Carol convinced herself that Troy was all right. After all, they had helped her to escape. Then she wondered why she had never run into him again down there. A seed of doubt was planted in her mind. She squirmed. *Damnit. We don't really know one way or the other. It's uncertainty again. I hate uncertainty. It's unfair.*

A profound sadness, a deep and disturbing feeling from the past, stirred in Carol. She felt helpless, without any control of the situation. Tears filled her eyes. Nick had come up beside her without saying anything. He saw the tears in her eyes but didn't comment. He just put his hand over hers for a moment and then removed it.

"Troy was becoming a good friend," Carol said, starting to hide what she was really feeling. All of a sudden her need to share her true emotions overcame her normal protection mechanisms. She looked down at the water. "But that's not really why I'm upset just now. I'm crying because of the uncertainty. I can't stand not knowing." Carol paused and wiped her eyes.

Nick was quiet. He did not understand exactly what she was saying, but he sensed that something special was about to happen between them. The gentle waves lapped against the side of the boat. "It reminds me of my childhood, right after my father left," she continued softly. "I kept believing that he would be coming back. All three of us, Richie, my mom, and I, would tell each other that it was just a temporary separation, that someday he would walk through the door and say 'I'm home.' At night I would lie in my bed and listen for the sound of his car in the driveway."

The tears were flowing now, big drops cascading down her cheeks and falling into the vast ocean. "When he would come to pick us up for dinner, or on a Saturday, I would help Mom fix herself up, choose her clothes for her, brush her hair." Carol choked up for a moment. "After I hugged him at the door, I would always take him to Mother and say, 'Isn't she beautiful?'

"For six months this went on. I never knew what I was going to feel from day to day. The uncertainty destroyed me, made me sick. I begged my father to give my mom one more chance. Richie even suggested that he could buy the house next door if he and Mother couldn't get along. So we could at least all be close together." Carol smiled grimly and took a huge breath.

"Then my father took my mother to San Francisco for the weekend. I was so excited. For thirty-six hours my heart soared, my future was assured. I was the happiest ten-year-old girl in the San Fernando Valley. But when they came home on Sunday night my mother was very drunk. Her eyes were swollen, her mascara was running, she was a mess. She marched right past Richie and me and went to her room. My dad, Richie, and I stood in the living room, all hugging, and wept together. In that instant I knew it was all over."

Carol was calming down now but the tears were still there. She looked at Nick, her eyes entreating. "It would have been so much easier if I could have cried one time and been done with it. But no. There was uncertainty, so there was still hope. So every day, every goddamn day, my little heart was broken again." Carol wiped her eyes one more time. Then she looked out at the ocean and shouted with all her might, "I want to know now, or at least soon, what happened to Troy! Don't make me wait forever. I can't take it."

She turned to Nick. He opened his arms. Without a word, she put the side of her face against his chest. He closed his arms around her.

ICK reached above the door to Troy's duplex and found the key on the ledge. He knocked on the door again and opened it cautiously. "Hello," he called out, "is anybody there?"

Carol followed him into the living room. "I didn't know you two were such close friends," she said, after she glanced with amusement at Troy's motley collection of furniture. "I don't think I've ever told anyone where I keep my key."

What Nick was looking for was not in the living room. He walked down the hallway, past the large bedroom with its storehouse of equipment, and into the smaller bedroom where Troy slept. "Actually," Nick yelled at Carol, who had stopped behind him in the hall opposite the first bedroom and was gawking at the jumble of electronics filling every conceivable cranny, "it was only yesterday that I came over here for the first time. So I don't really know where . . . oh, good, I think I've found something." He picked up a sheet of computer printout that was underneath a paperweight on the end table beside Troy's bed. It was dated January 15, 1994, and contained about twenty names, addresses, and phone numbers.

Nick met Carol in the hallway. He read quickly through the page and showed it to her. "There's not much here. Phone numbers and addresses for electronics and software supply houses. A bunch of numbers for Angie Leatherwood, probably while she was still on tour." He pointed at one entry. "This must be his mother, Kathryn Jefferson, in Coral Gables, Florida. But there's no phone number listed with the address."

Carol took the sheet from Nick and checked it herself. "I never heard him mention anyone but Angie, his mother, and his brother Jamie. No other friends or family. And I somehow have the impression that he hasn't seen much of his mother recently. Did you ever hear him say anything about any other family?"

"No," Nick replied. They had wandered together into the game room and Nick was idly turning knobs and switches as he walked past the arrays of equipment. He stopped and thought for a moment. "So that means Angie is the one. We'll tell her right away and then wait—"

Carol and Nick both froze as they distinctly heard the front door open and close. After about a second, Nick called out in a loud but uncertain voice, "Hello, whoever it is, we're back here in the bedroom." There was no answer. They could hear soft footsteps in the hallway. Nick instinctively moved over to protect Carol. A moment later Troy came around the corner and into the room.

"Well, well," he said, grinning broadly, "as I live and breathe. I have found a pair of burglars in my home."

Carol ran up to Troy and threw her arms around his neck. "Troy," she said, her comments coming in quick staccato bursts, "is it ever good to see you. Where have you been? You scared the shit out of us. We thought you were dead."

Troy returned Carol's hug and winked at Nick. "My, my. Such a reception. I should have vanished before." He extended a hand to shake the one that Nick was offering him. For a moment his face became serious. "On second thought, one experience like that is definitely enough."

Carol backed away and Troy saw the computer sheet in her hand. "We were going to try to notify your family . . ." she started. Troy reached out to take the page and Carol noticed a bracelet on Troy's right wrist that she had never seen before. It was wide, almost an inch and a half, and looked as if its twenty or so links had been made from flattened gold nuggets. "Where did you get this?" Carol asked, holding his wrist up so that she could see the bracelet more clearly.

Nick was unable to restrain himself any longer. Before Troy could answer Carol's question, he jumped into the conversation. "According to Carol," he said, "you were last seen disappearing down a corridor in an underwater laboratory. With a six-foot amoeba in hot pursuit. How the hell did you escape? We searched all over the area . . ."

Troy held up his hands. He was enjoying being the center of attention. "Friends, friends. Wait a minute, will you? I will tell you the story as soon as I take care of the necessities of life." He turned and walked into the bathroom. Nick and Carol heard a familiar sound. "Get some beer out of the refrigerator and go into the living room," Troy shouted from behind the closed door. "We might as well enjoy this part of it."

Two minutes later Nick and Carol were sitting together on the large couch in the living room. Troy plopped into the chair opposite them just as Nick took a huge swig from his beer. "Once upon a time," Troy began with a mischievous grin, "there was a young black named Troy Jefferson, who, while diving with his friends, vanished for almost two hours in a strange building underneath the ocean. When he emerged from his underwater adventure, he was rescued by divers from the United States Navy, who just happened to be in the area at the time. Soon thereafter young Troy was flown in a military helicopter back to Key West. There he was interrogated at length about why he was swimming in the Gulf of Mexico, all by himself, ten miles from the nearest island. An hour later he was released without anyone believing any part of his story." Troy looked back and forth from Nick to Carol. "Of course," he added, now more serious, "I didn't tell them anything that really happened. There's no way they would have believed the truth."

Carol was leaning forward on the couch. "So the Navy picked you up. Just after we left." She turned to Nick. "They must have been following us for some reason." *The missile must have been there after all,* she thought to herself. *But where did it go? Did the Navy find it? And how are they involved with this crazy laboratory? Nothing makes sense . . .*

"We spent over an hour looking for you," Nick was saying. He was feeling remorseful because they had abandoned the search for Troy so quickly. "It didn't occur to me that you might still be down in that place, whatever it was, and of course we couldn't hang around forever. All of our electronics were zapped by this funny carpet thing that came out of the sea. So we lost all nav—" He stopped in mid-sentence and looked at Troy. "I'm sorry, friend."

"Don't worry about it," Troy replied with a shrug, "I would have done the same thing. At least I now know that you have met one of the bizarre characters in my story. You didn't, by any chance, also meet one of the wardens did you? Great big globs of clear jelly, amoebalike, with little boxes in the middle and removable rods hanging out all over the top?"

Nick shook his head. "Warden?" Carol asked quickly, her brow knitted. "Why do you call that thing a warden?"

"Warden, sentinel, whatever," Troy answered. "*They* told me the warden things protect the principal cargo of the ship." Troy stared into the blank gazes of his friends. "Which leads me back to the first question," he continued. "*They* gave me this bracelet. It is some kind of two-way communications device. I couldn't begin to explain how it works, but I know that *they* are listening and watching as well as transmitting messages to me. Only a few of which I understand."

Carol was starting to feel overwhelmed again. In her mind this already complex situation had added a new dimension. Hundreds of questions were crowding into her brain and she could not decide which one to ask first.

Meanwhile Nick stood up. "Hold it a minute," he said, looking dubious and just a little confused. "Did I hear you right? Did you say you were given a communications bracelet by some extraterrestrials and then released into the ocean? And then the Navy picked you up and brought you back to Key West? Christ, Jefferson, you do have an imagination. Save your creativity for that computer game. Please just tell us the truth."

"I am," replied Troy. "Really—"

"What did they look like?" Carol interrupted, her journalistic training taking over. She had pulled a small tape recorder, the size of a fountain pen, out of her purse. Troy reached over and switched it off. "For now, angel," he said, "this is strictly between us . . . I don't think I saw any of them anyway. Just the wardens and the carpets. And my guess is that they're just robots, machines of some type. Intelligent, yes, but controlled by something else—"

"Jesus," Nick interrupted, "you're serious." He was becoming exasperated. "This is turning into the most amazing shaggy dog story that I have ever heard. Wardens, carpets, robots. I am lost. Who are *they*? What are *they* doing in the ocean? And why have *they* given *you* a bracelet?" He picked up one of the little pillows on the couch and threw it across the room.

Carol laughed nervously. "Nick's not the only one feeling frustrated, Troy. I was with you down there and I must admit that I'm having a hard time tracking your story. Maybe we should stop interrupting and let you talk. I've told Nick what happened in that solar system room up until you ran out and the thing or warden followed. Start from there, if you would, and tell the story in logical sequence."

"I'm not sure there is such a thing as a logical sequence, angel," Troy replied, echoing Carol's laugh. "The whole episode defies logic altogether. The warden thing eventually trapped me in a blind alley and sort of anesthetized me with one of its rods. It was like I was dreaming, but the dreams were real. I remember a similar feeling, after a fistfight when I was a teenager. I had a small concussion then. I knew that I was alive, but I was very very slow to react. Reality seemed toned down, out there in the distance somewhere.

"Anyway, another warden character showed up, same kind of body but different fixtures sticking in the jelly, and carried me to what I think was an examination room. I don't know exactly how long I was there. I was stretched out on the floor and touched by all kinds of instruments. My brain felt as if it were in superfast motion, but I don't recall any specific thoughts. Some images I do remember. I relived my brother, Jamie, breaking through the line on a trap play and going forty-five yards for a touchdown in the Florida state championship. Then the bracelet was put on my wrist and I had the distinct impression that someone was talking to me. Very quietly, perhaps even in a foreign language, but every now and then I understood what was being said.

"What they told me," Troy continued with an intense and distant expression on his face, "was that what we call the laboratory is really a space vehicle from another world. And that it has crash-landed, in a sense, on the Earth to allow time for some difficult repairs. *They*, that is, whoever built the ship, need help from us, from me and you, to obtain some of the specific items necessary for the repairs. Then they can continue on their journey."

Nick was now sitting on the floor just opposite Troy. Both Carol and he were hanging on every word. They sat in silence for almost thirty seconds after Troy had finished. "If this story is true," Nick finally spoke, "then we are—"

There was a loud knock at the door. All three of them jumped. Several seconds later the knock repeated. Troy went to the door and partially opened it.

"There you are, you little shit," Carol and Nick heard a gruff, angry voice say. Captain Homer Ashford pushed through the door. He didn't see Nick and Carol at first. "We had a deal and you've welshed on it. You have been back two hours already . . ."

Out of the corner of his eye, Captain Homer saw that there were other people in the room. He turned around to talk to Greta, who had not yet entered the house. "Guess what?" he said. "Nick Williams and Miss Dawson are also here. No wonder we couldn't find her at the hotel."

Greta followed Homer into the living room. Her clear, expressionless eyes spent no more than one second staring at each of the trio. Carol thought she saw just a trace of disdain in Greta's look, but she wasn't certain. Homer turned to Carol, the tone in his voice markedly more civil. "We saw you two return from your excursion around two o'clock," he said with a fake smile. "But somehow we missed Troy." He winked at Carol and turned to Nick. "Find any more exciting trinkets today, Williams?"

Nick had never made any attempt to hide the fact that he did not like Captain Homer. "Why of course, Captain," he answered, sneering the epithet, "would you believe we found a veritable mountain of gold and silver bars? Looked like that *Santa Rosa* stack we had on the boat one afternoon, must be about eight years ago. Remember? That was before Jake and I let you and Greta unload it."

Homer's voice had a nasty edge to it. "I should have sued you for slander, Williams. That would have shut your loud mouth once and for all. You had your day in court. Now knock off the crap, or one day you'll have more trouble than you can handle."

While Nick and Homer were trading insults and threats, Greta was strutting around the living room as if she were in her own house. She seemed to be oblivious to the conversation and even to the presence of the other people in the room. She was wearing a tight white muscle shirt and a pair of navy blue shorts. When Greta walked, she carried her arms high, her back straight, and her breasts erect. Carol was intrigued by her behavior. She watched Greta stop and sort through Troy's compact discs. Greta pulled out the disc with the cover picture of Angie Leatherwood and licked her lips. *This pair belongs in a kinky novel*, Carol thought, as she overheard Troy tell Captain Homer that he was busy this afternoon but would get back to him later. *What's their story?* wondered Carol. *And where does fat Ellen fit in?* Carol remembered that she was scheduled to interview the three of them later in the evening. *But I'm not sure that I really want to find out.*

"We were calling to tell you to bring your swimming suit tonight," Captain Homer was addressing Carol. She had missed the first part of his statement while she was watching Greta parade around the room.

"Pardon me," she said politely. "Could you repeat what you just said? I'm afraid I had drifted away for a few seconds."

"I said that you should come early, about eight o'clock," Homer replied. "And bring your suit. We have a most interesting and unusual pool."

During this exchange, Greta walked up behind Nick and quickly reached both arms around him. With everyone else in the room watching, she lightly twisted his nipples through his polo shirt and laughed when he jumped. "You always did like that, ya, Nikki," she said, releasing him after an instant. Carol saw anger flash in Homer's eyes. Nick started to say something but Greta had already walked out the front door before he could register a protest.

"Be sure to call me when you're through here," Homer said to Troy after an embarrassing silence. "We need to straighten out a few things." The older man turned around, awkwardly, and without additional comment followed Greta toward his Mercedes parked in front of Troy's house.

"Now where were we?" said Troy abstractedly, as he closed the door behind Homer and Greta.

"*You*," said Nick with emphasis, "were telling us an amazing story and had almost reached the punch line, where you were going to tell us what we could do to help some aliens who landed here on Earth to repair their space vehicle. But first I, for one, would like some explanations. I don't know if I believe any of this wild fairy tale you're telling us, but I will admit that it is extremely creative. What concerns me at this minute, however, is not the issue of creatures from another world. It's those two real-life sleazebag human beings who just left. What did they want? And are they somehow involved in our current adventure?"

"Just a minute, Nick," Carol intervened. "Before we become sidetracked, I would like to know what kind of help these ETs of Troy's want from us. A telephone? A new spaceship? Let's find this out now and talk about Homer and your girlfriend Greta later." Her reference to Greta was light and playful. Nick accepted it with good humor and feigned a wound. Then he nodded his assent to Carol's suggestion. Troy pulled a sheet of paper from his pocket and took a deep breath.

"Now you guys must understand that I'm not yet absolutely certain that I am properly receiving all their messages. But this particular transmission, where they list the things they need from us, is repeated every half hour. My interpretation of it hasn't changed for the last ninety minutes, so I'm fairly certain that I have it right. It's a long list and of course I don't pretend to comprehend why they want all this stuff. But I am certain you will both find it very interesting."

Troy started reading from his handwritten list. "They want an English dictionary and grammar, plus the same thing for four other major languages; an encyclopedia of plant and animal life; a compact world history; a statistical tract defining the current political and economic status of the world; a comparative study of the world's major existing religions; complete issues covering the last two years of at least three significant daily newspapers; summary journals of science and technology, including surveys of weapon systems both deployed and under development; an encyclopedia of the arts, preferably including video and sound where appropriate; forty-seven pounds of lead; and fifty-eight pounds of gold."

Nick whistled when Troy was finished. At Carol's request, Troy handed the sheet to her and Nick read it another time over her shoulder, absorbing every item. Neither of them said anything. "Believe it or not," Troy added as an afterthought about a minute later, "the first eight items are not too difficult to obtain. I stopped by the Key West Public Library on the way home from the marina and, for a fee, they are preparing for me a set of compact discs that contain virtually all of the requested information. The difficult items are at the end of the list. That's where your help is needed."

Troy stopped for a second to see if Nick and Carol were following him. "Just to make certain I understand," Nick was now walking slowly around the room with the list in his hand, "what you want, or *they* want if you will, is for us to return to their laboratory or vehicle or whatever it is with all this information plus the lead and gold?" Troy nodded. "But fifty-eight pounds of gold? That's about a million dollars' worth. Where would we get it? And what would they do with it anyway?"

Troy acknowledged that he didn't know the answers to those questions. "But I have the feeling," he added, "again based upon what I think they are telling me, that partially satisfying their needs will make their task that much easier. So I guess we do what we can and hope that it's enough."

Nick shook his head back and forth. "You know, Carol," he said as he handed the list back to her, "never in my wildest flights of imagination could I have concocted such an intricate and crazy scheme. This entire thing is so unbelievable and fantastic that it just begs to be accepted. It's pure genius."

Troy smiled. "So you will help after all?" he asked.

"I didn't say that," answered Nick. "I still have lots of questions. And of course I can't speak for Miss Dawson. But somehow, even if it's all make believe, the idea of playing the good Samaritan for an extraterrestrial ship is very appealing."

During the next half hour both Carol and Nick questioned Troy extensively. Troy dismissed Homer and Greta in a hurry, simply stating that he had agreed on Thursday night to keep them informed about what was happening onboard the *Florida Queen* in exchange for a short-term loan. He also indicated that he never intended to really give them any information, but that was all right because they were crooks anyway. Nick was not completely satisfied with Troy's explanation. He felt that he was not being told the whole truth.

In fact, the more questions he asked, the more doubt there was in Nick's mind about the entire story Troy was telling. *But what are the other options?* Nick thought to himself. *I have seen that carpet with my own eyes. If it is not an ET, or at least made by one, then it must be a very advanced robot designed by us or the Russians.* As he continued to question Troy, Nick's facile mind began to construct an alternative scenario, admittedly wild and improbable, but one that nevertheless explained all the events of the previous three days in a way that Nick found just as reasonable as Troy's crazy story about the alien space vehicle.

Suppose somehow Troy and that turd Homer are working with the Rus-

sians. And this entire thing is just an elaborate cover for a rendezvous where illegal information will be passed. Homer would do anything for money. But why would Troy do it? Having Troy participate in a scheme to sell U.S. secrets to a foreign country was the acknowledged weakness in Nick's alternative explanation, but he rationalized it by convincing himself that perhaps Troy needed a lot of extra money to pay for all the electronic equipment in his computer game.

He certainly couldn't have saved enough money from his paltry salary, Nick continued thinking. *So suppose these computer discs of Troy's have secret military data instead of all that crazy information he just listed. Then the gold could be his payoff. Or someone else's.* Nick asked several more questions about the gold. Troy admitted he did not understand very well what *they* were telling him, through the bracelet, about why they needed the lead and the gold. He just mumbled something about those two elements being difficult to produce by transmutation and then added nothing else.

For her part, Carol grew more and more convinced that the story Troy was telling was true. His inability to answer all the questions did not disturb her; as a matter of fact, given the rather fantastic nature of his story, if he had had pat answers to all the questions, she would have felt less assured of its truth. Despite her critical journalistic background, she found herself intrigued and a little enchanted by the idea that some superaliens from another world needed her help.

Carol's intuition was just as important as her rational thought processes in the formation of her opinion. First of all, she trusted Troy. She watched him very carefully when he answered the questions and did not see the slightest indication that he was lying. She had no doubt that Troy believed he was telling the truth. But whether Troy was indeed telling the truth, or was instead being manipulated and directed by the very ETs that he was purporting to represent, was another issue altogether. *But for what purpose?* she reasoned. *There's not much that the three of us can do for them. Even the information they requested, except for the weapons stuff, is relatively innocuous.* She temporarily set aside the notion that her friend Troy had become some kind of pawn for the aliens.

Carol could tell that Nick was growing more suspicious. Nick thought it was very peculiar that there were three Navy divers in the water at the exactly correct location when one of the carpets ushered Troy to the surface. And Troy's report of the interrogation process after they had flown him to Key West was so confused that Nick became exasperated again.

"Christ, Jefferson," he said, "you either have a very short or a very convenient memory. You tell us that the Navy kept you in custody for almost an hour, yet you hardly remember any of their questions and have no idea why they were interrogating you. That just doesn't sound right to me."

Troy was becoming a little angry. "Shit, Nick, I told you that I was tired. I had been through a traumatic experience. Their questions didn't make sense to me. And the entire time I felt as if a little voice was trying to make itself heard inside my head."

Nick turned to Carol. "I think I'm changing my mind. I don't want to play in this game, no matter how clever it is. Homer and Greta annoy me, but I can deal with them if it's necessary. On the other hand, the Navy scares me. There was some reason they were following us. It's just too damn unlikely to be a coincidence. Maybe Troy knows something about it and maybe he doesn't. I can't tell. But I don't like the smell of it."

He stood up to leave. Carol motioned for Nick to sit down and took a deep breath. "Look, you two," she said in a low voice. "I have a confession to make. And it seems as if this is the perfect time to make it. I did not come down here to Key West to look for whales." She glanced at Nick. "And not for treasure either. I came here to check out a rumor that a new Navy missile had gone astray and crashed in the Gulf of Mexico." She paused several seconds to let her message register. "I probably should have told you earlier. But I never found the right time. I'm truly sorry."

"And you thought the missile was in the fissure," said Troy a few seconds later. "Which was why you came back yesterday."

"We were going to salvage it for you and give you a worldwide scoop," added Nick, his feeling of betrayal softened somewhat by the obvious sincerity of her apology. "You were using us all the time."

"You could call it that," Carol conceded, "but as a reporter, I don't see it that way." She noticed the tension in the room. Nick seemed especially guarded. "But now it doesn't matter anyway," she continued. "What is important is that I have given an explanation for the Navy's presence at the dive site. During the last two days I have made several inquiries at all levels about the clandestine activities that the Navy currently has underway to search for the missile. Last night that Mexican lieutenant got a good look at our best close-ups of the missile in the fissure. Undoubtedly someone put two and two together."

"Look, angel," Troy spoke after another short silence, "I don't know anything about a missile. And too much is going on for me to be hurt because you lied to me. I'm sure you had your reasons. What I need to know now is whether or not you will help me take this stuff back to the ETs or aliens or whatever you want to call them."

Before Carol could answer, Nick stood up again and started walking toward the door. "I'm very hungry," he announced, "and I want to think through this entire situation. If you don't mind, Troy, I'll have an early supper and meet you later on tonight with my answer."

Carol realized that she also was extremely hungry. It had been a long, exhausting day and she had not eaten anything significant since breakfast. She was also a little concerned about Nick's response to her confession. "Why don't I join you for a bite?" she said to Nick. He gave a noncommittal shrug, as if to say suit yourself. Carol gave Troy a hug. "Let's all meet at my room in the Marriott around seven-thirty. I have to go there anyway to dress for my interview with the triple creeps. You guys can give me some pointers."

Her humor did not lighten the atmosphere in the room. Troy was clearly worried about something. His face was very earnest, almost stern. "Professor," he said to Nick in a soft and deliberate monotone, "I know I didn't have all the answers to your questions. I don't even have the answers to my own. But I do know one thing for certain. Nothing like this has ever happened on the Earth before. At least not in recorded history. The creatures who built that spaceship are, when compared to us, as we would appear to the ants or the bees if they could comprehend us. They have asked the three of us for help in repairing their vehicle. To say that this is a once-in-a-lifetime opportunity would be a colossal understatement.

"It would be great if we could sit around and debate this issue for weeks or even months. But we can't. Time is running out. The Navy is certain to find them soon, maybe they have already, with possibly dire circumstances for the human beings on this planet. *They* have made it clear to me that their mission must be fulfilled, that they must repair their vehicle and continue their voyage, *even if* they must interfere with the Earth system to achieve their goal.

"I know all this sounds incredible, maybe even absurd. But I am going to collect some lead weights from my diver friends and pick up the compact discs at the library. With or without your help, I want to be over their spaceship at dawn tomorrow."

Nick studied Troy very carefully during this speech. For an instant in the middle, it seemed as if it were not Troy speaking at all, but someone or something else speaking through him. An eerie chill raced down Nick's spine. *Shit,* he thought. *I'm as bad as they are. I'm now caught up in this thing too.* He gestured to Carol to follow him and walked out the door.

"**A**S I have told you twice before," the voice sounded tired and bored, "I was out diving with my friends, Nick Williams and Carol Dawson. She had a problem with her equipment and decided to make a quick return to the boat. We had found a particularly interesting reef, with some very unusual features, and we weren't certain we would be able to locate it again. So I decided to stay and wait for her to come back. When I finally surfaced half an hour later, there was no sign of them or the boat."

The recorder clicked off. The two lieutenants stared at each other. "Shit, Ramirez, do you believe that bastard's story? Any part of it?" The other man shook his head. "Then why the hell did you let him go? That black shitass sat there for an hour, making fools out of us with ridiculous answers to our questions, and then you summarily released him."

"We can't detain someone without positive evidence of wrongdoing," responded Ramirez, as if he were quoting from a military manual. "And swimming in the ocean ten miles from the nearest island, although strange, does not constitute wrongdoing." Ramirez could see that his colleague was scowling. "Besides, he never slipped up. He always told exactly the same story."

"The same bullshit, you mean." Lieutenant Richard Todd leaned back in his chair. The two men were sitting around a small conference table in an old room with white plaster walls. The tape recorder was on the table in front of them next to an empty ashtray. "*He* didn't even believe his own story. He just sat there, that cocky grin on his black face, knowing that we couldn't charge him with anything." Todd put all four of his chair legs back on the floor and pounded the table for emphasis. "An experienced diver would never stay down by himself for five minutes, much less thirty. Too many things could go wrong. As for his friends, why the hell did they leave him?" Now Todd stood up and made gestures in the air with his hands. "I'll tell you why, Lieutenant. Because they knew he was all right, that he had been picked up by a Russian submarine. Shit, I told you we should have taken one of the new vessels. We probably could have spotted the sub with the upgraded electronic gear."

Ramirez was playing idly with the glass ashtray while Todd was giving his lecture. "You really believe that those three are involved with the Russians in this, don't you? It sure seems farfetched to me."

"Fucking A," replied Todd, "nothing else makes even a little sense. Every engineer we have talked to says there are no conceivable failures that are consistent both with the observed behavior of the missile and the telemetry we received at our tracking stations. So the Russians must have commanded it off course."

Todd grew excited as he explained the rest of the plot. "The Russians knew they would need some local help to find the exact location of the missile in the ocean, so they hired Williams and crew to search for the bird and then tell them where it was. They planned to pick it up with one of their subs. Adding that Dawson woman to their team was a master stroke; her inquiries have slowed down our own search by making us more concerned about the press."

Lieutenant Ramirez laughed. "You always sound convincing, Richard. But we still do not have even one shred of evidence. I don't believe Troy Jefferson's story any more than you do, but there could be many reasons why he lied, only one of which is any of our business. Besides, there still is a fundamental problem with your explanation. Why would the Russians go to all this trouble just to seize a Panther missile?"

"You and I and even Commander Winters may not know the true story of the Panther missile," Todd countered quickly. "It may be designed to carry some new breakthrough weapon that we haven't even heard about. It's not all that unusual for the Navy to represent a project falsely and to keep its true purpose hidden." He stopped to think. "But what's motivating the Russians is not that important to us. We have evidence of a conspiracy here. Our job is to stop it."

Ramirez did not reply right away. He continued to push the ashtray around on the table. "I guess I no longer view it that way," he said at length, gazing directly at Todd. "I see no substantial evidence of any conspiracy. Unless Commander Winters himself orders additional work from my department, I am abandoning my investigation." He looked at his watch. "At least I can still spend Saturday night and Sunday with my family." He rose to leave.

"And what if I bring you proof?" Todd asked, making no effort to hide his disgust with Ramirez.

"Proof will convince Winters as well," Ramirez answered coldly. "I have taken enough risk on this project. I will not take any more action unless instructed by the proper authority."

Winters wasn't really certain he would find something appropriate. Ordinarily, he carefully avoided shopping malls, especially on a Saturday afternoon. But while he had been lying on the couch, watching one of the NCAA basketball games and sipping a beer, he had remembered how pleased he had been when Helen Turnbull, who had played Maggie, had given him a set of unusual tile coasters after the opening weekend of *Cat on a Hot Tin Roof*. "It's a fading tradition in the theater, I fear," the experienced actress had said when he thanked her, "but giving small presents after the opening night or nights is still my way of congratulating those people I have enjoyed working with."

The mall was crowded with Saturday shoppers and Commander Winters felt oddly conspicuous, as if everyone were looking at him. He walked around for several minutes before he even thought about what kind of gift he might get for her. *Something simple of course,* he thought. *Nothing that could be misinterpreted. Just a nice memento or souvenir.* He saw Tiffani in his mind's eye as she had appeared in his fantasy just before he had fallen asleep the night before. The image embarrassed him in the shopping crowd and he nervously called up another picture, this one wholesome and acceptable, of the little girl Tiffani during his conversation with her father. *Her hair,* he thought, remembering the pigtails. *I'll buy her something for her hair.*

He walked into a gift shop and tried to make some sense out of the jumble of bric-a-brac that lined the walls and was assembled on top of an assortment of tables in no identifiable pattern. "Can I help you?" Winters jumped when a salesgirl approached him from behind. He shook his head. *Now why did you do that?* he said to himself. *Of course you need help. Otherwise you'll never find anything.*

"Excuse me, young lady," he almost shouted at the retreating salesgirl, "I guess I could use some advice. I want to buy a present." Winters again felt as if everyone were watching him. "For my niece," he added quickly.

The salesgirl was a brunette, about twenty, very plain, but with an eager face. "Did you have anything in mind?" she asked. Her hair was long, like Tiffani's. Winters relaxed a little.

"Sort of," he said. "She has beautiful long hair. Like yours. What could I get her that would be really special? It's her birthday." Again he felt a strange anxiety that he did not understand.

"What color?" the girl asked.

The question didn't make sense. "I don't even know yet what I want," he replied with a puzzled expression, "so I certainly don't know the color."

The salesgirl smiled. "What color is your niece's hair?" she said very slowly, almost as if she were speaking to a mental retard.

"Oh, of course," Winters laughed. "Reddish-brown, auburn," he said. "And it's very long." *You said that already,* a voice whispered inside of him. *You are acting like a fool.*

The salesgirl motioned for him to follow her and they walked back to the rear of the store. She pointed at a small round glass case full of combs of all shapes and sizes. "These would make excellent gifts for your niece," she said. There was an inflection in her voice when she said the word "niece" that bothered Winters. *Could she know something? One of her friends? Or maybe she was at the play?* He took a breath and calmed himself. Again Winters was astounded by the volatility of his emotions.

On one of the small shelves were two beautiful matching brown combs with gold filigree across the top. One of the combs was large enough to hold all that magnificent hair in a chignon against her neck. The other smaller comb was a perfect size to adorn the side or back of her hairstyle. "I'll take those," he said to the girl, "the ones with the gold work along the top. And please giftwrap them for me."

The efficient salesgirl reached inside the display case and pulled out the combs. She told Winters to wait a couple of minutes while she wrapped the present. She disappeared into the back of the store and Winters was left alone. *I'll leave them on her dressing table at the end of intermission,* he was thinking. He conjured up a picture of Tiffani going into the dressing room, by herself, and finding the present under her nameplate against the mirror. Winters smiled as he imagined her reaction. At that moment a woman with her eight- or nine-year-old daughter brushed by him in the store. "Pardon me," the woman said, without looking around, as she and the little girl rushed to finger some Easter baskets hanging on the wall.

The salesgirl had finished wrapping the present and was standing next to the computer cash register. When Winters reached the counter, she handed him a small card that had "Happy Birthday" imprinted on the upper left corner. Winters stared at it for a few seconds. "No," he said finally. "No card. I'll buy another at the stationery store."

"Cash or charge?" the girl asked him.

Winters panicked for a moment. *I don't know if I have enough cash on me*, he thought. *And how would I ever explain the charge to Betty?* He opened his wallet and counted his money. He smiled at the girl and said "Cash, please" when he realized that he had almost fifty dollars. The bill was only thirty-two dollars, including the tax.

Commander Winters felt a rush of joy as he nearly skipped out of the store. His earlier nervousness had completely disappeared. He even began to whistle just before he pushed open the door and left the enclosed air-conditioned environment of the mall. *I hope she likes the combs*, he said to himself. Then he smiled again. *I know she will.*

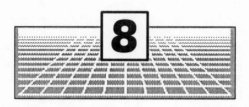

NICK poured the last of the bottle of Chablis into Carol's glass. "I don't think I could ever be a journalist," he said. "To be successful it sounds to me as if you have to be a sneak."

Carol moved a piece of broiled catfish mixed with some cauliflower onto her fork and put the bite in her mouth. "It's not that much different from any other job. There are always questions of ethics, as well as places where your personal and professional lives come into conflict." She finished chewing her food and swallowed before she continued. "I had thought that maybe I would tell you and Troy on Friday evening. But things just didn't work out, as you know."

"If you had," Nick pushed his plate away to indicate that he was finished with his meal, "then everything would have been different. I would have been aware of the possible danger and most likely it would have been you and I in that place together. Who knows what might have happened then."

"I've had worse conflicts before." Carol took a drink from her glass of wine. She wanted to finish with this subject. In her way. "Right after I graduated from Stanford, I worked for the *San Francisco Chronicle*. I was dating Lucas Tipton a little at the time that the Warrior drug scandal broke. I used the social contacts I had made through him to obtain a unique slant on the story. Lucas never forgave me. So I'm used to problems. They go with the territory."

A waiter came by and poured them some coffee. "But now that I have finished apologizing, for the third time," Carol said pointedly, "I hope we can go back to more important matters. I must tell you, Nick, that I find your Russian plot idea absolutely off the wall. The weakest element is Troy. There's simply no way he could be a spy. It's preposterous."

"More preposterous than a super-alien space vehicle in need of repairs at the bottom of the Gulf of Mexico?" Nick countered stubbornly. "Besides, I have a definite motive. Money. Did you see all the equipment he has wrapped up in that computer game?"

"Angie probably makes enough off her royalties in one week to cover all that computer stuff," Carol replied. She reached across the table and put her hand on Nick's forearm. "Now don't overreact, but you know there are some relationships where the woman carries the financial load. I can tell that she loves him. There's no doubt in my mind that she would offer to help him."

"Then why did he try to borrow money from me and then Captain Homer on Thursday night?"

"Hell, Nick, I don't know." Carol was becoming slightly frustrated. "But it's irrelevant anyway. I can't imagine any set of conditions, unless I was convinced that I was going to be killed, that would prevent my going back out there with Troy. Whatever the truth is, it is certainly a sensational story. I'm surprised you are so hesitant. I thought you were an adventurer."

Carol stared directly across the table at Nick. He thought he saw a flicker of flirtation hiding behind her unwavering gaze. *You are one fascinating woman,* he thought. *And you're taunting me a little now. I caught your double meaning.* He remembered how good he had felt when he held her on the boat in the afternoon. *Underneath that aggressive veneer is another person. Beautiful and intelligent. Hard as nails one minute and a vulnerable little girl the next.* Nick was certain that any hope he might have of continuing his relationship with Carol was dependant on his helping Troy. She wasn't interested in men who were not willing to take chances.

"I used to be," Nick finally replied. He twirled his empty wine glass in his hand. "I don't know what happened. I guess I got stung a couple of times and that has made me more cautious. Particularly where people are concerned. But I will admit that if I stand back from this situation and imagine myself as simply an observer, I find the whole affair absolutely fascinating."

Carol finished her wine and put the glass back on the table. Nick was quiet. She drummed her fingers on the tabletop and smiled. "Well," she said, fixing him with her eyes and picking up her coffee cup, "have you made a decision?"

He laughed. "Okay. Okay. I'll do it." Now it was his turn to reach out and touch her arm. "For lots of reasons."

"Good," she remarked. "Now that something has been decided, why don't you help me prepare for my interview with Captain Homer and the crew. How much was the stuff worth that you pulled up from the *Santa Rosa*? And who was Jake? I must act as if I'm serious about this story." Carol put her fountain pen tape recorder on the table and turned it on.

"We officially cleared a little over two million dollars. Jake Lewis and I each received ten percent, Amanda Winchester was reimbursed for the expense advance plus twenty-five percent of the profit. Homer, Ellen, and Greta kept the rest." Nick stopped but Carol indicated for him to continue. "Jake Lewis was the only close friend I have ever had as an adult. He was an absolute peach of a person, honest, hard-working, intelligent, and loyal. And completely naive. He fell for Greta like a ton of bricks. She manipulated him completely and then used his love to her own advantage."

Nick looked away, out the window of the small seafood restaurant, at some seagulls who were soaring over the water in the fading twilight. "The night we came back with the big haul, Jake and I agreed that one of the two of us would always be awake. Even then there was something peculiar in the Homer-Ellen-Greta triangle. At that time they were not yet all living together, but I still didn't trust them. While Jake was supposedly on watch, Greta balled his brains out. 'To celebrate,' he said, when he apologized to me for falling asleep afterwards. When I woke up, more than half of the treasure was gone."

Anger long buried was seething in Nick. Carol watched him carefully, noting the intensity of his passion. "Jake didn't give a shit about the money. He even tried to talk Amanda and me out of going to court. That's the kind of guy he was. I remember he told me, 'Hey, Nick, my friend, we made two hundred thousand apiece out of this. We cannot prove there was more. Let's just be thankful and get on with our lives.' Homer had cheated him and Greta had shit all over him, but Jake still wasn't pissed. Not much more than a year later, he married a water ski queen from Winter Haven, bought a house in Orlando, and went to work as an aerospace engineer."

The light was vanishing outside. Nick was deep in a memory, recalling the full measure of his storm of righteous indignation from eight years before. "I've never understood them," Carol said quietly. She switched off the recorder. Nick turned and looked at her, a quizzical frown on his face. "You know," she added, "the people like your friend Jake. Infinite resiliency. No harbored grudges. Whatever happens to them they just shake off, like water, and go on living. Cheerfully." It was her turn to feel a little emotion. "Sometimes I wish I could be more like that. Then I wouldn't be afraid."

They stared at each other in the soft light. Nick put his hand over hers. *And there's that vulnerable little girl again.* He felt a deep emotional longing stirring in his heart. *She's let me see it twice in a single day.* "Carol," he said gently, "I want to thank you for this afternoon. You know, for sharing your feelings with me. I feel like I saw an entirely different Carol Dawson."

"You did," she said, smiling and making it clear that her protective shield was going up again. "And only time will tell if it was a huge mistake." She pulled her hand slowly away from his. "For the moment, though, we have other business. Back to the menage à trois. What kind of facility is it that they manage and what do they do there?"

"Excuse me?" replied Nick, obviously confused.

"A friend of mine, Dr. Dale Michaels of the Miami Oceanographic Institute, told me that Captain Homer and Ellen have some kind of high-tech operation here. I don't remember exactly how he described it—"

"You must be mistaken," Nick interrupted. "I have known them for almost ten years and they are never anywhere except in that fancy house of his or onboard the *Ambrosia*."

Carol was puzzled. "Dale's information is always correct. He just told me, yesterday in fact, that Homer Ashford had field tested the institute's most advanced underwater sentries throughout the last five years and that his reports—"

"Hold it. Hold it." Nick was leaning forward on the table. "I'm not sure I'm following you. Back up. This could be very very important."

Carol started again. "One of MOI's newest product areas is underwater sentries, robots, essentially, that protect aquaculture farms from sophisticated thieves as well as large fish or whales. Dale said that Homer contributes money for the research and then field tests the prototypes—"

"*Son of a bitch*." Nick was standing up. He was bursting with excitement. "How could I have been so stupid? Of course, of course."

Now Carol was lost. "Would you mind telling me what's going on?"

"Certainly," Nick answered. "But right now we're in a hurry. We have to go by my apartment to look at an old map and pick up another navigation system for the boat. I'll explain everything on the way."

Nick put his key card in the reader and the garage door opened. He pulled his Pontiac into his reserved spot and stopped the car. "So you see," he was saying to Carol, "he knew that we wouldn't find anything. He let us search both his house *and* the lot that he had bought for his new mansion, down at Pelican Point. We found nothing. At that time it was still hidden somewhere out in the ocean."

"Did you look in the water around his new property at that time?"

"Yes, we did. Jake and I each dove there, on separate days. We found a very interesting subterranean cave, but no sign of any of the *Santa Rosa* treasure. But we must have given him the idea. I bet he moved the stuff there a year or two after Jake left. He probably figured it was safe by then. And he had doubtless worried himself sick that someone would discover the treasure out in the ocean. You see, it all fits. Including his involvement with underwater sentries."

Carol nodded and laughed a little. "It certainly makes better sense than your idea that Troy was working for the Russians." They opened the doors and climbed out of the car. "So how much do you think they have left?" Carol asked as they headed for the elevator.

"Who knows?" Nick answered. "Maybe they stole three million out of five." He thought for a minute. "They must still have a bunch. Otherwise Greta would have split by now."

The elevator doors opened and Nick pressed the button for the third floor. Carol heaved a big sigh. "What's the matter?" he asked.

"I'm exhausted," she said. "I feel as if I'm on a carousel that's spinning faster and faster. So much has happened in the last three days. I'm not sure I could deal with much more. What I need now is a second wind."

"Magic days," Nick replied as they walked out of the elevator. "These are magic days."

She looked at him with a curious expression. He laughed. "I'll explain an old theory of mine later," he said. He entered a sequence of numbers into the small plate on his door and the lock disengaged. Nick moved to the side with feigned gallantry and let Carol enter first. What she saw was chaos.

The place was a total shambles. In the living room, just beyond the kitchen area, all of Nick's precious novels had been scattered randomly about on the floor, the couch, and the chairs. It looked as if someone had taken each book out of the bookcase, held it up and shook it (trying to find loose papers perhaps), and then either dropped it or thrown it across the room. Nick pushed by Carol and stared at the destruction. "Shit," he said.

The kitchen had been plundered as well. All the drawers were open. Pots, pans, and tableware were strewn on the counters and on the floor. To Nick's right, the cardboard boxes containing his memorabilia had been pulled into the middle of the second bedroom. Their contents had been partially dumped onto the floor around them.

"What hurricane hit this place?" Carol asked as she surveyed the mess. "I didn't expect you to be a good housekeeper, but this is ridiculous."

Nick was unable to laugh at Carol's comment. He checked the master bedroom and found that it also had been ransacked. He then returned to the living room and started picking up his beloved novels and stacking them neatly on the coffee table. He winced when he found his worn copy of *L'Etranger* by Albert Camus. The spine of the book was destroyed. "This is not the work of vandals," he said as Carol knelt down to help. "They were searching for something specific."

"Have you found anything missing yet?" she asked.

"No," Nick replied, picking up another novel with a mutilated cover and shaking his head. "But the bastards have really screwed up my books."

She stacked his Faulkner collection on the easy chair. "I can see why Troy was impressed," she said. "Have you really read all these novels?" Nick nodded. Carol picked one up that had fallen under the television stand. "What's this about?" She held up the book. "I've never even heard of it."

Nick had just arranged another dozen books on the coffee table. "Oh, that's a fantastic novel," he said enthusiastically, forgetting for a moment that his condominium had just been trashed. "The whole story is told through this exchange of letters among all the principal characters. It's set in eighteenth-century France, and the main couple, socially prominent and bored, cement their weird relationship by sharing details of their affairs. With other lovers of course. It caused quite a scandal in Europe."

"That doesn't exactly sound like your typical Harlequin romance," Carol remarked, trying to commit the title of the book to her memory.

Nick stood up and walked into the smaller bedroom. He began to sort through the contents of the cardboard boxes. "There are things missing in here," he called out to Carol. She stopped arranging books and joined him in the bedroom. "All my photographs of the *Santa Rosa* treasure and even the newspaper clippings are gone. That's odd," he said.

Carol was beside him on the floor, in front of the boxes. She frowned. "Is the trident still on the boat?"

"Yes," he answered. He stopped rifling through the papers. "Down in the bottom drawer of the electronics cabinet. You think there's a connection?"

She nodded. "I think that was what they were after. I don't know why. It just seems right."

Nick picked up a large yellow folder that had been on the floor and replaced it in one of the cardboard boxes. A photograph and some sheets of typing paper fell out. Carol picked up the picture while Nick scrambled after the papers. She studied the photo and read the French inscription. She was surprised to feel a twinge of jealousy. "Beautiful," she commented. She noticed the pearls. "Also very rich and sophisticated. She doesn't look like your type."

She handed Monique's photograph to Nick. Despite his attempt to be nonchalant, he was blushing. "That was a long time ago," he mumbled as he hastily stuffed the photo back into the folder.

"Really?" Carol said, eyeing him carefully. "She looks as if she's about our age. It couldn't have been too long ago."

Nick was flustered. He packed some more loose material in the boxes and glanced at his watch. "We'd better leave soon if we're going to meet Troy at your hotel." He stood up. Carol remained kneeling on the floor, looking up at him with a steady gaze. "It's a long story," he said. "Someday I'll tell you all about it."

Carol's curiosity was piqued. She followed Nick out of his condominium and into the elevator. He was still ill at ease. *Bullseye,* she thought to herself. *I think I have just discovered a major key to Mr. Williams. A woman named Monique.* She smiled as Nick motioned for her to precede him out of the elevator. *And the man does love his books.*

Carol's room at the Marriott had two entrances. The normal approach to the room was by way of the corridor that led to the lobby. But there was another door that opened on the garden and the pool. When she exercised in the morning, Carol always used the garden entrance.

Nick and Carol were talking casually but quietly as they came toward her room from the lobby. She pulled out her electronic card key just before they arrived. As she started to insert the card into the lock, they heard an unusual sound, like metal banging against metal, from the inside of her room. Before Carol could say anything, Nick shushed her by putting his finger to his mouth. "You heard it too?" she whispered softly. He nodded his head. Using gestures, he asked her if there was another entrance to the room. She pointed out the door to the hotel grounds at the end of the corridor.

Palm trees and tropical hedges covered most of the area to the east of the Marriott swimming pool. Nick and Carol left the walkway leading to the pool and crept up to the windows of her room. The venetian blinds were drawn but they could still see into the room through a crack under the bottom of the blinds. At first the room was completely dark. Then a solitary beam from a flashlight reflected for an instant off one of the walls. In that split second they saw a silhouetted figure in the neighborhood of the television set, but they could not identify him. The flashlight came on again and it paused for a moment on the door to the corridor. The door was bolted. In the brief flicker of the light beam, Carol also saw that all her dresser drawers were open.

Nick crawled over next to Carol in the flower bed just under the windows. "You stay here and watch," he whispered. "I'll go get something from the car. Don't let them know you're here." He squeezed her shoulder and disappeared. Carol stayed glued to the window. Once more the flashlight came on, illuminating electronic parts spread out on the far bed. Carol strained for a look at who was holding the flashlight. She couldn't see him.

She became acutely aware of the passage of time. Her intuition told her that the intruder was getting ready to leave. She suddenly realized she was completely exposed sitting out there underneath the window. *Come on, Nick,* she said to herself. *Hurry it up. Or I may be chopped liver.* The figure in the room moved toward the garden door and then stopped. Carol felt her pulse rate increase. At just that moment Nick returned, out of breath. He had brought back a long crowbar from the trunk of his car. Carol motioned to him to stand by the door, that the intruder was about to come out.

She saw the figure put his hand on the doorknob and she flattened herself against the dirt. Nick was behind the door, poised to deliver a powerful blow to whoever exited from the room. The door opened, Nick started to strike. "Troy," screamed Carol from the flower bed. He jumped back just in time, barely missing the downward swoop of Nick's crowbar. Carol was on her feet in an instant. She ran up to a shaken Troy. "Are you all right?" she said.

His eyes were wide from fright. "Jesus, Professor," he said, glancing at the crowbar that Nick was wielding, "you might have killed me."

"Shit, Jefferson," Nick replied, the adrenaline still coursing through his system, "why didn't you tell us it was you? And what were you doing in Carol's room?" He looked at Troy accusingly.

Troy backed into the room and turned on the lights. The room was a disaster. It looked like Nick's condominium when Carol had first walked through the front door.

Carol turned to Troy. "Why on earth . . ."

"I didn't do it, angel," he replied. "Honest Injun." Troy looked at his two friends. "Sit down," he said. "This will only take a second."

Meanwhile Carol's eyes were scanning the room. "Crap," she said angrily, "all my cameras and film are gone. And virtually the entire telescope system, including the post-processor unit. Dale will shoot me." She looked in one of the open drawers. "The assholes took my photographs from the first dive as well. They were in a large envelope on the right side of this top drawer."

Carol sat down on the bed looking a little dazed. "All the film from the photographs that I took inside that place has been stolen. So much for my sensational story," she said.

Nick tried to comfort her. "Who knows. Maybe they'll turn up. And besides, you still have all the negatives from the first dive."

Carol shook her head. "It's not the same thing." She thought for a minute. "Damnit," she said, "I should have kept the exposed film with me when we left the hotel to go to Troy's apartment." She looked at the two men and then brightened a bit. "Oh well," she said. "There's always tomorrow."

Troy was still waiting patiently to give his explanation. He indicated for Nick to sit down on the bed next to Carol. "I'll make this short and sweet," he said. "Just the facts. I arrived here about seven o'clock. I came early because I wanted to make some modifications to your television set. I'll explain why in a minute.

"The people in the hotel wouldn't give me a key to your room so I came down here and fooled the card reader." He smiled. "It's no problem for someone who knows how these things work. Anyway, as soon as the green light came on and the guard bolt released, I heard the garden door slam. Someone had been in the room while I was opening the door. I caught a fleeting glimpse of him as he hightailed it around the corner of the building. He was a big man, not someone I recognized immediately. He was moving with difficulty, as if he were carrying something heavy."

"Part of the ocean telescope," Carol said.

"Go on," added Nick. "What happened next? I want to hear why you were in Carol's room working in the dark. I bet you'll come up with a good story for that too."

"That's easy," Troy said to Nick. "I was afraid the thief or thieves might come back. I didn't want them to see me."

"You're amazing, Jefferson," Nick responded. "You're the kind of person who would tell a cop that you were exceeding the speed limit because you wanted to get to a filling station before you ran out of gas."

"And the cop would believe him," Carol remarked. They all laughed. The tension in the room was diffusing.

"All right," said Nick. "Now tell us what you've done to the television. Incidentally, how did you get inside it? I thought these hotel sets were all alarmed."

"They are," Troy replied, "but it's very simple to disable the alarm system. It always cracks me up. Somebody sells the hotel the idea that they can protect their property with these alarms. But the burglars can easily find out what system has been installed, buy the circuit data sheets, and completely disable the protection."

Troy glanced around the room. He then checked his watch carefully. "Let's see," he said. "Why don't you two move over here in these chairs. I think you'll be able to see better." Nick and Carol exchanged puzzled looks and arranged themselves as Troy had requested. "Now," he continued in a surprisingly serious tone, "you will see what I believe is incontrovertible proof that my story about the aliens is true. They have told me, through this bracelet, that they are going to televise a short program from inside the vehicle at exactly seven-thirty. If I have translated their directions properly and made the correct modifications, this television should now be able to receive their transmission."

He turned on the set and put it on channel 44. There was nothing but snow and static. "This is great, Troy," Nick commented. "It will probably steal rating points from soap operas and music videos. Watching this requires even less intelligence—"

A picture suddenly appeared on the screen. The lighting was poor, but Carol immediately recognized herself in the scene. She was standing with her back to the cameras, her fingers moving around on top of what appeared to be a table. An orchestral version of "Silent Night," featuring an instrument not unlike an organ, accompanied the picture.

"That's the music room I told you about," Carol said to Nick. "I guess that warden thing had a video camera in all his paraphernalia."

The television scene switched immediately to a close-up of Carol's eyes. For five seconds her marvelous, frightened eyes filled almost the entire screen. She blinked twice before the camera pulled back and revealed her in front view, terrified, standing and shaking in her bathing suit. Carol shuddered as she recalled the horror of those seconds when the warden's appendages intruded upon her person. It was all shown in the video, some parts even in slow motion. One of the featured scenes was the deliberate movement of the bristles across her chest, including both her erect nipples. *Oh my God*, she thought. *I hadn't realized they were erect. Maybe fear does that.* Carol squirmed. She felt surprisingly embarrassed in front of Nick.

There was a jump discontinuity in the program. In the next scene the three of them were looking at Troy, lying on his back on the floor somewhere, with enough wires and cords attached to him that he could have been Gulliver bound by the Lilliputians. The camera panned around the room. Two wardens were in one of the corners. Their upper body attachments were not even similar, but they both had the same central body, amoebalike, that had confronted Troy and Carol. On the other side of the room a pair of carpets were standing together. From their motions it looked as if they were engaged in a conversation. Nick and Carol and Troy watched while the camera stayed fixed for about ten seconds. The carpets apparently finished conferring and then flipped off in separate directions.

The final frames of the transmission were a close-up of Troy's head showing more than a hundred probes and inserts connected to his brain. Then the screen went back to snow and static. "Wowee," said Nick after a moment. "Can I have an instant replay?" He stood up from the bed. "You were terrific," he remarked to Carol, "but I think your scenes will have to be edited if we want a PG rating."

Carol looked up at him and blushed slightly. "Sorry, Nick, but I don't think you make a good comedian. We have one already," she nodded at Troy, "and I think that's enough." She glanced at the clock beside her bed. "Now I figure we have fifteen minutes or so to make plans. No more. And I have to dress as well. Why don't you tell Troy about your decision and what you have concluded about the *Santa Rosa* loot while I change my clothes." She grabbed a blouse and a pair of pants and headed for the bathroom.

"Hey, wait a minute," Nick protested. "Aren't we going to discuss who it was that broke into my condominium and your hotel room?"

Carol stopped outside the bathroom door. "There are only two possibilities that make any sense," she said. "It's either the Navy or our sicko friends from the *Ambrosia*. Either way we'll find out soon enough." She stopped a moment and an elfin smile played across her lips. "I want you two to see if you can figure out a way to steal Homer's gold. Tonight. Before we go back to meet with our extraterrestrials tomorrow morning."

CAROL and Troy went over the details one last time and she checked her watch. "It's eight-thirty already," she said. "If I'm much later I know they'll be suspicious." She was standing outside Nick's Pontiac in the parking lot of the Pelican Resort, a restaurant about three-quarters of a mile from the Ashford mansion at Pelican Point. "Where is he?" she fretted. "We should have finished with this fifteen minutes ago."

"Just calm down, angel," Troy replied. "We have to test this new unit first. It could be very important in an emergency and I've never actually used it." He gave her a reassuring hug. "Your friends at MOI originally developed it."

"Why did I have to suggest such a wild-ass idea?" Carol said out loud to herself. "Where's your brain, Dawson? Did you leave it in the . . ."

"Can you hear me?" Nick's garbled voice interrupted her. It sounded as if it were coming from the bottom of a well.

"Yes," Troy answered into a tiny walkie-talkie shaped like a thimble. "But not too clearly. How deep are you?"

"Say again," said Nick. "I did not copy completely."

"Yes, we can hear you," Troy shouted. He carefully enunciated each word. "But not very clearly. You must speak slowly and distinctly. How deep are you?"

"About eight feet," was the response.

"Go down to sixteen and try it again," said Troy. "Let's see if it will work from the deepest part of the cave."

"How's he doing that?" Carol asked, while they waited for Nick to descend.

"It's a brand-new system, built into the regulator," Troy answered. "You have to speak while you're exhaling for it to work. There's a small transmitter/receiver inside the mouthpiece and an earphone attachment. Unfortunately, it doesn't work much below ten feet."

Almost a minute later Carol and Troy heard something, very faint, not even recognizable as Nick's voice. Troy listened for a moment. "We cannot read you, Nick. There is too much attenuation. Come on back now. I'm going to send Carol on her way." Troy pressed a button on the walkie-talkie that would repeatedly transmit this last message.

He handed the communications unit to Carol. "Okay, angel," he said, "you're ready. We should be in the water around nine o'clock and out, if all goes well, by half an hour later. Keep them occupied with your questions. You should leave by ten-thirty at the latest and drive directly to Nick's apartment. We will meet you there with your wagon." He raised his eyebrows. "And the gold, I hope."

Carol took a deep breath. She smiled at Troy. "I'm scared," she said. "I would rather face a carpet or even one of those warden things than this trio." She opened the car door. "Do you really think I should go in Nick's car? Isn't that certain to make them suspect something?"

"We've been through all this twice before, angel," Troy laughingly replied. He gently nudged her into the car. "They already know we're friends. Besides, we need your wagon for the diving gear, the backpacks, and the lead and gold." He closed the door and planted a light kiss on her cheek through the open window. "Be safe, angel," he said. "And don't take any unnecessary chances."

Carol started the car and backed into the middle of the parking lot. She waved at Troy and pulled into the dark lane that led through the marsh to the end of the island. The only light was from the nearly full gibbous moon that was already above the trees. *All right, Dawson,* she thought to herself. *Now you're in the middle of it. Just stay calm and alert.*

She drove very slowly. She reviewed the plans for the evening several times in her mind. Then she started thinking about Nick. *He holds on to things. Like I do. He still hates Homer and Greta for cheating him. He couldn't wait to dive for the gold.* She smiled as she turned into the circular drive in front of Homer Ashford's house. *I just hope there is some left over for him.*

A split second after Carol rang the doorbell, Homer opened the door and greeted her. "You're late," he said in a pleasant monotone. "We thought maybe you were not coming. Greta is already in the pool. Do you want to change and join her?"

"Thanks, Captain Homer, but I decided not to swim tonight," Carol answered politely. "I appreciate the offer, but I'm mostly here on business. I would prefer to start the interview as soon as possible. Even before dinner, if that would be all right with everyone else."

Homer led Carol into a gigantic family room and stopped by a large wet bar. A magnificent hand-carved wooden statue of a swimming Neptune, about four feet long altogether, was on the wall above the bar. Carol asked for some white wine. Homer tried without success to talk her into something stronger.

The family room had a billiards table at one end. On the other side, a sliding glass door opened onto a covered patio that narrowed into a cement walkway. Carol followed Homer in silence, sipping from her white wine every twenty steps or so. The walkway wound past big trees and a lighted gazebo off to the left before it spread out around the huge swimming pool.

Actually there were two pools. In front of Carol was a classic, rectangular, Olympic-sized pool under strong lights. At one end was a slide and waterfall that ran down an artificial mountain into the swimming area. At the other end, in the direction of the second pool and the ocean, there was a sunken Jacuzzi constructed out of the same decorated blue tiles that rimmed the top of the main pool. The entire complex was cleverly designed to create the impression of moving water. There seemed to be a steady flow from the waterfall, to the large pool, down into the Jacuzzi, and then into a stream that meandered off in the direction of the house.

The second pool was circular and dark. It was off to Carol's left at the edge of the property, near what looked like a small cottage for changing clothes. Greta was in the rectangular pool in front of Carol. She was swimming laps, her powerful body moving rhythmically through the water. Carol, who was an excellent swimmer herself, watched Greta for a few seconds.

"Isn't she something?" Homer walked over next to Carol. His admiration was obvious. "She won't let herself eat a big meal unless she works out beforehand. She can't stand fat."

Homer was wearing a light brown Hawaiian shirt with a pair of tan slacks. Brown loafers were on his feet, and a big drink, crammed with ice cubes, was in his hand. He seemed relaxed, even affable. Carol thought he could have passed for a retired banker or corporate executive.

Greta continued to swim relentlessly through the water. Homer was hovering over Carol and she was beginning to feel uncomfortable, as if her space were being invaded. "Where's Ellen?" she asked, turning to the large man and moving just slightly farther away from him.

"She's in the kitchen," Homer replied. "She loves to cook, especially when we have guests. And tonight she's making one of her favorite dishes." There was almost a twinkle in his eye. He leaned down to Carol. "She made me promise not to tell you what we're having," he whispered confidentially, "but I will tell you that it's a powerful aphrodisiac."

Ugh, said Carol to herself as she caught a whiff of Homer's breath and listened to his leering chuckle. *How could I have forgotten how repulsive this man is? Does he really think that . . .* Carol stopped her thought. She reminded herself that people with excessive money very often lose touch with reality. *Probably some of the women respond. For what he can give them.* She almost gagged. The thought of having any kind of sexual liaison with Homer was totally repugnant.

Greta had finished swimming laps. She climbed out of the pool and dried herself off. Her all-white racing uniform was like a transparent body stocking. Even from a distance, Carol could not avoid seeing the full detail of her nipples and breasts as well as her clump of pubic hair through the thin suit. She might as well have been naked. Homer stood beside Carol, unabashedly staring as Greta strode across the cement.

"No suit?" Greta said just before she reached them. Her eyes were trying to bore holes in Carol's. Carol shook her head. "I'm sorry," said Greta. "Homer had hoped that we might have a race." She looked at the captain with an odd expression that Carol did not understand. "He loves to see women in competition."

"It would have been no contest," Carol answered. She thought she saw Greta tense. "You would have won easily," she added. "You swim beautifully."

Greta smiled, accepting the compliment. Her eyes roamed over Carol's body. She made no effort to hide the fact that she was doing an appraisal. "You have a good body too for swimming," Greta said. "Maybe a little too fat on the ass and upper legs. I could suggest workout—"

"Why don't we show Miss Dawson the other pool?" Homer interrupted. "Before you go inside and change clothes." He started walking toward the little cottage near the ocean. Without saying another word, Greta turned and followed him. Carol took a sip from her wine. *Who knows what goes on here,* she thought. *Those three have not had to work for eight years. They take people out fishing and diving for amusement.* A strange mixture of disgust and depression started to spread in her. *So they manufacture entertainment to keep from being bored.*

Moments after Homer entered the cottage, a bank of floodlights down underneath the second pool was illuminated. Homer gestured for her to hurry and Carol skipped into the cottage. They led her down a flight of steps. Under the ground was a walkway that completely encircled the large glass aquarium that had looked, in the darkness, like a second swimming pool. "We have six sharks now," Homer said proudly, "as well as three red occi, a pair of cuttlefish, and of course hundreds of more standard species of fish and plants."

"Occi?" inquired Carol.

"That's the slang plural of octopus," Homer responded with a smug, self-satisfied smile. "Actually, the correct plural is octopodes, even though everyone now accepts octopi because it has been used so much."

Greta was standing with her face pressed against the glass. A couple of bat rays swam past. She was waiting for something. After twenty seconds or so a grayish shark appeared. The shark seemed to notice Greta and stopped, watching her, its face about five feet away from the glass. Carol could see the long sharp teeth and identified it as a mako, a fierce smaller cousin of the man-eating great white shark.

"That's Greta's pet," said Homer. "His name is Timmy. Somehow she has trained him to recognize her face against the glass." Homer watched a few more seconds. "From time to time she goes in there to swim with him. When the sharks have finished eating, of course."

The shark remained in place, staring blankly in Greta's direction. She began to drum her fingers against the glass in regular cadence. "Now this is exciting," Homer said, walking over next to Greta and the aquarium. "What you are going to see is what biologists call a typical Pavlovian response. I've never seen it quite this way before in a shark."

The mako began to be agitated. Greta started increasing the tempo, the shark responding by whipping the water back and forth with its tail. Suddenly Greta disappeared up the stairs. Carol thought she noticed a faraway look in her eyes when Greta zoomed by her. Carol looked at Homer for an explanation. "Come down here closer," he gestured to Carol. "You don't want to miss this. Greta cares for the rabbits herself. And Timmy always puts on a grand show."

Carol wasn't exactly sure what Homer was talking about. But she was enjoying the lovely aquarium. It contained crystal-clear sea water, obviously filtered and recycled regularly. Carol noticed several species of sponges and coral, as well as urchin and anemone. Someone had gone to great trouble and expense to re-create the conditions in the reefs just offshore Key West.

Suddenly a beheaded white rabbit impaled on a long vertical staff, the blood still spurting from its arteries, appeared in the aquarium just opposite where Carol and Homer were standing. It was over in an instant. Driven to immediate frenzy by the blood in the water, the mako attacked, its teeth ripping half the hapless rabbit off the stave with the first bite. The second swoop captured the rest of the rabbit and snapped the rod as well. Carol barely had time to recoil and turn her head. When she jumped back, she spilled wine all over her blouse.

Trying to appear calm, she reached in her purse for a tissue to wipe her blouse. She said nothing. She had had a perfect view of the shark's attack and could still feel the adrenaline imbalance that the fright had produced. *Great way to start a dinner party*, she thought. *Why haven't I ever thought of it. Dawson, these people are weird.*

Homer was still excited. "Wasn't that spectacular? Such raw, savage power in those jaws. Driven by pure instinct. I never get tired of it."

Carol followed him up the stairs. "Good show, Greta," she heard Homer say when they walked out of the cottage. "It was right in front of us. Two bites. Wham, wham, and the rabbit was gone."

"I know," said Greta. She was holding a diving mask. What was left of the staff was on the ground beside her. "I could see from up here." Greta was staring at Carol, obviously trying to discover her reaction. Carol averted her eyes. She was not going to give Greta the satisfaction of knowing she had found it repulsive.

"Greta has the whole thing down to split-second timing," Homer continued as they walked back through the gardens to the house. "She prepares the live rabbit on the chopping block an hour early. Then, when Timmy is ready, she . . ."

Carol tuned his gruesome story out of her mind. *I don't want to hear this*, she thought. She glanced at her watch. *Ten minutes after nine. Come on guys. Be swift. I'm not certain I can stand these people for another hour.*

Nick and Troy swam silently along the shoreline in the moonlight. They had carefully rehearsed the plan. No additional light until they were in the cove beside Homer's property and at least ten feet under water. Troy would lead, searching for alarm systems he could disable with the tools stuffed in the pockets of his wet suit. He would also keep a lookout for the infamous robot sentries. Nick would follow with the buoyancy bags they would use to carry the gold.

They had walked along the beach from the Pelican Resort parking lot, wearing their heavy diving suits as well as the backpacks, until they were only about a hundred yards from the thick fence that marked Homer's property. Then they had set down the packs containing their clothes and eased into the water. During the walk Troy had had several problems with his tools, and a decision to reduce his arsenal of gadgets had delayed their arrival at the embarkation point by five minutes. Just before they went into the water, Nick had given an uncharacteristic squeal of excitement and grabbed Troy by the shoulders. "I hope that fucking gold is there," he had said. "I cannot wait to see their faces after we steal it."

It was time to submerge. Holding hands in the darkness, Nick and Troy dropped about five feet under the water. They stopped, equalized the pressure in their heads, and repeated the procedure. When they were down about ten feet, Troy turned on the searchlight. They quickly worked out their directions and headed around the corner, deeper into the cove adjoining Homer's estate.

Troy was in the lead. He had no trouble finding the entrance to the natural tunnel that led to the subterranean cave. As they had planned, Nick waited outside the tunnel while Troy went inside to look for alarms. The rock cliffs closed over his head. The watery entryway was about five feet across and four feet high. Troy immediately found a metal box affixed to the left wall, where it was partially hidden from view. When he examined the box, he discovered that it was emitting two laser beams separated by about three feet.

On the other side of the natural tunnel were the receiving plates for the beams as well as the alarm electronics. Troy swam over carefully, pulled out his screwdriver, and dismantled the housing. The system was very simple. Failure of either plate to receive a beam would trigger the opening of a relay. When both relays were open, current could flow to the alarm. Thus an object had to be large enough to break both beams simultaneously to set off an alarm. Troy smiled to himself as he validated the operating principle by passing his hand in front of one of the beams. Then he jerryrigged one of the relays permanently closed. Satisfied with his work, he swam back and forth in the tunnel, breaking both beams at the same time, assuring himself that he had rendered the alarm system ineffective.

He swam back out to meet Nick and gave him the thumbs-up sign. The two men passed through the fifty yards of natural tunnel into the subterranean cave. Where the narrow passageway widened, Troy again gestured to Nick to remain behind while he, Troy, went into the cave to check for boobytraps. Nick let his feet fall to the bottom of the tunnel and switched on his own small flashlight. He was in a perfect place for an ambush. The tunnel was so small here that there was virtually no maneuvering room. He wondered what an underwater sentry would look like. *What a place to die*, he thought suddenly. Fear swept over him as he turned off his flashlight and looked down at his illuminated diver's watch. He watched the glowing second hand sweeping around the face. He tried to calm himself. It had been three minutes since Troy had left. *Why is he taking so long?* he asked himself. *He must have found something*. Another minute passed. Then another. Nick was having a hard time quelling the onset of panic. *What do I do if he doesn't return?*

Just as Nick was about to swim into the cave on his own, he caught sight of Troy's searchlight coming toward him. Troy waved and Nick followed. Within thirty seconds they were in the shallow part of the cave, where the water was only about four feet deep. The two men stood up with their flippers lodged against the rocks to protect themselves from falling in the intermittent tidal surges.

Nick pulled his regulator out of his mouth and flipped his mask back on his head. Before he could speak, Troy put a finger against Nick's lips. "Speak very softly," Troy's whisper was barely audible. "The place could be alarmed for sound as well."

There was no light in the cave except Troy's searchlight. However, over their heads, in the highest corners of the rock ceiling, Troy pointed out two separate banks of fluorescent lighting. The cave itself was an irregular oval, about thirty yards in its longest dimension and maybe fifteen yards across at its widest point. The ceiling was only about three feet above the water near the entrance to the tunnel out to the ocean, but it was twenty feet high in the corner where they were standing in the shallow water.

"Well, Professor," Troy continued whispering, "I have good news and bad news. The bad news is that there is no treasure here in this cave. The good news is that there are two other tunnels, both manmade, that lead away from this place and go under Captain Homer's property." He paused for a moment and watched his partner. "Shall we go for it?"

Nick looked at his watch. It was nine-twenty already. He nodded. "The bastard spent a lot of money down here. They must have stolen more than I figured." Nick adjusted his diving equipment.

"We'll start with the tunnel on the left. As before, I'll lead to look for trouble." Troy cast his searchlight around on the ceiling. "This is a strange place. But beautiful. It looks like another planet, doesn't it?"

Nick pulled his mask back over his face and slipped the regulator in his mouth. He flopped backward into the sea water. Troy followed and, once under the surface, showed Nick the way to the first manmade tunnel. This tunnel was on the other side of the cave, about twelve feet below the water at its lowest point. It was made of normal circular sewer pipe. The diameter of the pipe was about five feet, making the tunnel approximately the same size as the natural passageway between the ocean and the cave. Troy entered the tunnel gingerly. He swam back and forth from side to side, examining one wall for a few yards and then going across to the other. He almost missed the long, slender alarm box. It was embedded in the ceiling at a junction between two sections of sewer pipe and Troy just happened to look up before he triggered the alarm.

This system worked on a different principle. A camera or other optical device in the box on the ceiling took repeated images of a square foot of the tunnel bottom that was backlit by an illuminated square cleverly concealed below the normal concrete floor. Apparently some kind of data comparison algorithm in the alarm processor contained logic by which the consecutive pictures could be assessed, in terms of threat, and an alarm triggered if necessary. It was the most complicated device of its kind that Troy had ever seen and he quickly recognized the similarities between this system and the ocean telescope that had been onboard the *Florida Queen*. *That means MOI designed and developed it*, he thought to himself. *So I'd best be careful. I bet the algorithm is set so that disturbances to the camera trigger the alarm as well.*

Nick had swum over to the side of the tunnel, out of the way, and was watching Troy try to open up the alarm box without jiggling the optical instrument. To accommodate the almost two-inch width of the box, there was a gap of that size everywhere around the circle connecting the two sequential sections of pipe. Throughout the rest of the tunnel, all adjoining sections were cemented together. Here the passageway was discontinuous.

Curious, thought Nick. He idly shone his small flashlight into the blackness in the gap beside him, expecting to see nothing but a wall of rock. *What in the world is that?* he wondered, as his light fell upon some metal object that looked like a large grating. The grating was resting upon an old piece of railroad track. Nick looked more carefully. He could make out a gear box and some pulleys, but he had no idea how all these mechanical devices fit together.

Meanwhile Troy had managed to remove the housing from the alarm box without disturbing the camera and was busy trying to understand the inner workings of the system. *Whew,* he thought. *This is much too complicated to figure out in five minutes. If I can just isolate the alarm, that should be enough.* It was tough work under the water. But Troy was clever and the electronics were packaged in a logical fashion. He was able to find the alarm and disable it. Afterward Troy lingered for several seconds trying to determine the purpose of the other circuits connected to the alarm subassembly.

Nick had intended to show Troy what he had found in the gap; however, as he watched his friend struggling with the complex circuitry of the alarm box, he became again worried about the passage of time. It was now almost a quarter to ten. He caught Troy's eye and pointed at his watch. Troy reluctantly abandoned his investigation of the alarm and proceeded down the tunnel.

Thirty yards farther the tunnel passed what looked like a door to a submarine on their left. Both Troy and Nick tried pulling on the handle of the large and very heavy round door but nothing happened. With gestures Troy told Nick to continue trying to open the door while he swam on down the tunnel.

The gold bars and other objects that remained from the *Santa Rosa* treasure were sitting in the tunnel another thirty yards beyond the round door. The passageway itself came to an abrupt halt against a rock wall. In front of the wall was an array of gold and silver objects, stacked to an average depth of a foot or so across the width of the tunnel. The treasure was not hidden in any way, it was simply scattered in random piles on the concrete floor at the end of the tunnel. Troy was ecstatic. *There's plenty here,* he thought. *Enough for the aliens. Enough for Nick. Maybe even some left over for Carol and me.*

He swam back to find Nick. Nick was absolutely exultant when he saw the unmistakable smile on Troy's face. He raced around his friend to the end of the tunnel. When Nick first reached the treasure, he spent a minute or two swimming around, picking up each object that was different and dropping it back into the piles on the floor.

Holy shit, Nick said gleefully to himself as he and Troy started putting gold bars into the buoyancy bags. *I was right for once. There must be over a hundred pounds in bars alone.* They had agreed before the dive just to bring out the bars, provided there were enough. The bars were the only objects they could be certain were pure gold. *Even if we take fifty-eight to Troy's friends, that might leave fifty or so for us.* He did a quick mental calculation. *That could be over three hundred thousand dollars apiece. Whoopee.*

Joy and excitement surged through Nick. He was having difficulty containing himself. He wanted to sing, to dance, to jump with joy. He had been right after all. The bastards *had* stolen most of the treasure and now he was stealing it back. There's no happiness quite like the redressing of an old and painful grievance. And to do it with panache . . . Nick was already celebrating in his heart. This was his day.

Filling the bags took no time at all. Nick and Troy both felt as if they had infinite energy. When they had finished picking up the gold bars, Troy gestured down the tunnel. Nick looked down at the other treasure objects remaining on the floor. *We should take it all,* he thought. *We should leave Homer and Greta nothing. Nothing at all.* But he had to be practical. Each of their bags was virtually full and they would be heavy enough as they were.

Nick swam off in the direction of the ocean, his buoyancy bag full of gold trailing behind him. Troy followed. As they passed the bulky door on the right, Troy found himself thinking again about the circuitry leading to the alarm in the box just ahead, between the two sections of pipe. *What could those other connections be for?* Suddenly he remembered seeing a diagram in an electronics magazine about advanced timers that could reinitialize systems and swap out failed parts. By now the component that Troy had disabled might have been declared a failure by the smart processor in the alarm box, in which case it would have either been replaced by a redundant part or the system would be ignoring its output. *In either situation,* Troy thought, *that means the system could be active again.*

It was too late. Nick swam into the field of view of the optical device and lights came on throughout the tunnel. A metal gate started closing behind Nick and his bag of gold. It was only with a burst of speed that Troy propelled himself through before the gate shut completely. But his buoyancy bag full of gold bars was left behind, on the other side of the gate.

Nick stared at Troy's lost bag as it floated to the floor. He reached through the bars, grabbed the bag, and tried to pull it through. It was useless. He shook the gate. The metal was extremely sturdy. Angry and frustrated, he punched the gate with his fists. As Nick caught his breath in between punches, he became aware of a strange droning sound, like a motor, somewhere in the distance behind him. He turned around to find Troy. He could not see him anywhere.

Troy had been exhausted by his swimming sprint through the closing gate. His energy spent, he had let himself fall to the floor of the pool in the deepest part of the cave, halfway between the two manmade tunnels. He took several deep breaths through his mouthpiece and checked his air supply. He had about ten minutes remaining. He watched for a moment as Nick, almost out of sight to his right, tried fruitlessly to pull Troy's bag through the gate.

Shit, Troy thought, disappointed that he had lost the gold, *if only I had been thinking. I should have known . . .* He heard an unusual sound off to his left. Curious, Troy swam over to the entrance of the other tunnel and right into the path of the robot sentry.

Even though the original distance between them was over fifty feet, the guidance mechanism of the sentry fixed on Troy as soon as he appeared. Startled and fascinated, at first Troy did not try to avoid the onrush of the bullet-shaped submarine. The sentry was three feet long and a foot wide in its midsection. When it was about eight feet away, the sentry slowly loaded and fired a small but powerful spear, the size of a table knife, that Troy just managed to avoid as it hurtled past. The spear crashed into the wall beside him.

Adrenaline surged into Troy's system and he swam out into the middle of the pool. The sentry did not follow him immediately. Instead it moved over in front of the natural passageway to the ocean, thereby cutting off the escape route, and then turned around to make a systematic search of the pool. *Damnit,* Troy was thinking, *why didn't I leave while I had the chance?* He wondered if Nick was still over by the gate.

The sentry had now found Nick in its field of vision. He was swimming slowly toward the exit with his buoyancy bag. He was unaware that he and Troy were not alone in the pool. By the time Nick saw the sentry, he was fifteen feet away and within easy range of its underwater gun. Troy watched the sentry load a spear. *Oh no,* he cried out to himself. *Watch out, Nick.* There was nothing he could do.

It happened so fast that neither Nick nor Troy knew exactly what occurred. Troy would later explain that he felt a sudden warm tingle on his wrist and then something, a light beam or a laser burst or a stream of plasma perhaps, fired out of his bracelet and zapped the robot sentry into silence and motionlessness. Nick would say that the sentry, just when it was going to fire at him, was first distracted by Troy and then recoiled as if from an impact. Whatever happened, the sentry stopped all activity. Immediately thereafter the two men swam together over to the shallow part of the cave. They were temporarily safe.

Carol could not believe how plump and succulent the oysters were. Ellen was sitting at the other end of the table, opposite her, and was beaming with pride. "Would you like some more, dear?" she smiled, lifting the huge pot containing the oyster stew. *I'm now going to eat a second portion,* Carol thought. *In addition to the catfish with Nick. Greta would be disgusted.* She smiled to herself and nodded at Ellen. There was at least one thing she had learned this evening. Ellen was certainly a fantastic cook.

And a very sad person too, Carol thought as she spooned herself some more spicy stew rich with the fabled Appalachicola oysters. Homer had personally answered all the questions during the twenty-minute interview before dinner. Whenever a question had been controversial or delicate, such as when Carol had asked about the allegations that part of the treasure haul had been secretly stolen and hidden by the three of them, he had looked only at Greta before he made a response. *No wonder Ellen eats all the time. She's the odd man out. Or is it woman?*

"This stew is fabulous," Carol remarked to Ellen. "Would you mind giving me the recipe?"

Ellen was delighted. "Certainly, dear," she said, "it would be my pleasure." Carol remembered Dale's reference to Ellen's behavior at the MOI awards dinner and wondered if there was, indeed, any sexual component to the warmth Ellen was displaying. *I don't see it,* Carol decided. *This is just a lonely and profoundly disturbed woman. I don't feel one iota of sexual tension.*

"You've been asking the questions all evening, Miss Dawson," Homer was saying. "Now why don't we ask you a few?" He had been surprisingly pleasant and subdued since the bizarre preprandial shark feeding. *They must be normal sometimes,* Carol thought. *Otherwise they couldn't survive. But who knows when Mr. Hyde will show up again.*

"Ya," Greta said. It was the first time she had spoken directly to Carol during the meal. "Homer told me you were with Dr. Dale. You are lovers, no?"

You don't beat around the bush, do you Greta. Carol partially evaded the question. "Dale Michaels and I are very good friends. We spend quite a lot of time together, both socially and professionally."

"He is a smart man," Greta said. Those clear eyes stared at Carol and a smile played at the corner of Greta's lips. *What is she trying to tell me?*

The conversation was interrupted by the sound of a sharp alarm. Carol knew immediately that something had gone wrong. "What in the world is that?" Carol asked innocently as the strident alarm continued with its loud bursts.

Homer and Greta were already up from the table. "Excuse us," Homer said, "it's our burglar alarm. Probably an error. We'll go check it out."

They hurried out of the dining room, leaving Carol and Ellen alone, and headed down a nearby hallway. *I must follow them and find out what's going on,* Carol thought, her heart and mind racing together. She sneaked a peek at her watch. It was five minutes past ten o'clock. *They should have finished by now.* "I'm going to the rest room," she said to Ellen. "Don't bother," she added, as Ellen started to explain the directions. "I'm sure I can find it myself."

Carol walked quickly into the hall and listened for sounds of Homer and Greta. Moving very quietly, she followed them until she was just outside a large den on the opposite side of the house. The door to the den was ajar. "It will focus in a second," she heard Homer say. There was a pause. "Shit," he shouted, "it looks like the gold bars are already gone. They must have moved very fast . . . The picture is really not very clear. Here, you take a look."

"Ya," said Greta. "The bars are gone, I think . . . But Homer, the gold vould be very heavy. Maybe the thieves are trapped in the tunnel . . . Timmy could search for them."

"That would fix the bastards," Homer's nervous laugh sent chills down Carol's spine. She backpedaled slowly until she had retreated to the main foyer of the house. She heard an outside door slam in the direction of the den. *They've gone out to turn the sharks loose. Jesus. I must warn Nick and Troy.*

Carol walked into the nearest bathroom in the hallway, pushed the door closed, and turned on the water faucet. Then she flushed the commode and untaped the small walkie-talkie that was hidden inside her shirt. She put the unit right next to her mouth. "Mayday, mayday," she said. "They know you're there. You are in danger." She repeated the message and then pushed the button that would automatically recycle the communication several more times. *I certainly hope this damn thing works*, she thought.

She started to affix the tiny unit to the inside of her blouse again. While she was taping it down, she happened to look in the mirror. Her heart nearly stopped. Ellen was standing in the doorway, staring at her, the baleful glare in her eyes indicating that she had seen and heard everything. She took a step toward Carol.

"Just hold it right there, Ellen," Carol said. Carol put her hands up. "I have no quarrel with you." The fat woman hesitated. "Homer and Greta only use you anyway," Carol added softly, "why don't you leave them and make a life for yourself?"

Anger broke across Ellen's face. Her eyes narrowed, her cheeks reddened, and she raised her huge fists to threaten Carol. "It's none of your damn business how I live my life," she said menacingly. She moved again in Carol's direction.

Carol grabbed the thick metal towel rack beside her and pulled with all her might. The bar sprung free from the wall, dumping two peach bath towels and a wooden end piece on the linoleum floor. Carol brandished the bar over her head. "Don't make me hit you," she said. "Just move aside and get out of my way."

Ellen did not slow down. Carol aimed carefully and struck her hard, on the right shoulder. The heavy woman collapsed. "Greta," she wailed in a monstrous voice, "Greta, help me."

Still waving the bar from the towel rack, Carol walked carefully around Ellen and backed toward the door. Once in the hall, she sprinted to the family room and headed for the front door. Right beside the wet bar she was tackled from behind. Carol fell forward, hard, and smashed her nose on the carpet. She tried to squirm out of Greta's arms but it was impossible. She was pinned. A few drops of blood trickled out of Carol's nose and fell on the carpet.

Both women were breathing heavily. Carol managed to turn her body around so that she was facing Greta. She struggled vainly to free herself. Greta's strong arms slammed Carol's wrists against the floor. Greta bent down until her face was only inches away from Carol's. "You were trying to get away, ya, and just why vere you in such a hurry."

There was something feral in Greta's eyes. On impulse, Carol lifted her head and kissed Greta, full on the lips. Startled, her assailant's arms momentarily relaxed. That was all Carol needed. Gathering all her strength, she smashed the bottom of her palm into the side of Greta's head. Greta was stunned. Carol pushed her off and made a dash for the door.

Carol was already calculating when she ran out the front door and down the steps. *Greta will be up in an instant,* she thought. *I won't have time to open the car door. I might as well run for it.*

The German woman was only fifteen yards behind her, and gaining fast, when Carol turned onto the lane that led from Homer's house to the Pelican Resort. *For ten years I have run three times a week. But this is the only time my life has ever depended on it.* She tried to accelerate. Greta continued to close the gap. Carol was certain she was going to be caught at any minute. Once she thought she felt Greta's hand on her blouse.

But after two hundred yards Greta began to drop back. When she was a quarter of a mile from Homer's driveway, Carol dared to look over her shoulder. Her pursuer was clearly struggling and was now fifty yards behind her. Carol felt a renewed burst of energy. *I'm going to make it,* she thought. *I'm actually going to escape.*

Greta slowed to a walk. Eventually Carol did too, but not until she was almost to the restaurant. Even then she continued to look back, to try to find her antagonist in the moonlight. *Now I'll call a taxi,* she was thinking, *And go over to Nick's apartment. I hope that the two of them heard my warning and are safe.*

She could no longer see Greta. She stopped and strained her eyes. *She must have turned back,* Carol thought. While she was looking back down the lane, a pair of very strong hands grabbed her shoulders. She spun around and stared into the laughing eyes of Lieutenant Richard Todd.

H E had purposely waited until all the rest of the actors had left the dressing room. The package itself was inconspicuous, about the size of a large bar of soap, wrapped in white paper with a dark red ribbon. *You don't even know if it's from her,* Winters thought as he pulled the bow on the ribbon. The commander was full of anticipation. The show had been even better tonight. And in the bedroom scene he had felt, for just a second, the touch of Tiffani's tongue against his lips. *She didn't have to do that,* Winters told himself, suspending for a moment all vestiges of guilt.

His hands trembled a little as he opened the package. It was a plain white box. Inside was a silver cigarette lighter, simple but handsome, with the initials VW engraved on the outside at the bottom. His heart raced. *So she does feel it too.* Commander Winters felt a powerful burst of lust in his groin. Now he was imagining a scene no more than three or four hours in the future. He was taking Tiffani home and they were kissing at her front door. "Would you like to come in," she would say . . .

"I feel pretty . . . oh so pretty . . . I feel pretty and witty and gay . . ." He heard her singing as she came down the hall. She pushed open the door to his dressing room and twirled around. Tiffani's hair was stacked high on her head, showing the lines of her elegant neck. The gold filigree along the top of the comb that the commander had given her blended in perfectly with the rich red and brown of her hair. Her dress was white, low cut, with her shoulders exposed except for tiny straps in the corners.

"Well?" she said with a big and eager smile. She turned around again. "What do you think?"

"You look beautiful, Tiffani," he replied. He stared at her with such intensity that she blushed.

"Oh, Vernon," she sighed, now changing her mood, "the combs are wonderful." She pulled a cigarette from his pack on the dresser table and lit it herself with his new lighter. She took a deep drag, her eyes fixed on his, and put the cigarette down in the ashtray. "I don't know how to thank you," she murmured.

She walked over to him and put her hands in his. "It's already been another wonderful evening." She put her left hand behind his head and reached up to kiss him. His heart was about to explode within his body. She could feel his arousal as her lips nestled softly against his. She pulled his head down to meet hers and subtly increased the pressure of her kiss. At length he put his arms around her and pressed her body against his.

Commander Winters thought he was going to drown in the pleasure of that kiss. Never had he felt such longing. He was certain he would gladly die in the morning if he could just continue to kiss her all night first. For a moment, as he let himself experience fully the rush of joy and love and lust, all his worries and despair were pushed aside. He wanted to wrap himself around Tiffani, somehow zip her inside his skin, and close out everything else in the universe.

Melvin and Marc had come to the dressing room to find the commander. They had not approached with stealth and were not even being especially quiet, but neither Tiffani nor Commander Winters heard them walk up. The two men could see the pair kissing through the open dressing room door. They looked at each other and reached out instinctively to touch hands for an instant. From their own experience they knew about the difficulty of love affairs outside the accepted norm.

Tiffani and Winters finally broke the kiss and she put her head against his chest. Her back was to the door. Winters opened his eyes and saw Melvin and Marc standing there in front of him. He blanched, but the director made a gesture with his hands that said, "It's all right. It's your business, not ours."

Melvin and Marc considerately waited several seconds so that it would look as if they had not arrived until after the kiss. The commander patted Tiffani on the shoulder and turned her around in a fatherly manner. "Great show, Commander," Melvin said as he walked into the room. "And another super performance from you too, young lady." He paused. Marc smiled his compliments and Tiffani unconsciously straightened out her dress. "There's a Lieutenant Todd waiting outside for you, Commander," Melvin added. "He says it's urgent. He asked me to tell you to hurry."

Winters face was creased with wrinkles. *What in the world is he doing here?* he thought. *It's after ten o'clock on a Saturday night.* "Thanks, Melvin," he answered. "Tell him I'll be out in a few minutes."

The director and his friend turned and left the dressing room. Tiffani reached over for the lit cigarette, whose ash had grown so long it had nearly fallen out of the ashtray. She inhaled and handed it to Winters. "Did they see us kissing?" she asked anxiously.

"No," lied Winters. But already he was realizing how untenable his fantasy was. *Precious Tiffani,* he thought. *My teenage lover. We were lucky. But we cannot kid ourselves. We will be seen eventually.* He looked into her eyes and saw the flame of adolescent passion. Again he felt the surge in his loins. He reached down and pulled her forcefully to him. *And if the wrong person sees us,* he thought as his lips tingled with her kiss, *there is no limit to my risk.*

Winters threw his cigarette down on the ground and stomped it out. He shook his head in disbelief. "You are telling me that you have taken those three into custody? And you're holding them at the base?"

Lieutenant Todd was confused. "But sir, don't you understand? We have an entire set of photographs. In three of them you can clearly see the missile. And there are other pictures that show the black guy in some kind of underwater structure down there in the ocean. Just as I had guessed. What more could we possibly need? We also caught them, redhanded no less, coming back from a dive with fifty pounds of gold bars in their backpacks. *Fifty* pounds!"

Commander Winters turned around and went back in the theater. "Go back to the base, Lieutenant," he said disgustedly. "I'll be there in five minutes."

It was apparent that Melvin and Marc were just waiting for Tiffani and the commander before they locked up the theater and went to the party. "Can you take her over, Melvin?" he asked. "There's a big mess out at the base tonight and it looks as if I will have to straighten it out." The conversation with Todd had been sobering for Winters on at least two levels. First, it had reminded him that there was a real world out there, outside of the theater, a world that would not look kindly on a forty-three-year-old Navy commander having a sexual relationship with a seventeen-year-old high school student. Secondly, Todd's astonishing announcement that he had indeed detained three civilians, one of whom was a well-known reporter, jolted the commander into realizing that his preoccupation with Tiffani had affected his work. *I should never have let this thing get so far out of control,* he thought. *From here on out that lieutenant makes no move that I don't personally approve.*

"I'm sorry, Tiffani," he said in a fatherly voice. He gave her an ambiguous hug and a light kiss on the top of her head. "I'll come to the party as soon as I can."

"Hurry or you'll miss the champagne," Tiffani said with a smile. Melvin turned off the lights in the theater. The four of them walked out the door.

Winters had parked down the street almost a block away. He waved to Tiffani as she climbed into Melvin's car. *I wonder if you will ever know, young lady,* he thought. *Know how close I came tonight to throwing everything away.* In his mind's eye it was twenty-four years before, on a cold night outside of Philadelphia, and he had just gone berserk and virtually raped Joanna Carr. Winters started his Pontiac and eased into the street. *It would be so easy,* he thought. *Just one time to forget the rules and constraints. To dive into the water without looking first.* He remembered his pact with God after he had spent the night with Joanna. *So You kept your part of the bargain. I guess. And I became an officer and a gentleman. And a killer.*

He winced. He turned the car past the swank Miyako Gardens and headed for the base. With great effort he forced himself to stop thinking about Tiffani and Joanna and sex. *It's not enough that I have this trial with Tiffani. At the same time I am assigned a redneck lieutenant who runs roughshod over civilians in his attempt to prove some cockamamie . . .*

Commander Winters stopped at a signal. Slowly, the full impact of what Todd had told him began to sink in. *Jesus. I may be in trouble too. Unlawful entry. Wrongful detention. They'll throw the book at Todd . . .* He eased his car through the intersection. He mechanically put a cigarette in his mouth and lit it. *So I should be apologetic. But shit. That Dawson woman is a reporter. Bad bad news.*

He had arrived at the base. He waved to the security guard and drove on to where Todd had said they were keeping the trio. Winters stopped in front of a plain white building situated on a small hill about fifteen feet above the street level. A nervous Lieutenant Roberto Ramirez was waiting at the edge of the road. He was holding two large, thick envelopes in his hands. Ramirez turned and called something toward the front door. Todd came out in a moment. He locked the door carefully, came down the steps, and walked toward the other two officers. Ramirez was already showing the photographs to Commander Winters when Todd joined them. The three men had a short but animated discussion.

* * *

"So what happened after you received my message?" Carol turned to the other two as soon as Todd disappeared out the door. They had not had many chances to talk in private since Todd and Ramirez had taken them into custody in the parking lot at the Pelican Resort.

"Troy was ready to split," Nick laughed. "But I thought your warning only referred to the robot sentry. And since he had been quiet for several minutes, I figured we were already safe. I was still really pissed off about the second bag of gold bars. So I hurried back over to the gate.

"I was concentrating so hard on finding a way to pull the bag through the opening that I must have been oblivious to everything else. Suddenly I felt Troy jerk me backwards. Maybe a second later two or three sharks, one definitely a mako, slammed hard into the gate. I was certain the gate was going to fall into pieces."

"Those sharks were really nasty, angel," Troy interjected. "And stupid too. The big one must have banged against the gate a dozen times before he gave up."

"The buoyancy bag with the gold bars was immediately ripped to shreds by the crazy sharks. They may even have swallowed most of the bars themselves. It was not fun being that close to them." Nick shuddered. "When I close my eyes I can still see that mako's teeth three feet away from me. I'll probably have bad dreams for years."

"I pulled Nick toward the ocean. I didn't want any part of those mean bastards and I didn't trust the gate to remain intact in case they launched another attack. We made it out in record time. Of course, neither of us expected to be greeted by the U.S. Navy when we returned to the station wagon." Troy paused. "This Todd character, what's his problem anyway? He sure thinks he's a badass. Is he just pissed because the professor decked him last night?"

Carol smiled. She reached her left hand over and put it on Nick's leg just above the knee. Her hand remained there while she was talking. "Todd is one of the naval engineers trying to find the lost missile. I'm certain that he and his men must have been responsible for the break-ins at Nick's apartment and my hotel room. Otherwise they wouldn't have detained us."

"What grounds do they have for holding us?" Nick inquired. He dropped his hand down and wrapped it around Carol's. "It's not against the law to have gold bars in a backpack. Don't we have rights as citizens that prevent this kind of thing?"

"Probably," Carol replied. She squeezed Nick's hand and then retracted her own. "But as a reporter, I find this part of our adventure extremely inter-esting. You can tell that Lieutenant Ramirez is very nervous. He wouldn't let Todd even ask us any questions until Commander Winters was contacted. And he has been very concerned about our comfort."

As if on cue, the front door opened and the three naval officers walked in. Winters was in the lead with the two lieutenants just behind. Nick and

Carol and Troy were sitting on gray metal auditorium chairs on the left of a partitioned area that served as a waiting room for the larger offices in the rear of the building. Winters moved into the area and half leaned against the large gray desk opposite them.

"I'm Commander Vernon Winters," he said, his eyes meeting each of theirs in turn. "As Miss Dawson knows, I'm one of the senior officers on the base here. I am currently in charge of a secret project, code named Broken Arrow." He smiled. "I'm sure you are wondering why you have been brought to the base."

Winters reached out with his left arm and Ramirez handed him the infrared blowups that showed the missile in the most detail. He waved the photos at the three detainees. "One of the goals of project Broken Arrow is to find a Navy missile that has been lost somewhere in the Gulf of Mexico. Lieutenant Todd here believes, based on these photographs, that you know where that missile is. That is why he has acted to bring you here for questioning." Winters' voice rose in pitch and he began to wave his arms. "Now I'm certain I don't need to remind you that state-of-the-art weapons systems are what keep our nation free and secure—"

"Spare us the patriotic lecture and the histrionics, Commander Winters," interrupted Carol. "We all know that you are searching for a lost missile and that you think we may have found it. Sorry. We went out looking for it today but were unable to locate it again." She stood up. "Now you listen to me a minute. Your zealous lieutenant there and his men have broken more laws than I can count. In addition to kidnapping us, they have looted and vandalized my hotel room and Mr. Williams' apartment. They have also stolen some photographs and valuable equipment." She fixed Winters with a hard gaze. "You sure as hell better have good reason for dragging us down here or I swear I'll see to it that all three of you are court martialed."

Carol glanced at Ramirez. He was squirming. "In the meantime," she continued, "you can start by giving us an official, written apology, returning all our property, and making adequate payment for all the damages. In addition, I want exclusive access to all Broken Arrow files from this moment on. If you don't agree to all these terms, you might as well prepare right now to read about the Gestapo tactics of the United States Navy in the next edition of the *Miami Herald*."

Uh oh, thought Winters. *This is not going to be easy. This woman reporter intends to play the bluff and threat game.* He pulled out a cigarette while he was thinking. "Would you please not smoke in here?" Carol broke into his train of thought. "We all find it offensive."

Damn these aggressive nonsmokers. He replaced the Pall Mall in the pack in his pocket. Winters had been thrown off at first by Carol's rapid attack, but he eventually regained his composure. "Now, Miss Dawson," the commander began, a minute later. He looked away from the trio, in the direction of the front door. "I can understand why you might be upset by what has happened.

I will admit that our men may indeed have acted in an unwarranted manner while they were searching your rooms to find evidence. However . . ." Winters stopped in mid-sentence, turned around, and came back toward Nick and Carol and Troy.

"However," he repeated. "We are talking about treason here." He waited to let *his* threat register. "And I don't need to tell you, Miss Dawson, that treason is serious business. Even more serious than journalism." He hesitated again for effect and his voice became very stern. "If any of you have knowledge of the whereabouts of this missile and have conveyed that knowledge to a member of *any* foreign government, especially one viewed as inimical to our national interests, then you have committed treason."

"What kind of dope have you been smoking, Commander?" Carol replied. "We freely admit that we've been looking for your missile. But that doesn't make us spies. You have no case against us." She glanced at Nick. He was admiring her performance. "I'm simply a reporter covering a story. This treason business of yours is pure fabricated bullshit."

"Oh, yeah," said Lieutenant Todd, unable to restrain himself. "Then where were these pictures taken?" He showed the photo of Troy in full diving regalia in the initial underwater room with the red and blue walls. He then turned and pointed to the backpacks sitting in the opposite corner of the room. "And what were your two friends doing with fifty pounds of gold after their dive tonight?"

"All right, man," Troy remarked in an exaggerated manner. He took a step toward Lieutenant Todd. "All right. You've figured it out, haven't you? We found the missile and sold it to the Russians for fifty pounds of gold." His eyes widened as he looked at Todd. "And now the missile is onboard a submarine on its way to Moscow or wherever . . . Come on, man, get serious. We're not that stupid."

Lieutenant Todd's temper flared up. "You black bastard—" he muttered before Commander Winters jumped between them. Winters needed some time to think. Todd's questions were, after all, still unanswered. Even if there were good answers, it was not difficult to understand how someone could have come to the conclusion, based on the photographs, that there might be a conspiracy involved.

In addition, there was the issue of defending the actions of his junior officers and the investigating team. *If I let these three go now,* thought Winters, *then we are essentially admitting that we made an error in the first place . . .* Ramirez was gesturing at the commander. He nodded outside with his head. Winters did not understand at first, but Ramirez repeated the motion.

"Excuse us a second," Winters said. The two officers walked out on the porch above the steps, leaving Todd with Nick and Carol and Troy. "What is it, Lieutenant?" Winters asked.

"Commander, sir," Ramirez answered, "my career is the Navy. If we release these three now, after no formal questioning—"

"I couldn't agree more," Winters interrupted abruptly. "I wish that none of this today had happened. But it did. Now we must finish it up properly and thoroughly or we have no defense for what we did." He thought for a minute. "How long would it take you to get the video and sound equipment set up for a formal interrogation?"

"About thirty minutes," Ramirez replied. "Maybe forty-five at the most."

"Let's do it. While you're getting ready, I'll prepare the list of questions."

Shit, said Winters to himself as he watched Ramirez walk briskly toward his office on the other side of the base. *I am indeed going to be here all night.* He thought of his missed chance with Tiffani. *I'd better call her and explain while I'm drafting these questions.* He felt a sudden burst of anger toward Lieutenant Todd. *As for you,* he thought, *if we come out of this unscathed, I will personally see to it that you are transferred to Lower Slobbovia.*

It was after eleven o'clock. Lieutenant Todd stood near the front door. He was holding a billy club in his hand. Once before in the evening, just after Nick and Troy had reached the Pelican Resort parking lot, Todd had used the club on Nick's back to coerce him into the car. Nick could still feel the welt.

"How long is all this going to take?" Troy asked. He was standing near the desk. "Can't we go home now and get some sleep and come back on Monday morning . . ."

"You heard what the man said," Todd replied. He was definitely gloating. "They've gone off to prepare for a formal interrogation. You should be using this time to get your story straight." Todd pounded his palm with the billy club.

Troy turned to his companions. "All right, team," he said with a wink. "I move we blow this joint. Let's overpower this geek and blast out of here."

"Just try it, you shits," Todd rejoined. He smacked one of the empty folding chairs with his club for emphasis. "I'd like nothing better than to report that you tried to escape."

Nick had not said much since Winters and Ramirez had left. He now looked across the room at Todd. "You know what annoys me the most about this, Lieutenant?" he said to his captor. "It's that people like you," he continued, without waiting for an answer, "end up in positions of power or authority all over the world. Look at you. You think that because you have us under your control, that makes you somebody. Let me tell you something. You aren't shit."

Todd did not try to hide his dislike for Nick. "At least I can find white men to be my friends," he replied sarcastically.

"I do declare," Troy chimed in swiftly. "I believe our associate Lieutenant Todd may be a bigot. We may be talking to a true life honky. Let's see if 'nigger' is his next—"

"Boys, boys," Carol interceded as Todd started to move toward Troy.

"Enough is enough." The room became quiet. Troy walked back over to his friends and sat down in his chair.

A minute later Troy leaned over to Nick and Carol. As he was whispering to them, he put the gold bracelet right next to his mouth. "You know, folks," he said, "if we don't get out of here soon, we may be here all night. I can well imagine the questions taking three or four hours. And that means the Navy will get to the dive site before us in the morning."

"But what can we do?" Carol asked. "It would be a miracle if they let us just walk out without any questions."

"A miracle, angel," said Troy with a grin, "is just what we need. A good old-fashioned miracle. Like the blue fairy."

"What are you shits whispering about over there?" The truculent Lieutenant Todd began to walk toward the bathroom at the west end of the long room. "Knock it off. And don't try anything. The outside door is locked and I have the key." He didn't close the bathroom door. The urinal was fortunately out of view to the right.

There was not much light in the back of the small bathroom. As Todd was finishing his piss, he became aware of a strange sensation all over his right side, as if a thousand very small needles were sticking in him. Puzzled, he turned toward the corner. What he saw there sent an incredible shock of terror racing through his system.

In the corner, partially hidden in the poor light, was what could only be described as a six-foot carrot. The thicker end of the creature was balanced on four webbed pads planted on the floor. There were no arms, but about five feet above the ground, just under a maze of blue spaghetti of unknown purpose on top of its "head," four vertical slits, each a foot long, were cut in what might have been its face. Out of each of these slits something strange was hanging. Troy would later explain to Nick and Carol that these were sensors, that the carrot saw, heard, smelled, and tasted with these dangling extensions.

Lieutenant Todd did not wait to study the creature. He let out a whoop and backed quickly out of the bathroom. He did not stop to retract his penis or zip his fly. When the weird orange thing next appeared in the light at the door to the bathroom, the lieutenant was certain it was going to follow him. He stared at it, petrified and immobile, for half a second. Then, when it did indeed move toward him, Todd immediately turned around, unlocked the front door, and burst through it.

Unfortunately he forgot about the eight concrete steps. In his panic he tripped and fell. He smacked his head hard on the second step and tumbled down to the bottom. He lay unconscious on his back on the sidewalk in front of the building.

Carol had cowered against Nick when she had first seen the carrot. Then they had both glanced at Troy. He was smiling and humming to himself, "When you wish upon a star . . . makes no difference who you are." He seemed so blasé about everything that Nick and Carol even relaxed temporarily.

However, after Lieutenant Todd disappeared out the front door and the carrot turned to face them, it was difficult to remain calm.

"Nuts," said Troy with a big smile. "I was really hoping for the blue fairy. I thought she might make me rich, or maybe even white."

"All right, Jefferson," Nick said. His face looked as if he had just eaten a lemon. "Please explain what that thing in front of us is."

Troy first walked slowly over to the corner of the room to pick up their backpacks. "This, Professor," he replied as he then walked directly up to the carrot, "is what we might call a holographic projection." He put his hand into and through the orange body. "Somewhere in the universe there is supposedly a real life creature like this, but *they* have only sent his image to help us escape."

Even with Troy's explanation Nick and Carol did not want to come any closer to the stationary carrot than was absolutely necessary. They moved with their backs against the walls until they reached the door. "Don't worry," Troy laughed. "It won't hurt you."

The sensor hanging out of the slit on the far right of the carrot's head was totally incomprehensible. Carol could not take her eye off of it. It looked like a wad of gooey honeycomb stuck on the end of a majorette's baton. "What does it do with that?" Carol asked, pointing as she preceded Troy out the door.

"I don't know, angel," Troy answered. "But it must be fun."

Nick and Troy joined Carol on the platform at the top of the stairs. They all saw Todd at about the same time. They were naturally surprised to find him lying at the bottom of the steps. His head was bleeding. "Should we help him?" Carol wondered out loud as Troy bounded down the stairs in front of her.

"No way," Nick replied quickly.

Troy bent down beside Todd and carefully examined the unconscious lieutenant from head to toe. He slapped the big man lightly on the cheek. Lieutenant Todd did not move. Troy winked at his friends at the top of the stairs. "The professor was right, my man," he said, breaking into a grin, "you really aren't shit."

"So I kissed her," Carol said with a laugh.

"You did *what?*" asked Nick. They were in Troy's old Ford LTD, driving toward the Hemingway marina. After leaving the base they had walked the mile and a half to Troy's duplex to pick up his car. Carol was beside Troy in the front seat and Nick was in the back next to the backpacks containing the gold and the information discs.

Carol turned around to Nick. "I kissed her." She laughed again as Nick screwed up his face in disgust. "What was I supposed to do? The woman is stronger than most men. She had me pinned on the floor. There was something just a little suggestive about the way she was holding me . . ."

"Whoooee, angel," Troy slapped the dashboard with his left hand. "You are amazing. What did superkraut do next?"

"She released her grip on my wrists. Just for a second. I think she was deciding whether to kiss me back."

"Yuch," said Nick from the back seat. "I think I'm going to be sick."

"So you smashed her up side of the head and then ran off?" asked Troy. Carol nodded. Troy laughed heartily and then became more serious. "Be careful if you ever see her again, angel. Greta does not like to lose."

"But you're wrong about her in one respect, Carol," Nick remarked. "Greta's not into women at all. She likes sex with men too much."

Carol found Nick's comment smug and even irritating. She spoke across the front seat to Troy. "Why is it, Troy, that men naturally assume that any woman who has sexual relations with men could not *possibly* be interested in having sex with another woman? Is this another example of their fundamental belief in their own innate superiority?" She didn't wait for an answer. Carol turned around again to talk to Nick. "And in case you're wondering, the answer is no, I'm not a lesbian. I am relentlessly heterosexual, as much because of my San Fernando Valley middle class background as anything. But I will admit that sometimes I grow extremely tired of men and what I call their baboon demonstrations of macho."

"Hey," Nick replied, "I didn't mean to start an argument. I was just suggesting—"

"Okay, Okay," Carol interrupted, loosening up a bit, "no harm done. I guess I am a little quick on the trigger." She was quiet for a few seconds. "By the way, Nick," she remarked then, "there's one part of this that I still don't understand completely. Why did Captain Homer go to such great lengths to hide the rest of the treasure all this time? Why didn't he just sell it off as soon as he could?"

"Lots of reasons," Nick replied. "Not the least of which was fear that he might somehow be discovered and indicted for the perjury he committed during our trial. But this way he also escapes the IRS, the value of the gold appreciates in time, and, most importantly, Greta has to hang around if she wants her whole share. He almost certainly converts some of it to cash from time to time, probably through a third party. But never enough to call attention to the transaction."

"So you see, angel," Troy said, "that's why there's no way he can call the police. Because he would have to admit everything. I bet he's really pissed off."

Troy pulled into a left-hand turn lane and waited for the signal to change. A car pulled up beside them on the right, next to Carol, and she just happened to look idly in that direction. It was a Mercedes.

Later on Carol would recall that time seemed to dilate for her. Each second of the next minute was recorded in her memory in super slow motion, as if it were covering a much longer period of time. Greta was driving Captain

Homer's car and was staring at Carol. Homer was sitting beside her, waving his fists, shouting something that Carol couldn't hear through her closed window. Carol focused on Greta's amazing eyes. Never had she seen such hatred. For just an instant Carol looked away to alert Troy and Nick. When she turned back she saw that Greta had a pistol pointed directly at her.

Three things happened almost simultaneously. Carol ducked, Troy pulled into the intersection against the red light, barely missing a speeding car, and Greta fired the gun. The bullet ripped through Carol's window and crashed into Troy's door, somehow miraculously missing them both. Carol sat cringing under the dashboard in the front seat. She fought against panic and tried to catch her breath.

The chase was on. It was after eleven-thirty on a Saturday night in Key West and the traffic in the residential area was light. Troy's Ford was no match for the Mercedes. Twice more Greta maneuvered into position and the Ford was sprayed with bullets. Windows were broken and pitted but none of the occupants of the car was injured.

Nick was lying on the floor in the back seat. "Get downtown if you can," he shouted at Troy. "Maybe we can lose them in the traffic."

Troy was hunkered down behind the steering wheel as far as he could go. He could barely see the roadway in front of them. He was driving like a lunatic, swerving across the four-lane street into oncoming traffic, honking frantically, and making it impossible for Greta to predict his next move. "Where are the cops when you really need them?" he said out loud. "We have maniacs firing guns at us in the middle of Key West and there are no men of blue anywhere in sight."

After Nick's suggestion Troy suddenly spun around in the middle of the street and started heading in the opposite direction. Greta was not prepared. She hit the brakes on the Mercedes, went into a skid, caromed off a parked car, and then resumed the chase.

There were now no cars on the street in front of them and the Mercedes was closing the gap. "Uh oh," said Troy, fearing another attack. He violently pulled the steering wheel to the left, shot through an alley, into a parking lot, and back onto a narrow street. A few moments later he made a quick turn into a driveway. The car became flooded with light and Troy jammed on the brakes. "Everybody out," he hollered. While Nick and Carol were trying to determine what the hell was happening, Troy was giving his car keys to a tall figure dressed in a red uniform.

"We're just having drinks," he said. They heard the screech of the brakes on the Mercedes. "And those people behind us," Troy said in a loud voice to the half dozen onlookers, including two parking attendants, who were standing nearby, "have guns and are trying to kill us."

It was too late for Greta and Homer to escape. Troy had driven into the parking entrance of the Miyako Gardens Hotel and already another car had come into the circular drive behind the Mercedes. Greta threw the car in reverse, smashed against the grill and bumper of the Jaguar behind her, and then tried to make a run for it by squeezing around Troy's Ford. Troy and the uniformed attendant dove for cover as Greta hit the open door of the Ford, lost control of the Mercedes, and eventually crashed into the parking kiosk in the middle of the driveway. As Nick and Carol stumbled out of the car, four hotel security men surrounded Greta and Homer.

Troy walked over to join his friends. "Anybody hurt?" Both Carol and Nick shook their heads. Troy broke into a grand smile. "I guess that ought to take care of those characters," he said.

Carol gave him a hug. "It was a brilliant idea to drive here," she said. "What made you think of it?"

"Birds," Troy answered.

"*Birds?*" Nick responded. "What the fuck are you talking about, Jefferson?"

"Well, Professor," said Troy, opening the door to the elegant hotel and following his colleagues inside into the open atrium, "when they were about to catch us that last time, I realized that they were probably going to kill us for stealing their gold. And I wondered if there really were birds in heaven. My mother always told me that there were."

"Troy," Carol said with a smile, "you are so full of shit. Come to the point."

"Exactly, angel," he answered. "Look around you." In the atrium of the Miyako Gardens was a magnificent aviary whose tiny, threaded wire rose four stories into the air under a bank of skylights. Hundreds of colored birds played among the vines and palm trees and brought the real sound and feel of the tropics to the lobby of the hotel.

"When I thought about birds," Troy could no longer restrain a crazy laugh, "I realized we were in the vicinity of this hotel and the plan sort of jumped into my mind."

The three of them stood together and gazed up at the aviary. Carol was in the middle. She reached out her hands to both men.

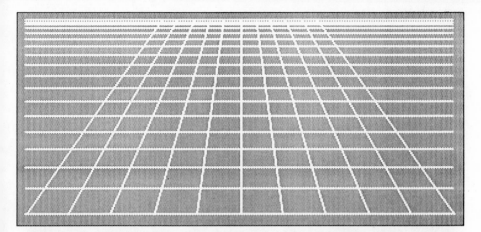

REPATRIATION

B ENEATH the emerald-green ocean the spacecraft rests quietly. Odd fishlike creatures swim by, observe the visitor from the heavens, and then continue on their journey. The final checkout before deployment is underway. When the checkout is completed, a door near the bottom of the craft opens and a gold metallic sphere with a diameter of about five inches appears. The sphere is tied down on top of a long, narrow platform. The treads underneath the platform propel it down a small ramp and then across the sandy ocean floor.

The flatbodied vehicle and its cargo disappear in the distance. After a long wait the strange moving platform returns to the spaceship without the golden sphere. The ramp slides back into the vehicle, the door closes, and the spacecraft is prepared for launch. Soon thereafter the great ship eases forward in the water, rising until it is just beneath the surface of the emerald ocean. It then reconfigures itself, adds wings, steerable flaps, and other control devices, and breaks the water looking temporarily like an airplane. Its ascent into the blue sky filled with light from the twin suns is rapid and breathtaking. Orbital velocity is reached in almost no time. Once in orbit above the atmosphere the aerodynamic surfaces are retracted and the spaceship makes one final voyage around the planet Canthor. When it reaches the proper true anomaly of its orbit, the craft accelerates quickly and hurtles again toward the cold and dark of interstellar space. The third delivery has been completed; nine more remain on its sixty-millicycle mission.

Three millicycles pass. The next target planet is only six systems away, another oceanic planet orbiting around a solitary yellow sun of unusual stability. The fourth cradle will be deposited there, on the third body away from the star, a planet whose period of motion about its central sun is so short that it makes fourteen revolutions in one millicycle.

Before reaching the target, the spaceship makes a detour. It dives deep into the hydrogen-rich atmosphere of the largest planet in the new system, thereby accomplishing two goals. Its velocity with respect to the central star is significantly slowed through conversion of kinetic energy to dissipated heat, and its reservoir of raw elements and primitive chemical compounds, from which the onboard manufacturing equipment creates all the backup and replacement parts, is partially replenished. After exiting from the dive into the thick atmosphere, the interstellar voyager covers the final distance to its target in a leisurely six hundred nanocycles.

During the approach, the automatic software in the central computer goes through a well-tested sequence designed to discover whether any of the conditions on the target planet have changed since the last complete set of systematic observations three cycles ago. Since the contents of each cradle have been uniquely designed, based upon the environment of the specific planet where the zygotes must grow and flourish, any major change in that environment could drastically reduce the probability of survival for the repatriated species. Upon command from the computer, a battery of advanced remote sensing instruments is deployed to confirm the original design specifications for the planet.

But the instruments do not, as planned, validate the set of design assumptions. The environment has changed. Not markedly, not as if it had been reworked on a massive scale by an advanced intelligence for some specific purpose. The initial data strongly suggests instead that during the last cycle or two some indigenous intelligence has emerged that has had a nontrivial impact on both the planet's surface and its atmosphere.

As the remote sensing instruments continue their survey of the target planet, something even more unusual is discovered. There are artificial satellites, thousands of them, in orbit around the body. A spacefaring species now makes this planet its home. An alarm is triggered in the central computer of the spaceship. The zygotes and the cradle system destined for this planet were not designed to deal with any other advanced species.

However, the brilliant engineers of the Colony had anticipated that at least one of the dozen target planets might have changed significantly during the three cycles since the last regular observations. A contingency protocol for handling new situations has been programmed into the approach sequence. Essentially, this protocol calls for careful analysis of the new conditions on the planet, assessment of the impact of those conditions on the key probability of survival parameters, and then, assuming that the impact assessment is not unsatisfactory, transfer, where possible, of new information into the electronic infrastructure responsible for the education of the repatriated species after cradle deployment.

One of the special subroutines in the contingency protocol handles the surprise emergence of a new spacefaring species. The first action in the sequence is the examination of one of the orbiting satellites to assess its technological sophistication. With great care the interstellar spaceship eases into a rendezvous position with one of the artificial satellites that remain mostly stationary above a single region on the rotating planet below. Using superfast burst algorithms stored in the communications macro, the spacecraft searches for and establishes the command and telemetry frequencies of its neighbor. But attempts to actually command the satellite fail, suggesting an elaborate protective code embedded in the receivers and/or a complicated redundant command procedure.

Without being able to command the satellite and thus assess its capabilities, the visiting spaceship cannot conclusively establish the technological stage of the new spacefaring species. The contingency protocol calls, in this situation, for trying to "capture" the satellite to perform in situ analysis, *provided* there is no obvious danger from devices onboard the satellite itself. This particular branch in the software logic for the spaceship was the subject of intense debate by the oversight board of the Committee of Engineers back during the design process several cycles earlier. Many of the more experienced engineers thought that it was risky to include such a logic loop, primarily because of the possibility that a paranoid emerging culture might arm their satellites with destructive devices that could not be easily recognized and disarmed.

However, it was argued, on the basis of historical evidence from throughout the galaxy, that since most incipient civilizations abolish warfare and aggression before they become spacefaring, absence of a clearly identifiable destruct or protective device was sufficient additional evidence to allow the careful capturing and dismantling of a satellite. And everyone agreed that the detailed information about the technological status of the new species that would result from such "reverse engineering" would be extremely valuable in completing the assessment of the risk to the repatriated species.

Great remote manipulator arms extend from the spacecraft, seize the surveillance satellite, and pull it into a large room with vaulted ceilings. An army of small electronic robots attacks it at once, scurrying all over its surface with probes and attachments. Trillions of bits of data about the satellite are fed into the primary data storage device in the spaceship computer. The new spacefarers are not very advanced technically. In fact, the computer algorithm concludes, it is very surprising that they have even mastered launching and maintaining so many satellites.

An explosion starts to rip through the room. An astonishing sequence of events takes place almost instantaneously after the explosion, as the spaceship deploys its protective resources to stop the spread of the fireball and mitigate the damage caused by the small nuclear device that has vaporized its host satellite. The explosion is quickly contained by unknown techniques, but not until considerable destruction has been caused onboard the interstellar craft.

An elaborate self-test occupies the great spaceship after the explosion. Detailed computer analysis of the damage indicates that the probability of successfully deploying the cradles at the additional eight planets would be measurably increased if the mission were temporarily interrupted to allow some repair processes to take place. A safe haven to conduct the repair operations, in a known environment with very few variations, is the concomitant requirement. The master computer decides, based on the system and subsystem constraints that must be applied during the repairs, that the shallow ocean floor on this target planet is a perfect place for such a hiatus in the mission plan.

*   *   *

The spaceship descends into the atmosphere, again reconfiguring itself to expose a set of aerodynamic control surfaces. During its rapid descent, the flight path is crossed by a bullet-shaped vehicle that has just been released from a high altitude airplane. The spaceship approaches and then flies alongside the missile. The missile telemetry is intercepted by the spaceship and correlated with the types of downlink data extracted from the satellite earlier. The spaceship computer uses its enormous processing capability and cross-correlation algorithms to try to break the command code of the tiny missile. Eventually it is successful and the visitor is able to interact with the guided projectile.

The spaceship commands the missile to read out its guidance subroutines. Performing quadrillions of computations per second, the intelligent computer at the heart of the interstellar craft deduces the targeting strategy for the missile. A target image that would result in the missile landing in the ocean, close to the chosen location for the space vehicle, is commanded into the missile's guidance algorithm. The spacecraft and missile plunge in tandem into the Gulf of Mexico.

The two vehicles come to rest about two miles apart on the ocean floor. Within the carefully coded fault protection software of the great spaceship, which took over operation of the craft immediately after the explosion of the satellite, four separate activities are being conducted in parallel. One of the processors is sorting through the data archives associated with this particular planet to determine what possible indigenous species could have gone through an evolutionary burst and become spacefaring with such rapidity. Coupled with this first set of computations is an evaluation of the impact of such a local advanced intelligence on the survivability of the repatriated zygotes. Among the questions addressed by the evaluation is what active steps can be taken by the spaceship now to increase the likelihood of successful embryo germination and development.

A third processor in the central computer performs a thorough, detailed analysis of the spacecraft state, including careful assessments of repair techniques and materials needed to fix each and every damaged component. The fourth major parallel subroutine directs the effort of the small flat robots that go out into the ocean, first to verify that the nearby missile is harmless and can be safely brought back to the ship, and second to catalogue all the flora and fauna in the neighborhood in case any kind of camouflage becomes necessary.

The carpets bring the missile to the spaceship for additional analysis. No major new insights are gleaned from this study. The engineering similarities between the missile and the earlier artificial satellite are simply catalogued in the data archives. The concurrent spaceship damage assessment concludes that all the raw materials and tools necessary for the repairs are available except for the proper quantities of lead and gold, both of which are difficult and time-consuming to make in the transmuter. If somehow enough additional lead and gold can be found, then the spaceship can be ready to leave this planet in three local days; if the spaceship has to make the lead and gold by itself, including leaching the elements in trace amounts from the ocean around it, then the total repair effort might take as long as thirty days.

The other two processors reach some equally interesting probabilistic conclusions. Mostly based upon the data taken during the endangered species roundup seven cycles earlier, two separate types of animals, one land-based and one water-based, are identified as the only possible candidates for the evolutionary burst that produced spacefarers in such a short time. Actually, according to the computer, if the land-based human beings survived their earlier nadir (around the time when some specimens were removed by the zoo ships of the Colony) and did not become extinct, they had by far the better chance of becoming the space voyager, especially in view of the results of the experiments conducted on them at the Zoo Complex. But if, indeed, the descendants of those bipedal, upright, aggressive creatures have become spacefarers, the processor warns, then the chances for survival to maturity by the zygotes in the cradle are extremely low. Unless somehow significant design changes in the cradle can be made on the spot or the development of the repatriates can be kept a secret from the humans for as long as a millicycle.

More worrisome for the extraterrestrial spaceship from the point of view of the overall mission is the tentative conclusion that it may well be discovered by the intelligent and potentially hostile inhabitants of the target planet in a comparatively short period of time. If discovered and seriously threatened, the spaceship could depart from the planet quickly and search for another haven to make repairs; however, traveling in the space environment in its current damaged state would be very risky. Another option would be for the spacecraft to send its own robots to the mines on this planet to extract the lead and gold that would virtually guarantee safe arrival at the next target, where the heavy metals are plentiful.

In either case, premature discovery by uncooperative Earthlings would almost certainly doom the zygote cradle that would be left on the Earth, if it is known that the cradle system came from the alien spacecraft. Thus the first action that the spaceship takes is to check out, deploy, and then hide the Earth cradle away from the vehicle. The carpets locate a sequestered spot six or seven hundred yards away on the nearby ocean floor and the platforms move the gold metallic cradle into that place under a rock overhang.

To reduce the probability of being discovered, the spaceship changes its outer surface to match the ocean floor around it. After a complex set of analyses of its entire decision matrix, the central computer concludes that the maximum likelihood of success path for the overall mission involves trying to enlist either the whales or the human beings to supply the extra lead and gold, as well as the new information to be transmitted to the cradle. So the spacecraft implements those repairs that are straightforward, puts itself into a standby for launch mode, and begins the task of communicating with the Earthlings.

The data taken by the Zoo explorers seven cycles ago (about a hundred thousand Earth years) suggested that the whales and human beings, at that time, had approximately the same potential for intelligence. The whale language was richer and more complicated at the time of this earlier investigation. The Zoo explorers studied it briefly and recorded in the archives its fundamental tenets. Based upon that old data, while at the same time trying to develop a scenario for communicating with the humans, the spaceship attempts to make contact with the humans. Because the whales have not substantially changed in the intervening time, the attempts are partially successful; the whales understand that they are being called, but they are mostly confused by the messages and unable to figure out how to respond.

Two small pods of whales do, however, decipher the message transmitted in the ocean by the alien ship and swim toward its source. The robots in the extraterrestrial spacecraft examine the whales carefully, even showing the captive missile to one of the pods to elicit recognition, and conclude absolutely that the whales cannot be the spacefarers. Therefore it is the human beings who have made the great evolutionary strides and must be contacted and somehow induced to provide the lead and the gold and the requisite information. Further attempts to communicate with the whales are abandoned.

Before the alien ship has determined the method it will use to contact humanity, chance provides it with an excellent opportunity. During the final interactions with the whales, three human beings are swimming in the neighborhood. By incredible luck, these three find the deployed cradle and take it to the land. As a cautionary move, the spaceship computer commands temporary changes inside the cradle to ensure its protection and to provide for more frequent status monitoring; however, there is no major concern yet. The humans do not recognize the connection between the cradle and the spacecraft. In addition, with the zygotes in their early stages of pullulation, the cradle has an extremely robust design. Having the cradle in the possession of humans at this time can also be viewed as an advantage for the superaliens; receivers in the cradle can be commanded to listen to the conversations and then telemeter to the mother spacecraft information that will permit learning the rudiments of the human language.

The logical processes in the extraterrestrial computers are strained to the limit to figure out a way to contact human beings for help without creating undue risk for both the Earth cradle and the rest of the mission. The computers are about to decide on a rapid strike at mines for the lead and gold when they realize, based on their partial understanding of the human language, that the three humans who found the cradle may be coming back into the vicinity. All of the spaceship processors are strapped together to design a scenario that will induce these humans to help them. The inside of the spaceship is even reconfigured from scratch for the arrival of the humans. For if the scenario is successful, there is a high probability that the spaceship can continue on its mission, having successfully deposited the millions of repatriated zygotes, but without having disrupted the main flow of life on Earth. This was the original goal of the mission.

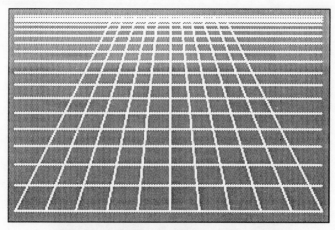

SUNDAY

I T was after two o'clock in the morning by the time the *Florida Queen* left the marina and headed out into the Gulf of Mexico. Carol and Troy stood together against the railing while Nick steered the boat through the harbor. "Well, angel," Troy said, "it has already been an unbelievable experience, hasn't it? And I must admit that I myself am a little nervous about what we're going to find out at the dive site this time."

"I thought you knew what was going to happen, Troy," Carol replied, pointing at his bracelet. "Don't *they* tell you everything?"

"*They* tell me a lot. And I'm getting better at understanding their messages. But how do I know if they're telling the truth?"

"We have had the same problem with you at times," Nick interjected from under the canopy. The boat was almost out in the open ocean. The lights from Key West were receding behind them. "In the final analysis, particularly when nothing makes sense anyway, it comes down to a question of trust. If I were to ask myself logically why I am going out into the Gulf of Mexico in the middle of the night to take lead and gold and information to some extraterrestrials who stopped here on the Earth to make repairs—"

Carol laughed and interrupted. "But there's no logical way to discuss this entire series of events. Troy already pointed that out. We're not operating on logic. And I don't even think it's a question of trust so much." She paused and looked up at the stars. "It's more like faith."

Troy put his arm around Carol and smiled. "I agree with you, angel. After all, we don't know shit. Only *they* know."

Carol yawned. There was silence on the boat. Everyone was very tired. After the security men had surrounded Homer and Greta at the Miyako Gardens, the police had of course been called. They had arrived within ten minutes but it had seemed as if their questions were going to last forever. Carol, Nick, and Troy had each been required to file a separate written statement. Homer and Greta admitted nothing, despite the fact that the security men had taken two handguns from them and matching bullet fragments were found inside Troy's car. Homer had phoned his lawyer and was expecting to be out on bail within four to six hours.

When the trio did finally reach the marina (they had to walk from the hotel because the police impounded Troy's car as evidence) carrying the backpacks, Troy remembered that he had not yet connected the new navigation equipment. Maybe it was because Troy was tired or perhaps having his two friends watch him part of the time over his shoulder made him nervous; whatever the reason, Troy was very slow in installing and verifying the new navigation processor.

Meanwhile, Carol and Nick had been checking to ensure that there were three complete sets of diving apparatus onboard the boat. The diving gear the men had used earlier in the evening was still out at the base in the possession of the United States Navy. Nick thought he recalled putting enough extra equipment on the boat to handle the large party from Tampa that had originally chartered the *Florida Queen* for the weekend. He was correct, but one of the regulator systems did not function properly during the checkout and had to be exchanged for a spare.

During the walk from the hotel to the marina, Nick and Carol and Troy had come to the unanimous conclusion that they would all three keep the underwater rendezvous with the superalien spaceship. There was no other reasonable solution. The boat could certainly be safely anchored. And none of the three of them could bear to think of missing the climax to their adventure.

Nick entered the ocean coordinates of the dive site into the navigation processor and put the boat on autopilot. He saw Carol yawn again. It was infectious. As he opened his mouth for a long, relaxing yawn, Nick realized how exhausted he was. He walked around behind the canopy and found two light air mattresses in a jumbled pile of supplies. He started inflating one of them by blowing into a valve at the end.

Carol came around to the back of the boat when the first mattress was almost inflated. The light on top of the canopy gave her face a glow. *She's even beautiful when she's tired*, Nick thought. He motioned to the other mattress. Carol bent down to pick it up and started inflating it. *And very capable. I've never met a woman who was so good at so many things.*

Nick finished with his air mattress and laid it down on the bottom of the boat. Carol was tiring, so he helped her inflate the rest of her mattress. He grabbed some towels and wadded them up like pillows. "We all have to sleep some," he said to her as an explanation. "Otherwise we'll be punchy when we try to dive."

Carol nodded and walked back to the edge of the canopy. "Is it all right with you if Nick and I take a short nap?" she said to Troy. He smiled his assent. "Wake one or both of us in an hour," she continued, "if you want to use one of the air mattresses." She turned around and started to leave. "Uh, Troy," she asked, before she left the side of the canopy.

"Yes, angel?" he answered.

"Do you know where *they* came from?" She pointed at the sky. Not too many stars were visible because of the brightness of the gibbous moon. It was well past its zenith and already into its western descent.

Troy looked up at the heavens and thought for almost a minute. "No, angel," he responded at length. "I think they've tried to tell me, maybe even twice, but I can't understand what they're saying. But I do know that they come from another star."

Troy now walked over beside Carol and gave her a kiss on the cheek. "Sleep tight and don't let the bedbugs bite," he said. "And maybe you can ask *them* yourself after you wake up."

Where do you come from? Carol was thinking. *And why did you land here, in this place, at this time?* She shaded her eyes from the glare of the moon and concentrated her attention on Sirius, the brightest true star in the sky. *Do you have a home there, around another star? With mothers and fathers and brothers? Do you have love and oceans and mountains and music? And longing and loneliness and fear of death?* For reasons she could not understand, tears found their way into Carol's eyes. She dropped her gaze and walked back to the air mattresses. Nick was already stretched out on one of them. He was on his back and his eyes were closed. Carol lay down on the mattress beside him. She reached out and put her hand in his. He pulled her hand to his lips, kissed it softly, and dropped it on his chest.

Nick's dream was confusing. He was in the main lobby of a huge open library with twenty floors of books. He could see the spiral staircases ascending to the stacks above him. "But you don't understand," he said to the clerk standing behind the long counter. "I must read all these books this weekend. Otherwise I won't be ready for the test on Monday."

"I'm sorry, sir," the diffident clerk replied quietly after scanning Nick's list a second time. "But all copies of these books are currently checked out."

Nick started to panic. He looked up at the enormously high ceiling and the floors of shelved books above him. He saw Carol Dawson up on the third floor, leaning against the railing and reading a book. His panic subsided. *She'll know the material,* he thought to himself in the dream. He raced over to the staircase and bounded up the two flights of curving stairs.

He was out of breath when he reached Carol. She was reading one of the books that had been on his list. "Oh, good," he said between gasps, "I knew as soon as I saw you that there was no worry."

She looked at him quizzically. Without warning she thrust her hand down into the top of his jeans and grabbed his penis. He responded immediately and leaned forward to kiss her. She shook her head and backed up. He pursued her, pushing her against the railing. She fought him. He pressed hard against her body and succeeded in kissing her. The railing gave way and they were falling, falling. He woke up before they hit the floor in the lobby of the library.

Nick shuddered himself awake. Carol was watching him intently. Her head was resting on her hands, propped up by her elbow. "Are you all right?" she asked as soon as he opened his eyes.

It took Nick a few seconds to acclimate after the vivid dream. His heart was still racing out of control. "I think so," he said. Carol continued to stare at him. "Why are you looking at me like that?" he asked.

"Well," she began, "I woke up because you were talking. I even thought I heard my name a couple of times. Maybe I imagined it. If you don't mind my asking, do you often talk in your sleep?"

"I don't know," Nick answered. He laughed a little. "Nobody has ever mentioned it to me before."

"Not even Monique?" Carol said. Her eyes did not leave Nick's. She could tell that he was trying to decide what kind of answer to give to her question. *You're pushing again*, a voice inside her said. *Let the man do things at his own pace.*

Nick looked away. "We did not sleep together that much," he said softly. There was a long pause. "Besides," he said, now turning back to Carol, "that was ten years ago. I was very young. And she was married to someone else."

While they had been sleeping Troy had switched off the light on the top of the canopy. The only light on their faces now was the reflection from the moon. They continued to look at each other in silence. Nick had not said very much to Carol about Monique, but it had been more than he had ever told anyone else, including his parents. Carol knew how much of an effort it had been for him to answer her question honestly. She rolled over on her back again and extended her hand to Nick.

"So here we are, Mr. Williams. Two solitary voyagers on the sea of life. Both of us are now past thirty. Many of our friends and classmates have already settled down into that house in the suburbs with the two kids and a dog. Why not us? What's different about us?"

The moon was accelerating its downward arc through the sky above them. As it descended, more stars could be seen on the opposite horizon. Nick thought he saw a shooting star. *There would be no way to hide from feelings.* Nick was jumping ahead of the conversation, imagining for the moment that he was going to be involved with Carol. *She would not permit it. At least I would not have any doubts about where we stood.*

"When I was over at her house on Friday morning," Nick finally replied to her question, "Amanda Winchester told me that I'm looking for a fantasy woman, someone absolutely perfect. And that mere mortals always come up short in my estimation." He propped his head up and looked at Carol. "But I think it's something else. I think maybe I'm not willing to make a commitment because of fear of rejection."

Did I really say that? wondered Nick, shocked at himself. Instantly he felt as if he never should have shared the thought. His defenses began to build and he braced himself for a flippant or insensitive reply.

But it did not come. Instead Carol was quiet and thoughtful. At length she spoke. "My protection is different from yours," she said. "I always play it safe. I pick men I admire and respect, intellectual pals if you will, but for whom I do not have any passion. When I meet a man who sets off the banjos and bells, I run the other way."

Because I'm afraid, she thought. *Afraid that I might love him as much as I did my father. And I could not survive if I were abandoned like that again.*

She felt Nick's hand on her cheek. He was caressing her gently. She reached up, took his hand, and squeezed it. He pulled himself up on his side where he could see her better. She could tell that he wanted to kiss her. She squeezed his hand again. Slowly, tentatively, he dropped his mouth on hers. It was a tender, adoring kiss, without pressure or overt passion, a subtle, artful question that could have been either the beginning of a love affair or the sole kiss exchanged between two people whose paths just happened to cross in life. Carol heard banjos and bells.

WINTERS stood on the deck by himself, smoking quietly. It was not a large boat, this converted trawler, but it was very fast. They had not left the dock until after four o'clock and they had almost caught up with their prey already. The commander rubbed his eyes and yawned. He was tired. He blew smoke out over the ocean. On the eastern horizon there was just a faint suggestion of dawn. To the west, in the direction of the moon, Winters thought he saw the dim light of another boat.

These young people must all be crazy, he thought to himself as he reflected back on the events of the evening. *Why the hell did they leave? Did they push Todd down those stairs without his knowing it? It would have been so much easier if they had just stayed there until we returned.*

He remembered the look on Lieutenant Ramirez' face when he had interrupted the telephone conversation that Winters had been having with his wife, Betty. "Excuse me, Commander," Ramirez had said. He had been out of breath. "You must come quickly. Lieutenant Todd is injured and our prisoners have escaped."

He had told his wife that he had no idea when he would be home and then joined Ramirez for the short walk back to the administration annex. On the way Winters had been thinking about Tiffani, about the difficulty he had

had in explaining to the seventeen-year-old why he could not just drop everything and meet her at the party. "But you can work any day or night, Vernon," she had said. "This is our only time to be together." She had already drunk too much champagne. Later in the conversation, when Winters had made it clear to her that he almost certainly would not make it to the party at all, and that he would probably ask Melvin and Marc to take her home, Tiffani had become petulant and angry. She had stopped calling him Vernon. "All right, Commander," she had said, "I guess I'll see you at the theater on Tuesday night."

The phone had clicked off and Winters had felt an ache tearing through his heart. *Oh fuck,* he had thought for a moment, *I've blown it.* He had imagined himself jumping in the car, forgetting Todd and Ramirez and the Panther missile, and driving over to the party to sweep Tiffani into his arms. But he had not done it. Despite his incredible longing, he was not able to pull himself away from his duty. *If it was meant to be,* he told himself consolingly, *then those flames of passion will burn again.* But even with his limited romantic experience Winters knew better. Timing is everything in a love affair. If momentum is lost at a critical moment, especially when the rhythm of the passion is heading for a climax, it will never be regained.

Ramirez had already called the doctor on the base and he had arrived at the annex just after the two officers. While they were standing there together, Ramirez had insisted to Winters that it must have been foul play, that Todd could not have fallen so hard unless he had either been pushed or thrown down the concrete steps. The lieutenant had begun to stir during the doctor's examination. "He has a bad concussion," the doctor had said after he first checked Todd's eyes. "He'll probably be all right but he'll have a ferocious headache in the morning. Meanwhile, we'll take him over to the infirmary and sew up that gash in his head."

To Winters it didn't make sense. While he was waiting patiently in an adjoining room for the doctors and nurses to finish the stitches in the lieutenant's head, Winters tried to figure out what possible motive Nick and Carol and Troy could have had for attacking Todd and then escaping. *The Dawson woman is smart and successful. Why would she do it?* He wondered if perhaps the trio might have been involved in some kind of big drug transaction. *That would at least explain all the gold. But Todd and Ramirez did not find any indication of drugs. So what the hell is happening?*

Lieutenant Todd had been kept awake during the procedure in the emergency room. He had been given only a local anesthetic to reduce his pain. But he had not been very lucid in response to the doctor's simple questions. "That sometimes happens with a concussion," the medical officer had told Winters afterward. "He may not be very coherent for the next day or two."

Nevertheless, around two o'clock, immediately after Todd's head had been shaven, stitched, and bandaged, Commander Winters and Lieutenant

Ramirez had decided to ask him about what had occurred at the annex. The commander could not accept Todd's answer, even though the lieutenant repeated it twice verbatim. Todd had insisted that a six-foot carrot with vertical slits in its face had hidden in the bathroom and had jumped him while he was trying to take a piss. He had escaped that first assault, but the giant carrot had then followed him into the main room at the annex.

"And just how did this thing—"

"Carrot," interrupted Todd.

"And how did this carrot attack you?" continued Winters. *Jesus,* he had thought, *this man has cracked. One bump on the head and he has finally flipped.*

"It's hard to describe exactly," Lieutenant Todd had answered slowly. "You see, it had four doodads hanging out of these vertical slits in its head. They were all mean looking—"

The doctor had come up and interrupted. "Gentlemen," he had said with a perfect bedside smile, "my patient desperately needs rest. Surely some of these questions can wait until tomorrow."

Commander Winters remembered an overpowering sense of bewilderment as he watched the gurney take Lieutenant Todd from the emergency operating room to the infirmary. As soon as Todd was out of earshot, the commander had turned to Lieutenant Ramirez. "And what do you make of all this, Lieutenant?"

"Commander, sir, I'm no medical expert . . ."

"I know that, Lieutenant. I don't want your medical opinion. I want to know what you think about the, uh, carrot business." *Damn him,* Winters had thought. *Does he have so little imagination that he can't even react to Todd's story?*

"Sir," Ramirez had replied, "the carrot business is outside my experience."

To say the least. Winters smiled to himself and flipped his cigarette into the water. He walked over to the little wheelhouse and checked the navigator. They were only seven miles from the target boat and converging rapidly. He pulled back on the throttle and put the boat into neutral gear. Winters did not want to draw any closer to the *Florida Queen* until Ramirez and the other two seamen were awake and in position.

He estimated that it was still about forty minutes until sunrise. Winters laughed again about Ramirez's unwillingness to venture a comment on Todd's carrot story. *But the young Latino is a good officer. His only mistake was following Todd.* Winters remembered how quickly Ramirez had organized all the details of their current sortie, picking the high-tech converted trawler for speed and stealth, rousting the two bachelor seamen who worked for him in Intelligence, and establishing a special link between the base and the trawler so that the whereabouts of the *Florida Queen* would be known at all times.

"We must follow them. We really have no choice," Lieutenant Ramirez had said firmly to Winters after they had verified that Nick's boat had indeed left the Hemingway Marina just after two o'clock. "Otherwise there's no way we could ever justify our having taken them into custody in the first place."

Winters had reluctantly agreed and Ramirez had organized the chase. The commander had told the younger men to get some sleep while he formulated the plan. *Which is simple. Okay, you guys, come with us and answer the questions or we'll charge you under the sedition act of 1991.* Now, after putting the boat in idle, Winters was ready to wake Ramirez and the other two men. He intended to apprehend Nick, Carol, and Troy as soon as it was daylight.

The wind around the boat changed direction and Winters stopped a minute to check the weather. He turned his face toward the moon. The air suddenly felt warmer, almost hot, and he was reminded of a night off the coast of Libya eight years earlier. *The worst night of my life,* he thought. For a few moments his resolve to carry out his plan wavered and he asked himself if he was about to make another mistake.

Then he heard a trumpet blast, followed maybe four seconds later by a similar but quieter sound. Winters looked around him in the placid ocean. He saw nothing. Now he heard a group of trumpets and their echo, both sounds distinctly coming from the west. The commander strained his eyes in the direction of the moon. Silhouetted against its face he saw what appeared to be a group of snakes dancing out of the water. He went inside the wheelhouse to fetch a pair of binoculars.

By the time the commander returned to the railing a magnificent symphony surrounded him. *Where is this incredible music coming from?* he asked at first, before he succumbed completely to its mesmerizing beauty. He stood powerless against the railing, listening intently. The music was rich, emotional, full of evocative longing. Winters was swept away, not only into his own past where his deepest memories were stored, but also onto another planet in another era where proud and dignified serpents with blue necks called to their loved ones during their short annual mating rite.

He was spellbound. Tears were already flooding into his eyes when he at last mechanically lifted the binoculars and focused on the strange, sinuous shapes underneath the moon. The ghostlike images were completely transparent; the moonlight went right through them. As Winters watched what was a thousand necks dancing above the water, cavorting back and forth in perfect rhythm, and as he heard the music build toward the concluding crescendo of the Canthorean mating symphony, his tired eyes blurred and he swore that what he saw across the water in front of him, calling to him with a song of longing and desire, was an image of Tiffani Thomas. His heart was devastated by the combination of the music and the sight of her. Winters was aware of an intense sense of loss unparalleled in his life.

Yes, he said to himself as Tiffani continued to beckon in the distance, *I'm coming. I'm sorry Tiffani darling. Tomorrow I will come to see you. We will* . . . He stopped his interior monologue to wipe his eyes. The music had now entered the final crescendo, signaling the actual mating dance of the pairs of Canthorean serpents. Winters looked through his binoculars again. The image of Tiffani was gone. He adjusted his glasses. Joanna Carr came into focus, smiled briefly, and disappeared. A moment later the little Arab girl from the Virginia beach seemed to dance just under the moon. She was happy and gay. She too was gone in an instant.

The music was all around him. Bursts of sound, powerful, full, expressing pleasure no longer anticipated but now being experienced. He looked through his binoculars one more time. The moon was setting. As it fell into the ocean the image created against its illuminated disc by the dancing serpents was unmistakable. Winters clearly saw the faces of his wife, Betty, and his son, Hap. They were smiling at him together with a deep and abiding affection. They remained there in his vision until the moon sank completely into the ocean.

C AROL struggled to adjust her diving equipment. "Do you need some help, angel?" Troy asked. He came over and stood beside her in the predawn dark. He was already fully prepared for the dive.

"I haven't worn anything like this since my first set of scuba lessons," she said, fidgeting uncomfortably with the old-fashioned gear.

Troy tightened the weight belt around her waist. "You're scared, aren't you, angel?" Carol didn't answer right away. "Me too. My pulse rate must be twice normal."

Carol's equipment seemed to please her finally. "You know, Troy, even after the last three days my brain is having a hard time convincing the rest of me that all this is really happening. Imagine writing it down for someone to read. 'As we were preparing to return to the alien spaceship . . .' "

"Hey, you guys, come here," Nick called from the other side of the canopy. Carol and Troy walked around to the front of the boat. Nick was staring out across the ocean to the east. He handed a small pair of binoculars to Carol. "Do you see a light out there in the distance, just to the left of that island?"

Carol could barely make out the light. "Uh huh," she said to Nick. "But so what? Isn't it reasonable that somewhere out in the ocean there would be another boat?"

"Of course," Nick answered. "But that light hasn't moved for fifteen minutes. It's just sitting there. Why would a fishing boat, or any other kind of boat, be—"

"Sh," interrupted Troy. He put his fingers to his lips. "Listen," he whispered, "I hear music."

His companions stood quietly on the deck. Behind them the moon disappeared into the ocean. Above the gentle lapping of the waves all three of them could hear what sounded like the climax of a symphony, played by a full orchestra. They listened for thirty seconds. The music reached a peak, faded slightly, and then ceased abruptly.

"That was beautiful," Carol remarked.

"And weird," Nick said, walking over beside her. "Where the hell was it coming from? Is someone out there testing a new stereo system? My God, if the sound travels five or ten miles, it must be deafening up close."

Troy was standing off to the side by himself. He was concentrating on something. Suddenly he turned to his companions. "I know this sounds crazy," he said to Nick and Carol, "but I think the music was a signal for us to dive. Or perhaps a warning."

"Great," said Carol. "That's what we need to reassure us. A warning of some kind. As if we're not nervous enough."

Nick put his arm around her. "Hey, lady," he said, "don't wimp out on us now. After all those brave comments about a once in a lifetime experience . . ."

"Really, let's go," Troy said impatiently. He looked anxious and very serious. "I'm definitely getting the message that we should dive now."

Troy's solemnity changed the mood of the trio. The three of them worked together in silence to secure the two buoyancy bags containing the lead, the gold, and the information discs. The eastern sky continued to brighten. It was only about fifteen minutes until sunrise.

While they were working, Carol noticed that Nick seemed a little distracted. Right before they left the boat she walked up beside him. "Are you all right?" she said quietly.

"Yes," he answered. "I'm just trying to figure out if I've completely lost my mind. For eight years I have been thinking about what I would do if I ever had my full share of the treasure. Now I'm about to give it all away to some extraterrestrials from God knows where." He looked at her. "There's enough gold here to last three people a long time."

"I know," she said, giving him a little hug. "I must admit that I've thought about it too. But in reality, part belongs to Amanda Winchester, part to Jake Lewis, most of it to the IRS . . ." She grinned. "And it's only money. That's nothing when you compare it to being the only humans to interact with visitors from another planet."

"I hope you're right," he said. "I hope I don't wake up tomorrow and feel as if I've made a terrible mistake. This entire episode has been so bizarre that I suspect my normal faculties aren't working properly. We don't even know for sure if these aliens are friendly . . ."

Carol pulled her diving mask over her face. "We'll never have all the answers," she said. She took his hand. "Let's go, Nick."

Troy was first into the water. Nick and Carol followed. It had been agreed before the dive that Carol would take the searchlight and lead the group. She was the most mobile of the threesome because each of the men was dragging a buoyancy bag. The trio had been concerned that they might have difficulty finding the ship and had discussed an elaborate set of contingency plans for locating it. They needn't have worried. Thirty feet under the *Florida Queen*, in virtually the exact place where the fissure had been on Thursday, there was a light in the water. Carol pointed at it and the two men swam up behind her. As they drew closer, they saw that the light was coming from a rectangular area about ten feet high and twenty feet wide. They could not see anything except what looked like some kind of material or fabric with a soft light behind it.

Carol hesitated. Troy swam right on by her, into the lighted area, his buoyancy bag trailing behind him. Everything disappeared. Nick and Carol waited. Carol felt herself tightening up. *Come on now, Dawson,* she thought, *it's your turn. You've been here before.* She took a deep breath and swam into the material. She felt something like plastic touch her face and then she was in a covered tunnel. A swift current was pulling her to the right. She went down a small water slide and was deposited in a shallow pool at the bottom. She clambered out of the pool and began removing her diving equipment.

Troy was standing on the floor about ten feet beyond the end of the pool. Next to him a warden had already taken the buoyancy bag, opened it, and adroitly separated the gold bars and the lead weights from the information discs. As Carol's eyes adjusted to the dim light around her, she saw that the warden was now loading the gold on a small platform sitting on top of tank treads about a foot above the floor. Immediately thereafter, the warden placed the information discs and the lead weights on two other platforms. A carpet that had been lying inconspicuously over against the wall on the left then rose up, apparently activated the treads under the platforms, and directed them toward a nearby hallway leading out of the room.

Carol pulled off her mask and finished removing her diving gear. She was in a medium-sized room somewhat like the ones she and Troy had encountered at the beginning of her last dive. The curved wall partitions were colored black and white. There was a small window to the ocean next to the splash pool on her left. The ceilings were low and tight, only a couple of feet above her head, giving her a feeling of claustrophobia. *So here I am again,* she thought, *Back in Wonderland. This time I will take plenty of pictures.* She photographed the procession of the carpet and three platforms just as it disappeared from the room. She then changed lenses and took a dozen quick close-up pictures of the warden standing next to Troy. It had the same amoebalike central body as the one she had confronted the day before, but there were only five implements sticking out of its upper half. The warden had probably been customized for its particular job of taking the objects from the trio.

Troy walked over beside her. "Where's Nick?" he asked. *My God*, Carol thought as she turned around and looked back at the slide and splash pool. *I almost forgot.* She chastized herself for not having waited for Nick. *After all, he's never been down here . . .*

Nick's big body careened out of control against the sides of the slide and he hurtled into the splash pool. The heavy buoyancy bag came down behind him and hit him hard, just above the kidneys. He stumbled to his feet, fell down in the pool, and then stood up again. In his diving apparatus with the thin plastic material from the bag tied around his wrist, it was he who looked like the visitor from outer space.

Carol and Troy were laughing as Nick climbed out of the splash pool. "All right, Professor!" exclaimed Troy. He reached forward to give him a hand. "Good show. It's a shame we don't have that entry on tape."

Nick removed his mouthpiece. He was out of breath. "Thanks a lot for waiting, team," he stammered. He looked around him. "What is this place, anyway?"

The warden meanwhile had approached him from the side and was already tugging at the bag with one of its appendages. "Just a minute, weirdo," Nick said, suppressing his fright. "Let me get my bearings first."

The warden didn't stop. A knifelike appendage cut the bag below where it was attached to Nick's wrist. Next the warden took the entire bag, including its lead and gold contents, and somehow pushed it through its own semipermeable outer skin. The bag could be seen intact, adjacent to the rectangular control boxes, as the warden turned and hurried across the floor. It went through the same exit that the carpet and platforms had used earlier.

"You're welcome," Nick managed to say as he watched the strange creature disappear with the loot. He finished taking off his diving gear and walked over to Troy. "Okay, Jefferson, you're the main man here. What do we do now?"

"Well, Professor," he answered, "as far as I can tell, our job is finished. If you guys want, we can suit up again and jump through that window wall over there. We'd be back in the boat in less than five minutes. If I've read the messages right, these alien dudes will be ready to leave very shortly."

"You mean that's it? We're done?" Carol asked. Troy nodded. "This is the most overrated experience since my first sexual encounter," Carol commented.

Nick was walking across the room, moving directly away from the splash pool and his two friends. "Where are you going?" Troy asked.

"I paid a hefty admission price," Nick replied. "I'm at least entitled to a tour." Carol and Troy followed him. They crossed the empty room and walked through an exit between two wall partitions on the opposite side. They entered a short, dark, covered corridor. They could see light at the other end. They emerged into another room, this one circular and significantly larger. It had the high cathedral ceilings that Carol had liked so much on her last visit.

This room was not empty. Sitting in its middle facing them was a gigantic, enclosed, translucent cylinder, about twenty-five feet high altogether and ten feet in diameter at its base. A horde of orange pipes and purple cable sheaths attached the cylinder to a group of machines built into the wall behind it. There was a light green liquid filling the inside of the cylinder and eight gold metallic objects floating at different heights in the liquid. The objects were many different shapes. One looked like a starfish, another like a box, a third like a derby hat; the only thing the objects had in common was their gold metallic outer covering. Upon close inspection of the cylinder, thin membranes could be seen inside the liquid. These surfaces effectively partitioned the internal volume and gave each of the golden objects its own unique subvolume.

"All right, genius," Nick said to Troy, after he stared at the cylinder for almost a full minute. "Explain what this is all about." Carol was in a photographer's paradise. She had nearly finished recording all hundred and twenty-eight pictures that could be stored on one minidisc. She had photographed the cylinder from all angles, including a close-up of each of the objects suspended in the liquid, and was now working on the machines behind it. She stopped taking pictures to listen to Troy's reply.

"Well, Professor . . ." Troy started. His forehead was knitted as he tried to concentrate. "As far as I can make out from what they've been trying to tell me, this spaceship is on a mission to a dozen planets that are scattered in this part of the galaxy. On each planet the aliens leave one of those golden things you see in the cylinder. They contain tiny embryos or seeds that have been genetically engineered for survival on that specific planet."

Carol walked over beside them. "So the ship goes from planet to planet, dropping off these packages containing seeds of some kind? Sort of a galactic Johnny Appleseed?"

"Sort of, angel, except that there are both animal and plant seeds inside the container. Plus advanced robots that nurture and educate the growing things until they reach maturity. Then the creatures can flourish on their own without help."

"All in that one little package?" Nick asked. He looked again at the fascinating objects floating in the liquid in the cylinder. He loved the golden color. All of a sudden he thought of the trident. He imagined thousands of tiny swarming embryos inside its outer golden surface and in his mind's eye he projected the growth of the swarm into the future. There was something fearsome about creatures genetically engineered to survive on the planet Earth. *What if they are not friendly?*

Nick's heart sped up as he realized what had been bothering him, partly subconsciously, since he started believing Troy's story about the aliens. *Why did they stop on the Earth in the first place? What do they really want from us?* His mind raced on. *And if that trident contains beings destined for Earth that are extremely advanced,* he thought, *then it doesn't matter if they are friendly. We will be finished sooner or later anyway.*

Carol and Troy were talking in general terms about the way an advanced civilization might use seeds to colonize other planets. Nick wasn't listening carefully. *I can't tell Troy or even Carol. If the aliens know what I'm thinking they will stop me. I'd better do it soon.*

"Troy," he heard Carol say as she began to take another set of pictures of the objects in the cylinder, "is it just coincidence that the trident we found on Thursday looks so much like one of these seed packages?"

Nick did not wait for Troy to answer. "Excuse me," he interrupted in a loud voice. "I forgot something very important. I must go back to the boat. Stay here and wait for me. I'll be right back."

He burst out of the room, down the corridor, and across the room with the low ceiling and the window on the ocean. *Good,* he said to himself, *nothing is going to stop me.* Without even pausing to put on his diving gear, Nick took a huge breath and dove through the window. He was afraid that his lungs were going to explode before he reached the surface. But he made it. He climbed up the ladder and onto the boat.

Nick went immediately to the bottom drawer underneath the racks of electronic equipment. He reached in and grabbed the golden trident. He could feel that the axis rod had thickened considerably. It was now nearly twice as thick as it had been the first time that he held it. *Carol was right. Damnit, why didn't I listen to her at the time?* He pulled the object completely out of the drawer. The sun was just about to come up behind him. In the dawn light Nick could see that the trident had changed in several other ways. It was heavier. The individual tines on the fork end were much thicker and had almost grown together. In addition, there was an open hole into a soft, gooey interior on the north pole of the larger of the two spheres.

Nick examined it carefully. Suddenly he felt powerful arms wrap themselves around his chest and upper body, forcing him to drop the trident on the floor of the boat. "Now just hold steady," he heard a lightly accented voice say, "and turn around slowly. We won't hurt you if you cooperate."

Nick turned around. Commander Winters and a tall, fat seaman that Nick had never seen before were standing in front of him in wetsuits. Lieutenant Ramirez was still holding him from behind. Ramirez gradually released Nick and bent down to pick up the trident. He handed it to Winters. "Thank you, Lieutenant," Winters said. "Where are your companions, Williams?" he then asked Nick. "Down there with my missile?"

Nick didn't say anything at first. Too much was happening too fast. He was having difficulty integrating Winters into his scenario for returning the trident to the spaceship. As soon as Nick had felt the changes in its outer surface, he had known for certain that the trident was one of the seed packages.

Winters was studying the trident. "And what's the significance of this thing?" he said. "You guys have taken enough photographs of it."

Nick was doing some calculations. *If I am delayed here very long, then Carol and Troy will undoubtedly leave the ship. And the aliens will launch.* He took a deep breath. *My only chance is the truth.*

"Commander Winters," Nick began, "please listen very carefully to what I'm about to say. It will sound fantastic, even preposterous, but it's all true. And if you will come with me, I can prove everything to you. The fate of the human race may well depend on what we do in the next five minutes." He paused to organize his ideas.

For some reason Winters thought about the ridiculous carrot story that Todd had told him. But the earnestness he was seeing in Nick's face persuaded him to continue to pay attention. "Go ahead, Williams," he said.

"Carol Dawson and Troy Jefferson are right now onboard a super-advanced extraterrestrial spaceship that is directly under this boat. The alien vehicle is traveling from planet to planet depositing packages of embryonic beings that are genetically designed to survive on a particular planet. That golden thing in your hand is, in a sense, a cradle for creatures that may later flourish on the Earth. I must return it to the aliens before they leave or our descendants may not survive."

Commander Winters looked at Nick as if he had lost his mind. The commander started to say something. "No," Nick interrupted. "Hear me out. The spacecraft also stopped here because it needed some repairs. At one time we thought it might have found your missile. That's partially how we got involved in the first place. We didn't know about the creatures in the cradle. So we were trying to help. One of the things the aliens needed for their repairs was gold. You see, they only had three days—"

"Jesus K. Christ!" Winters shouted at Nick. "Do you really expect me to believe this crap? This is the looniest, most farfetched story I have ever heard in my entire life. You're nuts. Cradles, aliens who need gold for repairs . . . I suppose next you'll be telling me that *they* are six feet tall and look like carrots—"

"And have four vertical slits in their faces?" Nick added.

Winters glanced around. "You told him?" he said to Lieutenant Ramirez. Ramirez shook his head back and forth.

"No," Nick continued abruptly as the commander looked completely confused. "The carrot thing wasn't an alien, at least not one of the superaliens who made the ship. The carrot was a holographic projection . . ."

The perplexed Commander Winters waved his hands. "I'm not listening to any more of this nonsense, Williams. At least not here. What I want to know is what you and your friends know about the location of the missile.

Now will you come with us over to our boat of your own free will, or do we have to tie you up?"

At that moment, six feet above them, a ten-legged, black, spiderlike creature with a body about four inches in diameter walked unnoticed to the edge of the canopy. It extended three antennae in their direction and then leaped off the side, landing on the back of Lieutenant Ramirez' neck. "Aieee," screamed the lieutenant during the pause in the conversation. He fell down on his knees behind Nick and grasped at the black thing that was trying to take a sample chunk out of his neck. For a second nobody moved. Then Nick grabbed a large pair of pliers from the counter and thwacked the black thing once, twice, and even a third time before it released its grip on Ramirez' neck.

All four men watched it fall to the deck, scuttle rapidly over to the cradle that Commander Winters had put down so that he could assist Ramirez, shrink its size by a factor of ten, and disappear into the cradle through the soft gooey opening on the top of the sphere. Within seconds the goo hardened and all the external surfaces of the cradle were again rigid.

Winters was flabbergasted. Ramirez crossed himself. The seaman looked as if he were about to faint. "I swear to you that my story is true, Commander," Nick said calmly. "All you have to do is come down with me and see for yourself. I left my diving gear down there so that I could hurry up here to retrieve this thing. We can go together with my last working tank and share the air supply."

Winters' head was spinning. The ten-legged spider was the straw that broke the camel's back. He felt that he had now entered the Twilight Zone. *I have never seen or heard anything even remotely like this before in my life,* Winters thought. *And only half an hour ago I had wild hallucinations with musical accompaniment. Maybe I am the one losing touch with reality.* Lieutenant Ramirez was still on his knees. It looked as if he were praying. *Or maybe this is finally my sign from God.*

"All right, Williams," the commander was surprised to hear himself say. "I'll go with you. But my men will wait here on your boat for our return."

Nick picked up the trident and raced around the canopy to prepare the diving equipment.

It took Carol and Troy a few seconds to react to Nick's abrupt departure. "That was strange," Carol said finally. "What do you suppose he forgot?"

"I have no idea," Troy shrugged. "But I hope he hurries back. I don't think it's very long until launch. And I'm sure *they* will throw us out before then."

Carol thought for a moment and then turned back to look at the cylinder. "You know, Troy, those golden things *are* exactly like the trident on the outside. Did you say—"

"I didn't answer you before, angel," Troy interrupted. "But yes, you're right. It is the same material. I hadn't realized until we came down here today that what we picked up on that first dive was the seed package for Earth. *They* may have tried to tell me before; maybe I just didn't understand them."

Carol was fascinated. She walked over and put her face against the cylinder wall. It felt more like glass than plastic. "So maybe I was right when I thought it was heavier and thicker . . ." she said, as much to herself as to Troy. "And inside that trident are seeds for better plants and animals?" Troy nodded his head in response.

There was now some motion inside the cylinder. The thin membranes separating the subvolumes were growing what appeared to be guidewires that were wrapping themselves around the individual golden objects. Carol reloaded her camera with a new disc and ran around the outside of the cylinder, stopping in the best positions to photograph the process. Troy looked down at his bracelet. "There's no doubt about it, angel. These ETs are definitely preparing to launch. Maybe we should go."

"We'll wait as long as we can," Carol shouted from across the room. "These photographs will be priceless." They both could now hear weird noises behind the walls. The noises were not loud, but they were distracting because they were erratic and so totally alien. Troy paced nervously as he listened to the gamut of sounds. Carol walked over beside him. "Besides," she said, "Nick asked us to wait for him."

"That's great," Troy answered, "as long as *they* wait as well." He seemed uncharacteristically nervous. "I don't want to be onboard when these guys leave the Earth."

"Hey there, Mr. Jefferson," Carol said, "you are supposed to be the calm one. Relax. You just said yourself that you think they'll throw us out before they leave." She paused and looked searchingly at Troy. "What do you know that I don't?"

Troy turned away from her and started walking toward the exit. Carol ran after him and grabbed his arm. "What is it, Troy?" she said. "What's wrong?"

"Look, angel," he replied, not looking directly at her, "I just figured it out myself a minute ago. And I'm still not sure what it means. I hope I haven't made a terrible—"

"What are you talking about?" she interrupted him. "You're not making any sense."

"The Earth package," he blurted out. "It has human seeds in it too. Along with the trees and insects and grasses and birds."

Carol stood facing Troy, trying to understand what was bothering him so much. "When *they* came here a long long time ago," he said, his face wrinkled with concern, "they took specimens of the different species and returned them to their home world. Where they were improved by genetic engineering and prepared for their eventual return to the Earth. Some of those specimens were human beings."

Carol's heart quickened as she realized what Troy was telling her. *So that's it,* she said to herself. *There are superhumans inside that package we've found. Not just better flowers and better bugs, but better people as well.* But unlike Troy, Carol's immediate reaction was not fear. She was overwhelmed by curiosity.

"Can I see them?" she asked excitedly. Troy didn't understand. "The superhumans, or whatever you want to call them . . . ," she continued, "can I see them?"

Troy shook his head. "They're just tiny zygotes, angel. More than a billion would fit in your hand. You wouldn't be able to see anything."

Carol was not dissuaded. "But these guys have such amazing technological ability. Maybe they can . . ." She stopped. "Wait a minute, Troy. Remember that carrot on the base? It was a holographic projection and must have come somehow out of the information base on this spacecraft."

Carol walked away from Troy into the middle of the room. She raised her arms and looked up at the ceiling thirty feet above her. "Okay, you guys, whoever you are," she invoked in a loud voice. "Now there's something that I want. We risked our ass to get what you needed for your repairs. You can at least reciprocate. I want to see what we might look like someday . . ."

To their left, not too far from one of the large blocky machines connected to the cylinder, two of the wall partitions moved apart to form a hallway. They could see light at the other end. "Come on," an exultant Carol called to Troy, who was again smiling and admiring her assertiveness, "let's go see what our superaliens have created for us now."

At the end of the short corridor, there was a softly lit square room about twenty feet on a side. Against the opposite wall, illuminated by a blue light that gave the entire tableau a surrealistic appearance, eight children were standing around a large, glowing model of the Earth. As Carol and Troy approached, they recognized that what they were seeing was not real, that it was simply a complex sequence of images projected into the air in front of them. But the diaphanous picture contained such rich detail that it was easy to forget it was just a projection.

The children were four or five years old. All were wearing only a thin white loincloth that covered their genitals. There were four girls and four boys. Two of them were black, two were Caucasian with blue eyes and blonde hair, two were Oriental, and the final boy and girl, definitely twins, looked like a mixture of all humanity. What Carol immediately noticed was their eyes. All eight children had large, piercing eyes of brilliant intensity that were focused on the glowing Earth in front of them.

"The continents of this planet," the little black boy was saying, "were once tied together in a single gigantic land mass that stretched from pole to pole. This was relatively recently, only about two hundred million years ago. Since that time the motion of the plates on which the individual land masses rest has completely changed the configuration of the surface. Here, for example, you can see the Indian subcontinent tearing away from Antarctica a hundred million years ago and moving across the ocean toward an eventual collision with Asia. It was this collision and the subsequent plate interaction that lifted the Himalayas, the highest mountains on the planet, to their current height."

As the little boy was talking, the electronic model Earth in front of him demonstrated the continental changes that he was describing. "But what is the mechanism that causes these plates and land masses to move with respect to each other?" the tiny blonde-haired girl asked.

"Psst," Carol whispered in Troy's ear. "How come they are speaking English and know all this Earth geography?" Troy looked at her as if he were disappointed and made a circular motion with his hands. *Of course*, Carol said to herself, *they've already processed the discs.*

". . . then this activity results in material being thrust upward from the mantle below the Earth's crust. Eventually the continents are pushed apart. Any other questions?" The black boy was smiling. He pointed at the model in front of him. "Here's what will happen to the land masses in the next fifty million years or so. The Americas will continue to move to the West, away from Africa and Europe, making the South Atlantic a much larger ocean. The Persian Gulf will close altogether, Australia will drive north toward the equator and press against Asia, and both Baja California and the area around Los Angeles will split off from North America to drift northward in the Pacific Ocean. By fifty million years from now Los Angeles will start sliding into the Aleutian Islands."

All of the children watched the changing globe with complete attention. When the continents on the surface of the model stopped moving, the Oriental boy stepped slightly out from the group. "We have seen this continental drift phenomenon that Brian has been describing on half a dozen other planets, all of them bodies mostly covered by a liquid. Tomorrow Sherry will lead a more detailed discussion about the forces inside a planet that cause the sea floor to spread in the first place."

A projected image of a warden entered the scene from the left and removed both the Earth globe and several other unidentified props. The small boy waited patiently for the warden to complete his task and then continued, "Darla and David now want to share with us a project they have been working on for several days. They will play the music while Miranda and Justin perform the dance they choreographed."

The mixed twins turned eagerly to their classmates. The girl spoke out. "When we first learned about adult love and the changes that we all can expect after we pass puberty, David and I tried to envision what it would be like to find a new desire even stronger than those we already know. Our joint vision became a short musical composition and a dance. We call it 'The Dance of Love.' "

The two children sat down away from the group, almost at the side of the image, and began moving their fingers rapidly as if they were typing on the floor. A light synthesized melody, pleasant and spirited, filled the room. The blond boy and the Oriental girl began to dance in the center of the group. At first in the dance, the two were totally separate, unaware of each other, each child completely absorbed in his own activities. The boy knelt down to pick a beautiful flower, its red and white coloring shimmering in the holographic projection. The girl bounced a large bright blue ball as she danced. After a while the little girl noticed the boy and approached him, somewhat tentatively, offering to share the ball. The boy played ball with her but ignored everything except the game.

This is magic, thought Carol as she watched the children's images moving with grace and deft precision in front of her. *These children are wonderful. But they can't be real. They are too orderly, too self-contained. Where is the tension, the strife?* But despite her questions she was profoundly moved by the scene she was witnessing. The children were acting in concert, as a group, flowing in harmony from activity to activity. Their body language was open and unafraid. No neuroses were blocking their learning process.

The dance continued. The music deepened as the boy began to pay attention to his partner and she began arranging her hair with his favorite flowers for their brief encounters. The body movements changed as well, the sprightly, exuberant bounces of the initial stages giving way to subtly suggestive motions designed to awaken and then tease the budding libido. The tiny dancers touched, moved away, and came back together in an embrace.

Carol was entranced. *How would my life have been different,* she wondered, *If I had known all this at the age of five?* She remembered her rich friend at soccer camp, Jessica from Laguna Beach, whom she had seen occasionally in subsequent years. *Jessica was always ahead, always had to be first. She had had sex with boys before I even started my period. And look what happened to her.* Three marriages, three divorces, just thirty years old.

Carol tried to stop her mind from drifting so that she could pay complete attention to the dance. Suddenly she remembered her camera. She had just taken her first pictures of the children when she heard a noise behind her. Nick was coming toward them through the corridor. And he was carrying the trident in his hand.

Nick started to say something but Troy hushed him by putting his finger against his own lips and pointing at the dance in progress. The tempo had now changed. The two mixed children had somehow put the music on automatic (it seemed to be repeating some of the early verses, but with additional instruments in a more complex pattern) and joined the blond boy and the Oriental girl in the dance. Carol's first impression before Nick spoke out loud was that the dance was now exploring friendships between the paired couple and other people.

"What's this all about?" Nick said. The moment he spoke the entire projected tableau vanished. All of the children, the dance, and the music disappeared in an instant. Carol was surprised to find that she was disappointed and even a little angry. "Now you've blown it," she said.

Nick looked at his companions' stern faces. "Jesus," he said, holding up the cradle, "such a greeting. I bust my butt to go retrieve this damn thing and you guys are pissed when I come back because I interrupt a movie of some kind."

"For your information, Mr. Williams," Carol replied, "what we were watching was no ordinary movie. In fact, those kids in that dance are the same species as the ones in your trident." Nick looked at her skeptically. "Tell him, Troy."

"She's right, Professor," Troy said. "We just figured it out while you were gone. That thing you're carrying is the seed package for Earth. Some of the zygotes in there are what Carol calls superhumans. Genetically engineered humans with more capability than you or me. Like the kids we just saw."

Nick lifted the cradle to eye level. "I had figured out myself that this thing was a seed package. But what's this shit about human seeds?" He glanced at Troy. "You're serious, aren't you?" Troy nodded his head. Troy nodded. All three of them stared intently at the object in front of them. Carol kept glancing back and forth from the trident to where the image of the superchildren had been. "It still doesn't seem possible," Nick added, "but then nothing else has for the last—"

"So what did you forget, Nick?" Carol interrupted. "And why did you bring that thing back?" There was no immediate response from Nick. "By the way," she smiled, "you missed the show of a lifetime."

"The trident was what I forgot," Nick answered. "It occurred to me, while I was studying the gold objects in the cylinder, that *our* trident might be a seed package. And I was worried that it might be dangerous . . ."

The sudden sound of organ music flooding down the corridor from the large room behind them stopped their conversation. Nick and Carol looked at Troy. He put the bracelet up to his ear as if he were listening to it and cracked a large grin. "I think that's the five-minute warning," Troy said. "We'd better make our last touchdown and clear out of here."

The trio turned and walked back down the corridor to the room with the cylinder. When they arrived, Carol and Troy were astonished to see a figure in a blue and white wetsuit on the opposite side of the room. He was kneeling reverently right next to the cylinder.

"Oh, yeah," said Nick with a nervous laugh, "I forgot to tell you. Commander Winters came back with me . . ."

Commander Winters had felt quite comfortable in the water even though he had not been down on a dive in five years. Nick had gone freestyle, swimming right beside the commander and using the emergency mouthpiece connected to the air supply on Winters' back. Despite his sense of urgency,

Nick had remembered that Winters was basically a novice again and had not rushed the first part of the dive. But when Winters had refused several times to follow Nick up close to the light in the ocean, Nick had become exasperated.

Nick had then taken a final deep breath from the ancillary mouthpiece and grabbed Winters by the shoulders. With gestures, he had explained to the commander that he, Nick, was going to go through the plastic stuff or whatever it was in front of the light and that Winters could either follow him or not. The commander had reluctantly given Nick his hand. Nick turned around immediately and pulled Winters into and through the membrane that separated the alien spaceship from the ocean.

Winters had been completely terrified during his tumble on the water slide inside the vehicle. As a result he had lost his bearings and had had great difficulty standing up after he landed in the splash pool. Nick was already out of the pool and anxious to find his friends. "Look," Nick had said, as soon as he could get the commander's attention, "I'm going to leave you now for a few minutes." He had pointed at the exit on the opposite of the room. "We'll be in the big room with the high ceilings just on the other side of that wall." Then he had left, carrying the strange golden object from the boat.

Winters was left alone. He carefully pulled himself out on the side of the splash pool and methodically stacked his equipment alongside all the rest of the diving gear. He looked around the room, noting the curves in the black and white partitions. He too felt the closeness of the ceiling. *Now according to Williams,* the commander thought to himself, *I'm in part of an alien spaceship that has temporarily stopped on Earth. So far, except for that clever one-way entrance that I did not have time to analyze, I see no evidence of extraterrestrial origin . . .*

Comforted by his logic, he eased across the room toward the opposite wall and into the dark corridor. But his newfound sense of comfort was totally destroyed when he walked into the room dominated by the enormous cylinder with the golden objects floating in the light green liquid. He arched his back and stared at the vaulted, cathedral ceilings far above his head. He then approached the cylinder.

For Winters, the connection between the trident that Nick had been holding and the objects inside the cylinder was instantaneous. *Those must be more seed packages, destined for other worlds,* Winters thought, his crisp logic disappearing in a quick leap of faith. *With six-foot carrots and who knows what else to populate a few of the billions of worlds in our galaxy alone.*

The commander walked around the cylinder as if he were in a dream. His mind continually replayed both what Nick had told him right before they descended and the amazing scene he had witnessed when the spiderlike creature had shrunk up and jumped into the golden object. *So it's all true. All those things the scientists have been saying about the possibility of vast hordes of living creatures out there among the stars.* He stopped for a moment, partially listening to the strange noises behind the walls. *And we are only a few of God's many many children.*

Organ music, similar in timbre to that which Carol had heard when she had finished playing "Silent Night," but with a different tune, began to sound in the distant reaches of the ceiling above him. It reminded Winters of church music. His reaction was instinctual. He knelt down in front of the cylinder and clasped his hands together in prayer.

The music swelled in the room. What Winters heard in his head was the introduction to the Doxology, the short hymn that he had heard every single Sunday for eighteen years in the Presbyterian church in Columbus, Indiana. In his mind's eye he was thirteen years old again and sitting next to Betty in his choir robes. He smiled at her and they stood up together.

Praise God from whom all blessings flow.

The choir sang the first phrase of the hymn and Winters' brain was bombarded by a montage of memories from his early teens and before, a suite of epiphanic images of his innocent and unknowing closeness with a parental God, one who was in the wall behind his bed or just over his rooftop or at most in the summer afternoon clouds above Columbus. Here was an eight-year-old boy praying that his father would not find out that it was he who had set fire to the vacant lot across from the Smith mansion. Another time, at ten, the little Vernon wept bitter tears as he held his dead cocker spaniel Runtie in his arms and begged the omniscient God to accept his dead dog's soul into heaven.

The night before the Easter pageant, the first time that Vernon had portrayed Him in His final hours, dragging the cross to Calvary, eleven-year-old Vernon had been unable to sleep. As the night was passing by the boy began to panic, began to fear that he would freeze up and forget his lines. But then he had known what to do. He had reached under his pillow and found the little New Testament that always stayed there, day and night. He had opened it to Matthew 28. "Go ye therefore," it had said, "baptizing all nations . . ."

That had been enough. Then Vernon had prayed for sleep. His friendly, fatherly God had sent the little boy an image of himself delivering a spellbinding performance in the pageant the next day. Comforted by that picture, he had fallen asleep.

Praise Him all creatures here below.

With the second phrase of the hymn resounding in his ears, the venue for Winters' mental montage changed to Annapolis, Maryland. He was a young man now, in the last two years of his university work at the Naval Academy. The pictures that flooded his brain were all taken at the same place, outside the beautiful little Protestant chapel in the middle of the campus. He was either walking in or walking out. He went in the snow, in the rain, and in the late summer heat. He would fulfill his pledge. He had made a bargain with God, a business deal as it were, you do your part and I'll do mine. It was no longer a one-sided relationship. Now, life had taught the serious young midshipman from Indiana that it was necessary to offer this God something in order to guarantee His compliance with the deal.

For two years Vernon went regularly to the chapel, twice a week at least. He did not really worship there; he corresponded with a worldly God, one that read the *New York Times* and the *Wall Street Journal*. They discussed things. Vernon reminded Him that he was steadfastly upholding his end of the deal and thanked Him for keeping His part of the bargain. But never once did they talk about Joanna Carr. She didn't matter. The whole affair was between Midshipman Vernon Winters and God.

Praise Him above ye heavenly host.

The commander had unconsciously bowed his head almost to the floor by the time he heard the third phrase of the hymn. In his heart he knew the next stops on this spiritual journey. He was off the coast of Libya first, praying those horrible words requesting death and destruction for Gaddafi's family. God had changed as Lieutenant Winters had matured. He was now an executive, a president of something larger than a nation, an admiral, a judge, somewhat remote, but still accessible in time of real need.

However, he had lost his all-forgiving nature. He had become stern and judgmental. Killing a small Arab girl wasn't like burning down the vacant lot across from the Smith mansion. Winters' God now held him personally accountable for all his actions. And there were some sins almost beyond forgiveness, some deeds so heinous that one might wait for weeks, months, or even years in the anterooms of His court before He would consent to hear your plea for mercy and expiation.

Again the commander remembered his desperate search for Him after that awful evening when he had sat on the couch beside his wife and watched the videotaped newsreels of the Libya bombing. She had been so proud of him. She had taped every segment of CBS news that had covered the North African engagement and then surprised him with a complete showing the day after he returned to Norfolk. It was only then that the full horror of what he had done had struck Winters. Struggling not to vomit as the camera had shown the gruesome result of those missiles that had been fired from *his* planes, Winters had stumbled out into the night air, alone, and wandered until daybreak.

He had been looking for Him. A dozen times in the next three years this rite would repeat itself and he would wander again, all night, alternately praying and walking, hoping for some sign that He had listened to the commander's prayers. The stars and moon above him on those nights had been magnificent. But they could not grant forgiveness, could not give surcease to his troubled soul.

Praise Father, Son, and Holy Ghost.

And so God became blackness, a void, for Commander Winters. On those rare occasions afterward when he would pray, there was no longer any mental image of God, no picture of Him at all in his mind. There was just blackness, darkness, emptiness. Until this moment. As he knelt there outside the cylinder, heard the final phrase of the Doxology, and prayed to God to forgive him his doubts, his longings for Tiffani Thomas, and his general lack of direction, there was an explosion of light in Winters' mind's eye. God was speaking to him! God had at last given him a sign!

It was not the sign that Winters had been seeking, not evidence that He had finally forgiven the commander and accepted his penance, but something much much better. The explosion of light in Winter's mind was a star, a solar furnace forging helium out of hydrogen. As his mental camera backed away rapidly, Winters could see planets around that star and signs of intelligence on a few of the planets. There were other stars and other planets in the distance. Billions of stars in this galaxy alone and, after the mammoth voids between the galaxies, more huge collections of stars and planets and living creatures stretching incomprehensible distances in all directions.

Winters' body shook with joy and his eyes flooded with tears when he realized how completely God had answered his prayers. It would not have been enough for Him to simply reveal to Winters that he was forgiven. No, this Lord of everything imaginable, whose domain embraced chemicals risen to consciousness on millions of worlds in a vast and uncountable universe, this God who was truly omnipotent and ubiquitous, had gone way beyond his prayers. He had shown Winters the unity in everything. He had not limited Himself just to the affairs of one individual on a small and insignificant blue planet orbiting an ordinary yellow sun in one of the spiral arms of the Milky Way Galaxy; he had also shown Winters how that species and its pool of intelligence and spirituality was connected to every part of every atom in His grand dominion.

As Nick walked across the room toward Commander Winters, the intermittent noises behind the walls increased in amplitude and frequency. Around on the far side of the cylinder, next to one of the larger support machines, a door opened and two carpets, moving inchworm style, came into the room. They were immediately followed by two wardens and four platforms on treads. The platforms were carrying stacks of building materials. Each of the wardens led two platforms to a corner of the room, where they started constructing secure anchor stanchions for the cylinder.

The two carpets confronted Nick in the center of the room. They stood up on end and leaned in the direction of the exit toward the ocean. "They're telling us it's time to go," Carol said as she and Troy came up beside Nick.

"I understand that," Nick replied. "But I'm not yet ready to leave." He turned to Troy. "Does this game have an X key at all?" he asked. "I could use a time out."

Troy laughed. "I don't think so, Professor. And there's no way we can save the game and try again."

Nick looked as if he were in deep thought. The carpets continued to beckon. "Come on, Nick," Carol grabbed him by the arm. "Let's go before they get angry."

Suddenly Nick advanced toward one of the carpets and extended the golden cradle. "Here," he said, "take this and put it with the rest of them, up there, in the cylinder where it belongs." The carpet recoiled and twisted its top from side to side. Then it pulled its two vertical sides together and pointed at Nick.

"I don't need a bracelet to interpret that gesture," Troy remarked. "The carpet is plainly telling you to take the trident back to your boat."

Nick nodded his head and was quiet for a moment. "Is this the only one?" he asked Troy. Troy didn't understand the question. "Is this the only seed package for Earth?"

"I think so," Troy answered after a moment's hesitation. He looked at Nick with a puzzled expression.

Meanwhile the activity level in the room had increased substantially. As Commander Winters ambled toward the trio in the middle of the hubbub, the wardens and platforms were actively building in the corners, moving equipment could be heard behind the walls, and the organ music was growing louder and slightly ominous. In addition, a giant sock or cover of some kind, lined with a soft, pliant material, had unfurled above them in the ceiling and was descending slowly over the cylinder. Commander Winters stared around the room with undisguised astonishment. Still serenely content in his heart from the beauty and intensity of his epiphany, he was not paying much attention to the conversation beside him.

"They *must* take this thing with them," Nick was saying earnestly to Carol and Troy. "Don't you see? It's even more important now that I know there are human seedlings inside. Our children won't have a chance."

"But *they* were so beautiful, so smart," Carol said. "You didn't see them like we did. I can't believe those children would ever hurt anybody or anything."

"They wouldn't mean to destroy us," Nick argued. "It would just happen."

The carpets were starting to jump up and down. "I know, I know," Nick said as he again extended the cradle toward them. "You want us to go. But first, *please* listen to me. We've helped you, now I'm asking that you help us. I'm afraid of what might be in this package, afraid that it might upset the delicate stability of our planet. Our progress as a species has been slow, in fits and starts, with almost as many backward steps as forward. Whatever is here could threaten our future development. Or maybe even halt it altogether."

The activity in the room continued unabated. There was no noticeable reaction to Nick's speech from the impatient carpets, who were now taking turns walking over to the exit in case the dumb humans still did not understand their message. Nick looked entreatingly at Carol. She returned his gaze and smiled. After a few seconds she came over and took his hand. Their eyes met for a brief moment as she started talking and Nick saw a new expression, something approaching admiration, in her glance.

"He's right, you know," Carol said in the direction of the pair of carpets. "You haven't thought carefully enough about the outcome of this mission of yours. Sooner or later your special embryos and the humans already on this planet will interact and there will be a catastrophe. If the seed package is found early in the development of your superhumans, I am certain the Earthlings will feel compelled to destroy it. What possible other reaction could they have? The magnitude of the threat may not be fully known, but it is easy to recognize that creatures genetically engineered by superaliens could pose a gigantic problem for the native species of this planet."

Troy was standing just behind Nick and Carol, listening attentively to what she was saying. Around him the preparations for launch continued. The wardens and platforms had finished constructing and installing the two pairs of stanchions that would be connected to the cylinder during launch to minimize vibrations. The golden cradles in the cylinder could no longer be seen; the cover had descended almost to the floor.

". . . So unless you take this golden package back with you, perhaps to place it on another world which does not yet have intelligence, there will be unnecessary death. Either your seedlings will perish before maturity or the native humans like us will eventually be swallowed up, if not killed outright, by the more capable beings you have engineered. That hardly seems to be a fair reward for our effort on your behalf."

Carol stopped to watch four strange cords extend themselves from the top and near the bottom of the cylinder, wriggle through the air, and end up attached to the stanchions in the corners of the room. The carpets were becoming increasingly agitated. The two wardens finished supervising their prelaunch procedures. They turned abruptly toward the four human beings and moved in their direction.

Carol tightened her hold on Nick's hand. "Perhaps it's true that our natural development is a slow and not altogether satisfactory process," she continued, fear creeping into her voice as the dreaded wardens quickly approached them, "and it's certainly true that we humans here make mistakes, both as individuals and as groups. However, you can't overlook the fact that this imperfect process produced us, and we had enough foresight or compassion or whatever you want to call it—"

"*Hold it,*" shouted Troy. He seized the cradle from Nick's hand and jumped directly into the path of one of the menacing wardens. He was only inches away from two whirling, threatening rods with cutting implements on the end. "Hold it," he shouted again. Miraculously, all activity ceased. The carpets and wardens stood still, the noises in the wall stopped, even the organ music was silenced. "Of all of us," Troy said in a loud voice, his head tilted back and aimed at the ceiling, "I have the most knowledge of what your mission is all about. And the most to lose by recommending that you abandon this part of it. But I agree with my friends."

Troy removed his bracelet and then dramatically jammed both the bracelet and the cradle *inside* the warden. He felt as if he were plunging his hand into a bowl of hot bread dough. He released both objects and withdrew his hand. The warden didn't move. The bracelet and the cradle remained where Troy left them inside the warden's body.

"From the very beginning I realized that the bracelet you gave me enabled me to have special powers, talents that were not naturally mine. I understood, without knowing the specifics, that there would be a substantial and continuing reward for my helping you. And I thought that finally, *finally*, Troy Jefferson would be somebody special in this world."

Troy walked past the amazed Commander Winters, who was following the proceedings with a peaceful detachment, and came up beside Nick and Carol. It was absolutely quiet in the room. "When my brother, Jamie, was killed," he began again softly, "I swore that I would do whatever was necessary to leave my imprint on society. During those two years that I wandered all over the country, I spent most of my time daydreaming. My dreams all had the same conclusion. I would discover something new and earthshaking and become both rich and famous overnight."

Troy gave Carol a quick kiss and winked. "I love you, angel," he said. "And you too, Professor." Troy then turned around and faced the covered cylinder. "When I left here on Thursday afternoon, I was so excited I couldn't contain myself. I kept saying, 'Shit, Jefferson, here it is. You are going to be the most important man in the history of the fucking world.' "

Troy paused. "But I have learned something very important these last three days," he said, "something that most of us probably never consider. It is that the process is more important than the end result. It is what you learn while you're dreaming or scheming or working toward a goal that is essential and valuable, not the achievement of the goal itself. And that's why you guys must now do what my friends have asked.

"I know that you ETs have tried to explain to me in these last several minutes, through the bracelet that you offered me for life, that the new humans you are depositing here will lead us primitive beings into a bold and wonderful era. That may be true. And I agree that we could use some help, that our species is full of prejudice and selfishness and all kinds of other problems. But you cannot simply give us the answers. Without the benefit of the struggle to improve ourselves, without the process of overcoming our own weaknesses, there will be no fundamental change in us old humans. We will not become better. We will become second-class citizens, acolytes in a future of your vision and design. So take your perfect humans away and let us make it on our own. We deserve the chance."

There was no movement in the room for several seconds after Troy finished. Then the warden in front of him jerked sideways and began to move.

Troy braced for an attack. But the warden moved in the direction of the exit next to the cylinder. The bracelet and cradle could still be seen inside its body.

"All right, team," Troy shouted happily. Nick and Carol hugged. Troy took Commander Winters by the hand. As they were leaving, the four of them turned around one last time to look at the large chamber. In this final view, each one of them saw the room in terms of his own amazing experiences. The noises had begun again behind the walls. And the carpets, platforms, and wardens were filing out of the room through the door beside the covered cylinder.

They had only been onboard the boat for three or four minutes when the water underneath them suddenly became very turbulent. They were strangely quiet, all four of them. A frustrated Lieutenant Ramirez paced about the deck, trying to get someone to tell him what had happened under the water. Even Commander Winters virtually ignored the lieutenant and just shook his head or gave simple answers to all his questions.

They were certain that the spaceship was about to launch. They didn't realize that it would glide gently away from their area first, so that it would not submerge them with a giant wave, before breaking the water and heading into the sky. The water stayed agitated for several minutes. All of them scanned the ocean for a sign of the vehicle.

"Look," yelled Commander Winters excitedly, pointing at a giant silver bird lifting into the sky about forty-five degrees away from the early morning sun. Its rise was initially slow, but as it rose it accelerated rapidly. Nick and Carol and Troy clasped hands tightly as they watched the awesome spectacle. Winters came over and stood beside the trio. After thirty seconds the craft had disappeared above the clouds. There was never any sound.

"Fantastic," said Commander Winters.